Intertwined

A REDEMPTION NOVEL

SASHA BRÜMMER

Intertwined
Copyright © 2016 Sasha-Lee Brümmer
Published by Sasha-Lee Brümmer

Editor:
Lisa Aurello

Cover Designer:
Sommer Stein, Perfect Pear Creative

Interior Design & Formatting:
Christine Borgford, Type A Formatting

This is a work of fiction. Any references to historical events, real people, or real places are used fictitiously. Other names, places, characters, and incidents either are products of the author's imagination or are used fictitiously. The ideas, characters, and situations presented in this story are strictly fictional and any unintentional likeness to real persons, living or dead, or real situations is completely coincidental.

The following story contains mature themes, strong language, violent circumstances, and sexual situations. It is intended for adult readers.

I dedicate this novel to those who are afraid to let go and let love take over. Trust in those around you because a love like the one in this story doesn't come by often.

Have faith in yourself instead of pushing others away. In loving yourself, you'll find yourself. Remember, those dark and challenging roads will lead to the most beautiful places and make perfect sense when you are able to look back at them.

Acknowledgments

THE NUMBER OF people who have been supporting me while I've brought this story to life has truly been overwhelming. First, I'd like to thank my family, Andrew, Vanessa, and Tynan, for allowing me to hole up in my writing cave and bringing me caffeine at the drop of a hat. There's nothing like family, and I wouldn't want any other than the three of you.

Belinda Brümmer, I will always be grateful for that random phone call. You helped steer me in the right direction with this book when I was lost and unsure where it needed to go. Thank you for having faith in me and my words.

Lisa Aurello, I'm not even sure where to start. You are beyond kind and selfless. You've been with me since day one of writing, and I could not see myself working with anyone else. You're one of a kind, and I'm ever so fortunate to know you. Thank you for the countless times that you've read through my works and helped me to better each and every word.

Heather White, A.F. Crowell, and Audrey Carlan, goodness, the three of you are rays of light in the dark. You have each been so supportive of me and my work when I wasn't sure of myself. Thank you for all that you do and for all of the support you each provide me with.

Linda Russell, I'm not even sure where to begin when it comes to your unconditional support. I'm beyond blessed to have you on my team. You're truly one of a kind, and I owe you the world. Thank you, Linda, for everything.

Sharon Renee Goodman, I'm hereby revoking your rights to

live anywhere else but in my pocket. I love your friendship and flair of sass that you bring into my world. Thank you for being you and for all of your support.

Ashley Scales, Linda Russell, Heather White, Holly Main, and Kimberly Lucia, you ladies are phenomenal. I love your brutal honesty and all of the effort that you put into helping me achieve my dreams. Thank you for all that you do.

Kimberly Lucia, I feel as if I've known you for years, and I probably have, but I'm delighted to have you on my side. You have the most beautiful soul, and I'm glad that I get to call you my friend. Thank you for all of your help in my chaotic world.

Kristi Webster, thank you from the bottom of my heart for allowing me to use the dark side of your mind when I was struggling. You're a talented writer and genuine inspiration to me.

Geneva Lee and Elise Lee, the two of you have the most beautiful souls. Thank you for your overpowering love and unconditional support. I will always remember being kidnapped in a taxi by the two of you. I adore you two hard!

Sommer Stein, holy . . . where do I start? You are beyond talented and a delight to work with. I'm not sure how you put what I see in my head onto my covers, but you do, and I love you for it. Thank you for always answering my early-morning messages and for being so willing to go above and beyond.

Lastly, I wanted to say the biggest thank-you to those bloggers, readers, and authors who have taken a chance on me. None of you will ever understand what it means to me for all of your help when we didn't know a thing about each other. Words have brought so many people together, and I'm delighted to be part of this community of bookish love.

Playlist

Back to Me—Daya

Blue Blood—Laurel

Breathin'—EDX

Closer—Chainsmokers feat. Halsey

Cold Water—Major Lazer feat. Justin Bieber and MØ

Coming Over (Filous Remix)—James Hersey

Crush—Campsite Dream

Don't Let Me Down—The Chainsmokers feat. Daya

Echoes—Revel in Romance

Fast Car—Jonas Blue

Feels—Kiiara

Go Flex—Post Malone

Gold—Kiiara

Kiss Me—Rebel feat. Sophie Simmons

Lost Boy—Ruth B

Pity Party—Melanie Martinez

Say It—Flume feat. Tove Lo

Scars to Your Beautiful—Alessia Cara

Sex—Cheat Codes

Show Me Love—Sam Feldt

So Alive—Goo Goo Dolls

Sweet Lovin'—Sigala

Unfold—Alina Baraz and Galimatias

Wicked Games—Parra for Cuva feat. Anna Naklab

One

Isla

A RESILIENT DEPRESSION has held me in a dense captive fog since I was able to understand the word *abandoned*. I carry the obscurities of my life around with me as I hang onto a thin thread. I know that the thread is too fragile to hold much more, and when it breaks, it may release the weight and free me of it, or it will pin me down and crush one meaningless bone at a time. It could make breathing difficult and screaming out for help an impossible feat as I watch a mirrored image of myself lose to a vehement and soundless internal war.

I've been told that I'm defective while I'm in my black state of misery, but how can someone who has not experienced the tumbling, sinking, clawing, festering, smothered emotions that I have over the years have anything to say about it? I've also been told that it's healthy to cry, but how can I force tears when I barely have the energy that it takes to sleep. Sleep has become more to me than just taking a moment of rest: it has become my escape from reality.

There's nothing tragically beautiful about depression. There's not always a reason for it either, but today and every day I sit alone in a dark forest.

I'm not living.

I'm purely enduring.

I consider myself to be a limited-edition empathetic target.

Someone who manipulative people seem to latch onto and try to exploit in any which way they deem probable. I've been surrounded by toxic people for my entire life, ones who have consistently cast the blame in my direction in order to hold me back. Regardless of the boundaries that I put up, there's always one asshole who manages to slip through and wreak havoc on my life. The ones that seem to know how to dowse my fires with a few drops of ice-cold water are always the ones that I don't see coming.

However, I've realized my potential since the last fucker barreled through my life, and no, I'm not talking about men taking advantage of me. I'm talking about spineless women who thrive on pushing another down instead of raising one up. Not only am I worried about my depression and anxiety suppressing me from being who I am supposed to be, but certain people have had the exact same effect on me as well.

In the end, I know that I'll be *fine*, but I still feel awful and weary all of the time. I've managed to fall in love with the pain, though, and it's drawn me in so deep that I want to stay. I'm unsure of what else there is in life without the daily dose of medication that diminishes my life.

I've begged more times than I'll admit to anyone to just make all of this shit go away, but it chooses to linger around instead. I am not the sort of person who will sit on the bathroom floor and cry and then walk out into a crowded room as if nothing happened. No. I'm able to control the depression in a way that others have learned to control me. I'm not ashamed to admit that I have an abusive relationship with the disease: I am well aware of how unhealthy it is, but I feel as if I finally have it under control.

In any woman, charm and beauty can be deceptive and not only to men but to other women as well. Most women will agree that they do not trust anything with a dick. However, I don't trust a bitch in heels.

Women are said to run the world because we have vaginas, but let's be frank here: having a vagina opens the door to manipulation and preconceived notions of needing a man to survive. It's all complete bullshit.

I was brought into this life and raised by women who hustle and overcome obstacles by tackling them with their feet on the ground. Those women, though, turned out to be the most manipulative people I have come across. Those women destroyed me at a young age and never bothered to look back. Not even once. I've accepted them for the women they are, but I've rejected them too because I now know that I deserve more. I have more internal scars than can be seen with the naked eye and it's all thanks to those who should have given me more in life than a padded room and restraints.

Who are these self-absorbed bitches? *Easy.* My mother who abandoned me and my grandmother who betrayed me until her dying breath—both of whom handed me over to others who thought they knew how to get a better handle on me: my mother to my grandmother and my grandmother to an institution.

Sure, I've accepted their faults, and I've moved on, but that doesn't take away the residual bullshit that it left me with. I'm exhausted from fighting my way through every day due to the depression that settled itself in when all of the pieces of who these women were fell into place. They kept their true selves hidden from me, but I understood.

I've always understood.

When manipulation takes away one's will to keep fighting, it's harder to stay than to pick up the pieces of yourself that another so arbitrarily cast off. I assume that they loved me—at least I'd like to think that—but love that was so easily discarded was not a love that was worth holding onto to begin with. Nevertheless, being abandoned takes away one's ability to realize that truth, as well as the ability to forget the instigators. The person that is left behind or handed over like a rag doll is never whole; that person won't recover, but will fight to make their lives whole again.

It's what I've been doing since day one. I've been fighting to find myself through a haze. I've been adamant about overcoming the thought of being thrown away and hastily left to the devices of people I didn't know.

A part of me has been missing ever since I can remember, and because of it, I don't believe that I'm living up to my life's fullest potential. I've gotten over it, though. I've said fuck it and kept on going on more occasions than I can count, and it's helped me to grow as a person.

At the age of fifteen, seventeen years ago, I was institutionalized at a psychiatric hospital for three years. My grandmother claimed that I tried to end my life because of all of the mental issues I had. Little did the nurses and doctors know that she was the senseless one out of the two of us. She left wounds on me that will never show or bleed because they go much deeper than flesh.

My grandmother made countless decisions to use her vile words against me. I don't believe that she was able to love anyone other than herself. She knew that she was inflicting pain but didn't care. She had a dark soul, one that if you listened closely, you could hear the laughter seep through the madness that resided inside of her. She drained me of my identity as a young girl and injected self-doubt into my already festering wounds.

Life inside of white padded walls wasn't one that I'd recommend or want anyone else to experience. At least when you go through the worst, it can be dimmed by a once-a-day pill. It was because I simply felt too much at a young age, too much of what

I couldn't understand.

I stopped eating as the depression worsened because what was the point, right? They documented every aspect of my life, every noise I had made or word that I chose to share. I had no light that could possibly morph into rays of hope. I just had a mind that plummeted downward into an immeasurable darkness. When I stopped eating, I ceased speaking as well because I didn't have anything to say while I was drowning in the bottomless gloom. Did I need help during those times? Undeniably. But did I require padded rooms, locked doors, and meals passed through a slot in those doors? No. Not at all.

What did help was the compassion of the nurses, something that I'd never experienced before. I was locked up and defeated yet I never felt as loved as I did within those four walls.

Through the process of healing, I saw a glimmer of my strength when I was told to look harder. I focused more on being released than I did on the illusion of my life, and because of that, I learned how to better myself instead of aimlessly wandering around in my own mind.

I was released from the institution a few days after my eighteenth birthday. My grandmother took me back in as if nothing had happened. As if she hadn't ignored my existence for three years during which I battled to keep hold of the woman I had become. I managed to get my GED while I was locked up, and I had applied to a few colleges, all of which were as far away from Portland, Maine, as possible.

After that summer, I left without so much as a goodbye to travel by bus and train to get to Chicago, Illinois. I only took with me what I could fit into my old school backpack—a few changes of clothes, toiletries, and my identification. I left everything else that belonged to Isabelle Madden behind.

I recall seeing the city for the first time, and I immediately knew that it was somewhere I needed to be. It's as if it was calling to me as I stepped down from the coach bus and into an empty parking lot that was lit up from the overhead streetlights.

I struggled for a week before my college classes started. I didn't have anywhere to go until move-in day, but I somehow made it work. I paid for cheap motel rooms with the money that I took from my grandmother and managed to keep any monsters at bay until I could afford the medication that did it for me. The biggest decision that I made that week was to change my name. I went into a courthouse to have my name legally changed from Isabelle, something that never suited me, to Isla.

I remember when I decided on Isla one night at a rickety bar. I was asked what I wanted to drink and wasn't even asked for any identification, so I went for it. The only thing that came to mind was Scotch whiskey. I remember the old man huffing out a breath as he reached up and grabbed a bottle from the back of the bar before placing it in front of me. The whiskey came from Islay, Scotland, and right then, I knew that I'd come to the bar for more than just a drink.

I'd come looking for a new identity, for a new me. For answers to who I am. Thanks to an old man and my request for whiskey, I found Isla Madden, the woman who has always been present inside me. The woman who kept pushing when everyone in her life decided that she wasn't worth their time and effort. For the first time in years, I felt like I could breathe without the fear of suffocation.

On freshman move-in day, I was delighted to have my own space. The roommate who I was assigned to live with eventually moved out because she couldn't stand my silence. I was lucky enough to have the room to myself for the remainder of my freshman year. I didn't have to worry myself about lining up outside of a nurse's station to receive my medication or when I'd be allowed out in the daylight again. This was the first time that I had complete and utter control over my life, and I was thriving in it.

I've since become accustomed to allowing people into my life, to let the love in if you will, even though I know that the moment you open the door is the moment that they destroy you. I have issues, and I'm aware of them, but that doesn't take away what I was forced into. It doesn't heal the aspects of life that I won't get back. It doesn't fix the fact that I'm not all that comfortable around other women unless they go out of their way to prove their loyalty to me. Nothing excuses the fact that pieces of my life were stolen, and I won't be able to ever get those years back.

I've let people control and consume me through the years, but over nine and a half years ago I met two men who have helped me see the potential in myself that wasn't brought to light before. Ever since I met them, they have repeatedly pushed me to my breaking points, and just as I'm about to fall over the edge, each of them reaches out and makes sure that I'm secure enough on my own two feet to stand once more before they let go of me.

To this day, the same two men help keep me in line, and quite frankly, they're the closest thing that I have to a family. It doesn't hurt that they are the most attractive men that I have ever met either. Each of them is aware of what I've been through, and they are the only two people whom I've trusted enough to delve deep into my memories and relive for them some of what I went through as a teenager.

Liam Jensen and Waylon Brass have been the sturdy rocks for me to stand on when I couldn't take another hit from life. I met each of them in college, and they were the ones that made me prove myself to . . . *myself*. They forced me to take a step back and figure out who I am and what I want out of life aside from changing my name.

It's because of them that I went from bartending at a strip club where I wore little more than the strippers did to my comfortable position today. The stripper joint helped me pay my way through college when I could barely afford ramen noodles, so I don't regret doing it. The plus side to it was that it forced me to be comfortable in my own skin. It made me realize that I had the potential to seduce others and engage in some of my darkest fantasies. I learned a lot that I wouldn't want to take back during my time of slinging cheap drinks down the bar rails, but I'd rather not relive it.

Thanks to those two fuckers, I went from indecent exposure to managing the most renowned whiskey library in the country and it's right here in Chicago.

"Isla? I need some help in the back. Do you mind?"

I'm snapped out of my daydream as one of my newer librarians calls out to me across the silent room. It's only his third day on the job, so I'm not expecting much from him at this point in time.

"Uh, yeah, just give me a second."

Before I make my way to the back, I pour myself a finger of Highland Park 50-Year-Old Single Malt Scotch and weave past the bar and into my office where I dig out the last of my prescribed depression medication and toss it back with the whiskey.

The taste of tobacco and dusty wood hits me before being replaced with smooth notes of raisins and nutmeg. The spicy and slightly smoky finish lingers as I walk into the back and straight into a conversation that seems to be going on about me, one that is obviously one-sided and obnoxiously obtuse.

"What the fuck is up with her? She's like damaged goods that no one wants to play with."

Eden looks over the new guy's shoulder at me and shrugs before turning back to her task of inventorying all of our new bottles.

I clear my throat and pick up a rare bottle of Macallan, inspecting it for a moment before speaking. "I think that you should grab your shit and get your sorry ass out of my library."

His rusty chuckle is unsettling as he turns to face me. "Yeah, sweetheart? What are you, the owner's chew toy?"

Eden giggles as she takes note of the bottle ID numbers on her tablet.

"The general manager, actually, and you're fired. I trust that you know your way out."

"You're firing me? I doubt anyone besides the owner is able to do that."

"Yeah?" I take my phone out of my pocket and dial Waylon before putting it on speakerphone.

"Isla?" he answers immediately.

"Hey asshole. I'm going to need security in here in two minutes to remove a disgruntled employee from the premises. He's refusing to leave."

"Jacobs is on his way. Give him five minutes."

"Thanks, Brass."

He hangs up while I watch the jerk's eyes go from arrogant to wide with fear before he runs over to grab his backpack and hightails it out of the back entrance.

"Such a pussy."

"I thought that you were going to eat him alive," Eden says from her post in front of one of the many shelves in the storage area.

I chuckle as I walk back to the front of the library. "I'm not particularly in the mood for anything inadequate at the moment. I'm sure that even house whiskey would taste better."

I don't hear her response as I close the door to my office, pull on my black leather jacket, and grab my phone before shooting off a text message to Wade about the fucker running. I yell out to Eden that I'm going to grab us coffee from one of my favorite coffee shops in Chicago before walking out of Blended and onto the bustling sidewalks of the Magnificent Mile.

Coffee sounds incredible right about now, but combining it with whiskey sounds oh so much better. I'm a whiskey girl at heart, so much so that I'm sure that's what runs through my veins.

Two

Liam

TO UNDERSTAND ME, you have to understand my past.

I do not and would not discredit those who have strayed away from me in recent years. I've disengaged myself from my social circles and immersed myself in alcohol, sex, and more recreational drug use than what is socially acceptable.

I've used drugs and alcohol as a pain reliever, as a sedative for death. A death that solely stains my hands. The boundaries of life and death took her from me, and today and every day, I ache in the vague shadows of what once was.

Loss. It's merely a word, but it is a word that is often underestimated. It does not take into account the years of longing for someone who will not return, or the power that it strips a person of. When Chloe vanished two days before our wedding day, I lost myself.

I have yet to come up for air even though it has been several long months since they found her mangled and distorted body in Mexico and seven years since I was last able to see her smile. She spent seven and a half years in hell: being exchanged for sexual favors and money should never be tolerated.

Grief is the last act of love that I will be able to give her. I failed her. Immensely.

Chloe was stolen from me and sold into sexual slavery on her bachelorette trip all of those years ago, but yet somehow, it feels like it happened yesterday. I can still hear the hysterics of her friend's voice over long distance and then she passed the phone to the other girl with her who was able to keep it together long enough to deliver the news. Wild chills break out on my forearms every time I think about answering that call, the call that changed my life in ways that I didn't know were even possible.

I should have been seeing a therapist about all of this for years—I'm well aware of that—but I didn't have the balls to man up and deliver my sorry ass to a chaise lounge chair and say my piece to someone who I probably won't be able to trust. Yet here I fucking am. In a leather chair, staring up at a white ceiling while some fucking asswipe with a doctoral degree is watching and taking notes as I spill my life story on dispassionate ears.

"I'm going to assume that you have trust issues from your past experiences."

"Yes, I have trust issues, and I know that what I'm about to reveal doesn't help with it in the slightest, but this is my life. Those trust issues? You can blame my mother for those because it's where they originate from. These are the cards that I was dealt, and I'm learning to play and manipulate them as well as I can before that last card drops, and I can't go back."

"Do you trust yourself?"

"Do I trust myself? That's an interesting question and one that I'll have to come back to, but right now the answer is fuck no. No, I don't. Not then. Not now. Not ever."

I clear my throat before I continue. "The truth is, I insisted that she go on her bachelorette trip with two of her closest friends, both of whom are alive, safe, and comfortable in their homes. Do they feel guilty that they left her alone in a club to hit up the bathroom with a man who ravaged the two of them long enough for his goons to snatch my bride? I have no doubt, but let's focus on the fact that this shit is about me and what I've done to remedy this fucked-up situation."

"Then we'll focus on you, Liam. What have you done, as you said, to remedy this situation that you've found yourself in?"

I cast a glance at the fucker with gray hair and glasses, and I swear to myself that this is the one and only time that I'll be coming here. I may as well get all of this shit out and in the open before I keel over from the weight of it.

"Between myself and my good friend, Waylon Brass, we've spent more time and coinage in an attempt to find Chloe than anyone would have thought possible. In a bid to save her, we assembled numerous teams of rescuers over the years. For years, we came up empty-handed until one monumental day when her last card dropped and I picked it up, added it to my hand, and tried to continue with life."

He clears his throat to draw my attention to him once again. "Are you telling me that you were the one who found her?"

"No. I had a team that is part of an organization that I started. They came across countless dead ends until they found her with a still heart, a heart that once belonged to me. I felt the absence of her for all of those years, but the knowledge that she's no longer alive to suffer soothes a side of myself that I'd rather not acknowledge," I confess and he nods.

"I'd like for you to try and explain it," he says in his cultivated Australian accent. I'm sure his blue blood runs thicker than even mine does. I scrub the thought from my mind before relaxing back into the chaise again.

"It's difficult to explain because when it's said out loud, I sound like a selfish dick, but that's not why I'm better off with this outcome as opposed to another. Yes, I've lost an important part of me, and she lost her life, but I'd rather her be dead than suffering under the hands of some fucking pricks." I pause to run my palm over my face.

"Go on."

I blow out a heavy breath before I continue. "I remember the pictures that the police and rescue teams showed me of her body when they found her in a shallow creek. She was barely recognizable with black hair that was too long and knotted and a body that hadn't been cleaned or seen the sunlight in years. There was irrefutably nothing left of the woman that she once was, the woman I loved. Her skin clung to her bones as if there was nothing left of her physical form. The worst part was seeing parts of her body dismembered, from her once-delicate fingers to her—*fuck.*"

"We only need to discuss what you feel comfortable discussing, Liam. Take your time, and when you feel ready, you may continue."

I watch him type something out on his device before I open my mouth to speak again. "Those images are permanently etched into the inside of my eyelids."

My mind starts running, and I go silent for a few seconds to think and sort out the shit in my head.

I have no doubt that she wanted to close her eyes and never open them again for those years that she was held captive and endured the sexual exploitation. To those fuckers that took her, she was nothing more than a paycheck, but to me . . . to me she was my entire life wrapped up in one gorgeous woman.

"She was it for me, and I lost it all because I did not think to take any precautions while sending her away. Her family has since disowned me, blaming the outcome of Chloe's life on me and my actions, but I really cannot blame them for their harsh judgment. It rings true for more reasons than one. I'm the reason why she went to Mexico. I'm the sole reason that she was taken and is now unable to experience life as a free woman again. Or any kind of woman, for that matter."

"Do you remain in contact with any member of her family?"

"Yeah, but just the one, and she doesn't exactly have a relationship with anyone in that family either. I mean, it wasn't her choice, but it is what it is."

"How is this woman related to Chloe?"

"She's her twin sister."

"I would imagine that relationship can be hard for you at times."

I chuckle and throw my head back, closing my eyes and forcing the images of Chloe out of my head. "At times, but I've managed to look past it. They weren't identical, but they did have many features in common."

"I see. Let's continue, shall we? What happened next?"

I nod and think back to the last thing I said about her family. I decide to skip over the fights and arguments that took place with my every visit and instead dive into something more important.

"In the last seven months, I've tried to find out where she was held and by whom, but I've come up empty-handed each and every time. With each attempt, I've delved deeper than the time before. I should never have trusted myself with her, and I will not trust myself with another woman again. It's better for me to be alone than to have someone need my protection, which is why I'm still in Australia."

"Where else would you have to go?" he asks as he adjusts himself in his seat. I don't even have to look at him to know that he's still staring at me like I'm on fucking stage giving my own eulogy.

"I moved away from Chicago, Illinois, after dropping out of college in my freshman year, and a couple of months later, I met Chloe. We were together for a year before I realized exactly how much she had changed me as a person. I wasn't the self-righteous prick with a never-ending bank account when I was with her."

I shut my eyes and think about the man I was before her and then who I became when I was with her. I was the man that she deserved at the time, but I can't go back to him. I'm not afraid to die; I'm afraid to live and be human. I swallow my pride before speaking again. It goes down hard.

"Once I proposed, she got busy and arranged the wedding in a few months, and I was more than ready to begin a new journey with her by my side. Unfortunately, it was stripped away from me when she was stolen. When some motherfuckers took away my reason for existing."

"We've been over this terrain before, but if you feel the need to clarify it, then please continue," he interrupts, and I allow him to finish his comment before I continue my story.

"I remember sitting up late each night, researching what it meant for her to be taken and what they might have been doing to her. The images that came across my screen destroyed me as well as any faith I had left in this sick, manipulative world."

"And you've witnessed this aspect of the world on multiple occasions?"

"Through the agonizing years of searching, yes, and I lost myself to the world of drugs and consenting women. I invested significant amounts of my trust fund into substances that should have been able to rid me of the constant sinking feeling, but honestly, nothing worked."

"Ah," he comments as he moves his fingers along the screen again.

"The drugs would steal me away from a conscious reality, but they would place me in a world where I would watch some sick fuck torture my bride. The images that were forced into my head were ones of her chained up in a dank, dark dungeon while men took turns on her, doing things I would never dream of doing."

"So what you're telling me is that nothing you did to alleviate the pain you were experiencing seemed to help. Is that correct?"

"I mean, yeah. When I'd come out of a drug-induced stupor, those visions would meet me in my dreams, and then again when I woke. I have not been able to escape them since the day she was taken, and over the last several months, they seem to have intensified. I swear that in my dreams I can still imagine her ear-piercing cries for help. It's a sound that won't soon disappear . . . it will haunt me until the day I die."

"Liam?"

"Yeah?"

"When do you believe that it will be acceptable to move on from your grief and misery?"

"When is it acceptable to move on? I mean, when is it acceptable to give up and go on with a normal life?" I ask to get a better handle on what he's asking from me. I shake my head as he waits for my answer, and I decide to go for one that I know I should have given myself a long time ago. "I don't have the answers to those questions for anyone in particular, but for myself, I do. My answer is unpretentious: *tomorrow.*"

These fuckers stole my life and put a limp in my stride, but I refuse to be a victim to them any longer. I will not remain silent about things that matter, but I also need to put distance between myself and the tyrants in my head that have seen more than their fair share of bruised and battered women.

"Tomorrow?"

"Yeah. It's never too late to change our paths, and this is me taking my strides back."

"I'm impressed," he says while trying to hide a smile. He doesn't know how long and hard I've stewed over all of this, and he won't ever know. Throwing my legs off of the chaise, I cup my face in my hands and rest my elbows on my knees as I think about what my tomorrow holds.

Fuck the world's expectations when it comes to what I do with my time and life; tomorrow is my day. It's the day that I will figure out what to do with all of my knowledge and be the one person to change lives, starting with mine. Again.

It's a late afternoon in Sydney when I decide to shut off my laptop after sending an email to inform my teams that I will be out of touch for a while. They will not be under any duress because of how I initially set up the organization. Wade Brass, Gage Cooper, and I hold the three lead positions in RW. Each of us has been in charge of three teams and three rehabilitation houses all over the world for those women who were saved while we were looking for Chloe. Neither of them advertises their involvement in this under-the-radar organization, Remission Worldwide, and neither of them physically put their lives on the line as I have in the past.

We've been fighting to improve the statistics and numbers of the women-lost to women-rescued ratio. Slavery is not a thing of the past—it's disgustingly common in today's society—but nobody pays enough attention to see it.

Remission Worldwide was established a couple of months after Chloe's disappearance, and we've been expanding the organization ever since. It is the sole thing in my life that I am able to say that I am proud of. Screw the money and all of my conquests because none of that means shit to me. This organization, though, is what I've put my life into.

In fact, my rehabilitation houses will remain where they are while I take this break. I will continue to prove that human trafficking isn't pretty. I've made a move in the right direction with their help, but it's my time to take a step back from the enslaved world and free myself.

I've dedicated my life to saving others, but we all need to put distance between ourselves and something vitally important every now and then. Both Brass and Coop understand my need to separate myself from this underground industry for a while until I can find whatever the hell it is I'm craving in my life. Right now, though, it is not this.

I cannot stomach one more woman begging me to save her while my own soul needs saving. Uprooting is my only option at this point, and nobody knows too much of my plan as of right now. I've decided what my next step will be, but I have no plans beyond that first footfall. As much as I loathe the thought of giving up control, it may possibly be what I need—a loss of self that the drugs no longer provide for me.

Since Chloe, I've managed to find some peace. There are two women whom I have taken an interest in, but I don't need anything more from them than what they are currently providing me with—their bodies. No, I'm not a misogynistic asshole; I'm merely an asshole who needs a sexual release once in a while.

Ever since Chloe's disappearance, I've emotionally detached myself from the two women who desire me, from two women who I need to keep myself afloat in the sea of slavery.

Shortly after Chloe was kidnapped, I fell into a black hole, the depths of which I would never have been able to get out of on my own—and then Adriana Hugh reached her hand in and gripped her fingers around mine. She's been pulling ever since, and as much as I try to fall back into the darkness, she refuses to let go and allow me to belong to the deep hell once more.

Between the two of us, we have been flying back and forth from the States to Australia every other month to be with each other, and we've kept it quiet until recently. Adriana works for

Wade in Brass Global as his personal secretary. Reassured that he'd understand since Wade himself found love recently, Adriana and I let it slip that we've been together. Needless to say, Wade was not impressed by my encroachment, nor was he shocked by my admission. I'm sure that he understands that celibacy is one thing that I would never agree to.

At first, Addy was someone who I was able to talk to about what was going on with the searches, but we somehow transformed into more. By more, I mean that we've been sleeping together for seven years, but neither of us has pursued anything beyond that from each other. I'm not entirely sure if she's content with my seeing her as well as Isla Madden, but she hasn't made any arguments against it.

Adriana has been my life raft while I've been trapped in a raging sea, where no one knows how close I have been to drowning. How close I've been to giving up and allowing my body to sink to the deepest parts of the ocean. I've hurt her more than I care to understand, though. I can see it in her eyes every time I'm with her lately, and I know that I need to do something about it.

Isla—Lord, help me—has been a constant in my life since my freshman year in college over nine and a half years ago. Unlike Addy, Isla is not my polar opposite. She sleeps around and enjoys being single as much as I do. She lives to raise hell and revels in getting a rise out of people. Isla manages a whiskey library called Blended, which is owned by none other than Wade Brass. The three of us have been close since day one, and we've all been blended together. I met Wade through our fraternity and Isla through him.

While I consider Wade family, Isla took herself out of that equation when we started fucking on a regular basis.

Now, it's the end of March, and I have not seen Isla or Addy since I left Scotland at the end of January. I've spoken to each of them on occasion, but I've not put too much thought into either one. I'm an asshole—*I know*, but I'm not looking for anything aside from someone to sink into, and they are both well aware of that. The mere thought of being in a relationship again and failing yet another woman is like a wooden stake to my already-mangled heart.

Tomorrow, I've decided, I will make my way back to the United States for a while. I haven't exactly told either woman that I'm flying back, nor have I told them that it will be a permanent move.

I've decided to give up my sanctuary here in Sydney, Australia, and say goodbye to those who were close to Chloe. I can no longer force myself to separate my two lives by oceans when I know more waits for me back home. I've decided that it's time for me to live instead of wading in the dark, endless waters while I wait to be taken under.

I'm not looking forward to the colder weather that Chicago has to offer, but it will be good to start fresh on my own once again. I'll keep this house in Sydney, as it hosts too many memories, both good and bad, for me to give it up.

The world enjoys spinning our lives out of control and watching us fall. This was my descent. I don't believe that I'd be able to stand up once more if the result will be the same if and when I find my reason for being here again.

Once I've finished packing one of my two bags that I'll be dragging through the airport tomorrow, I let out a heavy breath before grabbing my guitar, spliff, and lighter and stroll out onto my patio which overlooks the ocean.

I roll up my pants after I draw in a lungful of the tobacco and herb combination and sit down at the edge of the pool, dipping my feet and calf muscles into the crystal clear water. I exhale a breath of smoke for the last time, savoring the way it moves as it leaves the confines of my lungs and passes through my lips.

In order to get my life together, I've opted to give up this habit. Instead of running from something that I've had no control over, I'm going to take back that control, making it bend beneath me, instead of letting it twist me into distortion.

I run my fingers over the strings of my custom acoustic that Isla gave me for my birthday a few years back. I adjust it on my thigh and keep the spliff between my lips as I start to strum the hypnotic cords of *Nothing Else Matters*. The soothing quality of the notes touch a part of my soul that has been longing for more. Once I've played the song through, I set it down beside me and lie back on the edge of the pool.

My mind doesn't seem to take a break, though, as I argue with myself about my reasons for leaving.

I've enjoyed the freedom of doing what and whom I want these last few years, and I don't see the need to change that in the coming future. Nor do I feel the guilt that should be associated with fucking other women while Chloe was still alive. It was never done to rebel; it was done to get me through the hard-hitting times.

To save ourselves, we have to sacrifice pieces of who we are, and I've sacrificed more of myself than anyone should have let me get away with. I've got nothing to prove, but I've got a plan to get out of here that will ultimately allow me to get out of my own head.

I suck in another lungful and hold in the smoke for a couple of seconds before allowing it to escape. Once the immaculate high captures my body, I get up and drag my sorry ass into the living room where I remain until I pass out into an oblivion, a stupor that haunts me with images of Chloe's death and mutilations. Images that I eventually need to escape from.

When I wake up, all of the lights in the house are off, and

I'm veiled in a complete silence. Death transcends the physical form and makes itself known, especially in the dark. Right now, it's as if I can feel the dreams seeping from my mind and out into the air around me in an attempt to suffocate what I have managed to salvage of myself. I pull myself upright and run a hand down my face, realizing that the spliff was laced with something a whole fuck-ton stronger than simply tobacco and herb.

My phone goes off, and I groan at the instant headache that makes its claim around my skull. The crushing weight of the developing pain radiates down the column of my neck and eerily spreads over my shoulders. If I wasn't so used to the debilitating pain, I'd rip at my own jugular. I glance down at the screen, which is lit up with Adriana's name and picture, inviting me to answer it. I recollect what I can of myself before I answer with a swipe of my finger. Instead of bringing the phone up to my ear, I place her on speaker phone. The thought of having any sound that close to my head right now would drill little holes in all of my nerve endings and wholly wipe me out.

"What's up, Addy?"

"Hey you."

I clear my throat and pull my body up into a standing position. Steadying myself before taking the steps to get to the kitchen, I hold the phone down at my side. "What the fuck is the time?"

"It's just past eight in the morning here, so uhm, about eleven in the evening your time. You sound like you were asleep. I wouldn't have called if I knew that you'd be in bed."

There's more to that statement than I care for, and she knows it. She's been silently pushing for more out of this thing we have going on ever since we flew to Scotland together. In actuality, she might have been pushing for more before that, but I didn't take note of it. Right now, though, that little push was her way of telling me that she wants to know what I'm doing, and I'm not going to play pretend when I don't want to change. She'd have to break my fucking bed before I decide to tie myself down to one woman again.

"Yeah, well, I just passed out. Are you at work? Wade needs to let you come in later. It's far too early for you."

"I just got here, and there's a message from you on his office number."

I frown, not remembering what the hell I said or when I even called. "There is?"

"Yes. If that's how you feel, then please don't play dumb."

"Play dumb? When the fuck does it say that I called?"

She pauses for a beat too long. "About two and a half hours ago."

I go into the refrigerator and uncap a bottle of water, throwing half of it back before I pull open a cabinet stocked with my store-bought drugs. After popping four mind-numbing headache pills, I answer her. "Would you mind enlightening me as to what I said?"

"Why? Were you drunk? You sure didn't sound drunk."

Fuck me backward and in every other direction that this woman can think of. She's been so damned persistent about knowing more each time we talk, and the more she asks, the less I give her. How can a woman not take note of the pattern?

"No, Addy, I wasn't. I was—"

I cut myself off because I know that she does not favor my use of recreational drugs. She's part of the reason that tonight was my last jaunt with them. No, I'm not kicking the habit for her per se. I'm kicking it because of her influence.

"You were high," she says with a heavy sigh.

"Does it matter?"

"Yes, actually. How about I forward you the message and

you can call me back once you're done listening to yourself ramble on and on?"

I frown and slide my hand down the side of my face. "Go for it."

"Goodbye, Liam," she murmurs before she hangs up and I set the phone down on the counter, watching the light dim and then turn off, providing my head with a much-needed reprieve. I attempt to remember calling Wade, but nothing surfaces. Why the fuck would I call his office phone instead of his cell?

My phone pings, the noise further exacerbating my headache. I slide my finger to play the message that Addy sent me to listen to. I hit play and keep it on speaker, placing one hand on either side of the counter and ducking my head down between my arms to keep the nausea at bay for as long as possible. I don't get migraines too often, but this one is going to be a heavy hitter.

My voice comes over the speakerphone, and I cringe at my obvious stupor.

"Hey fucker," I say and it's followed by a pause, "I'll be flying into Chicago tomorrow at some point. I haven't told Isla or Addison yet. Wait, that's wrong, it's got to be wrong. The last Addison that I nailed must have been at that frat party where you fucked our little Isla."

I chuckle before speaking again. "Adriana, yeah, there we go. That's the right kind of pussy that I'm talking about. Fuck, she's got a pussy that I'd sing to, but let me tell you, she's fucking relentless. She understands where I stand regarding relationships, but she's going to keep pushing me but passively. Passive-aggressively. You know, she reminds me of Chloe. Maybe too much, and no, not in the physical way because let's be honest here . . . we know who that thought will lead me to."

I hear myself whistle, and I pinch the bridge of my nose. "There's not a chance in hell that I'd be the someone who she wants me to be. She's not Chloe, and she never will be, so she needs to quit pushing her shit on me, ya know? For fuck's sake, she's just trying too damn hard. Wade? You there, you asshole? Hello?"

The line goes silent for a while before I'm able to hear a rustling around, and then I hang up, ending the message that was supposed to be for Wade.

Fuck.

My phone chimes again with an email alert, but I ignore it and dial Addy instead. She must answer because it stops ringing on the second ring. "Adriana?"

She chooses to remain silent.

"I don't remember calling or saying any of that. I apologize."

"I can't do this any longer," she says so softly that it rips at something inside of me, something that should have died off a long time ago.

"You don't mean that. I was fucked out of my mind—"

She cuts me off before I am able to spew out another excuse. "No. You might not have been sober, but your words sounded truthful. I'm sorry that I remind you of her, but knowing how you truly feel . . . I'm sorry. I can't be your side piece any longer."

"You've never been a side piece."

"No? It sure has felt like it for years now. I should have realized that you wouldn't want anything more when you brought Isla into the equation. I was simply blinded by the charm you used to have. I need to go—Mr. Brass just walked in. Oh, and don't worry, I'll ensure that he gets your message."

"Shit, Adriana, don't—"

"Goodbye, Liam."

The phone beeps once, informing me that the call has indeed ended. I form a fist and slam my bare knuckles against the marble countertop, welcoming the sting that cracks around each one of them.

My gut is telling me to call her again and apologize, but my mind refuses to let that happen. If I do follow through and call her, then I'm allowing her into more than just my bed. I'm risking more than just my dick's happiness here; I do not want nor need more than what we've been doing. Either path will lead me to a dark place, and I will regret doing one or the other without a doubt. The thought of letting her down and pushing her away makes me drop my head in dissatisfaction with myself, but I quickly remind myself that it's better that it happens now before our hookup goes beyond what I want it to be. Although, I'm beginning to realize that it's gone well past that point for her.

I push myself up and off of the kitchen countertop and trash the now-empty bottle of water before retiring to my bedroom for the evening. Each step I take up to my bedroom seems to intensify the jarring and brutal daggers in my head. I crash on the bed without undressing or pulling the covers down as my body seizes in pain. The phantom pain festers, and I want to fucking perish underneath its pervasive hold.

The next morning goes by in a rush as I'm herded through security lines at the Sydney Airport until I'm on board and headed in the direction of Los Angeles. A lingering headache doesn't help either as the jet engines roar to life. I may be free of the gnarled claws of a migraine, but the agony brought on by every person's voice reminds me just how much I wish I was sitting on the tarmac alone. Flights like these make me grateful for my own jet, but when it's out for maintenance, I don't have any other choice but to fly with the rest of society.

As soon as we're in the air, I push my seat back and hit play on my phone to drown out the soft hum of the plane as well as the two women who have not shut up beside me in first class.

I'll have to endure some level of discomfort, and right now, I'm choosing something that I have control over rather than their fucking cackling.

It's the same shit, just on a different level, and I need to keep the headache contained before I get swallowed whole by its bitter pangs of unmedicated perdition.

I force my eyes to shut and focus on the soothing guitar riff that's passing through my headphones before sleep attempts to take me.

Fuck the turmoil of my yesterdays.

Fuck those almighty tomorrows that I think may bring me something to live for.

As of this moment I decide that I will live for each day and enjoy it as it comes and is given to me. Silver platter or not, I'll breathe life into myself once again. Regardless of the ragged struggle that I'll need to brutally confront, I know that there's something beyond the clouds of pain to live for. I just have to find it for myself.

Three

Isla

INCIDENTALLY, I'M NOT someone who needs saving any more than I need a drink. I don't need nor do I want a knight in shining armor, but as a woman, I do need a few things. The only things I'm certain about in life are orgasms and whiskey, and right about now, I could use one of each.

I'm not afraid to tell it like it is, and I've been called a total bitch because of it, but it doesn't bother me. I understand that words are more powerful than we assume them to be, and as much as they seemed to have controlled my life, I won't play the victim for another second. The majority of the time, I have to remind myself to dust myself off and don the crown to remember who I am.

My life seems to be a revolving door of sorts, nowadays, of whiskey, men, orgasms, and repeat. I don't mind it, but I'd like a little bit more out of life at some point . . . not right now, though. Today and every day to come, I see myself exactly where I am. I'm content, and I don't plan on changing the way I live my life anytime soon. Yes, I'm selfish and a bitch, but I've been living a life that belongs to me and only me. It's honestly the first time in my life that I've felt more than the drowning emotions of depression. After years of being in a medicated coma of sorts, I've managed to wean myself off of it for the first time. Today is day one without the slightest dose, and I'm excited to see how it goes.

I'm not someone who tends to hold back on anything when it comes to something I want that is attainable. I hold my own, and I'm damn proud of it. Fuck the world's perceptions of women who make a life for themselves. I'm single, I'm independent, and I'm happy.

At least that what I tell people.

I look up from my post at the bar and scan the crowded room in front of me. This is the other thing I live for. Blended is my sanctuary, and it's the one place that I don't feel like I have to try to convince people of who I am. I smile to myself before I readjust some of the bottles of whiskey along a wooden shelf before it happens again. A heavy hand lands on my ass, leaving a stinging pain in its wake. I spin around to see who the hell just had the audacity to land one on me again. It's him. The same dude from ten minutes ago and I swear to God, I'm going to have to toss a fucking bottle of whiskey at this asshole's head if he touches me once more.

My customers at Blended are usually laid back and tend to be higher on the social ladder than regular bars, and I've never seen this fuck here before, but I can tell that nothing good comes along with him.

One of my librarians, Eden, has been keeping an eye on him for the majority of the evening, but he's recently fallen in love with my ass while I reach for bottles of some of the world's most unique and expensive whiskey.

"Hey Isla?"

I spin around in the direction of Eden's voice and give her a weak, exhausted smile. "Yeah?"

"I think that we need to call the cops or something on him. He just leaned over and groped that woman's breast," she says, pointing to one of my regulars.

"Dear God. I'll get his tab taken care of, and you call Colin

Jacobs. His number is in my phone."

"Mr. Brass's driver, right?"

"You've got it."

With our little plan underway, she walks to my office while I purposely give him a great view down the front of my shirt as I hand him his bill back. I don't know how that amount cleared his card, but it did, so I'm not complaining. His eyes remain on my breasts as he scribbles on the receipt, leaving Eden a tip that is twice the amount of his bill. I try to hide my laugh as Eden comes back out and hands me my cell.

"Liam Jensen said that he's on his way with Jacobs."

"Liam?"

"Yup, Jacobs answered and then handed the phone off to him."

I raise my brows and take my phone from her, glancing down at it and expecting to see a missed called from Liam or even a text message, but there's nothing. Odd.

A good fifteen minutes pass while I serve my regulars throughout the library before a pair of muscle-laced arms come around my waist from behind.

"There she is."

I throw a glance over my shoulder and roll my eyes at his beautiful cocky grin. "What the actual fuck are you doing here, Liam?"

This man will, at some point, be the death of me. He does what he wants when he wants. He's reckless, stubborn, and inconsistent. Needless to say, he's untamable, even though countless numbers of women have tried. He brings chaos wherever he goes, but through all of it, I wouldn't change the man that he is. Most people look at him, and that's all that they can see. When they are able to look past his physical features, though, they'll see that there's more to him than that.

Although, I will admit that it's sometimes difficult to look past his sturdy and well-defined features and a body that was molded from granite. Liam is more than the full package, but not every woman out there will be able to handle him. He's got this dark-brown tousled hair that I'm dying to run my fingers through again, and that smile, fuck me. He's an Adonis that seems to make all other men pale in comparison. He's handsome all right, but inside, he's beautiful.

"Are you complaining? I swear that I could hear this pussy beg for me from across the ocean," he says through a cocky smile.

Damn, that smile.

Whenever Liam Jensen smiles like that, all that I can think is *oh shit.*

He moves his hand down as if he's about to cup my sex, but I stop him with one of mine and manage to cough out a laugh before moving out of his arms. I nod in the direction of the asshole sitting at my bar with his head on the counter. "Make him leave, and I'll blow you."

"Ah, doll, you'll blow me regardless."

I huff and push on his hands until he releases me. "Will you just help Jacobs, please?" I say as I glance over to where Jacobs now has the man over his shoulder, and he's leading the drunken loon out of Blended.

"It looks like I'm no longer needed."

"Neither is your cock," I shoot back at him and walk off in the direction of my office. I close my office door lightly behind me, and step to my desk, counting down the seconds before Liam barges in, and as if right on cue, the door swings open. He gazes at me with want in his eyes from across the room before slamming the door closed and turning the lock.

"I've missed you, Isla."

"Is that so? Did you miss me or my body?"

"Both. You're one hell of a bundle," he says as he walks up to me and slides a large hand down my ribcage to my hip. He pulls my body into his and I brace my hands against his chest.

"I didn't know that you were back. How long are you staying for this time? Just long enough to get the tip of your dick wet?"

His eyelids lower in deep need as his other hand moves to my back, pushing the thin material of my sweater out of his way until he's able to touch my bare skin.

"How about I keep my travel arrangements to myself, and you give me what I want?"

I toss my head back and laugh at him. To him, I'm a sure thing, but little does he know, I'm not so sure I want it anymore.

Isla Madden belongs to no man. At least not if I can help it.

I revolve around multiple men, just as he revolves around myself and Adriana Hugh, yet for some reason ever since we started fucking these last few months, the mere sight of her pisses me off. I cannot stand the fact that she gets to taste him after he's been inside of me, buried in my aching core while he made me cry out in pleasurable bliss.

I huff out a breath and look up into his dark, almost-black eyes. "Honestly. Why didn't you tell me that you were coming back?"

He must notice my body language change because his touch goes from demanding gropes to gentle strokes of his fingers.

"I didn't tell anyone."

"Chicken shit."

His light chuckle fills my office before he wraps my loose hair around his wrist. "Not one bit, but I thought that I'd need to ask your permission first before I just crashed at your place until I found my own. That's why I'm here."

"Ah, so you're here to use me." I pause and scrunch up my

face. "Wait. You're looking for your own place? How come?"

"I will be. I'll be staying longer than my usual week or two."

"And how long will that be, Jensen?"

"Indefinitely."

For some reason that I cannot explain, that one word calms all of the blood raging through my body at the thought of having to say goodbye to one of my best friends and fuck-buddy again.

I shrug to look as unaffected as I possibly can before moving out of his touch and grabbing my keys from the top drawer in my desk. "Grab your shit. Let's get you settled."

"It's currently all at Wade's place."

"Well, are you going to be crashing there or with me? You know that I won't approve of your fucking Adriana in my bed, so maybe it's wiser that you stay with Brass."

"Addy and I are over."

I don't think that I conceal the shock on my face enough to hide it from him because he gives me the cockiest of grins.

"Don't look at me like that."

"Like what?" I ask hesitantly.

"Like you thought that Addy and I may have developed into something more."

"Uhm, after all of those years, I'm not entirely sure how you two hadn't."

He clears his throat and pulls my winter coat off the back of my chair. "You know how I feel about having a woman rely on me. I don't trust myself enough to support someone."

"You've mentioned that more times than I care to think is true."

I slide my arms into my coat before buttoning it up and wrapping a scarf around my neck. He reaches for my hand without my having to prompt him, and he leads me out of the office and into the main room of Blended.

I scan the library for Eden, and when I spot her, I call out and tell her that I'll be leaving for the evening and that she's in charge to close up.

She gives me a thumbs-up as Liam and I walk out of the rear entrance and into the back lot, which is covered in more snow than it was when I first arrived. I dig my car keys out of my coat pocket and toss them to him.

He catches them and grins. "It's been a while since I've driven in this shit."

"Well, there's no time like the present to get back into the swing of things."

We walk up to my new pearl-white Porsche Cayenne, and I get into the passenger seat while he shuts the driver's side door and turns on the ignition.

"What happened to the Jeep?"

"I needed an upgrade. Plus, this baby has a lot more power behind her."

He winks at me and then gets a faraway look in his eyes.

"What is it? You look like a lost puppy."

"Fuck you," he chuckles before running his hand through his short, dark-brown hair and then down the side of his face, over his sideburns to his chin that is covered in just the right amount of growth.

My eyes automatically roam down this sexy specimen of a man, and I take in his six-foot-something frame, which is covered in jeans that fit him seamlessly, a plain black shirt, and a leather jacket. The man could kill with his looks alone, and it's one of the reasons why our friendship over the years has always harbored some sexual attraction. Sure, we've occasionally fucked throughout the years, but since December of last year when Wade and Hadley become something incredibly serious, so did my and Liam's naked antics.

We graduated from the occasional drunk fuck to multi-ple-times-a-week fuck when he's here, and I don't regret it. He knows how to work my body over, and I love watching him do it. It's a win-win situation without having to hardball anyone.

I unconsciously toy with the ripped fabric around the knee of my black skinny jeans as he pulls out of the lot and around the building onto the Magnificent Mile.

"So are you going to tell me what you're really doing here?" I ask while I stare out my window while we pass some of Chicago's most gorgeous architecture.

"I needed a change."

"That's it?" I turn to look at him as he slides a hand onto my knee and laces his fingers with mine, forcing me to stop toying with the frayed material.

"It is."

"You mean that you're done with Sydney? What about RW? I'm sure that it can't run itself without your taking control of every fucking decision that needs to be made."

"They'll survive without me for a while. I've decided to take a step or two back and try to salvage some of this messed-up life that I've been given."

I raise my eyes to the heavens and shake my head. "Liam, there are plenty of people out there who are in far worse situations than you are currently in. Maybe in the past, you could have beaten them in the *whose life is the worst contest*, but not anymore."

"I didn't say that. I'm not complaining, and no, I don't compare what I've been through with others because we are all living through challenges that we need to get through, and this just so happens to be mine. I've decided to move forward rather than dwell in the past."

"Liam Jensen, when did you become a man who knows

what he wants in life, and what did you do with my pessimistic best friend?"

"He's right here, doll."

I lift his hand up in mine and bring it to my mouth. Most men would assume that I'm about to kiss or suck on their fingers, but he should know better by now. I turn his hand and bite at the inside of his wrist.

"Fuck! What the hell was that for?" he says as he pulls his hand out of mine and pinches the inside of my thigh.

I screech and squirm away from him while I try to fight off the fit of laughter that wants to take over. "For not telling me that you were coming back. I may be a piece of ass for you, but we've always put our friendship first, and don't you dare forget that, you dickweed."

"Yeah, yeah."

I lean over and bite the outside edge of his elbow, causing him to swerve a bit in his reaction.

"When did you become this intent on biting me? This shit is new, and I might need you to take it to the bedroom with me."

He glances at me from the road and raises an eyebrow in question as he messes up his hair even more with his left hand.

"The bedroom? Who said that you'd be sleeping in my bed with me? I think that you deserve the couch . . . actually . . . nope. Scratch that. I'll give you a pillow, and you can sleep in the bathtub."

"Feisty bitch," he says with a laugh and places his hand back on my thigh, rubbing circles on the bare skin of my knee that's available to him.

We pull into Lake Point Tower's parking garage, and I don't have to direct him to my parking spot. He knows exactly which one belongs to me.

I've lived in Lake Point Tower for the last two years, and I'm in love with my loft apartment as well as its phenomenal views. The building itself sits directly in front of Navy Pier, providing me with a view that many won't have the pleasure of living with. It stands alone on a private two-acre park and is surrounded by Lake Michigan on three sides of the building. I was lucky enough to get one of the three sides when I purchased here.

Sure, I paid far too much for it, but then again, I get paid far too much for my own good. I know that from working similar positions throughout my life, but Wade has always spoiled me, and he refuses to take no for an answer. The first paycheck that he gave me a couple of years ago when he bought the hotel where I was working was more than my annual salary. I tore it to pieces in front of him in an act of rebellion. I remember his glare the moment I shoved all of the pieces back over his desk to him. A little later that week when I was checking the balance of my bank account, all of the money was already there, sitting pretty. Fucker.

I jump out of my SUV and check my pockets to ensure that I have my cell phone and walk around to Liam, who offers me his arm, but I nudge his side instead as we walk to the elevator banks and hit the up button.

Two women who I recognize as being my neighbors from a few floors below me walk up to us. Both of their gazes fall on Liam, and they both manage to look him up and down before turning to each other and sharing a knowing look.

A flash of heated jealousy rolls over my skin, and I couldn't have done anything to anticipate it or even stop it. *How fucking awkward and great*, I chastise myself. I'm jealous of two sets of fake tits eyeing one of my best friends.

I should be used to it by now—both of the guys who have been close to me for years are the two most gorgeous men I have ever laid eyes on. For some reason, though, one that I cannot explain right this minute, I want to pop these women's fucking silicone-enhanced breasts for staring at him like he's something attainable.

I shift from one foot to the other and Liam looks down at me, scowling before his attention is shifted to the two women standing beside us. He ducks his head down to whisper in my ear, "Do we not like them?"

I chew on the corner of my lip and stare up at him before saying, "Not with the way they are looking at you like they've already imagined you naked and hovering on top of them."

He glances from me up at them again and smirks. I know that I said that too loud, but I don't give a fuck. Fuck them for wanting him.

He shocks me when he bounds his arms around me and lifts me into his arms when the elevator doors open. He walks me into the metal death trap and pushes my back up against one of the four corners, causing me to lock my ankles at the small of his back.

I can feel his cock pushing into the apex of my legs as he gives me a sinful grin before taking my mouth smoothly. It's a rushed and heated kiss, one that would make any woman drop to her knees in submission. He must be enjoying putting on a show for the two of them as they follow us into the elevator, not caring that I'm clawing at his back.

Am I shocked by this kiss? Absolutely, but I'm more than stunned that he just turned both of them down for a threesome without having to say anything.

I have not, in all of my years of knowing this dickweed, seen him turn down easy pieces of ass like that before. He's like any other man when it comes to sex. He wants it and all of the time, but unlike other men, he gets it whenever he wants it, and dear God does he deliver.

Thoughts run through my head as if trying to come up with an excuse for his behavior but the moment his tongue flicks against mine as it would against my clitoris, I lose all of them.

.

Four

Liam

I CAN FEEL the warmth of her pressed against my cock as it swells. I can also sense the two pairs of eyes at the back of my head as the elevator comes to a stop.

Instead of hearing their heels against the marble flooring, all I hear is harsh, heavy breathing. I tear my lips from Isla's and turn my head to look at them as Isla runs her fingers into the back of my hair and tugs me back to look at her. The heat that's flaring in her eyes would scorch and damage any other man, but not me—I can't wait to provide her with the fuel to keep it burning. I grin and thrust my hips into her, conjuring a quiet whimper from her lips.

Fucking hell. I need her.

"Ladies, if you're not going to get off—the elevator, I mean—hit the close-door button, so I can finally bury my length inside of her while she's wet and ready. I cannot stand another second of not being inside her warmth. I need to fuck her until she's raw."

Isla bites down on my bottom lip, piercing the skin and drawing a drop of blood. She pulls back and cups her hand over her mouth once she realizes what she did. "Oops?"

Reality sets in at the same moment she pushes her chest up against mine. Our little game just ended and now pure, unadulterated need swims through my veins at the idea of having her on the floor of the elevator.

"You know," I tell her, "I wasn't really going to fuck you straight away, but . . ." I run my tongue over my bottom lip, tasting the rusty warmth from the blood she drew. "I may have to because of what you just did."

I watch her take the corner of her lip between her teeth as I hear the women exit, and the doors finally close. I don't let go of her for the remainder of the ascent, but I stare into her eyes, daring her.

She raises her brow at me, throwing the challenge back at me without saying a word. I watch her carefully as she shrugs her petite shoulders and leans into me again. Her tongue comes out, and she runs it over the bite mark on my lower lip. My eyes widen, but I cannot help my reaction to her as my lips start to move with hers again.

Fuck, I don't know what just went through her head, and as much as that should be inappropriate, it was anything but. The taste of her has made me realize that I've been starving to have her again. No amount of masturbation will ease this building need to have her once again.

The elevator doors slide open, causing our kiss to come to an abrupt end. I set her on her feet before leading her out of the confined space and down the hallway to her front door. I wait impatiently for her while she inserts the key into the lock and pushes the door in. She steps inside, and I have to do a double take of her place before I can look at her again.

"You redecorated?"

She nods and takes the key out of the door before closing it and shrugs off her coat to hang it up.

She's been quiet ever since she claimed me as hers in the elevator in front of people who we didn't know. She does this at times, and each time it baffles me the way she allows the silence to control her. When she's unsure of herself, she reverts back to being someone who she's fought to overcome. Instead of allowing her to think too much about what just transpired between us, I pull her back into the present with my words of distraction.

"It looks good."

"Thanks, I really like it."

I glance around and notice that the walls to the upper part of the loft are now glass, giving me an unhindered view of her bedroom. Instead of the dark colors that once graced the walls, everything is light and white, from the ceilings to the floors. I watch her remove her Converses from her feet and step onto a plush, dark-gray rug that covers the living room area. My eyes travel to the wall above her flatscreen where there is a four-piece painting of a close-up of a woman's face. She's stunning, and I groan when I see those fucking gorgeous lips, and I know that they belong to her because I've seen those lips in that shade of red swallow my cock on more than one occasion.

She's managed to outfit her place just as she does herself. Since I've known her, the only clothing that she'll wear is in blacks, whites, and grays. Aside from her red lips, and the occasional blue jeans, she doesn't do colors.

Over the years, Wade and I have tried to get her to put herself out there a little more, but it's the one thing that she refuses to change. I don't blame her, though, seeing as the world changed her heart. I remember purchasing a multi-colored thong for her once, and not even two seconds after handing it over to her, it was being consumed in the flames in Blended's fireplace.

"You know," she says, pulling me from my private thoughts, "it's kind of startling to be around you when you're not drunk."

"Yeah?"

"After the last few years, I've gotten used to you being fucked out of your mind while I'm around. I don't think that we've held an actual conversation in years."

"I call bullshit on that one, doll."

"I don't know, Jensen." She laughs and opens one of the cabinets in her kitchen, pulling out two tumblers before filling them with two fingers of Pappy Van Winkle's Family Reserve. She holds the glass out for me, and I take it in my hand while purposefully brushing my fingers along hers.

I enjoy teasing Isla. She might consider herself a tough bitch on her exterior, but through the years, I've seen her break down her walls, and I've seen the emotional side of her. She may not wear the sentiments on her sleeves, but she sure as fuck knows how to lock herself away and emotionally tear herself apart.

She's self-destructive in that way. She doesn't know how to handle the highs of her emotions when it comes down to it, just as I'm unsure how to manage my life.

"Just this one, Isla. I need to cut back, plus I'm tired as fuck, and I'll fall asleep on you."

She shrugs her shoulders, and I take a drink of the whiskey bourbon, groaning when the hints of vanilla, maple, and honey swim across my taste buds. She throws me a radiating smile over her shoulder and walks up the stairs into her bedroom.

I leave her be, and take a seat on the beige sectional in her living room, leaning my head back and propping my arm up on one of the throw pillows while I stare up at the glass walls of her bedroom. I watch her intently as she gives me a silent show, removing her jeans and shirt before stepping out of my sight as she undoes the clasps of her black silk bra.

No one should be this attracted to their best friend, but I'm well past caring about how frequently I see her flawless skin bared for me.

I shut my eyes and lean my head back after taking another healthy sip of the whiskey bourbon. This shit may not be the top of the line in the world of whiskey, but it's fucking incredible. It's premium through and through.

I'm jolted awake by the pinching of my skin between her teeth as she bites down on the inside of my wrist. I'm about to pull away from her when I realize that it's the hand that I've got my tumbler in.

"Fuck, Isla. Control your goddamn mouth, would you?"

"Uhh, rude," she says through a giggle and sits down beside me before leaning forward and pulling open a box of my favorite Chicago deep-dish pizza.

"When the hell did you order this?"

She moves strands of her wet ink-black hair over to one shoulder before she pulls out a slice and leans back against the couch.

"When your ass was well and passed out."

"I was resting my eyes," I shoot back and take a slice of my own, groaning when the taste of mozzarella cheese and pizza sauce hits my mouth.

She wipes off her mouth with a napkin before speaking. "Your stubborn ass was snoring. Don't try and deny it or I'll lock my bedroom door tonight."

"You'll do no such thing."

I finish my slice and reach for another. I had no idea how damn hungry I was, or maybe it's just because Lou Malnati's pizza is the shit. Isla sets her crust down, and I eye her suspiciously. "You're not going to eat that?"

"Uhh, nope. I need some more cheese and sauce," she tells me as she reaches for the pie again.

I put my hand out to stop her. "Uh-uh. Eat that. Nobody wastes this heavenly pie."

"Liam," she starts, staring me down, "if you'd prefer the bathtub to my bed, then you could have just said so." Her quirky smile inches its way onto her face as the words leave her mouth.

I sigh and move my hand away, allowing her another slice before she eats the crust.

"So," she says after taking a bite, "where are you going to look for a place to call home?"

"I've been thinking about it, and I'm not entirely sure. I'll have to get a realtor to help start my hunt. Do you have any ideas?"

"Well, it depends on what you want. Would you want a penthouse or apartment? Or even a house?"

I finish my slice while she sets her second one down, which she took one bite out of, and turns to face me. It's now that I notice that she's in leggings and a sweatshirt. She sits cross-legged and braids her hair while she waits for my answer.

"I think that I'll get a house. As much as I love living in the city itself, it'd be nice to have somewhere to escape to, but I'm unsure."

"So . . . something like your place in Sydney?"

"I'd like that."

She bites the corner of her lips as she ties the end of her braid. "What about Winnetka?"

"Winnetka? That's more than thirty minutes from the city, doll. Plus, I don't think those old-money rich bitches will approve of the parties that I plan on hosting there."

"Well, I'm not sure if you'll get the mansion that your heart desires any closer to the city, and you are part of one of those old-money families, so you can't say a word."

I chuckle and take a drink before laying my arm on the back of the couch. "I need another option."

She blows out a breath before replying. "What about staying on the Gold Coast? I know that it's in the city, but it's right on the water, which I happen to know you like. You'd be close enough to me too."

"I might scare you away if I'm too close to you."

She barks out a laugh and shoves my hand away from her shoulder. "You should just build your own damn house here in the city. I'm sure the realtor will never meet all of the wants you'll have."

"That's actually not a bad idea. I'll have to look into pieces of land that are for sale."

"So it's settled then?"

"For now," I say through a yawn.

"Great. So you're going to stay in the city if you can find a lot big enough for your ego?"

"Ah, there she is," I chuckle and trail my fingers down the column of her neck. I get an eye roll for that comment, and she shifts slightly beneath my touch.

"I'm going to bed," she tells me as she stands and stretches her arms up in the air, giving me a glimpse of her bare stomach. "You coming?"

"Am I?" I tease her and get up. I wrap my arms around her midsection and lift her over my shoulder as I make my way through her loft, turning off the lights as I go until we get up to her bedroom. I toss her onto her bed before pulling my shirt off over my head and tossing it onto one of the two chairs that are in the room.

She eyes me as she crawls underneath her large white comforter and relaxes back against a pillow that seems to be twice her size.

"If you need an orgasm, I'm happy to oblige, but I'm afraid that I'm too fucking tired to do more than that tonight, doll."

"You're turning me down?"

"Nah, I wouldn't do that. I just wouldn't be able to live up to the high standards that I've already set."

"As if."

I undo the button on my jeans and kick off my shoes. She's still watching me while I slide the material down my legs, toss it on top of my shirt, and climb in beside her.

"Keep those cold-ass toes to yourself tonight."

"Fine," she grumbles and turns on her side.

I reach over her to turn off the lights before winding an arm around her waist, and pulling her body up against mine.

"Sleep well, baby doll."

"Mmm."

I've never met anyone who has the uncanny ability to be a complete and utter grumpy bitch every morning without fail as Isla does.

I understand that waking up at five in the morning is not her forte. I mean, it's not mine either, but the time change fucks up my body each and every time I make this trip.

As I run my hand between her sweatshirt and her leggings she shifts and grabs a pillow, launching it at me. How she managed to hit me directly in the face without looking, I have no idea.

"Fucking hell, doll."

"I'm sleeping."

"Yeah? Well, I'm not."

"Liam," she moans and turns her head to face me as she hugs her pillow.

"Yeah?"

"You're an ass. Get out of my bed."

I move my hand under her leggings to touch her bare ass, enjoying the fact that she's not wearing any underwear. "All right. I'll give you ten more minutes while I go shower."

"Deal," she says sleepily and rolls back over.

I get up and stretch out my tired muscles before walking downstairs to grab my phone. I have a couple of emails from RW and a message from Addy: *Hey. I wanted to make sure that you made it back. If you need a place to crash, you're welcome to stay with me.*

I groan because as much as I still want to bury myself inside of her, I've already hurt her more times than what is acceptable of a man. I now know that she wants much more from me than just to hook up, because any woman who heard what I said about her as Addy did would have let me go without looking back.

Yet she still wants me in her life, proving to me that I mean much more to her than a simple cock to sink down onto. I type out a message and hit send: *Hey. Yeah, I made it, and I'm crashing with Isla. I don't think that this is going to work between us anymore, Addy.*

I walk over to the coffeepot and start a batch then make my way back upstairs to the bathroom when my phone goes off. I was not expecting her to reply to me at this early hour, but here she is: *You know what . . . fuck this. I thought that you'd just need time to figure out what you wanted, but it seems as if you've already done so. Goodbye, Liam.*

I groan and type out another reply: *I'm sorry, Adriana. I know that in time, we'll be able to hang like we used to. I'll see you around.*

To that, I don't get a response, so I set my phone down on the bathroom vanity and turn the shower on before I remove my boxer briefs. I step into the shower and allow the steam to fill the room while I rinse off my past with the scalding water.

I may not be getting high anymore, but I sure as shit could use something strong this morning. It's hard to see just how poisonous someone is in your life until you are able to walk away and take a deep breath of fresh air. For some reason, I'm breathing in that new air this morning, and I'm unsure if it has to do with saying goodbye to Addy, no longer getting high, or being around Isla.

For some reason, though, I believe that moving forward from Addy is, in a fucked-up way, moving away from the life I shared with Chloe. What's done is done, and now, as I watch a single water drop run down the wall of the shower, I realize just how small of an impact my life can have on the world. At the same time, I also realize just how much of an impact I'm making when I join with another drop. I'll figure out what is the best way to move forward with RW when I've regained the faith that I once had in myself.

I know that I need to get my shit together and that it's now or never.

By the time I emerge from the bathroom, Isla is still passed out under the mound of white covers. I head downstairs and pour a single cup of coffee before coming back up to her bedroom and slamming the door shut to jolt her awake.

Five

Isla

MOTHERFUCKING SHIT.

I sit upright and clutch at my chest. My heart is beating so hard that it's about to pound out of my body.

"You scared me, you asshole!"

"Mmm, good morning, doll," he says with a smug smile as he takes a drink of steaming-hot coffee.

I glare at him from my spot on the bed, but my eyes quickly travel the length of his body. He's still damp from his shower, and I squeeze my thighs to try and provide the apex of them with some sort of relief at the sight of this man. He's wrapped a towel around his hips and tucked it in right above the spot where his heavy cock lies.

I watch him as his corded arm lifts the white mug up to his lips, and I swear if this were a dream, then I'd already be drooling and naked beneath him. He's impeccably groomed—he always has been—and I cannot help but stare. My lady bits are begging for relief as he takes a step toward the bed.

"Want some?" he says as he takes another drink of the black gold and moves to the side of the bed that I'm seated on. I watch the muscles in his torso move as he lowers himself onto the bed and offers me the coffee mug. I take it with both hands and groan when the dark, pungent java aroma hits my senses. The comforting cloak of coffee and warmth take over my body as I take a sip and moan at the soothingly dark liquid. It's almost as good as whiskey. *Almost.*

I take one more sip before handing the mug back to him then crossing my legs. I watch as his mouth wraps around the lip of the mug and he takes a drink just as my insides pull together.

"Thank you," I say softly.

He raises his eyebrows as he hands me the mug again and I hold it with both of my hands to sip from. Instead of handing it right back to him, I hog it a little longer than I should. He shifts his large frame closer to me and takes the mug from me, downing the remainder of the coffee before placing the now-empty mug on my nightstand.

I pout at him because I need more coffee than that to completely wake up.

Chuckling, he gets up on his knees and moves over me, causing me to lie back down while he hovers on top of my rather needy body. Just because I'm a woman, doesn't mean that I don't need a release in the morning.

A chill runs through my body as he leans down and runs his nose up the column of my neck. I manage to swallow as his lips find mine, and as hard as I try, I cannot keep my hands to myself any longer. I slide them down either side of his long torso to where the towel sits low on his hips.

I dip a finger underneath the soft fabric of the towel and tug, slowly freeing his bare skin of it. He groans as his tongue moves alongside mine now. He tastes of coffee and Liam. It's a heady combination to wake up to.

One at a time, my thoughts creep in unwanted as our mouths move along each other's and our tongues intertwine in a private dance.

I know that I should stop messing around with him because one of us is going to get hurt in the future, and I have no doubt that that one will ultimately be me. He's too much of a player to hurt over someone like me. I mentally scold myself for wanting him like I do. I shouldn't, I know that, but I do.

Instead of pulling the towel off of him completely, I move my hands back up over his chest and push him off of me.

"I need more coffee."

"Seriously?"

"Uhh, yup." I slide out from underneath him and yank the towel off of his ass as I walk away from the bed. My sex is crying out to me, wanting me to go back to him so I can feel sated from a release, but I choose to ignore it as best as I can with my back turned toward him.

I head downstairs and pour myself a mug full of coffee and lean against the island. I swear, I almost spit out the coffee when he walks downstairs completely naked and comfortable with his erect cock aimed in my direction.

I swallow the sip of coffee as he comes up to me and takes the mug, taking a long drink of the hot liquid before passing it back to me. As I take a drink, he lifts me up and sits me on the island. My eyes widen as I almost spill the coffee on him, but I steady myself in time and take another drink.

As I move the mug away from my lips, he tilts my chin to the side and starts to kiss my neck. The soft kisses turn into nips and bites, and soon, I know that he'll start marking me if I don't push him away.

"Liam."

"Isla," he challenges.

Thank God that my phone starts to ring because I'm about to let him fuck me right here. "It's probably Wade."

"It's early, so he can wait."

"You're so demanding."

"I know what I want, doll."

"And what would that be?"

"You."

A long moment of silence follows the vibrations of my phone in which we just watch each other, our bodies paused while pressed together, neither of us wanting to make the first move.

He ultimately goes first when he cups my cheek and takes my lips again just as my phone starts to vibrate once more. He groans and pushes away from me to follow the noise. He's standing with his bare back to me in the living room, and I cannot help but drink in all of his masculinity. My eyes lower from his broad shoulders to his taut ass, and I take in a long, steady breath to help calm my need for him. Hell, to calm my own fingers.

I've always been attracted to him, but seeing him stark naked in my own space has intensified my desire to have him, and frankly, I'm not okay with that.

"Brass, what the fuck is so important that you need to interrupt my play?" I hear him say. He pauses a beat and then chuckles. It's a laugh that I haven't heard in a while, one that lets me know that he's got his mind on something other than his rescue efforts and more on things that he wants them to be on.

"Yeah. I'm going to crash here," he says. "I'll stop by later to pick up my shit." Another pause and then he adds, "All right, see ya, fucker."

He sets my phone back down and turns to face me with his cock hanging heavily between his legs. He's not as hard as he was a moment ago, and I blame Brass for that, but when I place the mug down and lift my sweatshirt up and off of my body, his cock bounces back to life.

He takes quick strides across the living room, and once he's in the kitchen, he pulls me off of the island and into his arms. I press my bare breasts onto his chest, loving the skin-on-skin contact as well as the heat it seems to create between us. He starts pushing my leggings down my ass as he takes two steps at a time to get us to my bedroom before he unravels me right here on the staircase.

I sink down into the mattress as he works my leggings off and tosses them aside before adjusting my body on the bed and crawling on top of me. He places kisses along my calf as he makes his way farther up. His lips and fingers still at my hips, daring me to thrust myself up to his mouth, but I force myself to hold back instead.

I don't usually let him lead the entire time, but I'm actually enjoying this early-morning fuck session by giving up my control to him.

His fingers dig into my sides as he runs his tongue up the middle of my body, pausing to sink it into my belly button and circle it once before making his way up to my breasts. I may not have those obnoxiously fake tits like those women last night did, but I'm proud of my girls.

He cups each of them and toys with my nipples with his thumbs as he bites down on my collarbone. Goose bumps break out over my skin as he moves up and seductively nips at my neck before trailing kisses back down the center of my body.

One of his hands slides down from my left breast to find my thigh and separate my legs enough for him to settle between them. My hips sway up to him of their own accord as he skims his knuckles over my now-damp entrance.

I lean up on my elbows just in time to watch him push his left ring finger inside of me, causing me to constrict around him immediately.

He throws a glance up at me while I bite at the corner of my lip.

"Let's see how fast I can make you come with my mouth."

Before I can protest, the flat of his tongue is dragging over my clitoris, making my entire body come alive with one solitary lick. I shove my hands into his hair as he continues his torturous devouring of my sex.

The addition of his middle finger in me as he bends them up to meet my spot makes me shiver. I tug on the strands of hair that I'm able to grab as my orgasm builds behind his tongue. He starts working my clit faster, and a rush of disorienting pleasure takes over until my body is surrounded in the sensation.

My mouth falls open in a silent moan for him as the sudden vibrations of the fast and vigorous orgasm leave me speechless. His tongue and fingers don't stop until I've come down from my high altogether.

"Record time, doll. That vibrator of yours must not be holding up."

"Fuck you," I hiss and shove his mouth off of me.

His chuckle fills my bedroom as he climbs up my body and grabs hold of his cock. "Are you still on the pill or do I need a condom again?"

"I'm on the pill, you dickweed. Now fuck me before I no longer want you to."

Liam is the only man who I've allowed to fuck me without a condom. Why? It's simple, really. I trust him. He told me that he's clean, and I swore the same. The trust between us is mutual, and it always has been.

He angles his head so it sits between my wet lips, and I swear that I can feel his cock twitch with need. I lean forward and bite down on his lower lip, reopening the cut that I made last night.

He lifts his hand and runs two fingers over his lip before he holds them away from his face, inspecting the blood on them. "You play fucking dirty."

I smile and lean up, capturing his mouth with mine. I get

lost in our kiss until I feel his heavy head sink into me, causing me to whimper against his handsome grin.

"Oh God."

"You've missed me."

"Shut up and fuck me, Jensen."

He closes his mouth on mine again as he slides the rest of his lengthy cock into me, filling me to my hilt. I bite down on his lip again, tasting the tinge of blood as he pulls out of me and achingly slowly fills me again.

"Liam."

"Isla," he grits out.

Six

Liam

SHE'S UNAPOLOGETICALLY HERSELF when I'm buried inside of her like this; she's thrashing underneath my hold as I nail into her with a sure and steady rhythm; she's looking up at me as if I'll devastate her with my very touch.

It only causes me to pick up my pace and start fucking her the way she's used to feeling me.

Her fingers are currently digging into my shoulder blades, and the moment she starts to drag her nails down my back is when I let out a rumbled grunt. She's not done this before, but I won't fight her on something that she wants. I adjust her, pushing her knees up until I'm able to bury myself deeper inside of her.

She expels a long, drawn-out scream as her body tightens around mine further.

"Jesus, doll. There you go. I need you to come all over my cock."

She whimpers at my demand and rotates her hips, causing me to throw my head back in pleasure. I need her to come. Right this fucking second because I'm unsure of how much longer I'm going to be able to hold out.

"Liam."

"Give it to me. Squeeze my cock, doll."

Her faces flushes with a wave of heat, she bats her eyelids

closed, and her body goes rigid beneath mine before she starts to tremble with the onslaught of a concentrated orgasm. Fuck, this woman is gorgeous both in and out of bed, and watching an orgasm rip her apart is breathtaking.

She digs her nails deeper into my back to the point that I feel them pierce my skin. I swear that I can feel the blood run over my skin, but I choose to ignore it as I slam my cock into her as she comes undone around me.

With a few more anxious thrusts, I'm able to let go and lose myself in her orgasm that is squeezing my entire shaft. She milks me for all that I've got, and I rest my face in the crook of her neck, breathing heavily as our bodies soar together.

A couple of moments pass by before I start to dislodge myself from her. She throws her head back onto the pillow, exhaling as her hands go to her now fucked-up braid, first loosening it and then running her fingers through the inky strands. I grab her wrist and hold her hand out in front of me.

The tips of her fingers are shamelessly stained with my blood. I raise an eyebrow and glance down at her.

"I wasn't aware that you were into blood play."

She frowns and pulls her hand from mine, glancing at her nails. "Holy shit. Did I hurt you?"

"Nah, you're all good."

"Are you sure? Let me see what I did, Liam."

I groan as I pull the rest of my semi-hard length out of her and watch my release leak from her before I sit up on my knees. She follows suit, but shifts off of the bed and walks to my back. Her gasp tells me all that I need to know. She truly let herself go with me this morning.

"You look . . . hot. I can't believe that I did that to you."

"Yeah? It can't be that bad, can it?"

"Liam, it looks like you were mauled," she says through a

snicker and walks into the bathroom. I get up and follow her when I hear the shower start. The bathroom is quickly filling up with steam when I turn my back to the mirror as it starts to fog up. I have multiple scratch marks running down my back with blood starting to dry up around them.

"You're a fucking beast."

"Hey," she scolds as she steps under the hot stream of water, throwing me the most innocent smile that she is able to muster up.

"Hey yourself. Quit hogging the shower," I say as I step in behind her. As the hot water hits my back, the cuts burn and I cringe. "Yeah, you're definitely an animal."

"I am not," she says as she spins around in front of me and smacks my chest. "Plus, you liked it."

"I won't give you the satisfaction of knowing that, but I would let you do it again."

"Deal," she says before leaning forward and placing her lips on mine.

We finish up our shower, and she gets dressed upstairs while I grab my shit and head down to the living room to get dressed.

An hour later, we're in her Porsche and on our way to Brass's place. Seeing as it's Sunday, I know that he'll be home with Hadley. When we arrive at the Waldorf Astoria Chicago Residence, Isla's Porsche gets valeted, and we make our way to the fucker's penthouse.

Once we're in the private elevator, I wind my arm around Isla's waist from behind, which causes her to look up at me.

"Hey."

"You haven't lost your touch, doll."

I think that she starts to blush, but she turns her face away from me so I'm unable to see. An odd want comes over me as I reach for her chin and lean down to lock our lips together. She doesn't pull away or protest as she normally would when we're about to be in the public eye. She turns her petite body into mine, and I don't hesitate to move my hand down the column of her neck before sliding it underneath the collar of her coat. It may not be much, but I'll take whatever skin-on-skin contact I'm able to get.

"Liam . . ."

"We could stop the elevator."

"I . . ."

As if on cue, the elevator comes to a stop, and I'm insulted by the fucking ping that it makes. Reluctantly, I remove my hand from underneath her clothing as the doors slide open. Instead of taking a step forward and into the lobby to Wade's front door, Isla lingers, leaning up on her toes to place a soft kiss on the line of my jaw and taking me by surprise.

I move her hair to one shoulder and bend down to take her lips once more before I lace our fingers together and lead her out of the elevator and to the front door, knocking twice before I turn my attention back to her.

"I wanted to ask you if you'd be interested in going to the Cubs' opening game with me next weekend?"

"Uhh, you bet your ass that I'm going. Do you still have your season tickets?"

"I do. Are you in?"

"Only if you swear that you'll be taking me to all of the games that you plan on attending. You know that I'm a Cubbie's girl."

"Don't push your luck."

"I'm not. I'm giving your whiny ass an ultimatum," she says as the front door opens. Instantly, the heat of her hand leaves mine, and for some reason, it pisses me off. It's not enough to be beside her. I need to be able to touch her without restriction, and

I'm not completely understanding why.

I look up to find Hadley and Isla hugging before they pull away from each other, and Isla walks into their two-story penthouse.

"Hi, you two," Hadley says as I draw her into a slight hug.

"How are you, Hads? Keeping Wade's dick happy?"

"It's good to see you too, Liam," she says with a laugh and leads us into the living room where we are met by Wade.

"There the fucker is," he says toward me.

"Oh? So what? Nothing for Isla? I see how it is, you asshole," Isla bites out but wraps her arms around his neck while she's on her tiptoes as a greeting.

"I'm glad you think so highly of me, Isla."

"I could tell you where to stick it, but I think that Hads takes care of you too much." Wade chuckles before she adds, "Hi, brass balls."

He tugs on her earlobe before letting her go. It's something that he's always done with her.

Hadley laughs as she joins us, carrying tumblers for whiskey and placing them on the coffee table in front of the couches.

"Keep those thoughts to yourself, Isla," Wade insists, and I shake my head at him. He loathes the idea of sharing anything of Hadley, especially while I'm around, and no, I do not blame him. I wanted her. I would have ruined her if I had the chance, and he knew where my thoughts ran when they were first dating each other.

"What do you want to drink?" Hadley asks to break up the tension that still revolves around Wade and I on occasion.

"Anything that you'd like, Rye," Wade tells her, and Isla takes a seat on the same couch as me, but distances herself by placing a cushion between us. That too pisses me off. Hadley and Wade both know that we do more than eye-fuck each other, and I do not see the issue with them seeing us together here this afternoon.

"You've got it, Whiskey," she replies and purses her lips as she walks away to the cabinet that houses some of their finest whiskeys.

Wade takes a seat on the other couch and winces.

"Does that shit still hurt?"

"Like a bitch."

"Fuck, man. I'm sorry."

"Don't concern yourself with it. I'm sure that you have more important fucking around to do."

"Waylon Brass," Isla interrupts and leans forward to take a drink from Hadley, "Control your ego, and I'll control Liam's cock."

"Jesus, Isla, I do not need nor do I want any more details about your lives together. I've had to deal with Adriana's off mood at work lately, and I will not put myself in a similar situation here with this hookup game."

Both Isla's and Hadley's jaws drop open, but Hads quickly recovers, whereas Isla seems to be speechless. *Motherfucker.*

I watch Isla swallow a healthy mouthful of Glenlivet 45-Year-Old, and instead of speaking, I follow her lead and take a drink of the single malt Scotch and throw my head back as the silky feel of the liquid clears my lips and opens up as it hits my tongue. Sweet fruit and vanilla syrup transform into a gentle spiciness of ginger once I swallow the sip.

"Thanks, Hads. This is great."

"Of course," Hadley replies and takes a seat on Wade's lap. I take another drink, forcing a swallow as I watch Isla purposely angle her body toward the armrest instead of toward me.

"Are you ready to go, Isla?"

"What?" She pouts as she turns to face me. "We just got here."

"Yeah, and I just needed to collect my shit."

"Uhh, all right." She places her tumbler down once she swallows the remainder and stands up. "Hads, we need to go out and get wasted without these two assholes. I swear they are worse than two women."

Wade chuckles, but I remain quiet. He knows that he's made me uncomfortable due to his uneasiness with me. We'll talk about it, but not while we are in the presence of these two. Between the two of us, we've thrown enough fists at one another to last us each a lifetime.

"We'll need another night with those red-headed-slut shots."

"Oh hell yes, we do," Isla replies to Hadley as I head upstairs to grab my two suitcases from their guest room before returning.

Isla has her coat on and is saying goodbye to Wade as I round the corner and grab my coat. I pull it onto each arm before buttoning it up and offering my hand out to Wade. "Let me know when you're free to go for a drink, Brass," I say, interrupting the two of them.

"Will do. We can head to Blended sometime this week."

"Sounds good."

Isla opens the door, holding it wide for me to get my bags through before we enter into the elevator.

"Bye, assholes," Isla shoots out as the elevator doors close, and we're suddenly surrounded by silence.

"I didn't know that things were still tense between the two of you," she says as she inspects her almost-black nails. I cannot help but watch her as she does it instead of answering her. Her eyes lift and meet mine, asking me for a response that I'm not entirely sure how to give. It's not often that Wade and I push each other, but I know that he's pissed about Addy and Isla more than he is about my sexual references around Hadley.

"We have our moments. Wade has issues with me whenever I make a comment in regard to Hadley that isn't innocent. I don't blame him, though." I decide to give her a half-truth because I don't need her disappearing on me just yet.

"You shouldn't be so hard on yourself, Liam."

"Thanks, doll, but it is what it is."

The elevator door opens and we walk across the lobby to the entrance and wait for the few minutes it takes for valet to pull up with Isla's Porsche.

After we've gotten my shit into the trunk, I get into the driver's seat and head over to her place. As I drive, the interior of the SUV remains silent as words that I struggle to speak aloud swarm my mind.

I've made my bed, and I'll lie in for the remainder of my life, but what I need is someone who will be there regardless of my past and my actions. I fucking know that my actions have spoken louder than my heart, but fuck, this is my fresh start, and I'd appreciate it if others saw it that way as well.

Isla's hand moves over mine on the steering wheel, taking me by surprise. "Liam? Are you all right? I feel like you are hundreds of miles away."

"I don't have a choice but to be, do I?"

"Okay, listen," she says as she shifts and turns her body to face me as I slow to a stop at a red light. "I know that these years haven't been kind to you, but you need to stop being so hard on yourself. Please, Liam, be that positive dickweed who showed up at Blended yesterday."

My eyes are focused on hers and the gold flecks that seem to glitter when she smiles. Her fingers intertwine with mine as she lets out a heavy breath.

"Please?"

I nod and run my thumb along the top of hers. "You've got yourself a deal."

Instead of letting go of me and relaxing back into her seat, she unbuckles and moves onto my lap, straddling me in the driver's seat.

"Isla, what the fuck are you do—"

I'm cut off when her lips come down on mine, and she bounds her arms around my neck, drawing my mouth closer to hers. Her chest is pushed up against mine, making my cock stir with need. She startles when the car behind us honks, interrupting the deadliest of kisses. She pulls back and places the palms of her hands on either side of my face. "Stay with me in the present and don't disappear into the past."

"Got it."

It's something that I used to say to her when we first met, when she divulged all of her insecurities that her past had saddled her with. Her saying my same words back to me hits me in the gut, and I know that I need to get my shit together now more than ever.

Her lips move down to mine once more as the vehicles behind us honk and give me the finger as they fly by on the wrong side of the road. She climbs off of me and buckles up before I start to inch the SUV forward again.

Somehow having her with me makes me feel complete. God, this woman is fucking trouble, and I have to let her go before she starts to need what Adriana did. I don't have the want or the will to put myself in the arms of a woman who needs something more from me than what I am willing and able to provide.

Once we've gotten settled back into her loft and I'm about to doze off on the couch, she comes bounding down from her bedroom in the shortest black spandex shorts, sneakers, and a long-sleeved shirt. She pulls a sweater over her head and grabs her headphones from the kitchen counter.

"I'm going for a run. It's gorgeous outside, regardless of the chill."

When she turns around to grab a bottle of water from her fridge, my eyes roam down her legs and then back up, stopping on the tattoo on the back of her left thigh, and I groan.

"When did you get that finished?"

"What?" She glances over at me and notices what I'm looking at. "Oh, my tattoo?"

"Yes."

It's fucking incredible. I get up and walk toward her to get a better look at it. I don't know how I overlooked it through our naked antics, but I did. It's a black and white detailed inking of an octopus pulling a ship under. I run the backs of my knuckles over it, and I feel her stiffen underneath my touch.

"Would you mind if I joined you?"

"Joined me?"

"Yeah. I know that your runs are personal and that you don't share that alone time with others, but I'd like to be a silent partner for you this afternoon."

I watch her process my question and shrug. "Sure. Hurry up, though. I want to catch the sunset."

I straighten up and head up the stairs to her bedroom to get changed before meeting her back down in the living room.

"All set. Let's go."

Minutes later, we've stretched on the front steps of her building, and now our feet are slapping the unforgiving concrete beneath us. We're keeping pace with each other as my lungs start to dry out from the fresh fifty-degree air. I glance over at Isla, who is lost in her own world with her headphones in and her black strands swinging wildly behind her. A sheen of sweat covers her forehead, and she must feel me staring because she glances over and me and throws me a radiant smile.

I shake my head, pulling myself away from her sexual allure to focus on each step I take. I pick up the pace, knowing that it will be grueling for her due to our difference in leg length, but she manages to keep up with me. My heart begins to throb inside of my chest as we leave the first two miles behind us. Together, we avoid the leftover snow from yesterday as we push harder. We might be pounding the sidewalk, but Isla takes each step gracefully.

She quickens her pace until she's sprinting, and pulling ahead of me. I watch her take a few long strides before I put forth more effort and go after her. She glances over her shoulder and squeals when she sees me taking faster strides to close the distance between us. I've barely broken a sweat because I'm used to running in the Australian sun, but when I catch her, my fucking heart jolts as I pick her up and keep running as I pull her onto my back.

"What the fuck?" she yells at me and smacks my shoulder blade.

I let out a breathy chuckle. "Hold on tight, doll."

She locks her ankles around my torso before pointing to an alleyway, which I take, and it opens up onto North Avenue Beach. Instead of stopping and allowing her to climb off of my back, I keep running until my feet are hitting soft sand instead of the taxing concrete.

I finally come to a stop where the waves are kissing the sand and set her down. I raise my arms and place both hands at the back of my head to catch my breath and to cool mysef down.

"Dickweed," she snorts and shoves me.

"What? I needed a little more weight to complete my workout. Although your buck-twenty didn't do much."

"Sure, you did," she says with a smile and sits down in the sand and starts to untie her sneakers.

"What are you doing?"

"Cooling off. What does it look like?"

"In there?" I ask as I look up at the waters of Lake Michigan.

"Yup," she says as she uses my shoulder as a post to take her sneakers off.

"Yeah, fuck no, that's not happening."

Her golden eyes find mine, and she blinks a few times while biting the corner of her lip.

"Fine. Hold my shit, you pussy."

I watch her as she strips down until she's only in her sports bra and a black silk thong. She takes a step away from me, but I reach out and grab hold of her forearm.

"Hold on," I tell her as I place her sweatshirt on top of her sneakers and pull my sweatshirt off, tossing it on top of the pile.

Once I'm down to my black boxer briefs, I walk up beside her, and hip-check her.

"Have you done this before?"

She looks up at me and shakes her head. "Nope, but the beach is empty, and the sun is about to set, so it's now or never, dickweed."

"I'm glad that my dick gets you high," I tell her as she takes off running. I'm quick to follow behind her as the water hits our feet before splashing up against our calves. She yells out and starts to retreat, but I grab onto her waist and pick her up, hauling her the remainder of the way into the water until it's deep enough for me to sink down below a wave. She squeezes my bicep as we surface together. I can feel her petite frame shivering in my arms, and I don't blame her. This water is fucking glacial at best.

"Liam! Let go of me, I'm turning blue," she shrieks at me and holds up her fingers, all the while giggling.

"Shit."

I cradle her and run as best as I can out of the water and onto the sand next to our things. I sit down and place her between my legs, locking her in before grabbing her sweatshirt and helping her to pull it over her head. I pull my shirt on and then drape my sweatshirt over our legs.

"That was possibly the rashest thing that I've ever done," she says, and I cannot help but laugh with her as her teeth chatter. She's right: it was fucking senseless, but I enjoyed the moment with her.

"It was unbelievably ill-advised, but I liked it."

She leans her wet hair against my chest, and I lock my arms around her, rubbing over the material of her sweatshirt to warm her up.

"It's beautiful, isn't it?"

"You shouldn't be so fucking sure of yourself."

She slaps at my hand and points to the sky. I look up and stop in my tracks. I've been so preoccupied with warming her up that I completely missed the peach, pink, and orange colors taking over the sky.

"Damn."

"This is why I love running out here. I can't ever get enough of it. The only thing that rivals this feeling is my relationship with whiskey."

"I don't doubt that."

Her entire body relaxes back against mine as she curls into a smaller ball. I fold my legs around her and move her wet hair to one shoulder before placing my lips to the cold column of her neck. A shiver runs down her spine, causing me to smile because I'm an ass, and I've been enjoying her reactions to me over the last twenty-four hours.

She turns to face me, and I don't hesitate to lean into her and link my mouth with hers. Our lips brush against each other's in an innocent tease, but I can tell that she's holding back the more demanding and fiery side of her need. I know what she likes, and it's usually fast and heady, not this passionate and slow tease.

"Isla," I say against her lips, prolonging each syllable.

She shifts her body until she's comfortably straddling me with the sunset to her back. I jolt when I feel her fingers run down my spine and pull her closer until there is no space left between the two of us . . . until I'm able to feel the beat of her heart against my chest. I don't have a moment to react as our lips meet again, and she takes what she wants, intermingling our breath until we labor for oxygen. I roll my tongue along hers, which causes her to unexpectedly inhale sharply.

I'm completely unprepared for the warmth that encircles us. It's uncontrollable, yet the faint feeling that swims through us as we share our lips with each other is penetrating. This right here might just be my salvation, but I know that this is all we can be because I don't trust myself to be more to her or anyone else.

If I could start this entire thing over with Isla, then I would. I wouldn't allow any of it to happen because by the way she's holding onto me and the shy look that she gives me when I pull away, I know without a doubt that I'll have to fucking hurt my best friend when I tell her that I don't want anything more.

I hesitantly pull back and look down at her, sliding a strand of hair behind her ear. She leans into my touch, and I know that I've already fucked up any form of anything between us. I can still feel the warmth that radiated in the spots where her body was touching mine, though, and it's messing with my head.

With a slightly shaking hand, she cups my jaw and leans into me, taking my mouth again. The sun has set, and we're surrounded by darkness as I lie back on the sand, bringing her down on top of me.

"We can't do this here, Liam," she says breathlessly as she grinds her hips onto my cock.

"Fuck it, it's something to do."

"Uhh, nope."

She gets up and starts to get dressed while I push myself up and off of the sand. "Rejection stings, doll."

"I'm sure you'll survive until we get back to my place."

"I might, but I'm not so sure about my cock."

"I am."

She gives me a glare that challenges me in her own little way. Fuck Netflix and chilling. With Isla, it's all about whiskey and adventure. Regardless of the amount of whiskey, though, she catches me off guard every time she's close, and instead of the whiskey, I often find myself to be intoxicated by her. I mentally chastise myself at the direction of my thoughts and get up without another word to pull my sneakers and sweatshirt back on.

By the time we arrive back at her loft, I'm exhausted from our run and then our sprint up the stairs. Both of us fall onto her couch and sprawl out.

"I don't think that I'll be able to lift my legs for the next couple of days."

She laughs and reaches over, bringing her palm down on my thigh with a heavy sting.

"What the fuck was that for?" I call out as I grab her wrist.

"For being a prick."

"Classic, doll."

"You like classics with red lipstick," she counters and puckers her lips, blowing a kiss my way.

"I could think of better things that mouth could be doing right about now."

"Oh yeah? Such as?" she taunts and lifts her sore body off of the couch.

"Shutting up so I can sleep," I spit at her, and she gasps.

"See. You're more than a prick than you dare to realize."

"Oh, I realize, doll. I just don't have the soul to care."

She shakes her head at me instead of replying and walks

upstairs. I hear the water in the shower turn on while I lay my head back and pass out into unconsciousness.

The next four days pass quickly with the amount of work I've been doing on Isla's body and my personal life. I met with a realtor, and she showed me a couple of places in the city, but I insisted that I needed to work from the ground up, and she's finally found a lot of land for sale that overlooks the lake. I haven't gone to see it, but it's on the Gold Coast, so I told her to send the papers over, and I'd make an offer on it.

Another day passes before I hear back from her, informing me that my cash offer was accepted and that I'd need to meet with her once more to fill out the remainder of the paperwork.

Energy transcends the bounds of my body, and I need to do something more than just sit here in Isla's living room and impatiently wait for her to get back from her shift. Instead, I decide to call an Uber and head out to Blended.

For some reason, I have the need to tell Isla before anyone else and celebrate with her, and it is something that should give me pause, but I choose to ignore that nagging feeling in my gut and go for what I want.

When I arrive, it's past ten in the evening, and my eyes find her as soon as I pull open the front door. She's on a wooden ladder that leans against one of the shelves, to retrieve a bottle of whiskey. I watch her body move up the rungs and cast a quick glance around the room, taking note of how many of the men present are watching her too.

My long strides take me across the large space to her in no time at all and I move behind the bar, despite the argumentative look that a few librarians give me. I spin Isla around just as her foot hits the floor and her eyes go wide, not expecting anyone to be close to her.

"Liam. You can't be back here."

"I do what I want, and you should already know that." She bites the corner of her lip and tries to push me out of her way. "Ah, she is getting sick of having me around. Well, it shouldn't be too much longer before I'm out of your hair. All I have to do now is hire a contractor and get some blueprints drawn up."

"Wait, what?" she asks as she pours out two fingers of amber.

"I got the lot."

The masterpiece that is her dark red lips part and she inhales a deep breath of air before responding. "Are you kidding me? That's incredible! Congratulations, Liam," she shouts and leaps into my arms as I grip onto her trim waist.

That odd sensation pulls at my insides, but I choose to ignore it just as her lips come down on mine. We have not had any public displays of affection other than on the beach a couple of days ago, but how can I count that when there wasn't another soul in sight?

She must realize her mistake because she pulls back and pushes herself out of my arms when I lower her back down to the wooden floor.

She wipes her mouth off as if it will, in some way, help erase the kiss. "That never happened," she snaps at the bartender beside us and strides past me with the bottle of whiskey in hand to her office in the back.

I follow her lead and close the door behind us. "If my lips revolt you enough to wipe—"

She moves toward my direction and reaches past me to lock the door before wrapping her arms around my neck as she stands up on her toes. My automatic response is to grant her my lips as I lean down and take hers forcefully. I shift my head to the side, allowing me better access to her mouth that will let me make her lose her mind as our tongues wrap around each other.

Her greedy hands move into my hair, tugging at the strands with more than the mere excitement of my purchasing a piece of land in the city should garner. She quickly pulls away and covers her mouth.

"Fuck. I don't know what has gotten into me. I'm sorry," she says with a frown before she steps away from me and takes a seat at her desk. I stand there, watching her for a minute while she pretends to occupy herself with something on her laptop, but I know that she's full of shit.

"Are you all right?"

"I'm fine," she spits out too quickly for my liking.

"I'm going to call bullshit on that, but I'll let you be. Come on, let's grab something to eat and then you can get some fucking rest for your day off tomorrow. The Cubs won't wait for us if you sleep the day away."

She lights up and pushes her chair back at my suggestion.

"Deal."

"Good. Now get that ass back in my hands. I wasn't quite done with appeasing your need to kiss me."

She attempts to hide her smile but fails miserably as she gets up, and I stride toward her. I lock my arms around her and rest my nose against hers.

"You've been drinking tonight. I can still taste the rye on my tongue."

"Would you like another taste?" she asks in the now-limited space between us.

"Please."

I satisfy her need for me by meeting my lips with hers, and swallowing the moan that escapes her.

I've been awake for a grand total of two minutes when Isla

comes back from her run and strips down bare in front of me. *God help me.* This woman is more than good-looking and more than a mere five-foot-three petite fuck. She knows the ins and outs of pleasing both me as well as herself, and she won't be one to deny it either.

"You're up early." My voice is raspy from sleep.

"I had a sunrise yoga class with Hadley before my run."

"Where the hell do you find this shit?"

"I'm not sure. She just asked me to go, so I did. It was on the terrace at Navy Pier."

"Are you cold?"

"I'm frozen," she says as she jumps underneath the comforter, not giving two shits that she's naked.

"Come here."

She moves toward me without so much as a complaint as I wrap my arms around her, and the moment she pushes her toes up against my calves I pull back. "Oh hell no. Keep that shit to yourself."

"What? I'm cold . . . and naked."

"Obviously, but doll, cold toes and I do not mesh well."

"You're the one in my bed, dickweed."

"Touché."

I stretch my arms out and push my body up and off of the mattress.

"What time does the game start?" she asks as she nuzzles into her pillow.

"Seven this evening, I believe, so we can leave at 5:30 and get a cab or Uber up there so both of us can drink."

"That sounds good. So wake me up at five?"

"Seriously?" I ask as I swing my legs off of the bed and stand, walking my horny ass to the shower to relieve the tension that's been straining my dick since she stripped down in front of me.

"I'm serious. Enjoy your hand."

I turn to face her as I reach the bathroom door, my cock wanting to go to her and that mouth of hers. "You're the one missing out."

She rolls her eyes and turns away from me in an attempt to fight off her own libido. I doubt that she'll win, though, and I know that she'll end up using her fingers instead of me to simply prove a point. I head into the bathroom and close the door behind me before I turn on the shower. I strip down and step in, the chilled tiles taking me off guard until the water has had enough time to heat them against my feet.

Thousands of warm drops of water cascade down my body, soaking me. The rivulets drip from my chin and run down my body as I'm heated from the outside in. I groan to myself as the steam starts to fill the room as I proceed with my shower instead of my hand.

Once I'm cleaned off, I turn the shower from the perfect pressure and temperature to frigid cold in order to rein in my dick that's been refusing to cooperate with me this morning.

By the time I'm done, and I walk out into the bedroom, Isla is fast asleep. If I didn't know any better, I'd swear that no one was under the covers, but considering her petite frame, it's easy for her to get lost in the warmth and comfort of her king-sized bed.

Instead of waking her up, I pull on my sweatpants and head downstairs where my laptop is located and pull up my email from Remission Worldwide. I may have nothing to prove, but RW has constantly been on my mind, and I finally give in to check on my organization.

By the time I return all of the emails that I've deemed important, it's well past one, and Isla is still asleep. I decide on a nap before we hit the ballgame. I lay my head down on one of the throw pillows and knock out until my alarm goes off.

By the time I force my eyes to open, Isla is downstairs moving her body to the music that's streaming from her phone on the kitchen counter. Her black hair is pulled back in a high ponytail, she's got on white jeans, and a red and blue Chicago Cubs shirt. It's the only time that she'll actually wear colors. A baseball cap sits next to her phone, and I groan in appreciation of her love for this team and the game.

"You're finally up."

"Look who's talking."

That earns me an eye roll before she pulls the cap onto her head, pulling her hair through the back of it.

"I'm ready when you are."

"What's the time?"

"Just past five-thirty. I have an Uber on its way. I figured that you could be ready in three minutes. Or does your taut ass need more pampering than that time would allow?"

"Speak for yourself." I get up and smack her ass with more force than I mean to as I pass her by to head upstairs to get dressed. She cries out as I take the steps two at a time.

When I come back downstairs, she has her phone and keys in hand while waiting beside the door.

"Come on," she grumbles and nudges me out of the door with her elbow as I pull the baseball cap over my bedhead. I catch her watching me while she waits for me to step foot out of the loft and into the hallway.

When I do, her eyes run down my torso and then back up to my face. I decide not to push her on her very obvious want. Instead, I place my hand at the small of her back and guide her forward toward the elevator bank.

Our trip from her apartment to Wrigley Field is mostly

traveled in silence. I can tell that she's overthinking something, but I'm too afraid to actually ask her what's on her mind out of fear of her wanting more than what is between us.

The tension must be too much because our Uber driver pipes in, "So the Cubbies, yeah?"

Isla cracks a smile and pulls the bill of her cap farther down.

"Always, man, always," I say.

"I'll be listening from here. Have fun out there."

"Will do."

He pulls to a stop, letting us know that the few blocks away is the closest he will be able to get us to the ballpark due to the traffic as well as the blocked-off streets.

I get out and offer Isla my hand, which she takes and doesn't let go of as we walk toward the ticketing entrance of Wrigley. She stops just shy of the ticket lines and lets go of my hand to spin around with both of her arms outstretched.

"I've missed this."

With her head held high, she effortlessly spins around once more as she scans the hundreds of people around us. The sheer determination I see in her eyes as she takes the few steps toward me has me almost intimidated. Something radiates from within her, and in this moment I find her irresistible. She knows that she's attractive and highly practiced in seduction, but today, she's just herself. Isla is not someone who is conventionally beautiful. She's hauntingly stunning.

Without thinking, I grab hold of her hips and pull her flush against my body. I run my hand over her jaw, before angling my head and taking her mouth with mine.

The majority of our kisses have been rushed and filled with ardor, but for some reason, this one right now seems to match the one that we had on the beach. Our breaths mingle as her arms reach up and tangle around my neck. Her smile breaks our delicate kiss as she pulls back and slides her hands down my chest, resting them on my torso as she looks up at me.

"That was unexpected."

I pull the bill of her cap down before taking one of her hands. "I couldn't help it. My hand did me no good earlier today." I give her the best excuse that I'm able to muster up because I don't have a single answer that would fit our friends-with-benefits relationship.

"Neither did my fingers."

She gives me a radiant smile as we walk toward the line, hand our tickets to the taker, and make our way inside of the ballpark to my season-ticket seats behind first base. We're in the first two rows so we won't have to bother getting up for hot dogs and beer, and these chairs happen to be cushioned. My ass is already thanking me.

"I knew that you had connections, but how in the ever-loving shit did you get these seats, Liam?"

"Honestly?"

"Yes, honestly." She must see me blanch because her smile falls. "On second thought, I don't need the details."

I shake my head and ask for two local Goose IPAs from the waitress who approaches us before I turn my attention back to Isla and ensure that no one is listening in on what I'm about to tell her.

"I bought season tickets, but my seats were up a couple of rows, the same ones that I had last season until . . ."

She places her hand on my knee and squeezes. "I don't need to know."

I shake my head and lean over, speaking against her ear for her alone to hear. "One of the higher-ups in Cubs' management has a daughter who was taken in Greece. Somehow she was sold to one of the rings that RW encountered when I flew back to Australia from Scotland. I had all of those woman flown to Australia, a total of eighteen of them, and helped them with their injuries. We eventually got her to talk and then I contacted her family. I told them that I didn't want anything in return, but he must have looked me up, and the next thing I knew, I got an email with my adjusted season tickets as a thank you. I really shouldn't have accepted them. I almost feel guilty about it. Almost."

I move back as the waitress hands me the two beers. I take a sip of the foam from one of them before giving that one to Isla. She scowls at me but takes it anyway.

"Thank you . . . and Liam?"

"Yeah?" I answer her shortly because this is not necessarily something that I want to speak about tonight. I'm here to have a great time with my best friend, not to delve into the tribulations of the world.

"I'm proud of you."

"Yeah? Well, I would have done it for anyone."

"I know that. You're an incredible person, and you need to stop disparaging yourself. You've put your life on the line to get women who you don't know out of sickening situations, and I'm sure that you've had your fair share of physical violence when it comes to your going in with the team. You should be proud of what you've accomplished."

I sigh and down half of my pint of beer before answering her. "Thanks, but I've never done any of this for the recognition."

"I know that, and you need to continue to live instead of being scared of life. You're alive, and you need to savor what the world has given you."

"This is some pretty heavy-hitting shit for a ballgame, doll."

"I'm sorry," she mutters, and I suddenly feel like shit. I take her hand and lift it up to my lips, placing a kiss on the inside of her wrist before intertwining our fingers together. I shouldn't encourage this public display of affection, but I cannot seem to help myself this evening. Especially after what she just said. She's not usually someone who speaks out about savoring life because she's still learning how to do it herself.

She glances down at our hands and murmurs, "Intertwined lives."

I'm not entirely sure that I heard her correctly. "What?"

She blanches and shakes her head back and forth quickly. "Nothing. I think I need another beer."

"I think I need something stronger than this crap."

"Whiskey?"

"Always, doll. Always."

We're at the top of the fifth inning, and I'm unsure if I'm seeing two pitchers on the mound, or if it's my vision. I lean over to Isla and tug on a strand of what I believe to be her dark hair. "Tell me that you see the second guy on the mound too, please."

She glances up at me slowly; clearly the couple of craft beers and other alcoholic beverages have had their effect on her as well. "I see four," she giggles and throws her head back before adding, "are we even winning?"

I chuckle and squint at the scoreboard. It takes me a minute to concentrate enough for the numbers to stop dancing around. "Fuck yeah, we are. It's four to one. Let's go, Cubs," I yell out and clap my hands together.

"Are you sure that's the score?"

I shrug and take a drink of her beer. "Not one bit."

She laughs and shoves my arm playfully. In retaliation of her trying to push me away, I throw my arm around her shoulders and pull her closer to my chest.

"I think that we both need food, doll."

"Mmm, nachos please."

"You sure you don't want a dog?"

"Nope, I'll get one later tonight," she says adamantly and runs her hand over the bulge in my jeans.

"Jesus. Keep that up, and I'll call an Uber before you get those damn nachos."

Her eyes go wide as she shakes her head then raises her hand to get our waitress's attention to place a food order.

She leans over me to place the order, asking for extra cheese and chips.

"Just make it two nachos and two dogs," I say, trying to help the waitress out.

"You got it," the waitress says before she struts off, swaying her ass for my double vision.

"Whore," Isla states and crosses her arms over her chest.

"Excuse me?"

"You heard me. You're obviously here with me," she snaps, gesturing to my drunken hand on her upper thigh, "but she is insistent on flirting with you each time we order."

"Ah." I nod my head and take hold of her chin in my free hand. "It's a damn good thing that I'm thinking about getting you naked and underneath me on the drive home rather than her then, huh?"

"You were?"

"Isla, I'm always thinking about ways to get into those tight jeans of yours."

She squeezes her thighs together, almost crushing my fingers at the same time.

"If I didn't know that you used to be a gymnast in your formative years, I might have been worried about the strength you harbor in your legs."

She leans forward and licks my bottom lip just as the

waitress returns to serve us. "All right, here we go," she says as she attempts to hand us our food.

I chuckle at Isla's audacity and lay my mouth against hers in a full kiss before pulling away and squeezing her thigh.

"You'll get it later, baby doll."

"I know I will," she says as she bites at the corner of her lip.

I turn back to the waitress and take the food, handing Isla a tray of nachos and putting the other on my thigh next to my second hot dog.

"Eat up. I'll need you somewhat sober to blow me."

She leans over and whispers in my ear. "You just like the lipstick stain that I leave behind."

"More than you know."

I watch her run her tongue over her bottom teeth, and my cock jumps to life. She'll get it good later for playing dirty while I'm trying to enjoy my Cubbies and buzz.

The Cubs won seven to four last night, and I'm not entirely sure how we got out of the park, ordered an Uber, or made it up to her loft. When I open my eyes, the morning light shines into her room, and I shut my eyes in an attempt to avoid the massive hangover that I know will hit me in three . . . two . . . *fuck me*. I groan quietly as my head starts to pound.

"Shh."

I shift and open one eye to look down at Isla, who has her head buried underneath her pillow, her Converses still on, and her shirt off.

"You're a fucking mess."

"If you don't shut your mouth, I'll sit on your face."

"That actually sounds rather intriguing."

That gets her to shift and glance up at me from her pillow fortress. "Shut it, dickweed."

"Glad my cock can get you high, sweetheart. I've told you that once, and I'll keep telling you."

She reaches over and tosses a pillow in my face for speaking.

"So I'll take that as no hangover sex?"

"Who has hangover sex?" she says with a groan.

"We do."

"As of when?"

"Now."

I pull her on top of me, and she steadies herself with her hands on my bare chest. My hands roam down to her sides, and it feels like I'm drunk all over again with the feeling of my hands being exactly where they belong.

Seven

Isla

FINE. I'LL ADMIT it.

I do, at some point in my life, want to fall in love with the right man. Yet as I stand behind the bar of Blended while Wade goes over the expansion plans, I'm afraid that my heart might be pulling me in a direction that I know it cannot go.

Should not, cannot, and will not. Nope. I refuse to fall in love with my best friend and be part of one of those couples that were always *meant to be.* He's not interested in more than what I'm giving him, and I know, regardless of how much and how often I lie to myself, that I am.

"Isla. Pay attention," Wade says and stares at me blankly.

"Huh? Oh. Sorry, Brass."

"Where's your head? I thought that you'd be more interested in the expansion."

"It's not important, trust me. So you've already bought the bar next door?"

"Yes, I have."

"And Hadley is all right with that? I mean, a lot happened to her in there."

"All of this was her idea."

I raise a brow at him and nod before looking down at the blueprints again.

"When will it be taking place?"

"The contractors will be here this afternoon before you open up, and they will start tomorrow morning."

"Wait. It's happening that fast?"

"I don't see why not. I've hired the best, and with the kind of money that I'm throwing at them, they have projected that it will be done two weeks from today."

"Two Sundays away?"

"Correct."

"Are we going to close for the duration of the expansion? I'm not entirely sure that the patrons or any of the members would enjoy the noise and dust that will occupy the space."

"Yes. We'll be closed for those two weeks, and I'll need you to send out an email to all of the members, informing them of the plans."

I glance at my watch before looking up at him. "If you say so, boss man."

"Fuck off with that. This will get us more business because we'll be able to house an additional eighty people without violating any fire codes."

I bite the corner of my lip and nod in agreement. "I'm just . . ."

"What? Hesitant to close so quickly?"

"Hell no. I'm just not sure where I want to go on vacation." I give him a warm smile and lean over the bar top to tousle his effortlessly styled hair.

He shakes his head at me and picks up his whiskey tumbler, taking a sip before pointing to the blueprint. "I'll be redoing your office as well."

"You're what?"

"You heard me, Isla. I believe that it can be upgraded."

"Well then, go ahead and don't let me hold you back. You won't find me complaining for a second."

"As I thought," he says before finishing off his whiskey and checking the time on his Rolex. "I need to get going."

"All right. I'll send out that email now and post about the expansion online as well."

"Thank you," he says as he stands to his full height and comes around the bar to wrap me in his arms, placing an innocent kiss on top of my head. I hold him close for a few seconds before letting go and patting his chest.

"I'll see you soon. Maybe you and Hadley should go on vacation with me as well."

"Possibly . . . but that would mean that Liam would be going as well."

"You seriously need to get over this jealousy or resentment . . . whatever you want to call it that you have been carrying around about him. He's just fucking around, and you know that he would not now or ever purposely go after your woman—your wife. I won't stand by and watch you two burn away years of friendship. It would also leave me in limbo between the two of you, and I refuse to go to that place again."

"You have a point. I'll talk to Hads about it and consider it."

"Thank you, Brass, for everything."

"You're welcome, Isla. I'll call you this evening."

"Bye," I call out to his back as he leaves through the front door and gets into the waiting BMW with Jacobs in the driver's seat.

I slide my hand along the bar top as I make my way into my office to send out the email informing our paying members of the expansion.

When I finally make it home, it's well past four in the morning, and I'm beyond exhausted. In addition to the typical bar work, we had to move some of the important and confidential crap out of my office, cover up the majority of the library's furnishings, and store the whiskeys. It feels like I had to move out of my damn apartment. It took every librarian I had on staff to get it done, and now all I want to do is crash in my bed and curl up under the comforter.

Liam isn't in my loft when I get home, and disappointment causes my entire body to sag. I should not, no matter what the reason, be this down about Liam-fucking-Jensen, but here I am. Sulking.

Damn it.

Instead of heading to bed, I go to the fridge and decide to make bacon and pancakes before I pass out. I ate dinner at Blended, but it feels like I haven't eaten in over a decade.

By the time I've made and eaten more pancakes than I can count, and I've cleaned up the kitchen, it's almost five. Yet there's still no sign of Liam. I force my mind to think about something other than him either talking about sex or having sex with someone besides myself. When I get into bed, it doesn't take me long until I'm passed out and dreaming of Liam's hard appendage hitting me deeply.

A sound echoes through the loft, causing me to stir and push the comforter off of my top half. I force the sleep to leave my eyes as they adjust to the light coming from my windows.

"Liam?" I ask, but there's no response. I move my feet off of the bed and stand up, throwing my arms into the air and stretching before checking the time. It's almost noon. I take a few steps but pause when I get lightheaded. I reach my arms out and grip onto the door frame in an attempt to steady myself, but it doesn't help.

A burning wave of warmth moves up my throat, and I haul my body into the bathroom just in time to reach the toilet. *Holy shit.* I blame the whiskey we drank last night when we were moving things around, or maybe even the pancake batter.

I decide on a shower once I've calmed down enough to get back up onto my feet and make my way to the other side of the bathroom.

By the time I emerge I'm feeling a tad better, but something still doesn't feel right. My phone chimes and I make my way across the bedroom with a towel wrapped around myself. When I unlock the screen, a text from Wade awaits me: *Get packing. We're leaving in three hours.*

I frown at the message and type back to him: *Leaving? What are you talking about?*

I watch the dots move on the screen as I wait for his reply: *You told me that you wanted a vacation, and I'm obliging you. Hadley's excited to get out of the city.*

Can I ask where we are going?

Yes. Iceland.

I stare at the screen and close the message application and then reopen it to make sure that I'm not reading anything incorrectly. Maybe I have a fever?

I read over the short pair of words three more times before I type out a response to him.

What? Are you serious? Brass, that's ridiculous.

Not ridiculous. Start packing. Jacobs will be picking you up in two hours.

I cannot help the slight smile that takes over as I give him a simple reply: *Thank you.*

Two hours pass, and I've packed two large bags with clothing that I doubt I'll need, but I'm unsure of what to expect or how long a trip it will be. I could have called Brass and asked him, but that would have taken away precious time to pack. I'm hauling the second suitcase down the loft's flight of stairs before I realize that Liam has yet to show up.

I frown at the thought, hoping that nothing tragic has come of his random disappearance. Once I've gotten all of my shit together there's a knock on the door, and I answer in hopes of it being Liam, but Colin Jacobs gives me a tilt of his head in greeting. "Afternoon, Miss Madden."

"Jacobs, how many times have I asked you over the years to call me Isla?"

"Countless, ma'am," he says, his Southern roots making themselves known.

Shaking my head in admonishment, I lock the door behind me before following behind him with my purse as he takes both of my bags and leads us to the elevator bank. While we wait for an elevator to arrive, I shoot off a quick text to Liam: *Hey, I'm leaving with Brass for a couple of days. You have my extra key. I'll see you when I get back.*

When we arrive at the airport, Jacobs pulls through a security gate and onto the tarmac where Wade's jet awaits. I haven't heard back from Liam, and I'm honestly more than a little concerned.

"Colin?"

He must hear the concern in my voice because he says, "Is everything all right?"

"I'm not entirely sure. I haven't heard from Liam in a while."

I see him smile in the rearview mirror before he tries to hide it. "I'm sure that he's well."

I huff out a breath, swinging the door open when the BMW comes to a stop, and get out. I turn my head and throw a wave at Jacobs. "Thanks for the ride."

"You're welcome. I'll get your luggage loaded."

"Thanks."

I know that I'm being curt, but I'm just peeved right now, and no number of smiles is going to curb my mood.

I head up the stairs to the jet, checking my phone one last time, hoping for a text from Liam, but there's nothing there. I'm scrolling through my social media feeds, thinking I might see something with him mentioned in it when I walk into the cabin.

"It's about damn time you showed up, doll."

My head shoots up as I lock eyes with Liam's. I swear that my heart starts to beat too hard to the point that it might be beating backward, and I may pass out right here.

"You asshole," I say as I walk toward him and push his shoulder. He has the audacity to look wounded at my nudge.

"What? I heard that you were a little concerned for my well-being."

"Fuck you," I spit at him and take a seat on the other side of the aisle from him.

"Ah, feisty. Just the way I like you."

I turn my shoulder to him as I set my travel purse on the seat beside me and buckle up, choosing to ignore the ignorant dickweed.

"Ouch. The cold shoulder?"

I turn to him, and I cannot help the emotion that rolls off of my tongue. "I thought you were dead, so excuse me for caring enough to possibly do something about it."

"Yeah? By doing what? Leaving the country?"

I ignore his little dig as I reply, "Where were you and where's my best friend?" I ask, referring to Wade.

"Another dig, doll? I won't pretend that one didn't hurt. Hadley had to stop and get the two of you some girly shit before arriving. To answer your first question, I was with Wade. After you and I had spoken about the tension between the two of us—Wade and I—I decided that I needed to do something about it. We spent the majority of the evening speaking and hashing out shit before diving into his whiskey stash when we apparently booked this vacation for the four of us. Seemingly drunk Brass and Jensen had plans."

"This was your idea?"

"It was ours," Wade says as he walks into the cabin with Hadley in front of him.

"Seriously? We're going because the two of you got too drunk to function, and this is how it ended up?"

"Yeah, pretty much," Liam says, and Hadley leans over to hug me.

"Hey. They were up all night, and I'm not entirely sure how they are not still drunk."

"Assholes," I say and roll my eyes. I should never be this worried about him. The first thing that I wanted to do when I saw him was to throw my arms around his neck and breathe him in with the knowledge that he's all right, but that's wrong on so many levels. I chose to ignore that initial instinct and opted to go with the one that followed it: bitter irritation.

I'm never this emotional, and the only thing that would make any logical sense is that my monthly crimson cockblocker is on its way. I frown at the thought and pull my phone out, clicking on the calendar application and scrolling back to the last time I had my period.

No.

Nope.

Oh no, no, no.

This cannot be happening. I take in a deeper breath than needed and lean my head back on the headrest. I shut my eyes and start counting the days that I've missed.

I'm two weeks late. Fourteen days. Surely that means absolutely nothing. I blow out a long breath as a hand settles on top of mine.

"What's going on?" Wade asks, but I decide to answer with a

shake of my head rather than trusting my words.

"He didn't mean to upset you, Isla."

"It's not . . . I'm fine. I'm just tired. We were at Blended for a lot longer than usual."

I doubt that he buys my excuse; he typically sees straight through me when I'm lying, but for now he lets it go and takes a seat opposite me and next to Hadley.

I close my eyes and pull my knees up to my chest, curling up on the plush seat as I start to count how late I am again. I decide at this moment to keep this little worry to myself instead of causing this entire vacation to go up in flames . . . at least until I can confirm or deny it.

I don't know how long I was asleep, but when I wake up, Liam is beside me in the adjacent seat. Wade and Hadley must have retired to the private bedroom in the back. It's just over a six-hour flight, and I have no idea how long I've been out.

I shift and unbuckle before reaching into my purse for my phone. Finding it, I unlock the screen to check the time, figuring that we've only been in the air for three hours. When I lean back in my seat and glance over at Liam, he's watching me.

"What?" I mumble.

"I'm sorry."

I shift uncomfortably. He has me considering moving to the other side of the cabin. As much as I was worried about him and wanted to be sure that he was okay, I feel the need to get away from him now.

"Don't worry about it," I say and turn into the seat, trying to get comfortable again as I recline it. I refuse to give up my seat now that I've gotten comfortable. He's the one who needs to move.

"Isla."

I force my eyes to close as I think about being sick this morning, and the outlandish amount of food that I consumed last night and the couple of days before that. My heart sinks at the thought of how much alcohol I've consumed in the last couple of days, and I'm suddenly begging for this not to happen.

"Doll?"

"What?" I ask him softly.

"Speak to me?"

"I've got nothing for you."

"Listen," he says as he reaches out and places his hand on my thigh, "I should have told you what was going on."

"No. I have no right to know anything about you or what you do, Liam. Just please drop it. I'm worn out."

"You have more right than most people to know about me, Isla. If anything, I owe it to you for helping me make this move."

"Liam, please. Just . . . stop talking."

His hand lifts off of my thigh, and a shiver runs through me at the loss of warmth his palm provided me.

I know that I'm being a bitch, but I just need to sleep off this nightmare until I can prove that my suspicion is wrong. It has to be because if the cards fall in a certain way, there's no getting out of it.

This cannot happen, I repeat to myself. Especially not with my best friend—a man who my feelings have grown for, but a man who is in no way interested in pursuing anything even remotely serious, let alone having someone rely on him.

Shit, having two people rely on him.

This is not me. I'm not this needy woman who needs a man to depend on. I've always been independent and quick to realize that I'm all that I need. I've always been someone who has sought respect and not the attention of others who are not going to give me security in life. I think that I was designed to be alone because I'm selfish, and I don't accept help well, especially after the period of time in padded cells. Most men want to offer their women the world, but I've always had my own.

Wade once told me a few years back that I'm feared. I remember asking him why, and he told me that it's because I require no validation in life . . . because I don't need anyone. I didn't understand him then, but now it makes sense. Men are intimidated by women who without any men's help are able to achieve the life they dream of living. I have no attachments, and frankly, attachments equal weaknesses and are the cause of suffering.

A tear leaks down my cheek, and I allow the next couple following it to fall before I squeeze my eyes shut tighter and will myself to fall asleep again.

I refuse to be scared to walk alone, regardless of what I'm put up against. Irrespective of that, though, I'm terrified of what my future now holds.

Eight

Liam

WE FLEW INTO Keflavik International Airport and drove thirty minutes to the resort where we'll be staying for the next week and some change. I've been ignored by Isla for the entire drive, and the only time she showed the slightest bit of emotion is when we arrived at the Blue Lagoon Geothermal Spa. The milky blue water seemed to put her in a trance by its otherworldly appearance.

As we head toward the hotel, I reach over and take her hand in mine. Instead of refusing, she allows me to lace my fingers through hers. I keep our hands between our thighs in hopes of not drawing attention to the fact that I'm allowing this display in front of Wade.

She looks at me before attempting to pull her hand out of mine, but I tighten my fingers around hers, keeping her in place. I know that I've upset her, but she should essentially be over it by now. My eyes meet Wade's as he glances up at me from my and Isla's intertwined hands, but he doesn't say a thing. He simply gives me a questioning look.

The vehicle comes to a stop, and I almost thank the heavens. I've got nothing to prove, but I need to make sure that she's all right. I need to figure out what is holding her back from enjoying the early stages of this vacation.

I open the door, and let go of her hand before getting out

and stretching. The cool temperature takes me off guard, so I lower my arms and slide each into my leather jacket. I knew that it would be colder than what I've slowly been getting used to in Chicago, but I didn't think that I'd almost freeze my nuts off.

As I reach out for her, I watch Isla retreat from me; I stare at her, pleading with her to tell me what is going on in her head. The two of us fall into step behind Brass and Hadley into the hotel's lobby. We'll be staying at the Silica Hotel, which is set in the heart of this lava landscape and is a mere ten-minute walk to the spa.

The hotel is modern with a minimal decor, and the view from my room has got to be award winning. On one side of the hotel, there are rooms facing the lava landscape, and on the other side of the hallway, the rooms face the milky blue waters of the hot springs. I scored the room with the milky blue views, and Isla has one across the hall from me with the lava field vista.

When Wade and I booked the place, we reserved two rooms, but Isla was insistent on having her own room, which leads me to think that there is more to what's going on than her simply being peeved at me.

We have all retired to our rooms for the remainder of the evening, but I have not been able to close my eyes, seeing as it's about ten in Chicago and three here in Iceland. I decide to head out to the hot springs instead of sitting around in the room awaiting the sunrise. I change into my swim trunks, then pull on a sweater and sweatpants before venturing out into the cold of the night.

I take steady steps on the wooden walkway that leads to the hot springs and undress, tossing my sweats on the lounger before immersing myself in the warm waters of the Blue Lagoon.

I allow the waters to swallow me, submerging fully into the heat of the springs. Breaking the surface, I take a few strokes through the water, leisurely extending my limbs out to slice through the water with organic fluidity. After a couple of laps in the heat, I lie back in the water and allow the peaceful tranquility to overtake me. The heat is somehow refreshing, which helps release all of the tension that I've been carrying around since Isla stepped onto the jet. I allow myself to drop down into the water, and when I come back up, my eyes scan the walkway because I can feel my body's want for her spark to life. Isla is sitting on the lounger that I dropped my sweats on, and she's watching me intently.

Cautiously, I move toward her and lift myself up and out of the heated waters. I quickly move to the rack that hosts the hotel towels and dry off before I step toward her, and she hands me my sweatpants.

She's curled up in a couple of layers, but she's still shivering. Once I've gotten my sweatpants on, she hands me my sweater, but I shake my head. "Put that on; you're shivering."

"But—"

I cut her off. "Put it on, Isla."

She hesitates at first but then pulls the thick fabric over her head before wrapping her arms around her waist.

I grab a dry towel and pull it over my shoulders before I sit down on the same lounger as her. She starts to shift, but I place my hand on her thigh, stilling her. I swing one leg over the seat and pull her back between my legs.

"Talk to me."

She rests back against me without any further argument, but chooses to remain silent.

"Isla, I won't beg."

"It's nothing, okay? Trust me."

I move her black hair to one shoulder and run my thumb from her jaw, down the column of her neck, and down to her collarbone underneath her layers of clothing.

"All right. I don't believe you for a second, but I won't push you tonight."

"Thank you," she murmurs and finally releases herself into my hold.

Isla isn't a woman who needs validation on anything. She's strong-willed and highly autonomous, yet I know that something is off and whether it be my fault or not, she needs to understand that I won't leave her in the dark alone with her shadows. She'll lose herself to them if she's allowed to become immersed in the suffocating darkness.

I know the feeling all too well, and I refuse to let someone this significant to me walk into it willingly.

———————————

I carried her back inside and to my room once she fell asleep. She might have refused to share a room with me earlier this evening, but I doubt that it's what she truly wanted, considering how she's curled up against my bare torso right now. I haven't been able to get in a minute of sleep, and I'm unsure if it's due to the time difference or the jet lag, but when the sun finally rises, she shifts beside me.

I know that she's awake, and I don't bother her until she's ready to move or speak. She tilts her head up to look at me, and I blink down at her. Somehow, I'm in awe at how attracted to her I am right now. The majority of her makeup has rubbed off, but somehow, her lips are still slightly stained my favorite color.

"Why am I here?"

"In Iceland?"

"No, Liam. Why am I in your bed?"

"I thought—"

She untangles herself from me and sits up, throwing the covers off of herself. "Well . . ." She clears her throat and gets out of bed slowly. "You thought wrong."

I don't bother going after her when she walks out of the room. She doesn't belong to anyone, let alone me. I wouldn't want that regardless, though. I've made it clear to her that I was uninterested in pursuing more with Adriana as well as her.

I know that once this trip is over with, I'll need to separate myself from her in order to distance myself from falling head-first into any sort of relationship. I'm not giving up: I'm simply allowing myself to be happy with what I want in and out of life.

As I lie in bed, thoughts of Chloe begin to flood my mind. I remember waking up to her hair splayed over my chest and her light breathing as she dreamt. Her entire body fit into mine flaw-lessly, but I cannot fight off the feeling or knowledge that Isla might feel even better.

Might? Who the fuck am I kidding?

She feels better in my arms than any other woman before her has, and that scares the shit out of me. The thought gives me even more reason to call it fucking quits once we're back in the States.

I run both of my hands down my face before sitting up, yawning, and tossing the white sheet off of my body. I head out to the gym on the premises and lay my fists into the speed bag repeatedly before I torture myself on the free weights and tread-mill. After what feels like a lifetime of physical exhaustion, I head back to the room and clean up. Once I've showered and dressed, I head out into the hallway and down to the lounge for breakfast where I'm met by Wade and Hadley, but not Isla.

"Morning," I say as I take a seat at the table for four.

"You look like shit," Wade comments, and I give him my finger to mull over while I pour myself some orange juice from the carafe.

"Where's Isla? I figured that she was with you earlier since she wasn't in her room," Hadley says as her and Wade's food is placed in front of them.

"Nah, she left earlier this morning. She should be in her room. When did the two of you get down here?"

"Not even five minutes ago. I went to her room right before coming down here, and she didn't answer the door."

"Odd."

It's the only response that I give them. She might be out at the spa already, or she could be in the waters; neither would surprise me. She seems to be in her own world, and unwilling to surface to ours.

Hadley watches me for a minute before setting her fork down. "I'll go check on her."

"You do that."

"Watch yourself, Jensen," Wade says as Hadley leans over and kisses him before she places her napkin down and walks away from the table.

"Yeah, yeah. How's your back?"

"Stop skirting around the issue. What the fuck is going on between the two of you?"

"The two of us?"

"Don't play coy."

"Can I at least get some vodka in my orange juice before the interrogation begins?"

"By all means. Go ahead," he gestures toward the waitress who brought their food by earlier.

I catch her attention and ask for two shots of premium vodka, neither of which I plan on sharing with Brassy boy over here. When she returns with them, I pour both of them into my glass and take a sip before downing the remainder of it.

"All right. What the fuck do you want to know?"

"Don't fuck with her, Liam."

"It may be a bit too late for that."

He shifts his body a few times before stilling. I'm assuming to get comfortable after the long flight. He still has issues with sitting still for long periods of time.

"Whatever the hell is going on between the two of you has obviously turned into something more for her than it has for you. Have you considered that?"

"I have, and it's part of the reason why I came by your place the night before. I need to pull away and do it as seamlessly as possible."

"I think that it's going to come down to all or nothing."

"What is that supposed to mean?"

"Truthfully, from what I've seen, you're fucked either way."

Nine

Isla

THE MINUTE THAT I left Liam's room earlier this morning, I returned to mine where I grabbed my purse and made a quick exit from the hotel. I did not care whether or not I looked appropriate to go out in public. I just needed to know, and I needed to know straightaway. The hours that had elapsed since I realized that I was late had been dragging, and it was difficult to distract myself through the agonizing tick of the clock.

I had the hotel front desk call me a car, which took me to the store located just north of where we are staying. I'm pretty sure I bought the last couple of boxes of pregnancy tests that they had on hand, and I got a sorrow-filled look from the clerk upon checking out. Damn her.

Upon returning to the hotel, I stole into my room, hoping to get away without being seen by Liam, and somehow, I got away with it. Once inside, I secured each lock on my door in every way possible before I ripped open the first box and read the instructions that came along with it. It seemed simple enough, so I did what I needed to do.

When the first little blue cross appeared, I belligerently threw the stick away, chugged a bottle of water, and tried again. I got the same result the next three times. The little blue crosses are mocking me now as I stare down at them with tears in my eyes. Slowly, I lower myself onto the cold tiles of the bathroom floor and cross one leg over the other while my fingers trace over one of the blue crosses.

How is it possible to let yourself down? Surely this all has to be in my head. None of it can be real, but then I think back to the sheets, kisses, and skin that I shared with Liam when he first arrived and I know that this is something I can't hide from.

This is happening whether I want it to or not.

This tiny development is currently budding inside of me, and I'm stunned, to say the least. Doubts start to churn ideas in my head as I cover my palm over my mouth to keep the emotions from spilling out into the world. How am I worth this pregnancy, much less a child? I've seen the monster inside of me. I know what I'm capable of and what it's capable of as well. I don't think that I deserve much more than what I currently have. Why would I? Why is the world offering me more than what I'm able to handle when I've barely got myself as well my dark shadow in check?

I have the obvious choice to interrupt it because I've caught it so early, but I do not think for a second that I would ever have it in me to do such a thing. I'm having a difficult time understanding how I can feel so much already for something so new to me. I wouldn't put the life of the little thing—or things—at risk because I'm self-centered.

I'm stranded, and I'm not sure where to go from here.

What happens next?

What do I have to do?

Will this hurt?

How do I tell him?

I'm terrified at the idea of being pregnant, but most of all, I'm terrified of the butterflies that have just started to flap their wings inside of my stomach.

A loud knock on the door startles me, and I wipe my tears

with the backs of my hands before standing and laying the tests down on the vanity. I take steady but slow steps to the door, trying to remain quiet as I look through the peephole. It takes me a moment to focus my watery eyes on the figure in front of me but when I see that it's Hadley, I undo the latches and pull the door open.

Mentally, I start counting down the seconds until she notices my swollen eyes and flushed face. She knows that I'm not one to cry, but there I was . . . on the fucking bathroom floor in tears.

"Hey. I was just coming to look for you." She pauses and then tries again. "Isla? What's wrong? Are you all right?" The expression on her face lets me know exactly how I must look because I didn't even have the door open all of the way. *Joy.*

"Uhm, it's just that . . ." The tears return unwanted, and I fight my body to take in a ragged breath. "I can't breathe."

Reaching for my hand, she walks me over to the bed, allowing the door to close on its own. She takes a seat, and I sit down next to her, wringing my hands together in an attempt to feel anything else aside from the devastating emotions that are teeming through my body.

"I know that you usually talk to Wade about the ups and downs of life, but if you feel comfortable enough to talk to me, then please know that I'm open to listening."

I give her a nod in reply as a sob pulls at my chest, threatening to be released into the noiseless room.

"Have you eaten? I can order you an omelet from room service," she says as she reaches for the phone on the nightstand.

My entire body reacts to the thought of eggs, and I almost double over in front of her, but I force the movement of my limbs to carry me to the en suite bathroom where nausea overtakes me once again.

Holy shit. My stomach lurches and heaves, but as hard as it tries, I can't get up anything more than I already have. I think that I've knelt down to the porcelain throne more times this morning than I did throughout my college career.

"Isla, are you ill?" she asks, but the question falls flat as she walks into the bathroom and pauses as she sees the tests. "Are you . . . ?" She looks at the little blue crosses and moves to me as I flush the toilet and straighten up, waiting for her harsh words, but the ones that I was expecting don't come.

She wraps her arms around me and doesn't let go as she speaks. "You're pregnant." It's a statement that she leaves hanging in the air between us instead of asking me about it outright. "Is it Liam's?"

I nod, not wanting to say the words out loud for myself because that would make it final. Somehow it seems as if it would be a lot more conclusive than hearing someone else state them.

"Did you just figure this out?"

"Yes," I answer, my voice hoarse from all of the crying that I've done behind these closed doors.

"Do you know how far along you are?"

I shake my head to answer her, but offer up my words as well. "If I had to guess," I say as I pull away from her and wipe the underside of my eyes, "I'd guess just over four weeks. Since he got back, really. We didn't wait very long to jump into bed. It's been six weeks since I got my last period"

She smiles at me, and it's not a forced smile or one that makes me feel guilty about my current plight. "That makes you six weeks pregnant. I read you're supposed to start counting from the first day of your last menstrual cycle. Does he know?"

"No, not yet. I'd like some time to digest this before I tell him or even Wade about it, though. It's just . . . it's a lot to take in all at once. I mean, I'm in no way fit to be a mother, let alone survive nine months without whiskey and sporting a pot belly."

I laugh miserably, but she puts her arms around my shoulders again and hugs me close.

"You're going to be great, regardless of what you think." She holds me at arm's length and glances down at my flat stomach. "It's kind of incredible. Maybe you should start thinking about it as a blessing in disguise."

"You think so?"

"Definitely."

I huff out and bite the corner of my lip as I pull Liam's sweater off and toss it into the bedroom. "I think that I'm going to shower and get ready for the day. I may need more concealer than usual, though." I try for a joke even though I'm the one who needs some cheering up at the moment.

"I'll text Wade and tell him that I'm going to spend some girl time with you and that they can go ahead to the spa and book us into as many packages as they wish."

"Are you sure?"

"Positive," she says as she walks through the doorframe. "Hadley?"

"Yes?"

"Thank you."

"Of course."

I'm not used to being vulnerable in front of a woman, and I wouldn't be comfortable with any one of them right now. Over the last decade, the only people to see me break at all have been Liam and Wade. Hadley and I have never been too close. We get along just fine, but we don't have that friendship vibe between us that she has with her best friend, Lola Marc. I don't mind it, though. I was not exactly welcoming when Wade first showed interest in her, but it was for his own good. Now, though, I'm glad that he has her in his life. They keep each other stable, and I've honestly never seen him so enthralled with life before.

I'm grateful for her right now because I have no idea what to do next.

After a long shower, I get dressed and spend a good amount of time on my hair and makeup before I even attempt to walk out of the bathroom and face the outside world head-on.

"Isla? Are you all right in there?"

"I'm fine," I say as I step out and into the bedroom where she's sitting on the bed, flipping the page of one of her romance novels. She closes the book and sets it on the white comforter before sitting up.

"Have you tried to eat anything? Maybe we can go get you a smoothie or something. I may not know what to do, but I was looking up morning sickness before I decided to dive into this novel."

I almost whimper in delight at the thought of filling my stomach with something. "A smoothie sounds incredible right about now."

"Smoothies it is, then."

We head to the hotel's restaurant and even though they are closed, they oblige us and make me a strawberry-banana-peanut butter smoothie with the mention of the name Waylon Brass.

I take a long sip from the straw when it's handed to me and sigh contentedly as the refreshing liquid moves down my throat.

"Thank you," I tell her before taking another long drink.

"You're welcome. Is there something that you want to do today? We can head over to the spa, but I'm not so sure that it's wise to get into the hot springs given your condition."

"What? Seriously? Well, shit. I guess I need to call my OB/ GYN and find out what I can and cannot do."

"Call her now. I'm sure that you've got some questions for her."

"I do, but I'll need to go in and see her too. She'll probably want to do a blood test to be sure. Maybe it's the water here that makes the little blue crosses appear?"

Hadley purses her lips and tries to refrain from laughing, but it doesn't help. I nudge her in the side as we start our walk to the spa, and I place a call to my doctor.

By the time my phone call ends, I've found out that I won't be allowed in the water because raising my body temperature could cause health defects, especially in the first couple of weeks in a pregnancy.

"Well, I'll be staying away from the hot springs, and I have an appointment in a week and a half. We'll be back by then, right?"

"I believe so. If not, I'm sure Wade won't be opposed to your flying back earlier."

I chew on my bottom lip as we walk into the spa's interior. A calming sense washes over me for a brief moment of time before I see Liam and Wade stand up together when they see the two of us enter.

My heart seems to speed up and slow down all at once, and I'm suddenly the definition of chaos.

I may look calm and collected on the outside, but on the inside, I'm screaming for help and gasping for a single breath of air. How do I convince myself that I don't feel anything for this man—a man who has always been by my side—when my heart knows the truth?

Hadley walks into Wade's arms, and I stay a couple of feet away from Liam, forcing a physical distance between the two us, even though I don't want it to be there.

Of course, he breaks it. He takes the three steps over to me and places his hand on my shoulder. "Everything all right?"

Do I tell him?

When I refuse to respond to him, he pulls me into a hug and my entire body stiffens, but my heart starts to beat faster, and I know that I'm in for a long, ugly ride ahead. I feel like I've just trapped the both of us with this illegitimate pregnancy.

My body loosens up slightly when he places his lips on the column of my neck. I glance over at Wade and Hadley, but neither of them are paying any attention to us as they walk to the spa's front desk.

"Isla?"

My entire body seems to thaw at my name coming from his lips, and I don't know when I became this girl, but here I am, swooning over one of my best friends.

"I'll be fine."

He pulls back to look at me, and I'm sure that he's able to tell that was a lie, but he decides to keep it to himself if he does.

He glances over his shoulder at our friends before speaking. "They're going in for a couple's massage. I wasn't sure what you'd want to do."

"What did you make an appointment for?"

He takes my hand and squeezes it once before answering. "The same thing."

I'm thrown off guard, and I know that this isn't a good idea, but I don't want him to realize that there's something wrong while we're here—where I can't easily escape.

"Okay. When is it?"

His fingers intertwine with mine as he leads me to the front desk. "In a few minutes."

Hadley glances over at me and mouths, "Are you okay?"

As much as I feel like I need to lie to protect myself and cover up my pain, I decide against it. She's the only one who knows where my head is in this moment. I shake my head from side to side in a negative answer, and her facial expression changes from one of delight to sorrow.

My eyes fall to my Converses because if she looks at me like that once more, I'll fragment and fall to pieces at Liam's feet. I can't lose it, at least not while he's around me. He'll just suggest some sexual healing bullshit, and I don't necessarily want that right now.

Lies, lies, lies. I always want him.

"Mr. Jensen? Your room is ready for the two of you." A spa attendant announces, and he tugs on my hand.

"Are you ready?"

"I suppose so."

As we follow the attendant to the back, she shows us around the interior of the spa and where we can get changed before leaving us to our own devices. Before we part ways, Liam pulls me to his chest, demanding my attention.

"We'll need to talk. If you don't tell me what's bothering you now, then I'm sure a tumbler of whiskey or two will do it."

"I need to get changed," I say as I pull back from him and walk toward the women's locker room.

"Isla?"

"Yeah?"

"You look beautiful."

Instead of replying to him, I cast him one last glance and disappear out of his line of sight to get changed into a fluffy white robe. I know that I'm going to end up messing things up at some point, whether it's with our friendship or more, but I don't want that point to be right now. I know that once I've hit that high point or that rock bottom with him, I won't be able to change it back to what it was before.

I'm scared of losing my best friend, but I'm terrified that I'll go on with life and never tell him exactly how I feel and how everything has developed into so much more than friendship for me. Liam Jensen currently carries my heart around with him whether he is aware of it or not.

I stuff my crap into an empty locker and huff out an annoyed breath. I know that I've taken our friendship for granted, and my getting pregnant is just my dumb luck. I mean, what girl wouldn't want to fall in love with her best friend if she was given the option? But what girl would potentially throw away or risk a friendship to possibly pursue those more intense yet way more fragile feelings? Me, that's who.

Once I've changed and locked my belongings away, Hadley struts her ass into the room with a larger-than-life smile on her beautifully pale face. If I didn't know any better, I'd take bets on her hair color being factory-developed, but it's not. Her almost white platinum hair has men drooling after her, and if I swung both ways, then I'd be doing the same thing.

"Hey, I'm glad that I caught you," she says as she pulls me into a hug.

Why does everyone feel the need to hug me? Do I look that pitiful?

I allow her to comfort me until the emotional buildup in my eyes is too much to take and is threatening to spill over. I rear back and wipe the corners of each eye, trying to not ruin my mascara.

"I think that this will be good for you. Just go in there and relax . . . even though it's with him. I remember the first time that I saw you two together in Sydney. You both seemed to calm each other down somehow. It's odd, but I'm sure that it has to mean something."

I have to laugh at her comment. "Hads, I was beyond drunk that night."

"You were happy. Now, I need you to be happy and pregnant."

I wish I could tell her that it's not that simple. If she got pregnant, she'd have Wade by her side every step of the way, but I know without a doubt that Liam will feel imprisoned and retreat from me.

"I'll see you afterward," I say before leaving her to get changed as I exit the room, only to find Liam leaning against the wall across the hall, waiting for me in a robe that matches my own.

He's too damn attractive for his own damn good. *Dickweed.* A smile cracks through my shame and I step toward him, telling myself to forget just for today, just enough to allow myself to enjoy being with him.

"All set?"

"Mmm-hmm."

Ten minutes later, I'm looking down at a dark wood floor while a female massage therapist is working on my lower back. Liam wasn't impressed when two males walked into the room earlier. He refused to have them lay a hand on me and insisted on two females.

For a moment, I allowed myself to enjoy the jealousy that he had over the idea of another man's hands running over my exposed skin. I confess that I actually like the fact that he might have been envious.

Our beds are directly beside each other, separated with just enough room for the massage therapists to walk in between. Once both therapists have moved to the other sides of our tables, he reaches for my hand. He finds it underneath the blankets that cover my body, and I don't fight him off when he laces his fingers through mine.

I've heard that slight touches help relieve stress from one's body, and if this massage doesn't do it, then I'm almost positive that Liam's touches will.

"You good?" he asks, and I squeeze his hand in response because if I speak right now, he'll hear the obvious emotion in my voice, and I think that I'll keep my pretty mouth shut for the time being.

"After this, we can head out to the hot springs."

He's pushing me to speak, and I really don't have a choice about it now, so I answer him, but I manage to keep my voice low. "I . . . uhm . . . I think I might skip that."

"Are you sure? I have us scheduled for a hot-springs water massage after lunch."

"I'm sure. I'm not too big on sharing large hot tubs." It's the single most pathetic excuse that I can come up with, but it's all that I have at the moment. He doesn't respond for a minute because experiencing the milky waters is what we're here for.

"All right. Is there anything else you'd like to do?"

"I'm not sure. I just want to enjoy this right now."

He runs his thumb along the inside of my palm, which causes me to adjust myself on the table. His touch seems to be distracting and healing me all at once, so I force my eyes to close and focus on the back-and-forth movement of his thumb against my palm. With each additional touch, though, the following one turns into more attachment.

This type of affection doesn't often come from him, so I find myself getting lost in thinking about my fondness of him rather than the hands moving up and down the length of my thigh.

He might not know it, but this simple touch between us is intensifying the already-deep affectionate feelings that I hold for him. It's become so much more than a sexual attachment for me. It's turned into a budding romance with beloved intimacy. He's my favorite place to go when things get rough in my mind. He knows how to dull the ache that the dark disease threatens me with.

Liam came into my life like a fucking train wreck. He changed my reality and made me question everything about myself. He's revolutionized my world in a matter of years, and when I'm with him, hours feel like seconds, and seconds feel like hours when we are apart.

Liam and I have always shared a mutual connection, one that is robust, bottomless, and complex, but I'm unsure if he sees it. He has to see it, but I think that he's choosing not to. This man helped me prove to myself that I was worth more than the hand that I'd been dealt.

I've fallen in love with the most unexpected person in a time of chaos.

When a fairy tale doesn't come true, do I fight for it?

Ten

Liam

I GET LOST in her, and it's the kind of lost that makes being found frightening. I want her. I want all of her. I want her flaws, her imperfections, and her dirty mouth. Isla. I simply want all of her, but my choices have been limited by my own decisions.

Here's my admission: I *like* her more than I originally planned for, which is reason enough for this week to be the last of what we're doing. Fuck, I even smile like an idiot when I think about her. Her roots are deeper than they appeared to be from the surface now that I've acknowledged the fact that she means more, but I need to dig those roots up. I have to remain in control of whatever this is, and I'll be unable to do so if I allow them to stay.

I've decided that once I'm back in the States and the construction of my place is well underway, I need to put all of my effort and energy back into RW. After speaking to both Wade and Gage on separate occasions, I've decided to go ahead and open up an RW recovery center in Chicago—a silent safe house—and focus on the trafficking that happens right in front of our eyes in our own city. If it's successful, I may venture out to other cities in the States as well.

I've been keeping up with my teams on the ground in Mexico as well, and I've been asked on more than one occasion to join them. A week ago, I wouldn't have considered going back into the bounds of hell, but I know that I need to go. They would not ask me once to simply fuck around, and seeing as they've asked twice, I cannot keep denying them.

With my mind made up, the hands that were massaging the back of my neck let up, and the two massage therapists excuse themselves from the room.

I turn my head to the side and wait for Isla to open her eyes and look at me. Isla wears her scars as she does her beauty. They aren't physically visible, but the actions and stance of a strong woman cannot be overlooked. When I look back on the time that I first met her, I would have never assumed that she would be so unbelievably significant to me.

"Doll?"

"Mmm?" she replies and stretches out her arms in soft movements.

"How'd that feel?"

"It was exactly what I needed today. Thank you."

"Can I get my spirited bitch back now? She's been missing since we left the States."

Her smile is hesitant, but it's there. "I can try, but I can't promise you a thing."

I swing my legs off the bed and stand, shamelessly naked in front of her as she peels her eyes open.

I watch as her eyes travel the length of my torso and down to my appendage that hardens beneath her glittering gaze. My want for her is inevitable and sure. The serenity of the room morphs into something more captivating and heady, and my entire body comes alive with it. She manages to catch her breath before I speak.

"If you didn't have a facial scheduled, I'd lock us in here for the remainder of the day."

She pushes herself up, and the sheet that was covering her

breasts slides smoothly down her skin, revealing them to me. I have to refrain from taking her on the fucking table as she loosens her hair from the braid that she put it in earlier.

"Tempting," she says before getting up and walking to her robe hanging from a hook near the door.

"Don't deny your need for me, Isla."

I can feel the energy shift in the room, and I'm well aware that she can too. I won't stand by and watch her deny it.

"Have I ever?" she asks while she ties the sash around her trim waist.

"I wouldn't know."

"Well . . ." She turns to face me. "I'll tell you the next time that I require you to satisfy a need within me. Deal?"

"I thought that deal was already in place."

She shrugs and pulls the door open, but I take quick and purposeful strides to intercept her before she can exit the room. I grab hold of her wrist and yank her back against me before closing the door and pushing her back up against it with more force than I mean to.

"I don't know what the fuck is going on with you," I hiss, fury slicing through each word, "but if it has anything to do with my disappearing on you, then I've already apologized, and I refuse to do so again. Clear your head of whatever the fuck it is that you're thinking and live in the moment instead of whatever the fuck you are doing right now. Get your shit together, Isla."

I don't expect it until it's over and the side of my face is left stinging. I turn my head to face her again, and she's got her hand cupped over her mouth, shaking her head from side to side.

"I'm—oh God, I'm so sorry."

Instead of pushing away from her, I press my entire body hard against hers and sweeping her hand away from her mouth, I crush mine against hers, willing her to part her lips for me.

When she does, I don't hesitate to take the kiss further and run my tongue along hers. Her arms link around my neck, and I lift her up by her waist to move her legs around my torso before carrying her over to one of the tables and sitting her down on it.

"What aren't you telling me?" I ask against her addictive lips.

Her grip around my neck tightens, and I pull her closer to the edge of the table until her front is flat against mine. I could easily slide into her right now and fuck the truth out of her, but I know her, and that's not what she needs. I won't allow my need for her to make her feel used.

"Nothing," she lies easily and then continues to kiss me as if I'm her air. As if she needs more of me than what I'm providing her at the moment.

I think I might be losing my mind, but I cup her cheeks and use all of my self-restraint to pull back from her. "It's something, doll, and I want to know exactly what is going on with you. I won't let you down, Isla. Have I ever?"

She shakes her head before leaning against my bare chest. "No. It's just . . . I just need time, okay? Please?"

"If you're sure."

"I am. Just don't take me for granted."

I pull back until I'm able to get her to look up at me. "Why would I do that? You know me, and as much as I enjoy fucking around, I don't play games like that."

She shrugs and wipes beneath her left eye quickly. "I'm a mess, I'm sorry."

The last time I saw Isla this frail was when I first met her. She was beside herself and wrapped in a depression so deep that you could physically feel the misery radiating off of her in waves.

"You've got nothing to apologize for. Why don't you cancel the facial, and we'll grab something to eat and possibly arrange something to do later—something other than the water massage?"

I know that I need to do something, but what? What can I do if she's refusing to let me in? Can I force my entrance? Or will that be too much for her. I know that she's learned to let me in, but if I do that, will she put up her guard against me? Fuck.

"All right," she says through a sniffle and slides off of the table, pushing on my chest with the palm of her hand to put some distance between the two of us. "I'm sorry."

"There's more to this shit than you're telling me. Just know that I will figure out what's going on. I won't let you sulk for our entire vacation."

She shrugs and kisses the cheek that she slapped before leaving the room and me standing bare with the door wide open.

I glance over my shoulder at her retreating back before I grab the robe off of the hook and cover myself up. I'm not entirely sure what the hell has gotten into her, but it's not necessarily something that I plan on sticking around for once she has that smile on her pretty face once more.

After I'm dressed, I head back into the main lobby, and Wade walks up to me from behind while he types something out on his phone.

"It looks like the women have decided to head to lunch."

"Without us?"

He glances up at me with a knowing expression. "What happened?"

I shake my head and move to the seating area as I pull on my jacket. "I'm not entirely sure. She won't tell me what the fuck is going on, and I refuse to dig any deeper." He knows that it's a lie; I'm merely unsure of where to start.

"Why?"

"Why what?"

He takes a seat in front of me and runs a hand through his hair. "Why don't you want to find out what's going on?"

"Because, frankly, it's none of my goddamn business."

"I beg to differ."

"Fuck off."

"I told you before we left that there is more to whatever is going on between the two of you on her side than you seem to think there is. I know that you've said that you'll pull away after this vacation, but I don't see that happening. You need to do something about this sooner rather than later. I've told you once, and I'll say it again: if she comes out of this wounded, then I won't be held accountable for what my fists do to you."

"You're not one to get physical, Brass. Unless it's over your wife."

"Or someone who I'm particularly close to."

I stand up and shove his shoulder. "Can you drop this shit long enough for us to get lunch?"

I don't want to think about what she wants or might need from this fucked-up bullshit that we've been putting each other through. Jesus, I thought my hookup with Adriana was bad, but this one just hit itself out of the damn park and into a whole different level.

"If that's what you want."

"Don't throw words at me that are meant to mean more than one thing."

"You choose to hear them as you need to understand them."

We make our way through the spa's interior until we come to its in-house restaurant. I spot Isla immediately, even though I wasn't purposely looking for her. I seem to be drawn to her nonetheless.

I walk up to the table and pull out the chair beside her. Once seated, I run my hand down her thigh. It's only when I have my hands on her that she looks over at me, acknowledging my presence.

"Hi."

"Do you need a drink or hand restraints?" she snaps. She glowers at me and shoves my hand off of her thigh.

"Neither." I know that I've hit a nerve, but I refuse to let her push me away like this when I know she's needing to speak to me.

"Good."

I replace my hand on her thigh and flip open my menu with my free hand before glancing at it, deciding on the Icelandic Lunch.

Returning my attention to her and ignoring the fact that we have an audience, I move my hand farther up her inner thigh. "Are you going to talk to me about this shit?"

She watches me for a moment before shrugging and leaning over the table. "What are you getting, Hads?"

Hadley looks from Isla to me and back to Isla. "I'm not sure. You?"

She bites the corner of her lip, and it makes me want to move my body over hers and take her right here . . . show her that she can't keep shit from me.

"I'm thinking about getting soup and crackers. I'm not too hungry."

"Are you sure?"

"Positive," Isla replies, and I'm slightly confused by the exchange, but I choose to ignore it.

When Hadley pulls up the menu again, I turn my full attention on Isla. "I'll drop it for now. However, I won't deal with this fucking attitude that you're giving me. We're here on vacation, one that I thought you'd appreciate."

"I . . . uhm . . . I do appreciate it, Jensen. It's just some personal stuff that I have going on right now. It's nothing that you have to worry about."

Hadley almost chokes on her water when she takes a sip but continues to try to ignore our conversation.

"Figure your shit out and start having a good time."

"Fine," she huffs and takes a drink of her water. "I could seriously use a fucking tumbler of amber right about now."

"I'll get you something," I tell her, but as I'm about to get up, she grabs hold of my forearm and shakes her head.

"No, it's okay. I don't need it."

"Are you sure?"

"Yes. I'm just hungry," she says, contradicting what she just told Hadley.

Once we've ordered and our food has arrived, we're still sitting in silence, waiting patiently for someone else to break the tension.

"Liam?"

"Isla."

"Can we just . . . I don't know . . . put everything from the last couple of days behind us and just move on?"

"I'm down with that if you are. It'll be good to have my baby doll back."

That gets her to smile, one that I haven't seen since I took her to the baseball game.

After lunch, we each retire to our rooms back at the hotel, but I cannot set aside the feeling that Isla needs me to be by her side more than she's letting on. Against my better judgment, I walk out of my room and across the hall to hers, knocking twice before I glance down at the bottle of whiskey in my hand.

She opens the door as she's pulling my sweater on over her head.

"Comfortable? I have a clean one if you want it."

Fuck, I'm all over the place with what I want and what I need from her.

"No, this one is fine. Thanks, though."

"Good. Can I come in?" She hasn't moved aside, and I'm beginning to think that I should have just gone to the bar instead.

"Sure," she says as she steps aside and holds the door open. I take the few steps to her bed and take a seat.

"Are you busy?"

"Not entirely," she replies, moving to her laptop and shutting it before joining me on the bed.

"I wanted to talk to you about something, and I figured the whiskey would help with the news."

"Uh . . . all right. What's going on?"

"Us."

"Us?"

"Yeah. I think that once this trip is over that we need to leave whatever is more than our friendship in Iceland."

I wait for her to show me any type of a response, but she doesn't so I continue. "You know that I'm not interested in more, and before you assume that it's because of you, you need to understand that it's not. You know what I've struggled with since Chloe disappeared, and I won't put anyone in my line of fire again. I don't trust myself enough with somebody else to search for more in any relationship. You need to understand that."

"Trust me, it's clear as glass," she says with more bitterness in her voice than I initially expected to hear.

"I need you to know that I didn't go into this with a goal to hurt you. I enjoy being around you, Isla, and you should know that, but I can't do anything more than that. Not now—or ever, if I'm being frank." As the last of the words vacate my mouth, I can taste the residual bitterness that the lie holds.

She nods and turns her head to look out the window instead

of at me while she formulates her response. "I think that you need to give me some time and space right now."

I stay seated and reach for her hand. "Isla."

"Don't," she snaps and pulls her hand away from mine.

"This is nothing new. I've always said—"

"Liam," she interrupts me, "if you don't leave, then I will."

"Don't give me shit. Just talk to me."

She turns to face me with tears in her eyes, but instead of saying a word, she gets up and walks out of the room, and before I know it, the door closes, and I'm left sitting on her bed alone.

An odd ache creeps into my chest, and there's suddenly a gravity there that wasn't present before.

I lie back and decide to wait her out. She'll be back in here sooner or later, and I'll get a better chance to fully explain myself then. I open the bottle of whiskey and take a long drink, welcoming the powerful burn down the back of my throat. It seems to ignite my body as well as my mind as I replay our little conversation.

The next time I open my eyes, they burn in the darkness of the room. I pull my phone out of my pocket and take note of the two missed calls, both of them from Hadley. I toss it to the side and sit up. The alcohol in my system comes back with a vengeance to remind me just how much I drank. I don't recall passing out, but I've clearly had my fair share. The room spins as I squint, trying to remember where I am.

Ah. Isla's room.

I stand up on unsteady legs and make my way to her bathroom. I'm almost surprised when I don't see her shit all over the vanity like she has it in her loft.

After relieving myself and walking back into the bedroom, I turn on the lights and am thrown when I don't see anything of hers in the confines of these four walls. Even my bottle of whiskey is gone.

I pick up my phone from the bed once it goes off, alerting me to a text message from Brass: *Be glad that we're not in the same room right now.*

I text back: *What the fuck is that supposed to mean?*

I wait for his reply as I do a once-over of her room for my bottle, but come up empty-handed. As I leave and stumble across the hallway to my room, his reply comes: *That you just fucked up one of the best things that could have happened to you.*

And what exactly would that be? I manage to type out and send.

Isla.

I toss my phone across the room. It hits the far wall before dropping to the floor. I don't need to hear this bullshit. It may take a bottle of whiskey to make me see what I've actually done, but there's no going back. Not only have I pushed Isla's feelings aside without a care, but I've also ruined an almost decade-old friendship because of my dick.

Regretfully, I walk over to my phone and pick it up, ignoring the now-cracked screen and typing out a message back to Wade: *Where is she?*

Two hours into the flight I put her on back to Chicago.

It takes me a minute or two to realize what he's saying, and when I do, the weight of what I've done hits home, and I know that none of this will get back to where it was.

Why does it feel like I just broke up with my best friend? We weren't together. I never intended to stay or have this aching feeling to chase her, but here I am, suffering in my own indecision.

I push these drunken sentiments aside and decide to let it go right here in my room. I won't regret ending something that I know I'd be no good at, something that I wouldn't be comfortable with.

I don't reply to Wade. I decide to leave my phone in my room as I go in search of another bottle and the hot springs.

I didn't find a bottle, and now I'm chest deep in the warm waters as I glance up at the night sky, which is littered with hundreds and thousands of stars.

I remind myself that the worst is over and that I am now able to move forward with my plans in life. I need to concentrate on the women who need me, the ones that are in trafficking situations. The ones who are actually suffering and being taken advantage of while other men watch. It's degrading and dehumanizing, and if I can put a stop to it in my own city, then I will, but first I need to head to Mexico with my team.

I decide at this moment that I'll email them with my answer once I'm sober enough to work my phone correctly. I turn my attention to the voice calling my name and groan when I see the look of horror on Hadley's face.

"You're a fucking asshole."

"That's nothing that I haven't heard before . . ."

"I'm serious, Liam," she calls out from the deck that she's standing on. "You've messed this up more than you care to know."

"Why are you trying to tell me about it if you know that I don't give a shit?"

As the words leave my mouth, I can taste the lie that comes with them, but I don't let on.

I don't get a response from her, and I turn back to the direction where her voice was coming from, only to watch her walk back to the hotel and back to Wade.

I lie back in the water and attempt to replay the words that I said to Isla, but my drunken mind is now hazy, and the only thing that I'm mildly interested in is my bed.

I'm woken by continuous knocking on my door, and I'm about to rip someone's fucking arm off. *Jesus.* I need to get my head on right and spend more of my free time back in the gym, laying my fists on the punching bag instead of resorting to the verbal outlet that I've been using lately.

I get up, my sweatpants hanging low on my hips, as I make my way over to the door. I pull it open without bothering to see who the fuck had the nerve to wake me up.

Hadley has both of her hands on her hips, and her eyes are boring into mine with an intensity that I've never before seen come from her.

"What do you want?"

"Obviously more for you out of your pathetic, drunken life than what you seem to want."

"Was that supposed to hurt?"

"Yes," she huffs and pushes my door open, striding past me and taking a seat on the loveseat in the room. "What happened?"

"With what?" I ask as I start the coffee machine up, placing a cup in the top and waiting for the hot liquid to pour out into the mug below.

"I know you're not stupid, Liam, so the only other reason why you'd be acting this way is if your decision has affected you more than you want to let on."

"If you say so. Why are you here, Hads?"

"Someone needed to kick your ass into gear, and trust me, you don't want that to be Wade right now. I've had to subdue him with sex more than once since Isla came to him about leaving."

"And? Should I give a shit? I'd prefer for it not to be anyone."

"She deserves better than you. You know that, right?"

"Why do you think I put an end to something that would have hit a wall and crashed regardless?"

"You may not understand, but she needs you now more

than I think you will ever realize, and you just let her down in the worst way possible."

"Listen here, Hadley. I've told her from the beginning of us fucking around that I didn't and wouldn't want more. I had to end shit with Adriana for the same reason, and she knew where I stood and still stand. I don't trust myself with the responsibility of caring for someone or having someone need me again like Chloe once did, because I'll disappoint and ruin shit."

"Oh really? Well, if it's not apparent to you, I'll be the first to tell you that you just did that with Isla."

"And? It's better to rip off the Band-Aid while she can still heal, rather than when shit gets too deep, and there's no going back."

"Liam, trust me when I say that there is no going back from this point. You've royally fucked up, and she won't be able to heal from you."

I run my fingers through my hair before standing and walking to the door, opening it up for her to leave.

"Seriously?" she asks with mock disappointment marring her features.

"Seriously. I don't need heat from you about this shit."

She stands up and strides past me and down the hall before I shut the door and head into the bathroom to shower—to rid myself of the ill and misconstrued feelings I'm harboring about myself at this moment.

Eleven

Isla

I'M THE DEFINITION of emotional chaos, and I've never been this torn up over anything in my life before. Not when I was locked away. Not when I found out the truth about my mother. Not when I figured out what's missing from my life.

This, though, is slowly drying me up from the inside out. It's taken me by what little balls I thought I had and tossed me around a time or two.

I've been home for just over a week now, and I've had Jacobs hand deliver Liam's crap to Wade's penthouse. I'm sure that Wade instructed him to make sure that I have everything that I could possibly want or need while I'm technically home alone.

As the sun rises, I decided that a run might help distract me enough to get away from the horrible thought processes going on in my head, so I get changed into my running gear and head out the door.

I've barely made it three miles when I realize just how much of a dumb idea this was. Every thought that I wanted to rid myself of seems to come to the surface now that I have nothing else to do but think as my feet hit the boardwalk beneath them.

I force my legs to dig harder as I run along the lake's shore, but when I see a mother run past me while pushing a stroller, I almost fall over my own two feet and crumple. I move to the side of the trail and bend over, resting each hand on my knees

in an attempt to catch my breath. This is what modern-day torture must feel like. Fuck the cat-o-nine tails; this shit is digging in
deeper than a multi-tailed whip ever could.

I'm pregnant, and I'm alone. It's a classic tale, really.

Once I've calmed my body down enough from the run, I
stretch my limbs out to ensure that I don't end up with a cramp.

I check my watch and decide to take a leisurely walk back to
my loft instead of running it. It will buy me some time between
now and my OB/GYN appointment that I decided to move up
since I left Iceland earlier than expected. I was lucky enough to
get into their only opening this week.

I'm a nervous wreck, and I'm not sure what to expect when
it comes to the appointment. I have no doubt that she'll need to
prod me with something or other, but I'd just rather not do it.
Especially *unaccompanied*.

After a quick shower, I get dressed into my usual dark jeans
and gray silk tank with a comfortable light sweater. I grab the
keys from the little bowl beside the door and head down to my
Porsche. Once I'm seated and buckled in, I lean my forehead on
the steering wheel and take a deep breath in an attempt to calm
my nerves.

Holy shit on sticks. I have no idea whatsoever what I'm
doing.

I'm petrified. Beyond petrified, I feel like I'm solely living in
fear, and I cannot see past its boundaries. I'm completely lost, but
here I am, having to woman up and take those next steps in my
life.

After a couple of minutes, I straighten up and drive the
twenty minutes that it takes to get to the doctor's office and park
my car.

I should text Liam at the very least. He needs to know what
I'm doing because this doesn't just involve me anymore.

I'm unsure how he will react, though, or if he'd even like to be here with me. So, with a heavy sigh, I decide against it and make my way into the doctor's offices for my appointment—the very one that will ultimately tell me what the remainder of my life will be like. I keep my fingers crossed as the appointment proceeds, praying that it's that damn blue water that made those little crosses appear. It has to be.

Forty-five minutes later, the doctor leaves me alone with my thoughts as I stare at the black and white image in my hands. It's tiny and blurry, but it's there. She or he, I've decided, just became the sole purpose of my life. This little thing knows exactly how to tug on the few strings of my heart that I have left. Right now, it's enjoying playing with them like a puppet as it draws out all of my emotions hidden in the cold and dark corners.

An unwanted tear falls, and I dash it away before it can ruin what's left of my makeup, but it falls onto the image in my other hand, leaving a mark the size of the baby in the picture. I wipe the picture off and swing my legs off of the bench, taking my time getting dressed before emerging from the room and walking out to the check-out area of the doctor's offices.

The only time I speak is when I'm asked a question. I'm drifting off into some distant world while everything comes crashing down around me . . . but at the same time, my entire body is filling with an anticipated delight.

If there's one thing that I know, it's that I won't let this little thing down. Not like the family I was born into let me down.

I make my way back home and get comfortable on the couch with a warm mug of apple cider, the television remote, and a throw blanket before I'm able to get the courage up to pull out the ultrasound image once again.

I mentally curse myself at the mark that the teardrop left beside the blurry baby's image. While I still have the courage, I set the image down on the coffee table and take a picture of it with my phone. I type out a message and attach it to a text message to Hadley as well as Eden.

This is happening.

I sit back and turn the television on to some lovey-dovey romantic bullshit on *Lifetime* and get comfortable.

"Well, little dude, it's just the two of us now," I say down to my stomach and the frown. What if it's a baby girl? Hell, I can't handle a mini-me running around. I can barely handle myself at times.

My phone vibrates in my hand, bringing me out of my thoughts. A text from Hadley lights up my screen, and I swipe my finger across it.

Holy shit, Isla. I know that you must be scared out of your mind right now, but try to see the light in this, okay? We just landed, and I'm telling Wade to drop me off at your place. I hope that's all right.

I'd actually appreciate the company right now. I reply.

I'll be there in thirty.

I toss the phone onto the couch cushion beside me and groan just as it goes off again and a message from Eden comes across the screen. I lean over and swipe my finger across it: *Isla. This better not be a late April Fool's joke because I bite.*

A tear falls onto the screen when I type out my reply: *I wish it were that simple. Can we get together when you get back from your trip?*

You didn't even have to ask. Stay strong, and I'll be there soon to kick whomever impregnated you in the balls. That way he won't ever be able to do it again.

I giggle-sob as I hit the little letters on my screen.

You know, I'm lucky as hell that you applied to work at Blended four months ago.

Her reply makes me smile for a brief second before it

disappears again: *Duh.*

Forty-five minutes and a second mug of apple cider later, there's a knock on my door. I take my time getting up and straightening myself up before I walk to the door and pull it open without looking through the peephole.

I freeze when I look up and see broad shoulders in my doorframe instead of Hadley's slim ones. Liam looks down at me but doesn't say anything.

"Let me through, Liam," Hadley says from behind him and squeezes through to me between the doorframe and Liam's sturdy build.

She pulls me into a hug and whispers, "I tried to get him to stay in the car, but he naturally refused. I'm sorry."

"It's okay," I tell her while my eyes are still trained on Liam's.

He's staring at me like I'm something that he might want, someone that means more than just a fuck, but I don't quite understand after every hurtful thing that he said to me. I might have understood what he wanted in life, and he understood what I wanted, but none of it matters anymore. Not when I'm going to be bringing another life into this world.

I've seen Liam passionately angry, vibrantly elated, and inconsolably dejected, but never have I seen him take a turn and aim all of that emotion that he harbors within himself at me before.

The only thing that is going through my head is that I've had much more than my share of dealing with all of his shit already. I mean, we're not going to be getting anywhere, and while I need him to care and to be there for me, I know that once he finds out that I'm carrying his baby, he'll push me away indefinitely.

I decide at this very moment not to put my love and life on the line for him. If he wants more, then he's going to have to be the one to fight for it because I don't have the strength or reason to do it anymore.

"Do you want me to get Jacobs to get him out of here?" Hadley asks while throwing her thumb in his direction.

I shrug and turn around, blanching when I see the ultrasound on my coffee table. "Uhm. I'm actually not feeling very well, so I'm not sure if it's a good idea for either of you to be here right now."

"Isla."

It's the first time that I've heard his voice in over a week, and my body betrays me by turning toward him and sending a rare spate of goose bumps down my arms and legs. All of which cause me to shiver and wrap my arms around my waist.

"I think you should leave."

Hadley looks down at the coffee table behind me before moving toward it. I know that she'll save me from him seeing the one thing that I'll care for and about for the remainder of my life. I take a step toward the door where's he's still standing.

"We need to talk," he says, and it's now that I notice that the fight that once shone so deeply and prominently in his eyes is gone.

"I don't believe that there's anything more that needs to be said after what you admitted to me in Iceland."

"There is, yet there isn't." He looks behind me, and I follow his eyes as Hadley lifts my purse from the floor and places it on top of the ultrasound image on the coffee table. I'm hoping that he doesn't notice what she's doing.

I physically sag in relief as my evidence is covered up, but I attempt to feign cold detachment when I feel Liam's fingers move over my arm.

It doesn't work. Not for a damn second.

My body betrays me as my chest heaves with a breath, and the rest of the world becomes an unimportant blur. I manage to clear my throat before he says anything else. "Just tell me what you came here for and go."

I watch as the frown lines appear on his face, and I feel like my knees are about to buckle. His leaving is the last thing that I want, but I refuse to hold him hostage when none of this, none of *us*, was meant to happen.

"I'm leaving for Mexico in a day."

"You're what?"

"I'll be joining one of my teams for about two weeks. They're struggling to have enough manpower to enter a compound that they've come across. I'll be flying down with two other teams of mine."

"Surely they don't need you there, Liam."

"They do, or they would not have asked."

I watch Hadley slip past us and out of my loft before I look back up into his eyes.

"But it's dangerous."

"It is, but it's what I live for. RW is one of the reasons why I don't need—can't have—commitments in life. I put my life on the line to save others, and I can't have the pressure of someone waiting for me back home."

I reach out to steady myself against the wall before I'm even able to come up with a reply. "But you do have . . ."

"Have what? What do I have, Isla?"

I want to yell at him and state that he has *me*, but I know that it won't be enough for him to stay behind while his team literally drags themselves through a man-made hell. I know that his finding out that he's going to be a father will, though, but I decide not to put that on him. I know that he's trying to find himself again, and if he believes that he needs to go, then who am I to stand in his way?

I force myself to believe my own feeble excuses as he pulls

my body against his and wraps his arm around me.

"I'll be fine, and I'll check in with you or Wade as often as I'm able to."

"This is senseless," I say against his chest.

"Don't be petulant, Isla. I wouldn't expect you to grasp any of this even if it was standing right in front of you."

I pull back to gape up at him and his cocky mouth. I refuse to let him or any other ever talk down to me after living through that exact thing for fifteen years with my grandmother. He knows that. He's one of the few people who do, and this is his way of making sure that he pushes me away for good. Congratulations, Liam, I do not want another moment of my life to be spent beside you.

"You need to leave."

"Isla."

"No." I take a couple of steps backward until the backs of my knees hit the coffee table. "I need you to leave. Go. Good luck out there."

"Don't be like this."

"Like what?" I ask as innocently as I'm able to. I don't know how much longer I'll be able to hold back the harsh emotions that are whirling around inside of me. I don't want him here to witness me break down into the pathetic piece of ass that he's come to regard me as.

"Forget it. It doesn't surprise me that you're unable to handle my shit. I'll catch you later," he says over his shoulder as he leaves his unborn child and me behind, and it hurts. Dear God, does the sudden stinging sensation in my core wound me in every way possible.

Once the door clicks closed behind him, I have to remind myself that he's not a stone-cold human. He just doesn't know. He has no idea what he's putting on the line and what he's leaving behind, and as much as I want to pull that door open and yell at him down the hallway, I hold back. He might not know about the baby, but he came here to spew vile words at me that he knew would knock the wind out of my sails.

I slump down against the door and cup my face in my hands. How can I feel so shut out and isolated when it's half of my own doing? I could have begged him to stay, but what good would that have done? Why would I put myself at any more risk?

My phone goes off, and I fish it out of my pocket.

I'll miss you.

The black and white words mock me as I try to come up with a reply to him, but my mind is twirling in a thousand different directions, so I simply close my eyes and pull my knees up to my chest as my body starts to hollow out.

Each and every sob rips through my muscles and bones until it guts me from the inside out. Heavy tears roll down my cheeks at the utter devastation and loss I feel. The overwhelming sense of vulnerability shatters what's left of the hold that I had on my emotions as I willingly stand by and let it rip me apart.

Another painful emotion slams into me as my phone goes off again. I look down at it, and I cannot help the silent scream that tries to leave my lips.

Don't cry, doll. I can hear you, and it's killing me.

I shouldn't let a man get to me like this, but he's not just a man: he's my best friend, and I think I'm feeling a lot more than those sorts of sentiments toward him. Another muffled sob leaves me as I clutch onto my stomach, as I will everything to go back in time. Back to when I wasn't pregnant and to the time I could have said no to him. I should have said no the first time we let things get too far all of those years ago.

I attempt to blink away the briny tears from my bloodshot eyes when the knock sounds on my door, and my phone vibrates at the same time.

Isla. Please. Let me in.

I start to type out a message to him, but everything I look at seems to be so far away and blurry. Black dots dance at the edge of my vision as my body heaves, trying to expel everything I've consumed today, which is a mere two mugs of apple cider.

An uncomfortable warmth settles over my entire body as the room spins, and I fall into nothingness, past oblivion, and into unconsciousness. The room dips and sways into a silent sanctuary as my eyes fall shut.

I open my eyes again to a continuous knocking on the door, but I close them quickly, willing all of this to go away. I must have been out for less than twenty seconds, but it feels like a lifetime.

I hear a key turn in the lock, and the door pushes against my back, making my nerve endings scream.

"Doll, let me in." This time his voice sounds heavy and thick with emotion instead of the annoyance and resentment that it was laced with earlier.

I manage to move my body a foot or two away from the door, and before I'm able to comprehend what's happening, he's on his knees in front of me, pulling me into his arms.

"Jesus."

I don't bother reaching up for him or holding onto anything. That sturdy and sovereign woman is nowhere in sight right now, and for the first time since being locked away, I truly lose myself to the monster buried inside of me.

"What the hell is going on in your head, huh?"

"Please," I manage to choke out with a wobbling chin and quivering lips.

"Let me get you into bed, and then I'll leave."

I don't reply because I know that he'll do what he wants regardless of what I tell or beg of him. He lifts me easily and carries me up the stairs in my loft to my bedroom. He sets me down and pulls the comforter over me as a series of blatant tears start up again.

"I'll have my phone with me, and if you can't reach me, I'll text you the satellite phone's number. We may be over, Isla, but that would never rule out our friendship."

I nod even though I very much disagree with him and pull a pillow into my arms, feeling as abandoned and sullen as I did all of those years ago. Why does it feel like my best friend keeps breaking up with me when he never truly held that responsibility to begin with?

He places a kiss on the back of my head, and I watch him as he walks around my bed with purposeful strides to the door and then out of my sight down the stairs.

He exits my world without even saying goodbye, and although I know it shouldn't hurt, it does. It hurts like a bitch. These pregnancy hormones are going to be the death of me, and I'm barely past my seventh week. This little dewdrop is turning my life into a hell storm, but I wouldn't ever consider the alternative.

I tried to cover up my pain, but it's turned out to be hopeless today. Instead of setting aside the sensitive part of who I am, it seems to have taken center stage. Every word and every action have fought straight past my resistance and grabbed hold of my heart. I'm exhausted from trying to be strong and fight my way through this battle between what I feel and what my heart knows. I'm trapped somewhere I feel I don't belong, and as much as it should not hurt, it's unambiguously painful.

I'm currently stuck between missing him and letting the asshole become someone else's problem.

My tears have gone from wrenching wails that rack my body to soundless and aching as my emotions whirl around me.

I've stepped into the rip current, and I'm already exhausted from swimming against it. It's time to lie back and allow it to lead me on my journey like the waves of an ocean, pulling me into its deep and uncertain waters.

Screw living in this hookup society when I'm a hopeless romantic at heart.

Screw the rest of the world as I struggle to go on.

Screw everything and everyone.

I'm done.

Twelve

Liam

I ACKNOWLEDGE THE fact that I've botched shit up for the third time. I know that I've made her question herself when the problem is me. I'm the guy who isn't enough, and he knows it. I question every part of who I am on a regular basis because of it. I've found my faults, and I don't know another way around them except to punish myself for them, and if that punishment harms another in the process then it's all fair in love and war.

Just not this time.

This time, the guilt I feel has transformed from something emotive into an entity that's somehow defying gravity. Instead of numbing her out, I've welcomed her in because I'm no longer immune to Isla Madden.

She's dug deep and made herself comfortable in my soul, and as much as my pride, experience, and reason argue, I know that I have to give her more. More than what I've allowed myself to give in years. I know that I somehow need to shift from toying with her emotions to providing her with the validation that she deserves, yet as of right now, I cannot bring myself to do it.

I'm not the lifeline that she needs me to be. I may be the help for those women who are held captive, but when it comes to my personal life, I tend to see things differently. I'm finally starting to see what it means to be alive again. What it's like to wake up each morning and take in that first deep breath of air that a new day provides, instead of attempting to suffocate me with my past.

I take a step into my private jet where I'm greeted by eight other team members who are mainly based in the States. The majority of them come from Gage's teams, and I'm glad that they have all volunteered to go along with me. In addition to the nine of us in total, another nine will be meeting up with us in Mexico City.

I set my shit down on one of the leather seats before making myself known.

"Listen up," I yell out to get their attention. They shut the hell up for a moment to let me say my piece. "We are well aware of what we are going into today and the days to follow. I know that all of you have read the prompt and legal contract on this one, but I'm going to reiterate the important parts before we take off. You all need to realize what you're putting at stake if you're still on the jet while it hurtles itself down the runway. The men who run the compound that we will be raiding are under the assumption that I'm there to buy as many women as my dick desires." I clear my throat and try to continue after my brash words.

"Slavery has a face. It's the face of my once-fiancée, the faces of daughters, sisters, mothers, and wives. We're going to alter that image one pixel at a time. In doing so, we're attempting to rid the world of this horror. In the future, I plan on putting together a new team that will focus on boys and men who find themselves in a similar predicament. This trip, however, will be focused on the women in this particular compound. It's one of the largest in North America and we will not go in unarmed. We will, nevertheless, be unwelcome when they realize what we're there to do. Keep your eyes open and feet on the ground. I'm going to need each and every one of you to get as many of these women out alive as possible."

A couple of the men and woman clap, but I continue, "Take this as your warning. We're each putting our lives on the line to save another's. Once we're in the air, I will not turn this jet around. If you'd rather not risk your life to save someone who once walked freely and was coerced into sexual exploitation and slavery, then get the fuck off of my jet."

No one makes the motion to move, and I nod once before taking my seat and my pilot returns to the cockpit to get us into the air.

This is the generation that might have the balls to say *enough*, and I'll be leading the way with a handheld flashlight as we force our way through the darkness that has captivated too many souls for my liking. I run a hand down my face and try to focus on the maps that I've been handed, but it's no use. My mind is too preoccupied to plot out an escape route if it comes down to it. I hand the physical maps over to one of my best men and pull out my phone, hoping for a text from Isla, but neither of the two that are waiting for me is from her.

I click on Wade's message first: *Godspeed* and then on the one from Adriana: *I was told that you were heading back to Mexico. I'll be thinking about you. Please be safe and call me when you get back to the States.*

Goddamn it. I don't understand why I feel like I'm letting Isla down when I have so many others telling me that I'm doing the right thing here. I shut my eyes and lean my head back against the cold leather as the jet lifts itself into the air.

We've landed in Mexico City, and started our trek a couple of hundred miles into the jungle where this camp awaits us. Every second we wait will see another woman suffer, which is why we're going straight into this fight.

I've successfully managed to get our military-grade arsenal shipped here without detection, and it's all currently loaded in the back of the truck that I'm driving. I know that showing up with this truck may be risky, but I'm banking on them assuming that I'll be packing it full of women.

Little do they know that I'll be taking them out in the blink of a fucking eye. Yes, I've killed men before, and no, I don't hold an ounce of guilt over it because I've done it to save others.

"Are you ready for this, Jensen? You've not done a sting this large before," my second-in-command, Grady Kent, says. He's been by my side since he found out about Remission Worldwide on the day that I launched it. He lost his sister to trafficking, and he's been fighting by my side ever since. He handles the field-work more than I do, which is why he's here today. He understands what I'm getting all of us into, but he wouldn't turn his back on his sister nor me to stay at home with a beer in hand.

"I don't think that anyone would ever be prepared enough for what we're about to witness."

"Truth, brother. I'm glad that you agreed to join us on this one."

"I was given the option, and I would not miss it."

"Yeah? Well, don't tell my wife that I had the opportunity to step down from the mission. She'll have my goddamn head."

I chuckle and shake my head. "Hence why I remain single. I don't need the extra trouble."

"Nah, it's no trouble at all. It's a good feeling to get home after days of dealing with the scum of the world and sinking into her."

"Spare me the details, mate."

"I'm sure you've got yourself a little lady back home, and I'm sure you understand what it's like to go home to her."

I pause as the image of Isla in tears comes to mind. In over nine years, I've never once seen Isla cry like that before. To say that it destroyed me is one massive understatement. I saw it at that moment, though; I saw the distance in her eyes. I took her for granted, and I lost her.

"No. There's no one back home."

"I doubt that. Don't screw yourself over, and get out of your own head. You've been too quiet on this drive. I'm used to you being an overbearing ass-munch, not this sedated beast. I know that there's something eating at you, and I'll bet coinage on it that she's fucking gorgeous."

"You pay too much damn attention, Kent."

He chuckles as we pull through the first checkpoint of the compound. I lay on the brakes and roll down my window, nodding to the fucker who has an assault rifle in his hands.

"Nombre?" he spits out, and I have to hide my smirk.

"Jensen."

"Qué hay en el camión?"

I don't bother responding in Spanish. I know that he's stationed at the first checkpoint because of the sole reason that he's able to understand and speak English. He's merely getting what little joy out of life that he can by trying to force me to speak Spanish.

"Space for my purchases."

He nods to the two men standing beside the heavily rusted gate. Both of them lean into it and push it across its rails until it's open. Dumb shits, I would never have let a truck like this onto my property without having it inspected first.

He signals for my crew and me to continue, and I do, stepping on the gas and moving forward.

We drive for another fifteen miles before we're stopped again, and after that, another ten before I shift the truck into park and swing my door open. I'm exhausted from the flight and travel, but as soon as my boots hit the rough jungle floor, all of my senses seem to awaken and heighten at once. It's go time, fuckers.

The process starts off slowly with a couple of handshakes and introductions, but the second my foot hits the last step of the underground maze, my team falls into action. The loud and abrasive noises last for a good hour before I'm surrounded by a deathly silence.

I don't count the number of men I've stepped over or how many rounds I still have available in my gun as I start the truck up as the last of my guys helps a couple more women out of the underground hell that they have been living in. Surviving in. *Dying in.*

The raid went as planned and we pulled more women out of that hole than I would have predicted. A total of a hundred and nine of them are now sitting pretty in my first safe house just outside of Guatemala City. We blew through the border last night, and now we wait for the plane I've chartered to get these women onto US soil. The few women who are from Central America, I've handed over to the Guatemalan authorities with a handful of my men to ensure that they get where they need to go once they feel secure enough to leave the safe house.

To my horror, we lost a total of two men out of the seventeen who were with me. I won't forgive myself for their deaths. It's another notch that the sculptor has taken out of who I am, but I remind myself that they knew what they were getting into. Like me, they dedicated their lives to saving others.

I'll be the one to knock on the doors of their homes to inform their families of their loss as soon as I get back tomorrow. Meanwhile, RW will start to help get these women settled into a safe house as close as we can get them to their homes where medical and psychological evaluations will be performed on each of them.

"Jensen," a heavy hand lands on my shoulder, drawing me away from my ongoing thoughts. I turn and look up at Grady.

"What?"

"You need to rest up. You haven't slept since you left Chicago. That's closing in on three days now."

A façade of a chuckle moves past my lips as I shake my head. "I couldn't even if I tried."

"Doubtful, brother. Listen, the team has put something together for your birthday. I'd appreciate it if you got your ass to bed so that they can attempt to surprise you with some apparently expensive-ass whiskey that one of the boys brought along."

"Fuck. That word should be scripted on my body somewhere. It's one of the few things that keeps my heart fucking beating."

"Quit being a pussy and get some much-needed rest before they barge in on you, mate."

"Yeah, yeah."

He leaves me be for a moment of silent reprieve before I get up from my seat on the porch and make my way to the truck where I plan on crashing for the night.

As much as I can cut back on the terrified screams of the women while they sleep, I will. Fuck, what I wouldn't do to feel stone cold after a long drag of something powerful and relieving.

The next day passes without consequence. The team handed me a bottle of the Macallan 30-Year-Old Sherry Oak that I'm currently sipping on in my hotel room in Dallas, Texas. The rich mahogany color looks impeccable behind the crystal tumbler.

I get up and walk to the window before taking a long drink of the deliciously smooth Scotch with dried fruits, sherry, orange, and wood smoke. The flavors sit on my tongue as the spice develops and the finish stays just long enough for me to take the next sip. There's no better way to drink this antique gold than straight.

Today may be my thirty-second birthday, but it's not worth celebrating while I'm here in Dallas to deliver the news of the death of a man who should still be alive to raise his three girls.

My phone vibrates with a text message informing me that my ride is here. I grab my wallet after swallowing the remainder of the smooth experience, savoring every moment of it that I'm able to.

As one would imagine, I wasn't welcomed with open arms. His wife and girls shut down the moment they saw me on their doorstep. I managed to tell them as little as possible in an attempt to avoid causing further distress. Yet as they sat in front of me while I informed them that they wouldn't have to pay for his funeral or even concern themselves with the arrangements, it was difficult to keep my mind clear. It's tough not to get carried away with the thought of who might be informed of my death if it was to happen while I was out in the field.

Sure, my parents would be the first to know, but whom would they tell next? Waylon? Isla?

Isla.

Fuck.

Once I've said my goodbyes I head to the airport to board my jet to Seattle, Washington, where I'll need to inform the next family and watch them fall apart in front of me as well.

By the time I get to the jet, I've received more than a handful of messages from people I've once considered friends, sending me well wishes on my birthday, but regardless of how many times I check my phone, the one name I'm longing to see come across my screen doesn't.

I burnt that bridge, but I can't stop myself from asking why she hasn't tried to cross it again, whether for our friendship or something more. I may still be alive after this mission, but I feel dead inside.

The beautiful thing about life, though, is that it's forgiving and allows us the opportunity to move forward. Isla might not feel either sentiment toward me right now, but I seem to have caught hold of these feelings for her like a motherfucking amateur. She tripped me, and I don't have the strength to stand and run again.

Moments of realization are some of the best things about life, but they are ones that we can't share with others because it would take the stark beauty out of them. I may not have the ability to love her as she deserves, but I believe in that click that I have with Isla, and it's more than enough to make me want to go after it, to pursue it until she has no other option but to allow me back in.

Clarity. It's what brings the lost home.

Thirteen

Isla

I TURN OVER and push the comforter off of my face before reaching onto the nightstand where my phone has lit up with an incoming call. My mind is foggy with sleep, so I squeeze my eyes shut as I blindly answer it.

"Hello?" I say, my voice too groggy.

"Hi, baby doll."

I inhale a fresh breath of air for what feels like the first time in five days. The sound of his voice is like ice-cold water on my face, breaking me out of any residual sleep.

"Liam? What time is it?"

"It's late . . . well . . . early. I just needed to hear your voice. I'm sorry to wake you."

A thick wave of chills ripples over my chest and move down through my body as I pull the comforter over my head again. He may not be able to see me, but I'm hiding nonetheless.

"You shouldn't say things like that to me. Where are you?"

"I just got to Seattle," he says, ignoring my comment altogether.

"Seattle? As in Washington State?"

"Yeah."

"I thought you were going to Mexico."

"I went, and we did what we needed to do. I lost two of my men, which is why I'm here."

I sit up straight in my bed while my heart struggles to pump enough blood and oxygen to the rest of my body. "Oh God. Please tell me that you're okay?"

His chuckle is sugar-sweet, and it makes me fall for his ass even more than I already have. It doesn't matter that I can't re-wind and make him shove those hurtful words back into his mouth because he broke the best part of me. What I feel for this man won't let up—not after what he's made me feel.

"Do you think that you're going to get rid of me that easily?"

I stay quiet because I'm unsure how he wants me to respond to that little statement.

"Isla?"

"Yes?"

"I'm fine if you look past the bruises and the couple of lines of scratches down my back. I'm just exhausted."

A thrill pushes its way into my heart, and I have to fight it down. "I'm glad that you're okay. Are you . . ." I pause because I don't know if I have the right to ask him questions like this any-more, but against my better judgment, I proceed anyway. "Are you going to be back in Chicago anytime soon? We need to talk."

"Yeah, I'll be back in about a week. I need to help with these funeral arrangements and ensure that the women are settling into their safe houses." The line goes quiet for a few seconds be-fore I hear his voice again. "Doll?"

"Yeah?"

"We can talk now."

"I'm not so sure that doing this over the phone will be the right way."

"Hang up and I'll FaceTime you."

"That's not what I meant."

"Do it, Isla."

I cast a glance at what I'm wearing and shrug. "Okay, sure."

I pull the phone away from my ear and hang up on him before he has the opportunity to respond or even change his mind about seeing me.

Deep down, the butterflies are stretching out their dormant wings as I wait to see him.

My phone starts to go off again, and I hold it out in front of me, while I reach over and turn on the lamp on my nightstand.

It takes a moment to connect, and when it does, Liam's face takes up the majority of my screen. He adjusts the phone in his hand until I'm able to see more of him. My bedroom seems to fill with his level of testosterone in a nanosecond even though he's thousands of miles away from me. His shoulders are sagging, and he's unshaven, but he's still one handsome fuck. Bastard.

"God, what I wouldn't give to be in that bed with you."

I swallow the lump in my throat and look away from the screen. "Please don't say things like that."

"It's the truth."

"I think we both want you here for two very different reasons."

"You're afraid," he states so easily.

"Of what? Don't be ridiculous, Liam."

"Of losing me."

I look down at my left hand as my fingers play with the edge of my comforter.

"You look beautiful, doll."

I look up at the screen and shake my head as tears threaten to dry me out again. "Please don't play with me, Liam. I can't hide what I feel for you anymore. It was never meant to happen, but it did, and I can't go back right now."

"I'm not playing. You know too damn well that we'd go insane without each other."

"Would we?" I feel insecure and empty right now, but seeing

him on my screen seems to somehow dislodge both of those feelings.

"Without a single doubt. Isla, I know that what I've said has hurt you and that my actions have been anything but what they should be. After living through all of this shit in these last few days, though, I'm beginning to realize that we can't be just friends when neither of us looks at the other in that way."

"What do you mean? You'd want me the other way?"

"I'd do almost anything to have you in that way."

We stare at each other for a few quiet moments before he speaks again.

"The animal inside of me aches for you, but more importantly, the chemistry that we share is too powerful to be ignored any longer."

"I thought that you didn't notice it."

"I've known that it's been there for a while, but I tried to cover it up. Being away from you right now, though, has made me realize just how fucked up that was."

I can see the hesitation in his eyes, and I somehow manage to gather up my courage to call him out on it. "Why are you telling me this as if you're afraid that you're going to fall in love with me?"

His answering smile almost makes me forget to draw in a sufficient amount of oxygen into my lungs.

"Take a deep breath and tell me that you love me too, baby doll."

"What?" I choke out.

"You heard me. I got a little lost between referencing the past and facing the future, but I'm here now, and I acknowledge that I've fucked up more than I care to admit, but I'm asking you to be patient with me. Let me be that lifeline for you while I still have the courage to ask you and tell you this. Isla?"

"Yes?"

"I'm in love with my best friend."

My breath catches and my entire body starts to vibrate in relief and an overwhelming amount of bliss. Suddenly, nothing else matters, not one second of it because I know he made me dance around his heart while he was trying to protect it. He watches me unfold as his words consume me.

"I—you're serious?"

"Exceptionally serious."

"Liam, I can't . . ."

"Tell me what it is that you're having a hard time controlling."

I chew at the corner of my lip because I didn't think that we would ever get here, especially not over some stupid video call. The more he shares with me, though, the more the emotion seeps through my recently constructed walls. He's cracked them, and he's well aware of the fact. I shift on the bed before looking back up into the screen.

"I—I love you, Liam Jensen."

"I know," he says with the most natural smile I've seen him wear in years.

"Don't look at me like that," I say through a blush.

"Like what? What am I looking at you like?"

"Like you're in love."

"You better get used to it then," he counters.

We don't speak for what feels like a lifetime. I lie down on my side and stare at his handsome face while he does the same. When I hear his voice again, I've realized that I've dozed off with the camera slightly askew and pointed toward me.

"Doll? I need to get off of here and get some sleep."

"Hmm?"

"Fuck, I could watch you sleep for eternity."

"Stop," I grumble and pull the comforter higher up and over my shoulder.

"I'll be back in Chicago as soon as I can, and I'd appreciate it if my girl sent me a couple of messages now and then."

"I suppose that it won't hurt to type out something or other," I tease.

He chuckles and turns off the light in his hotel room.

"Liam?"

"Yeah?"

"Happy belated birthday. I'm sorry—"

"You have nothing to apologize for. All yesterday did was make me realize just how much I was missing out on without you in my life. Honestly, it's the best thing that you could have given me."

I can just make out the outline of his face, and I'm contemplating telling him my truth. I don't know if it will be too much for one night, or if it's the right time. I suppose that no time would be the right time for what I have to tell him, though.

I sigh and turn off my light before pulling up my text message application while we're still on FaceTime together. In a message to him I attach the ultrasound image that I sent Hadley last week. I'd rather not say the words out loud right now, but I know that I need to tell him. My finger hovers over the send button for a few seconds, and then I send the image into the pixelated world and anxiously wait for his response.

"Did you just send me something?"

"Uhm, yes."

I hear him shuffle and then his face is illuminated by the brighter light from the messenger application.

"What did you send?"

One. Two. Three. Fou—

"What is . . . ? Isla, is that . . . ?"

I blow out a breath and push my head deeper into the pillow. "Happy belated birthday, Daddy."

"What?"

I can still see his face and it's masked in confusion, horror, and to my surprise, delight.

"This . . . it's mine?"

"Whose else would it be?"

His face turns dark again, and I know that he's searching for mine on the screen.

"You're pregnant? You're pregnant with my child?"

I nod but quickly realize that he can't see me. "I am. We are."

"Holy shit," he breathes out. "When did you find out? How far along are you? Are you sure? Are you sure that this is ours?"

I can't help the smile that forms on my face for the first time about this pregnancy. "Yes, it's ours. I figured it out while we were on the plane to Iceland and confirmed it when I flew back home. I'm just over nine weeks along."

"Jesus."

"I know, I'm sorry. I should have said something sooner."

"Don't apologize for holding this back while I put you through shit, Isla. Fuck, I had no idea. I'm the one who's sorry. This—this is why you deserve better than I can give you. This is why I don't want anyone relying on me, but God. I can't believe what's happening."

"You're okay with it?"

"I don't particularly have a choice, but yes, I am. I mean, as okay as I can be about it. Are you sure?" he asks me again.

"Positive, Liam."

"I'll message my pilot now, and I'll be on the jet in an hour." His lights turn back on, and I see the subtle smile on his face while he pulls a shirt over his head.

"No, it's okay. You have work to do, and I'm not much company with all of this morning sickness."

"You've been sick? I can't leave you to go through this alone, Isla."

He sets his phone down on the nightstand while he moves around his lavish hotel room.

"Liam?"

"Yeah?"

"Please stop. I'll be okay. I swear it. I just need you to focus on helping those that you're in the middle of helping and then you can come for me."

"For you and my baby. Isla, I've never been able to put things that actually matter first in my life until this moment," he says as he picks up his phone from the nightstand. "I'm going to do this right. Starting now."

"You're being ridiculous."

"I'm not. You need me."

"I . . ."

Do I? Probably not as much as those women who he just pulled out of Mexico do, but yes, I do. I've needed him before this baby came along, and I'll probably need him well past it.

"Exactly. Fuck, this is liberating."

I giggle and turn my light back on. "What is?"

"Doing something for me and not giving a shit about the consequences. I'm sorry that I let you down when you needed me."

"You didn't—"

"I did, doll. All of those nights when you were so distant from me make sense now. I forced you to go through the beginning of this alone, and I refuse to do that again." He stops stuffing things in his bag and stares at the screen. "Do you forgive me?"

"For what? Being who you are?"

"No. There's being who I am and being a fucking ass who was too goddamn afraid to admit what he had."

"Well, seeing as those are your words and not mine, yes, I forgive you."

"Thank you."

I watch as he runs a hand through his hair and down the back of his neck. God, what I wouldn't give to touch him right this second.

"Liam?"

"Yeah, doll?"

"I need you."

His eyes shoot up to the screen as pure elation crosses over his face.

"I won't let you down again, Isla."

I give him a shy smile as he picks up his duffel bag and swings it over his shoulder before I watch his hotel room disappear behind him.

"Give me ten minutes, and I'll call you right back. I need to make sure that I'm all set to leave, and I need to arrange for someone else to fly up and sit with this family tomorrow."

"You don't have to do all of this for me."

I move a strand of hair behind my ear and let a yawn escape my lips once the sentence leaves them.

"Yes, I do. Go back to sleep if you need to. I'll see you soon."

"I don't think that I could go back to sleep now even if I tried."

I watch him get into a car and tell the driver where to go before he responds. "All right, I'll call you right back. Love you, babe."

I can't begin to explain the wave of hope that runs through me at his last three words.

"You too," I say and then he's gone.

I look around my quiet room and pinch the skin on my forearm to make sure that I didn't just dream that all up. I open our text message conversation and see the solitary image that holds both my and Liam's future staring back at me.

I swallow the lump that's forming in my throat and get out of bed. I start cleaning up my bedroom, changing the sheets out and by the time I'm done, thirty minutes has passed without a word from him. I decide on a relaxing bath and then to get ready instead of just staring at the phone while the seconds tick by. Once I step into the warm water and am seated in a mountain of bubbles, my phone starts to go off. I giggle and cover my chest up with bubbles before I answer him.

His image blinks onto my screen, and I sag a little farther into the water now that I see he's already on his jet.

"That took longer than I thought . . ." he trails off and raises his eyebrows. "I should be in that water with you."

"Hi."

I swear it feels like I've just met him because I'm suddenly a nervous wreck. My stomach flutters and I notice that I have one of my arms wrapped around my midsection in a way to reassure myself. I'm gnawing at the inside of my cheek while he watches me.

"What are you thinking about?"

"Nothing. I don't know. I'm just nervous about everything."

Little does he know that he's my *nothing*.

"About what exactly? Us?"

I nod and lean my head back against the lip of the tub. "Yes, us, and the fact that I'm pregnant. I can't believe that both things are actually happening."

"Get used to it, doll."

My pulse is pounding against my temples as I take in a

shallow breath. "You're sure about all of this?"

"I'm not sure about a single fucking thing, but you have my word that I won't let you or that baby down."

My eyes flicker down to my stomach, and I run my fingers over it. "I know that you won't. You're not someone who goes against his word."

"Good. I'm glad that I haven't lost all of your trust. I'm about to take off, and you should get some sleep."

"Wait."

I feel absurd for asking him this, but I don't particularly want to be alone right now.

"Do you have Wi-Fi onboard?"

"Yeah, I'm using it right now."

"Would you mind staying on the call with me?" I ask and start chewing on the corner of my lip again in a sensitive manner until his answering grin causes me to smile back at him. I have a feeling that this smile might be permanent on my lips for a while, and hopefully, mend any fragments of my heart that broke off when he left.

"I'll stay, but I'm warning you that I might pass out. I haven't gotten a lot of sleep these last few days." I think that he reclines his seat because the angle I have of him seems to be from above rather than right in front of his handsome-as-fuck face.

"What do you think people will say? Specifically Wade?"

"Does he know?"

"That I'm pregnant? No, not that I know of. Hadley knows, though."

"That would explain why she's been so fucking peeved with me. She's been constantly up my ass about you."

I giggle and readjust myself in the tub. "Probably."

I let this sense of happiness soak right into my bones and savor it in the moment.

"To be honest here, I don't give a fuck what anyone thinks. Yeah, we've got a shitload to figure out, but I'm glad that we're going to be able to do this together."

"Me too."

"When were you planning on telling me?"

"I wanted to tell you the second I found out. I wanted you with me at the doctor's appointment, but I was frightened, and I tried to cover up my pain rather than let you see it. I guess these pregnancy hormones have a mind of their own."

"I'll be with you for all of the ones you have in the future. I'm sorry that I missed the initial one."

"Thank you," I say shyly. "Hold on one second for me." I set the phone down on the edge of the tub and start to wash up.

"You know, I'd prefer to watch you do that than stare at your ceiling."

"And how do you expect me to do that when I need both of my hands?"

"You'll figure it out."

"Liam," I scold and reach over to grab my phone, but the second I grab onto it, I know that I've made a mistake. It slips from my soapy hand and into the tub along with me.

"Fuck," I say under my breath and fish it out of the water. I manage to hop out of the tub without slipping on the tile with wet feet and tiptoe downstairs to the kitchen while I frantically push the buttons on it, waiting for any sign of life from the damn thing, but nothing happens.

It takes me a couple of minutes to find the rice and drop my now-dead phone into a bag of it before I make my way back upstairs to finish my bath.

"Sorry, dickweed," I say underneath my breath. Of course, this would happen on the day that I loaned Eden my tablet, and Wade's technical people have my laptop to install some bullshit state-of-the-art system that they insist will make my life easier when it comes to all things at Blended.

Shit on a stick. I need to figure out what to do. I'd take a short nap, but I would never wake up on time to meet him at the airport without my phone to wake me up. Let's be honest, no one has a freaking alarm clock anymore, and I'm afraid that I'll miss him.

I return to my bath and allow my body to soak in the fragrant water before making sure that I'm clean-shaven and ready for him in any which way possible.

I shuffle around the bathroom, getting ready, while occasionally glancing at myself in the full-length mirror, wondering how long it will take until I get to see any changes in my body.

Once I'm dressed, I make my way downstairs and start walking up and down the length of my loft.

I know that I'm being outlandish, but when something turns around in your life, you go for it. Liam's the biggest asshole that I know, but he's also one of the most giving and selfless men. I wipe at the tears leaking from my eyes and half-laugh at myself. I'm a mess.

I glance down at my outfit and shake my head before running back up the stairs and tearing my closet apart until I walk out with something better than what I had on.

Instead of my yoga pants and a baggy sweatshirt, I've changed into a deep blue skinny jean and a flowy, sheer black tank that I tuck into the front of my jeans and a pair of black strappy sandals.

I give myself another once-over in the mirror before heading downstairs and sitting down in the spot that Liam usually does when he's about to take a nap on my couch. *I told you that I'm being ridiculous.*

Three hours and forty-five minutes of foot tapping and endlessly checking the little hands on my watch have finally come to an end as I wait outside of the private airport's entrance for Liam's jet to land.

Regardless of how much I flirt with this woman at the gate who is obviously into me, she won't let me past the wall of steel to get closer to him.

I park off to the side of the gate, so hopefully he'll see me when he's leaving with a driver. I get out and move to the front of my Porsche to lean against the hood while I search the sky for any incoming flights.

Call me old-fashioned, but the second I see his jet land, I picture an old-time movie being played over a projector screen with *Kiss Me* playing softly in the background. It takes another fifteen minutes before the gate opens and a black vehicle starts to pull through, but it suddenly jerks to a stop and one of the rear doors flings open.

Liam steps out, stealing my breath and all of the heat from my skin at first sight. I stand up straighter as he takes long strides that turn into a jog across the distance between us until he reaches me and folds me into his arms. Before I draw in another breath of air, his lips move down to mine, making my entire body come alive with one desperate kiss.

He has all of my defenses down as his tongue asks for entrance, and I give it to him, allowing his calloused fingers to move underneath my tank to the bare skin at the small of my back.

His kiss is beyond gentle, and I can taste my briny tears as our lips move against each other. His free hand moves up into the waves of my hair until he's holding onto the back of my neck, securing me in place.

I think the two of us morph into a single being as I dissolve into the warmth of his body. Each time he moves his hands along my skin, more tears fall, and neither of us pulls apart. After what feels like months of fighting off these out-of-control and wild feelings I've held for him, I can finally let them go. I give myself the opportunity to fully experience what it's like to be with him without having to hold my breath or say something that neither of us wants to hear. *I won't lose him again*, I promise myself.

His large hand moves from the back of my neck and to my cheek as he releases my lips from his warm ones. His eyes catch mine in the dim light as he wipes away a tear that's rolling down my cheek.

"I'm sorry, Isla. So sorry."

"Shh," is all I can manage before I lean up on my tiptoes and lock our lips together once more in the deepest, most respectful silent language. He pulls me as close as he can possibly get me to his hard torso before lifting me off of my feet and taking a couple of steps toward my Porsche where he sits me down on the hood.

I ring my legs around his waist as our kiss becomes more than an unhurried tender tease. His hands are moving up the sides of my body as I shove my fingers through his hair, tugging him forward. He chuckles against my lips and reaches down to unbutton my jeans.

"Liam," I moan softly, "we can't. Not here."

"Just let me feel you," he says as he pushes his hand past the zipper and slides his fingers underneath the slight elastic of my panties to my lips. He lazily runs his fingers over me, causing my entire body to tighten up while it seizes with pleasure.

"Excuse me, sir?" A masculine voice breaks through the silence around us, and I want to yell at him for ruining what Liam was about to do to me.

"What?" Liam says while staring into my eyes as if he's searching for something more than he sees.

"Would you like me to unload your belongings?"

"Please," he replies as he removes his fingers from their prime position on my body and proceeds to zip and button me up all the while staring at me like he sees more in me than he ever has before.

I unlock my ankles from his back and move my hands farther up his chest. I feel his chest vibrate before I hear his voice, and it sends a massive wave of goose bumps running down my arms. "So you dropped your phone in the bathtub?"

"Guilty."

He chuckles and kisses me once more before helping me down from the hood. "The fucking plane wouldn't get me to you fast enough."

"To that, I agree."

"I bet, but shit, I could sleep for two days straight right now."

"It's a good thing that I have the most comfortable bed in the city then, huh?"

"It is. What do you say that I drive us home and then hold you against me until I wake up again? Then, I'll ravish you like you deserve. Deal?"

"Deal."

He starts to turn around to grab his things, but quickly stops and glances down at me before moving a hand to my midsection and over my stomach.

"She's there?"

A smile splits my face at his assumption. "She? What makes you think that it's a girl?"

"The fact that I've been saving them for years. Maybe this is my reward, you know? Having two for myself. When do we find out?"

"Actually, my guess is as good as yours. I'm new to all of this too. I guess that I need to order some pregnancy books because that one pamphlet did nothing for me."

"You'll need to share it with me."

"Not while you're half asleep. Let's go before you pass out on the gravel."

"I'll be fine to drive," he says as he grabs his duffel and a larger bag that looks like it should carry a rifle. I choose to ignore it and open the trunk for him to place it inside.

"I'll drive," I tell him.

"Are you sure?"

"Positive."

"All right. Let's get my sorry ass into bed."

I squeeze his hand, and he walks me to the driver's side and opens the door for me. I stare at him for a second, tempted to look behind him to see where he's hiding my best friend, but instead I ignore the little voice, placing a quick kiss on his cheek before I get in, and he closes the door behind me. Two seconds later he's getting into the passenger seat and buckling in as I start the car up and pull back onto the road, heading in the direction of Navy Pier.

The sun has started to rise when he reaches over and wraps his fingers around my inner thigh. I look over at him while I stop at a red light, but he's already drifted off to sleep. My heart constricts in my chest as I pull through the intersection.

I don't know how we went from one side of the ocean to the other in a single conversation, but I do know that both of us must have been ready to make the journey or it would not have happened so quickly. Being around him seems to be all of the therapy that I need because all of the negativity that was physically holding me down seems to have vanished the moment he drew me into his arms.

I've fallen in love with this man simply because he is who he is. Through the thick, the thin, and the good and bad, he hasn't lost the person who he's been since the first time I met him.

If someone told me almost ten years ago that I'd be dating this jackass and expecting his baby, I would have laughed in that fucker's face, but great relationships don't simply happen. Just like any relationship, this one is the product of a consistent investment of affection, patience, and time. We might just be starting out, but something tells me that this might actually last. That *something* is deep down in my belly where our love is growing to form a little human.

Before I know it, I'm pulling into my parking spot and shifting the vehicle into park before I turn it off. I unbuckle, trying to not disturb his hand on my thigh before I lean over and place my lips against his.

His chest expands on his inhale before he opens his bloodshot eyes and moves his hand from my thigh up to my waist as he pulls me over the center console and onto his lap.

"I didn't mean to fall asleep on you."

"It's okay, I just won't be able to carry you inside like you'd be able to if the roles were reversed."

His chest vibrates with a silent chuckle as he moves his hands down to my thighs.

"Bed?" I ask as his eyes start to droop again.

"Please."

I somehow manage to push the door open and climb off of him, and he follows behind me. "We can grab your stuff later."

"Sounds good."

He locks his fingers around mine as we make our way up to my loft and then up to my bedroom. Watching him as he lazily strips down to his boxer briefs, I take a moment to admire this masculine specimen in front of me and find myself insanely aroused by the simple act of his baring himself. Perching on my side of the bed, my eyes roam down the sharp ridges of his stomach and down to that bulge. He should really be painted or sculpted because he's just that beautiful. He puts me in a heady trance that brings back all of the butterflies. Every single one that was once lost has returned to its place of origin.

It doesn't matter how much I've tried to distance myself from him, my attraction to him only seems to grow. He gazes at me before getting underneath the covers and pulling me down next to him once I've kicked off my jeans. He holds me against his warm chest and seems to fall asleep almost immediately.

"Love you, babe," he mumbles.

I turn around to face him and run the palm of my hand against his cheek, which causes him to raise his eyelids for a brief moment before closing them again.

"Love you," I say as he pulls me as close as we can possibly get to each other. I tilt my head up and touch my lips to his in a slow kiss. I wasn't expecting him to kiss me back, but he does ever so lightly before his lips stop moving altogether and I know that sleep has finally claimed him.

I've got everything and nothing to lose with Liam Jensen. He's crossed the border into my heart tonight where he'll leave his love behind. My body jolts when he runs his hand down the side of my ass and to my thigh where it remains as I drift away from the conscious world.

Fourteen

Liam

WHEN I PEEL my eyes open, I'm surrounded by darkness and the sweet smell of roses and vanilla from Isla's Valentino perfume that she loves so much. I know it because I introduced it to her a year or two ago. I'd be able to recognize it anywhere. I shift onto my back on the bed and look over to her side where she's curled up into a ball and as far away from me as possible while she sleeps.

I grumble and reach over to her, pulling her petite frame toward my larger one. "What the hell are you doing all the way over there?"

When her skin comes into contact with mine, I almost pull back at how cold she is. I turn her around so that she's facing me and pull her flush against my bare chest. She exhales and nuzzles into me before pushing one of her legs between mine.

"What are you dreaming about, doll?" I ask as I run my thumb over the tension lines between her eyebrows. She doesn't respond to me, and I don't want to wake her up just yet. I'm unsure of when she actually fell asleep or what the time right now is. All I know is that I've slept the day away instead of spending it with her.

I throw a glance over my shoulder to the nightstand that holds my phone. I reach over and unlock it, squinting at the time and date. It's well past three in the morning of the next day. Jesus,

I've slept for almost a solid twenty-four hours. I set the phone back on the table before again looking down at her.

I cannot believe that she's carrying a part of me inside of her. I slide the palm of my hand up her front and underneath her clothing until I can rest it against her stomach. I place my lips against her temple before I move her out of my arms for a couple of minutes. I head into her bathroom and shower off my travels and clean myself up before heading downstairs to grab something to eat.

She's filled the freezer with more pints of ice cream than I've seen in a while. I question whether they are because of how I made her feel or if it's pregnancy cravings.

Holy fucking shit.

She's pregnant.

The weight of those words hits me hard and fast, but instead of the sudden sinking feeling that I'd expect to pull me down, a lighter one lifts me up, and I can't help the smile that it brings.

Despite the time, I start a pot of coffee and lean back against the kitchen island as it starts to brew. The bittersweet scent begins to fill the loft when soft footfalls draw my attention to Isla as she walks toward me.

"Morning, doll," I tell her as she reaches me and stands between my outstretched legs before leaning her body against mine.

"Mmm."

"I'm going to guess that pregnancy won't help with the grumpy mornings, will it?"

"This doesn't even count as the morning," she grumbles against my chest muscles.

"No?" I lock my arms around her shoulders and kiss the top of her head while I enjoy the warmth of her breath moving across the skin of my chest.

She sighs in response and tightens her arms around my torso. "I like having you here."

"You humble me, Isla."

"Quit bullshitting me."

I pull back to look down at her. "I wouldn't. I might be losing my mind because I've decided to stop fighting what I feel for you and follow the fucking arrows pointing in your direction, though."

"By arrows do you mean your dick?" she counters while I'm trying to be sincere with her, but I give in and laugh along with her. "We might be together, Jensen, but that doesn't mean that I'm going to change my spots."

"Thank God for that. I'm unsure if my cock can handle a prissy little bitch."

She shoves me, and I catch ahold of her wrist, trapping her hand behind my neck and then reaching for the other, placing it in the same position as she leans into me.

"You're such an ass."

"One that you have rather intense feelings for, so don't go bitching about my behavior. Plus, we're just getting started, and we wouldn't want to scare anyone away."

"Who the fuck would we have to scare away? Your parents?"

"Jesus, no. They seem to adore the fuck out of you."

"You should tell them that I'm pregnant. I'm sure that your sister will be beside herself. She's always wanted her younger brother to aspire to more than just a drunk bastard."

"Don't say that too loudly. My mother might cut your damn tongue off."

"We'll have to see what she does, won't we?"

"After having an affair and giving birth to me nine months later, what can she do other than be thankful?"

She shrugs and runs her fingers into the back of my hair.

"She loves you and so does your biological father as well as your dad. You were blessed to have so many people there for you."

"As much as that is true, it was difficult to grow up in a world that was surrounded by lies. Did I ever tell you that my mother lied about my being hers for the first eleven years of my life?"

"She did what?"

I nod and move my hands down her waist to her ass. "Yeah. She made up some story about her sister passing and her inheriting a nephew. It was all a cock-up, but it was my life. Shit, she had me believing that bullshit for years until my father came back into the picture when he found out about me."

"That's who you got your trust fund from, right?"

"Correct. It's more than likely the only reason why my mother confessed the truth about me in the first place."

"How did your dad react—the man who's married to your mother?"

I place my lips on hers before pulling back. "He told me not to look back and keep taking steps forward in my life because there's no use in throwing glances over your shoulder when you're not going that way."

"He sounds like a wise man."

"He is, and I'm sure my mother and both of my fathers would like to finally meet you."

"So the shared video calls over the nine-plus years don't count as meeting?"

"No, baby doll, they sure don't."

"Well, I'm so fucked."

I raise my eyebrows as she moves out of my arms and pours a cup of coffee before handing me the black gold.

"Why?"

"For one, I have to charm the pants off of not one but two fathers, and your sister, well, let's just say that I remember her calling me out on my whorish behavior our freshman year in college."

"Fuck that, and fuck her big mouth. We've never gotten along because of our eight-year age difference and because I'm literally the bastard in the family."

"You are, but I love you."

"Yeah?" I take a drink of my coffee and hold out the mug for her to take a drink, but she shakes her head no.

"I can't have caffeine for a while."

"Is that some pregnancy rule?"

"Apparently."

"Then who the fuck am I going to share my damn coffee with?"

She smiles and runs her hands up my abdomen to my chest and then skates her nails against my skin before dragging them down to the edge of my boxer briefs.

I groan as my cock jerks to life between us.

"I'll assume that this conversation is over."

"So over," she says breathlessly and pulls her sweatshirt up and off.

The next time I wake up, I have Isla's naked body wrapped around mine, and the room smells of her and the sweet, unforgiving scent of sex. It's a heady sensation that I'd like to get used to waking up to. I groan when I shift on the mattress: the muscles that I haven't used in a long while ache just below the surface of my skin.

Fuck, this little vixen likes to play.

"Shh," comes from the sexiest set of lips that I've ever used before I get up and make my way into her bathroom, and they inspire my next move.

I open more drawers than one would assume might be filled

up in the bathroom before I find what I'm looking for.

I walk back to the bed, hard as fucking stone, and sit down beside her.

"Doll?"

"Go away," she mumbles and pulls a pillow over her head.

"I have a favor to ask."

"Does it involve your woody?"

"You know that it does."

She pushes the pillow off of her face and glances down at my lap where my cock is straining against its own skin, and then to my hand that's holding her favorite tube of red lipstick.

"Sit up."

She does as she's told as I uncap the lipstick and hold it out for her.

"What's this for?"

"I like the stains that you leave behind after you suck on me."

"Oh? This is news . . . sort of," she says with a giggle.

"If you don't get on your goddamn knees in front of me in the next thirty seconds, I'll take matters into my own hands and fuck that pretty little mouth of yours until it's raw."

That gets her to react.

She frantically shoves the comforter off of her and takes the lipstick from my hand, applying it effortlessly over the surface of her lips. Fuck me running. Her cherry-red lips make me want to do more than just watch her suck me off right now.

She leans over to place the tube of lipstick on her nightstand and then sits back against her headboard and stares me down.

"Is that a dare?"

"Take it as you will, Jensen."

The deep rumble that leaves my chest surprises even me and causes her to jump as I launch myself at her and hold her body against the headboard.

Her lips part as her breathing becomes labored with a need for me. I grab hold of her jaw, and she opens wider for me, inviting me inside of her warmth. I manage to keep her in place as I stand up and position myself at her now-closed lips.

"Open."

She complies and I push the length of myself between her sex-red lips. She puckers them around my shaft as she swallows me whole. I pull out slowly, and she tongues me when she gets a drop of my pre-cum, red stains marking my skin already.

I slide back into her as she hollows out her cheeks. I grab hold of her ink-black hair as she shields her teeth and I start to fuck her pretty mouth.

Her tongue slides along the bottom of my shaft as I repeatedly pull out and shove back in. I feel the heavy pinch at the small of my back as my release works its way through my body. She must feel my shaft thicken and the skin tighten around me because her hands move to my chest as she starts sucking on me harder.

"Fuck, doll, you're gorgeous."

She hums against me and the vibrations fuck me over. I start to pour myself down her throat as I slide against her. She drags her nails down my chest, leaving stinging lines all the way down as I surrender myself to a desire laced in agony.

"Jesus," I spit out as she swallows me completely before I pull back and out of her mouth. She gives me a little show by keeping her lips around my crown awhile longer and sucking on me before I pop out from her lips.

My chest is heaving from the sheer pleasure, and I glance down at her before me. Her lipstick is smeared, and the majority of it paints my cock. I fucking thrive on this shit.

"Well?" she asks innocently as if she did not just ask me to fuck her mouth and enjoy it at the same time.

"Damn."

"Good," she replies and slinks away from me, walking her bare ass into the bathroom and closing the door behind her.

Once the two of us cleaned up, I had enough time to retrieve my shit from her SUV. I manage to open my laptop long enough to check my RW email, and I'm rather astonished at what I find.

To: Liam Jensen
From: Grady Kent
Subject: RW Break-in

Mr. Jensen,
It pains me to write to you like this, but I just received news that RW's central Sydney office was broken into last night. I have attached a detailed list of what was taken. Please feel free to look over it.

Best,
Grady Kent.
Office and Field Manager of Remission Worldwide.
"One woman at a time."

It's a small office, only containing the servers that host all of the organization's detailed information, as well as files of all of the men and women who work for me. I scan through the list of files that were taken from the office, most of which have a comment beside it saying that it has been recovered. Once I get to the end of the list, I see almost every file is shown as having been recovered with the exception of one. My own.

All of the video recordings have been scrubbed from the hard drive, which leads me to believe that it might have been an inside job, but I can't be sure, and I refuse to take any risks. I'll have a few of my trusted men dig around and keep an eye open for any suspicious activity, but there's nothing much else that I'm able to do right now. The authorities in Sydney have been notified, and detailed records have been taken on what happened, but beyond that, there's nothing that I am able to do from the States.

I type out an email to the head of the offices in each location of a safe house and copy Gage and Wade on it as well. I may not know what it means, but I do know that I won't be taking any chances. I instruct them to have the remainder of the physical copies of files destroyed once they have been transferred onto a server located in Brass Global's building here in Chicago. In addition to that precaution, I advise them to reset all of the passcodes to all of our offices and servers at every single RW site.

Isla's hands move to my shoulders and start massaging them just as I send out the email.

"Is everything okay? You seem tense."

"Hey babe. I'm trusting that everything will be fine, but we're dealing with a break-in in Sydney right now."

"Oh hell. At your house?"

"No, at Remission Worldwide. Someone got into the central office."

"Hopefully, nothing seriously important was taken. Surely you guys don't keep cash on hand there, right?"

"We do, but that's beside the point. The only thing that they have been able to identify as missing was a file containing my personal information in it."

"Why would someone want to take that?"

"Good question, doll, but let's not concern ourselves with that right now." I turn the barstool around to face her and pull her body between my legs. "The Cubbies are going to need us today."

"I thought that you might have forgotten."

"Not in this lifetime. Go get dressed and let me take my girl out."

"Deal."

———————————

It's Sunday and game day at Wrigley Field, and I swore to her that we wouldn't miss a game weekend together. This is me keeping that promise. My phone chimes as we get into her SUV, and I'm about to head out of the parking deck. I dig into my pocket to retrieve it and open up a text from Gage Cooper.

Jensen, are you able to get together today? We need to talk in regard to your email, and I'd prefer to do this in person.

I'll be at Wrigley. Swing your ass on by. I know that your seats are right next to mine, fuckhead. I type out and hit send before I pull out of the parking spot and head in the direction of one of my favorite places in Chicago.

During the drive, I start to run through the lists of men and trafficking rings that I've taken down over the years, but I don't know of any that would have access to my full name to find out any information about me or where I came from.

"You seem far away, Liam."

I squeeze her hand in mine before letting go to back up into a spot at the ballpark.

"Sorry, doll. I'm trying to piece together who knew anything about me to get to RW."

"That's more than understandable, and I'm sure that it's nothing."

"Let's hope that it's just some bored teenager. I can't risk my girls."

I lean over and kiss her while my hand moves underneath the thin material of her Cubs shirt.

"You have your heart set on it being a girl, don't you?"

"For now," I say against her red lips.

"We're not even to the twelve-week safe zone, Liam."

"You don't have a thing to worry about, babe. She's going to be perfect."

I take her lips once more before we head into the crowds of Wrigley when my phone vibrates in my pocket. I dig it out and open the message from Gage: *Be there in fifteen.*

"I hope that you don't mind, but Gage just let me know that he'll be joining us. Those two seats that were empty beside us at the opening game belong to him."

She laughs as we turn into the row to take our seats. "Do you really think that I'd give a fuck?"

"Nah, but I thought I'd try out being a gentleman for a few minutes before being true to the asshole that you know me to be."

"I prefer the asshole in you, dickweed," she says as she leans over the armrest that separates the two of us and runs her tongue down the left side of my jaw. My dick stirs behind the fabric of my shorts.

"You'll get yourself in trouble if you continue this, baby doll."

"Maybe I'll like it," she counters just as she leans in to do it again, but this time, I catch her lips with mine. She shamelessly moans against me as she digs her fingernails into my chest against my shirt. Fuck, I love what I'm able to do to her. She's damn near putty in my hands.

"Liam."

"Isla," I say right before I pull on her full bottom lip with my teeth and let go.

"Thank you for coming back early for me. All of this has been a lot to absorb on my own."

"Like I told you . . . it took me a while to realize exactly what you mean to me, but once I got the clarity that I needed, I didn't have to think twice about it. In retrospect, I've been fighting it off for a while, but I'm glad that I caved into those seductive red lips of yours."

I watch her as she almost shies away from me while moving her braided hair from the center of her back to her left shoulder.

"Don't do that."

"Don't do what?"

"Don't pull away from me when I know you, Isla. Yes, we've taken what we are to the next level, but I still know you."

"I know . . . it's just a different feeling. I don't want to wake up tomorrow morning and have this all be a dream, or have you tell me that you don't want it."

"Do you trust me?"

"Yes. Probably more than I should and more than any other woman would trust an ass like you. You're my best friend—how would I not?"

"Gee, thanks for the vote of confidence, and I damn well better be more than your best friend at this time."

While she's stewing over what to say, Gage turns into our row of seats, and I stand to greet him. "How's it going, fuckhead?"

"All good as of now."

I lean over Isla as we slap each other on the back, and he takes a seat beside her.

"It's good to see you again, Isla. How are you holding up with this shitface back in the States?" he asks her, and I stay quiet, interested to hear what she has to say.

"As good as I can be with him hogging up the majority of my bed each night."

Gage's dark chuckle bleeds into the air around us. "The bastard better be grateful that you haven't put him out on the curb yet."

"Oh trust me, it's come close a time or two. I'm going to grab you guys some beer. Do you want anything in particular?"

She knows that she doesn't need to get up to get anything during the game with the seats we have, and I'm grateful that she can pick up on Gage's need to speak to me in private.

"Goose IPA, please, babe," I say as she stands. My eyes move down from her tight ass to her tanned legs and then back up her body until her eyes are locked on mine, and she leans down, placing a kiss on my stubbled cheek.

"Gage? What about you?"

"I don't suppose that you snuck any whiskey in if he's getting a craft then, huh?"

"Sorry, Coop, not this time, and the only whiskey they have here is house."

"Get me what Jensen is getting then, thanks."

"Sure thing. You'll just owe me later," she winks as she steps past him and out of the row of seats.

Now that it's just Coop and me, he drops his smile and wrings his hands together as he decides on how he wants to open this topic of discussion. "I think that we may have a mole in RW."

"I've considered it, and it wouldn't shock me, but I wouldn't know where to start when it comes to figuring out who it is. I've had a lot of employees in and out of that office over the years, and it could be any number of them."

"It would have to be someone who knows the ins and outs of the office and possibly beyond that because it wasn't ransacked," he says as he opens his email application on his phone.

"Possibly, but that still leaves a hell of a long list of names to go through. I'll do it, though—I'll be the one to sit down and go through them all. And we're sure that the only thing that was taken was my file?"

"Positive. I asked Kent to double-check everything again

once I got his email earlier today. The poor shit hasn't slept since he helped get all of those girls where they needed to be."

I chuckle because I'm well aware of what he must be feeling like right now. "He'll survive. Now tell me, what are your thoughts on what needs to happen next, aside from an investigation into each employee who has had access to the office over the years? Do I need to step up security at all locations, or does this mean that it's personal?"

He shakes his head as I speak. "If I were you, I'd keep a tight grip on Isla if you two are together. Shit, man, I'd keep a close eye on your mother and sister as well."

The harsh reality of his words sucks me in, and I have to give myself a few seconds to recuperate.

"It can't be that serious, Coop. I've kept my full name as well as the organization under the radar as much as the government will allow it. The rings only know me as Jensen and nothing more."

"It's not—right now—but I don't have another explanation for it. The only other thing that I can come up with is some kid breaking in, but then that doesn't account for your file being the only thing that's missing. Hell, all of the fucking cash is still there, and I've had all of our investments as well as bank accounts checked. Every fucking thing is there, Liam. Not a single cent is missing. This might get ugly, and I'm going to insist that you keep your girls close."

"She's pregnant," I say under my breath as visions of repulsive men coming and snatching Isla from her bed fill my head.

His body movements still as he swallows my proclamation. "Who else knows?"

"Four people, I believe, but I'm not completely sure if she told anyone aside from myself, Hadley, and now you. Five if you include her co-worker. Surely this has nothing to do with her.

She's only nine and a half weeks along, so no one would fucking know even if they went digging."

"It may have everything to do with her. I'm going to assume that she's gone to see the doctor about this little addition?"

"She has."

"That there, Jensen, leaves an opening that wasn't there before. There's more documented information about her that can easily be hacked into."

I lean forward in my seat and run a hand down my face, cupping it over my jaw, trying to force myself to remember what was in that file. "I don't believe that my file contained any information in regard to her."

"But it held the right amount of information someone might need to find you and then her or any other females in your life."

"How would they even know where to look unless they've been watching me from afar for some time?"

"That's the only way that they'd know how to get to you. Keep your eyes peeled, especially while you have her at your side. It might be a good idea to separate yourself from her until we've got this shit on lockdown."

"Separate myself from her? Jesus, Coop, we just clarified all of what we are a day ago. I can't leave her, especially when I already have, and now that I know that she's pregnant . . . no. I refuse to compromise our relationship that much."

"All right. You have a valid point when it comes to keeping what you have with her secure, but it won't be secure if something happens. I just need you to be prepared. Outside of watching and mentoring my teams, this is what you brought me into RW for. You needed more than some asshole to help you see what needs to be done on the business side. This is business, Jensen. It might be a fucked-up side of business, but it is nonetheless."

I glance over my shoulder because I can physically feel her

when she's near, and every cell in my body is currently wanting to break away from who I am and go to her. I think I've always been able to feel her presence, but now I know why: *she's mine.* She's just started taking the stairs down to get to our aisle from the main concourse, so I turn back to Cooper.

"Don't repeat this conversation while she's around. The last thing that I need is her concerning herself over something that might not even mean a goddamn thing. I'll get with my head of security and arrange a watch over her as soon as I can get them here. Do you truly believe that I need to extend that protection to both my mother and sister?"

"If that were my file that was taken, Jensen, I would."

I nod as I look up and lock eyes with Isla as she steps into our row of seats. A vision of her in the dark hits me with a rough pang in the chest, but the second I hear her voice, I'm brought back to Wrigley, the Cubs, my girl.

"Cold brews, anyone?"

She doesn't look anywhere but at me, and I feel like I'm in a damn trance. I get to my feet to take the beers from her, handing one off to Gage before lacing my fingers through hers and taking a seat once she has.

My mind seems to be a thousand miles away as we stand for the national anthem and the first pitch. She moves her body against mine and looks up. I cast my gaze down at her and a wave of unease moves down my spine.

I won't let a single man lay his grimy hands on her. Not now and not ever. Isla Madden belongs to no man but me.

"What's eating at you, Jensen?" she asks as I shift her closer to me, tangling the hand that's not holding onto my beer into her long locks of hair.

"Don't concern yourself with it." I can hear the harshness to my tone, and I know that she does as well, but she doesn't mention it. She leans into my touch before turning to Gage.

"Coops? What are you up to nowadays?" Isla takes a seat between the two of us, which settles the anxiety rolling around like a fucking bouncy ball inside of me.

"Keeping busy, Madden. Between your boyfriend and best friend, I don't know how I keep my fucking head on straight."

Isla turns to me at that word, and I give her the best smile I can muster up while images of her being taken from me and strapped down to a mattress with its springs jutting out and scratching along her bare skin invade my mind.

"My boys know what they want out of life, and you're the one who wanted to be a part of what they do so quit your bitching."

He laughs along with her while I try to assemble a plan in my head to keep her and our baby safe. A couple of minutes pass without any banter or passing of words between the three of us before Isla shifts her full attention to me.

"What aren't you telling me?"

I move my hand to her thigh, pushing my fingers between her crossed legs until I'm content with where they are.

"I think that I'd like to take you to meet my folks."

Gage glances over at me and nods his approval before turning his attention back to the game on the field.

"Are you trying to induce the puking?"

With that, she forces me out of my inner war and gains my full attention. I bring the IPA to my lips and take a long drink before setting it back in the cup holder. "Fuck that. I think it'd be good for you to be there when I tell them that we're bringing another person into the family. Well, since I'm bringing another two in."

"Two?"

I nod and lean in to press my lips to the column of her neck while I speak the words I never thought that I'd be brave enough to state again. "I'm going to marry the fuck out of you, Isla Madden."

She gasps and grabs hold of my knee to steady herself in her seat as if it's started to move without her permission.

"You can't—"

"I can, and I will."

"No, I was going to say that you can't make those promises to me. I'm not even sure if I want that life. I'm not sure if I want to grow old with an asshole like you by my side."

"We're never getting older, baby doll."

She huffs out a sigh and looks up at me through her thick lashes. My eyes dart to her lips and train on them as she purses them together. "Don't get your hopes up. I've already noticed your balls wrinkling."

I throw my head back in a laugh as she tries not to choke on her water beside me. "Who the fuck needs whiskey when I have you to get drunk off of, huh?"

"Everyone needs whiskey, Jensen," Gage says at the same time that Isla murmurs something under her breath.

"What was that, doll?"

"Nothing."

"I'll show you nothing if you don't tell me what you just said."

She clears her throat but continues to watch the Cubs pitcher throw strikes. "I said that I probably wouldn't flow quite as well as whiskey does."

"Bullshit." The word leaves my mouth before I can fully understand that she thinks that there might be something else I'd rather be holding onto than her and this unexpected pregnancy.

"You're a storm I'd chase while I was blinded by whiskey."

"Liam." My name rolls off of her tongue, and something

inside of me hurts from not having her close enough to me. The need I have to feel her against me at all times is consuming.

Fuck it.

Without asking, I grab hold of her waist and lift her over the armrest effortlessly and onto my lap.

"I'll drink this whiskey until I'm dizzy with all things you. I'll drink it until I can no longer feel that burning sensation that heals my soul."

"What if my whiskey can't cure your soul?"

"I'd say fuck the whiskey and just give me you."

"So you're saying that I'm worth the shot?"

I chuckle and remove the baseball cap from her head. "Well worth it."

Gage groans and Isla doesn't hesitate to reach out and slap his shoulder. "Grow a pair."

"They're fully grown, Madden."

"As if," she counters, resting her head against my shoulder.

It's the bottom of the fifth when Gage gets up and shakes my hand, hugs Isla while she's still seated on my lap, and excuses himself from the game. I know that under normal circumstances, he would never leave a Cubbies game before the last pitch, but something tells me that he's going to dig a little harder into what happened at RW. I know that I should be doing the same, but I'll consider this keeping an eye on my girl instead.

If it's bothering him as much as it is me, then preventive measures need to be taken before I regret not having them in place.

I pull out my phone and type out an email to my head of security while Isla watches the game. My words are sharp and precise as I inform him that I want security around Isla, my mother, and my sister, twenty-four hours a day starting the second my security guys land in the States. I type out a short list of names to choose from. I won't accept anyone outside of those names. Once I hit send, Isla speaks.

"I can't believe that we're tied right now. Let go, Cubs!" she calls out and shifts on my lap. "You know, Liam, you have two seats for a reason."

I put my phone away and bury my face in the crook of her neck before baring my teeth against her skin and sinking them in deeper than I intended. She lets out a soft cry as I taste the faintest hint of warm copper on my tongue. I pull back to see exactly how I've managed to mark her before running my tongue over the now red marks where my teeth drove into her tanned skin.

"Holy shit, Liam," she says through gritted teeth.

"Don't act like you didn't enjoy that. By the way, I don't like these shorts. You should take them off," I tell her as I run my fingers underneath the hem of the tight black frayed material.

"That's justifiably forbidden in this country."

"Yeah? Well, there's something about breaking the rules that makes this unspeakably desirable."

"You're horngry," she says as she digs her sweet little ass into my crotch.

"Horngry?"

"Yes. Like hungry and angry, but you're more of the horny and angry type."

"Yeah, well, I've gotten a sample of what a real woman tastes like, and now, nothing else in the world will compare."

"I'd love to give you another taste or two. If the Cubs weren't the ones playing, then we'd both be well on our way to multiple public orgasms right now."

"My fucking luck."

The Cubs hit a ball out of the park with the bases loaded, causing us both to leap to our feet and cheer as the four team members make their away around the bases.

"See, you're good luck. Quit putting yourself down, Jensen."

The only thing that I can think of at the moment as I watch the joy wash over her face is that I cannot wait until I get to call her a Jensen. The threat of having her taken from me seems to have affected me harder and faster than what one might expect and as much as I try to convince myself that these feelings are making themselves known by the mere thought of her disappearing, I know that it's all bullshit.

They've been present for years.

"If you say so, Madden."

She shoves me, but I catch her off guard by grabbing hold of her wrist and bringing it up to my lips. I ever so slowly run my tongue along her skin before kissing her in the same spot.

"I'm serious about what I said before."

She works on swallowing before responding to me as the stadium calms down from their shared excitement. "Which was?"

"I want you permanently—not temporarily."

"Liam."

"I could start wildfires with the things I feel for you, Isla. You have to know that. It just took me longer to come to terms with it."

Instead of responding or reacting to the game when the Cubs gain another run on their opponents, she stares at me. Everyone around us is up and out of their seats again, but I couldn't give two shits. Their chants and cheers fill the stadium, but she's all that I can focus on at the moment.

"You're it, Isla. I could wait another four years, but that wouldn't change what I ultimately want with you."

"Liam," she says to try and stop me from speaking my truths.

"You, doll, have made me realize that you were the only reason that I didn't give up when I endured the flames of hell. Maybe there's no such thing as a happily ever after, but I'll take my chances with it if I get to wake up next to you every morning."

"I thought that you had Adriana for all of that."

Intentionally slowly, I take up the distance that's separating us from each other and slide my hands down her ribcage and then around her back. "She might have been there for me to know in the biblical sense, but you, Isla, were the one to keep my feet planted on the ground when I wanted to dive headfirst into the turbulent seas. I see that now, and you know that it's the truth, or you would have never stuck by my side. We've been providing each other with more than friendship over the years, but we've been blind to it. You have always been there while I silently promised you the world. I've already devoted myself to you by choosing you over everything else, but I need to know if you'll do the same."

I clear my throat and smile down at her. "You'll wear white for me one day, but I'll wear out three words that cause your skin to break out in goose bumps today."

"You're so sure of yourself and of us when you never were before."

"My entire world flipped when I saw you on the floor in your loft, and since then I've chosen you day after day, and I don't plan on ever stopping. I know that you've provided me with more than my share of second chances, but I'm tired of holding back. You want to be in my life as much as I want to be in yours, but in more of a way than we have been before. Show me, Isla."

I've noticed that the few people around us have gone quiet and are now seated as I'm reading the lines of my soul out loud. I can feel the energy moving off of her body, and if I weren't so sure of my stance, it would knock me off of my feet.

She hasn't said anything else, so I dare to push her over the edge with what I have to say next. "No one will ever love you as I do in this very moment. Until tomorrow, that is, when the love that I didn't think was able to grow any more does. Isla Madden, I'm in fucking love with you. I don't mean a childish, seeing-stars love. I mean a soul-deep, burning love that not even the burn of whiskey could hold a candle to."

As if on cue, I watch as she shivers in my arms and wild goose bumps break out over her exposed flesh.

"The fucked-up part of all of this," she says while looking down at her feet, "is that I think that it's always been this way."

I tilt her chin up and place my lips against hers. "You own me."

My entire world is focused on the woman in my arms as well as a tiny something that she's carrying around with her. When she pulls away from me, her cheeks are burning red, and I run my thumb underneath her bottom lip in an attempt to clean up the lipstick that I've managed to fuck up.

"Yes."

"What?" I ask as I move a lock of her wavy hair behind her ear. Our eyes are focused on each other's and if I was able to capture this moment in a photograph, I would.

"Yes, I'll wear white for you one day."

I can feel my heart thunder as she openly gives her commitment to me.

"You're serious?"

"Very much so."

"Holy shit, you're serious."

She nods and all I can think about is getting down on one knee in front of her, but she's holding onto me so tightly that I don't believe that it would be physically possible.

"I don't have a ring."

"I don't need one," she says while looking straight into my eyes. "This just got real, didn't it?"

"In more ways than one."

Fifteen

Isla

LIFE HAS A fascinating way of showing you what you need when you didn't know that you needed it. I didn't mean to fall in love with my best friend, or get pregnant, or get engaged, but here I am. I'm tangled up in all three, and as much as I should want to run, I'd rather be intertwined in this personal mess of mine.

It's Monday morning, and the cleaning crew is just finishing up in Blended as I sit at the bar and watch them move the furniture into their respective positions. I scroll through the limited number of pictures of Liam on my new phone and sigh contentedly to myself.

Eden walks in through the back door a moment later and gasps when she sees what they've turned Blended into.

"Holy shit, Isla. Did you know that they were going to do all of this?"

"Not one bit. You should go and check out my office."

"No way," she says as she stops walking toward me and backs up to stick her head through my office doorframe. "Fuck me stupid, Isla."

"I'm straight. Thanks for the offer, though."

"Funny," she says as she walks over and pulls out one of the new barstools, taking a seat next to me. "Mr. Brass has great taste."

"He sure does. I like how he's kept everything the same but just updated it. Do you remember my favorite wingbacks?"

"I do."

"He just had the leather replaced, and they are on the opposite end of the floor now."

She looks around again and nods at the larger space in front of us. "It's the same, but not, you know? It looks as if it was just built."

"It kind of was. They had to remove the exposed overhead beams and put in new ones so that they'd run the full length of the new expansion."

"I love everything about it. It's still so warm and inviting and just . . . whiskey. It's like this place breathes it."

"Very true," I say as I pull my phone out of my pocket and open it up to take a picture and send it to Hadley, but I get distracted by a message from Liam.

What time will you be taking a lunch break?

Probably at noon, why? I hit send and wait as the dots bounce up and down on my screen.

I need to take you ring shopping.

I gasp and glance at my left hand for a second before Eden butts in. "Is everything all right? How's pregnancy treating you?"

I can't hide this. Not from Eden who I let see all of my dirty laundry. "Honestly, good. All of it. Everything went from being blue to fucking radiant colors."

"Come on, you have to give me more than that. Is it about Liam?"

"It is," I say as I type out a message to him: *Will that make what we're doing official then?*

Official? You're already my fiancée, Isla. The only thing left to do is get you in front of someone who is ordained and make it legal.

I draw in a deep breath and slide my phone over the bar top

to Eden so she can read my text message exchange. It takes her a moment to scroll up and read them, but I know the second she gets to the one that he just sent me.

"Are you fucking with me? You're engaged? Am I being punked right now?"

I shake my head and cup my hand over my mouth before letting out a scream that I had no damn clue I was holding in. "I can't breathe," I say while the palm of my hand is still pressed tightly against my lips.

"Have you told anyone?"

"No. No one, not even Brass."

"Wait, does he know that Liam knocked you up?"

"Nope."

She looks up from my face and over my shoulder, her eyes widening. "Well, oops. I hate to be the one to tell you this, but he just found out."

"What?" I ask and turn around to see Wade standing there and watching me intently.

"If you wouldn't mind giving us a couple of minutes alone, Eden, I'd appreciate it," he says smoothly.

Oh shit.

I should have her call for help, and not for my own well-being, but for Liam's. Dear God, get that man an ambulance before Wade even leaves the library.

Eden gets up without another word and leaves Wade and I alone in Blended.

Traitor.

He joins me at the bar a moment later and removes his suit jacket before taking a seat on the barstool that Eden vacated.

"Something tells me that you've been keeping a lifetime's worth of shit from me."

"I'm not, I mean, I didn't mean to. It's just . . . it's been a really rough couple of weeks."

"Why don't we start from the beginning in order for me to understand?"

So, I do. I fill in all of the gaps with information that I've kept from him because I knew, regardless of what he said, that he'd be highly disappointed in me. I tell him about finding out I was pregnant in Iceland to having a mental breakdown, and to yesterday when Liam confessed his truths to me.

"Are you sure this is what you want?" He holds up his hand to stop me from speaking before he's done. "This is a lot to take on all of a sudden, and regardless of how you feel about him and the friendship over the last couple of years, I need you to be certain that this is what you would want even if you weren't pregnant."

"I don't think that what I feel for him has been drowned out or intensified because of the pregnancy, but I suppose that I can't say the same for him."

"I'll have a conversation with him about it. I won't get in the way if this is what you both want and if you're happy, but I don't want either of you to go into this because of old-fashioned moral expectations."

I reach over and wrap my arms around his neck, hugging him as if he's the lifeline I hold onto to prevent myself from sinking into the quicksand. "Thank you for being you and never holding back."

"You're both family to me, and I wouldn't want either of you falling into a routine instead of living."

"I wouldn't want that either, but I know what I do want and that's to be with him. I never meant to fall for him or feel this way about him, but I do, and I'm so sick of fighting it. I've learned a lot in this past year whether it's been from watching you follow your heart or something that I was forced into. I'm just ready to start living my life. If I screw up, and things go awry, then it'll happen, but I'm not willing to lose what I have with him. Not when he's one of the two people in this world who know me better than I've ever known myself."

"You've put yourself on the line for him, and I haven't seen you do that before. Do what makes you happy, Isla. The rest will fall into place."

"Thank you, brass balls."

"Now. How far along in your pregnancy are you?"

I start the count in my head before I answer him, "I'm closing in on ten weeks. I know that you aren't supposed to share it until twelve weeks when it's safe to, but I had to tell someone."

He nods and gets up to pour himself a tumbler of whiskey. When he returns to his seat next to me, he takes a long and slow drink of the Glenmorangie Pride 1981. I draw in a deep breath of the captivating and heady aromas of poached pears, pineapple, and nutmeg as he watches the liquid move around in the glass. My envy settles itself in my stomach when I know the flavors of honeydew melon, lemon, and vanilla are hitting his taste buds.

Ugh, what I wouldn't give to have that long-lasting taste of sultanas and toasted almonds lingering on my palate right now.

"Don't drool, Isla."

"Shut up, asshole," I laugh and nudge his side.

"Nine months without whiskey is a long fucking time. Are you going to be all right with working here? If not, we can make another arrangement."

"Do you really expect me to up and leave Blended?"

"I do not."

"Then why would you even ask?"

"I needed to make sure that you'd be comfortable."

"Well, thank you. Maybe if you're nice, I'll name the dewdrop after you."

"The dewdrop?"

"Yes, my baby."

He shakes his head at my nickname for it and swallows the remainder of his drink. "I need to get going. I have some things at the office that require my attention. Call me if you need anything, and Isla, I do mean anything at all."

"Will do. And Wade?"

"Yes?" he asks as he pulls his suit jacket back on.

"Thank you."

He leans in and places a kiss on my forehead before turning and walking out of Blended.

The rest of my morning passes quietly while Eden and I restock the remainder of the shelves with whiskey for our opening tonight. By the time noon rolls around, I'm so immersed in what I'm doing that I don't notice Liam standing behind the bar until he clears his throat.

"Baby doll?"

I straighten up and grab at my chest as my heart pounds against it. "Oh . . . holy shit."

His smile almost makes me drop the four-thousand-dollar bottle of whiskey that I'm holding.

"I didn't mean to frighten you."

"Hi. It's okay. My mind has just been running in a hundred different directions, and I'm trying to play catch up."

He walks around the bar and takes the bottle of whiskey from me, inspecting its label before placing it on a shelf and pulling me into his arms. "I didn't get a response from you earlier. Are you having a change of heart?"

"What?" I squeak out and shake my head, "No. Not one bit. Wade came in and we spoke, and then I got distracted with everything that I need to get done before we open up tonight."

"Mmm," he hums against my neck as he runs his firm lips

over my skin, causing my entire body to respond to him as every surface of my skin breaks out in thousands of little bumps.

Seriously? Does this little trait ever go away?

"And what did Wade have to say?"

"Not much. Too much. A lot. Nothing."

"Yeah?" He brushes his fingers over the mark that he left at the base of my neck the night before last before pulling away from me enough to make eye contact.

"He knows."

"About what?"

"Everything. You. Me. Us. The baby."

"Should I set up a wall of security around myself, so he doesn't castrate me?"

"No," I breathe out as I reach over to undo the top button of his black collared shirt.

"Am I allowed to take you ring shopping or will I have to go through him first?"

"Liam, don't be preposterous. Of course you can take me."

He leans in and sinks his teeth into my bottom lip as his hands move underneath the fine material of my shirt. I moan against his lips on instinct, completely forgetting that we aren't alone in the library.

"I swear to God, if you two don't get a room, I'll pull my pants down and start getting myself off because of all the sexual tension in here right now."

He laughs against my lips before moving away from me. "It's Eden, right?"

"It sure is."

"Take care of my girl while she's here. I don't need her lifting anything heavy either in the state that she's currently in."

She salutes the bastard and turns back around to stock the shelves. Liam knows how to get what he wants out of women, but who can blame her? I mean, *look at him!*

"Are you ready to go?"

"I guess. I'll go grab my keys."

"No need, doll. I did a little shopping of my own earlier today."

"Oh? Buying what? A sex doll?"

"You're all the doll I need, Isla. Come on, I'll show you."

He reaches down and takes my hand, leading me through the front door of Blended and into the sunshine to the only car currently parked in Blended's customer lot.

He reaches into his pocket and unlocks it before we reach the passenger door. "Wait. You bought this?"

"Yeah. I was going to go with something a bit sportier, but since we're expecting, I figured that this beauty could pass as a dad vehicle as well as Jensen wheels."

Instead of taking a seat in the blacked-out Maserati Quattroporte, I turn into his body and kiss him fervently. God, I love this man. He might know how to spoil himself, but he takes care of what's his, no matter what.

"I think that you've made a good choice," I say, feeling rather lightheaded from that kiss.

His hand lands firmly on my ass before he takes a step back and holds the door open for me. "Get in."

I do as I'm instructed and take a seat on the lush dark-brown leather, running my hand over the center console, and watch as Liam climbs into the driver's seat.

"I think that it's my turn to be horngry."

No man should ever look the way Liam does right now as he backs out of the spot he was in and pulls onto the street.

He glances behind us to the backseat, and a proud smirk appears on his chiseled jaw. "We could make it work in here, doll."

"I'd like to try."

"I think I'm digging these hormones. You're getting adventurous. Maybe next time, you'll let me fuck you while we're at the ballpark. It's always been a fantasy of mine."

I chew on the corner of my lip as he whips us around a corner and I squeal when he comes to an abrupt stop at the stoplight.

"Holy shit, cowboy, don't kill me before you've put a ring on it."

He shakes his head and starts driving like a grandma when the light turns green.

"Jesus. Liam, just drive the damn thing like you mean it."

His hand moves to my inner thigh, and he slowly edges his fingers between my crossed legs. He enjoys holding me like this, and I don't mind it one bit. It's as if he's securing himself to me while his body is otherwise occupied.

"I've been thinking about heading down to see my folks tomorrow. Are you game?"

"Tomorrow? Liam, Blended just reopened its doors after the expansion. I cannot leave them high and dry. Especially not now."

"Well, it's a fuck-lucky thing that we know the owner then, isn't it?"

"You didn't," I gasp and slap the back of his hand with mine.

"I did, and we're leaving after your shift tonight. My jet will be ready and waiting to take us down to the Keys."

I settle back into the seat and glance over at him. "All right. Whisk me away on your big boy toy. I could do with a tan, and I'd love to stick my toes in the sand. Plus, I'll get to see where you grew up."

"That you will. I'd prefer to get a hotel, but if you'd like to stay with my mother, then we can do that as well."

"I think that we'd knock the house off of its stilts if we stayed with them."

His warm chuckle fills the Maserati's interior, making me

shift in my seat as he pulls up in front of Harry Winston. I look out the window, and my jaw drops open.

"What? No, this is too much."

He puts the vehicle in park and swings his door open without a care in the world and walks around to open my door. "If you don't get out, we'll miss our appointment."

"You have an appointment?"

"Yes, *we* have an appointment. Now, are you going to let me do this or not?" he asks as he looks down at me like I've lost my mind. I squeeze my thighs together and unbuckle the seatbelt before taking his hand.

We're greeted as we walk inside and then shown around the boutique before we're given the space to walk around together. We're the only ones in here, and I'm taken aback by the attention that is provided to us. After looking over a couple of the rings, my eye keeps catching on a cushion-cut diamond micropave engagement ring. Liam seems to take notice and laces his fingers through mine before asking to see the ring.

"This is too much," I say under my breath, but he doesn't listen to me when the ring is placed on a velvet tray in front of him. He picks it up and admires it for a second before his striking dark eyes meet mine. He reaches for my left hand and slowly slides the cold metal onto my left ring finger.

"This one is three and a half karats set in platinum with the micropave frame and band," the saleswoman says, but all I can focus on is Liam.

"Do you like it, beautiful?"

"I love it," I say softly and move my frame into his larger one as his arms move around me, securing my body to his.

"I love you, Isla."

"Love you, dickweed," I say against his shirt.

His frame vibrates silently against mine as I rest my head

against his chest. This is where I want to be. Right here with him. The entire world could fade away around us, and I'd still be in this bubble with him.

"I'll give the two of you a moment," she says and starts to walk off, but Liam stops her before she can get too far.

"No, we're ready to finalize the purchase."

"Yes, sir. If you'll both follow me, we'll get everything squared away."

I haven't let go of Liam as they speak, but now I have no other choice but to detach as we follow her to a private room. I hand over the ring to her before taking a seat next to my *fiancé*.

Holy fuck me.

He reaches over and wraps his fingers around my thigh as they start to discuss the ring's lifetime warranty and payment methods. When she slides the detailed sheet of paper in front of him with the five-figure price tag on it, I almost pass out.

I grip onto the table and throw a glance at him. "Liam. That's too much."

He looks over at me and shuts me up with his lips before pulling back. "Stop putting a price on what we have."

I glance down at the paperwork and truly let the price of it sink in: it costs more than the average car does, but I know better than to argue with him. This man is stupid-crazy for loving me, and mad-crazy for making me tear up right now.

"Hey," he says to draw me away from my thoughts.

"I'm sorry, I'm just emotional."

He squeezes my thigh and genuinely smiles at me. "You're beautiful."

I blow out a deep breath while staring up at the ceiling to halt the tears that are begging to surface. Before he turns back to the saleswoman who I'm sure is going to make one hell of a commission on this purchase, he squeezes my thigh again. I rein in my emotions as they continue their conversation. Liam has his checkbook out and at the ready. This man is absurd.

As it turns out, they didn't have my size in this particular store, but Liam agreed to pay extra to have it flown in from New York City by tonight. Extra meaning that he spent the same amount as the ring on this little arrangement. He insisted that it was worth it when he'd show up at his parents' house with the ring sitting pretty on my finger.

Today he's being careless and reckless when it comes to his money, but I don't want to deny him what he wants. It's rather rare to have him spend this kind of money on himself when he has Remission Worldwide to concern himself with. I know that I shouldn't think twice about it because the amount of money that he has in stocks and bank accounts rivals what Waylon has. He's a smart man, despite what people assume. Once he signs off on the papers, he puts ink to his checkbook and writes one out for the full amount before handing it off to the saleswoman.

If this is how he's going to spoil me, I cannot begin to imagine what it's going to be like in seven months.

"You didn't have to do any of this, you know."

"I know that, doll, but I wanted to. I need to see that ring on you, or I might fucking combust with envy if one more man dares to look at you."

"You won't have to worry about that for too long. I'm going to be the size of a small whale before you know what hit you."

"Don't doubt yourself. I'm excited to watch you grow with my child. Now get your ass back to work."

I giggle and lean over to kiss his cheek, but he turns his face, and we spend the next fifteen minutes making out in the parking lot in his new ride like we're seniors in high school.

I break away from him long enough to open the door and

step out, but he reaches for me once more.

"I've been meaning to tell you that you'll have a security detail around you for a while after the break-in at RW. I've flown a couple of my men in from Australia. I trust them, and Grady will be the one taking care of you for a while."

"I have a bodyguard? What could be so bad that I need one?"

"Do you trust me?"

"Implicitly."

He nods and winks. "Then trust me."

I sigh at how absurdly handsome he is once I've closed the vehicle's door behind me and blow a single kiss in his direction as I walk back into Blended.

We've been slammed at Blended all night long, and I'm beyond worn out, but the bubbling excitement to head somewhere with Liam is what seems to be getting me through the long night.

I sit down at the desk in my office for the first time tonight and let out a soundless exhalation as I take in the silent reprieve and sore feet.

After a few moments of quiet, I dig my phone out of my pocket, and a giddy feeling slides over me at the sight of Liam's text: *I have Hadley over packing a bag for you. I hope that you don't mind.*

This man. I swear. He's so damn impatient.

Ever since I told him that I'm in love with him, he seems to go out of his way to make sure that I have everything that I need, but if I truly think about it, he's been doing that since day one.

I tap out a response on my phone before hitting send: *Hi, stranger. I'm sorry that I'm just now getting back to you. I don't mind, just as long as she packs all of my bikinis.*

He's the purest of distractions that my mind needs right now, and I'd much rather be naked and contorted around him than feeling run-down and too exhausted for my liking. My phone goes off, and I close out of Instagram to read his message.

I believe she did. I'm about to walk into Blended. We'll get a car to the airport.

I don't mean to, but I jump up and manage to knock over my new desk chair as I run out into the front room of Blended that is buzzing with people and the sweet smell of cigars and whiskey.

Eden walks by me and gives me a skewed look as she hands a patron his tumbler. "You all right?"

"I'm great. Have you seen Liam? He said that he was about to walk in."

She rolls her eyes at me and looks around the room. Thank God that she's able to see more from her taller height's vantage point than I can because she smiles and waves in the direction of the door.

"He just saw me. Have fun," she says, and hip-checks me before walking back behind the bar.

I watch as the bodies move aside as he takes the last few steps toward me. He doesn't slow down his rushed pace until he has me in his arms and my feet are off of the ground. His firm mouth claims mine, and I get absolutely lost in his scent, warmth, and love. He pulls his lips away from mine, and I almost whimper in need, but I somehow manage to contain it. Which, in turn, saves the patrons around me from figuring out just how fucking horny I am at the moment.

"I think that it's safe to say that I missed you."

"Liam Jensen, you have officially lost your mind, and you might be too young for this midlife-crisis bullshit."

"As young as you are old," he chuckles, and I smack his chest.

"Liam," I scold and try to pull out of his arms.

"Uh-uh. You're not going anywhere but with me."

"Make me."

He shrugs and lifts me up like I weigh five pounds before throwing me over his shoulder.

"What the fuck? Liam! I'm at work; you can't do this here."

"Oh, but I already am."

"Dick," I hiss as he walks us to my office and shuts and then bolts the door behind us before he sets me upright on my feet.

"I thought that you'd want to do this in the privacy of your office."

"Do what?" I ask as I try to wipe the giddy grin off of my face.

I watch him reach into his pocket and pull out a ring box.

I start to giggle uncontrollably because this is actually happening . . . again. "You could have done this in front of thousands of people, and you know that I'd still say yes."

"Yeah?" He raises his eyebrow and grabs hold of my hand.

Before I can complain, he's dragging me back out and into the main room in Blended where he leads me to the middle of the floor and yells out to Eden to bring him a glass of whiskey.

She complies by taking the one she's carrying to a member off of her tray and hands it to him instead. He takes a long drink before setting it back on her tray and turns to me.

"What are you doing, Jensen?" I ask hesitantly.

His answer? Well, the bastard drops down onto one knee, and my heart starts to beat wildly, almost knocking me out.

Holy motherfucking shit.

"Isla Madden. The first time I asked you this, I didn't have a ring," he says before he clears his throat and I slap my hands over my mouth to try and stop the tears that are already starting to roll down my cheeks.

The room has gone from bustling to a low hum with almost everyone's eyes trained on us.

"I've confessed my truths to you, and you know the baggage

I carry alongside me day in and day out. Yet you manage to look past all of that shit and see me for the man I am."

I watch his Adam's apple work as he swallows and opens the two sides of the navy ring box. Inside the box is the ring that I picked out earlier today nestled in a navy cushion.

The women around us who are able to get a good look at the ring all seem to gasp, and I cannot help the sob that escapes my lips as the tears blur my vision.

"Baby doll, will you walk down the aisle to me in white? Will you grant me those classic red lips whenever I need them? Will you allow me to choose you without pause? Will you start this journey with me? Be incandescently happy with me, and say yes when I ask you to marry me?"

I'm a blubbering mess as he speaks, but he's still looking up at me like I'm the only reason that he's still on this planet. Before I get the opportunity to give him my answer, he speaks again.

"So, Isla, will you do this thing with me and wear this rock that makes you look engaged?"

I'm about to suffocate if I don't allow my body to breathe. All I can do is start nodding down at him because I can't say the words if I can't get enough oxygen into my body.

He gets up and pulls me against his hard chest before engulfing me in his arms and whispering, *I love you, I love you, I love you,* over and over again into my ear.

I don't know what's happening around me, but all that I can concentrate on is the feel of his body along mine as I break down in his arms.

"Shh, beautiful," he says as I pull away from him long enough to wipe the smeared makeup off from underneath my eyes.

"Do we have a deal?" he asks me quietly as he tilts my chin up with two fingers.

"Yes. We have a deal," I somehow manage to get out through my quivering lips and all-too-raspy voice.

Another minute passes before I'm able to collect myself enough to move away from him, and when I do he reaches for my left hand and brings it to his lips. Instead of kissing me like I assume he's going to, he takes my ring finger into his mouth and sucks on it for a second, which earns him one hell of a reaction from those who are watching.

I can't help but be utterly turned on and anxious at the same time as I watch him pull my finger out from between his lips. He holds my hand out palm down as he slowly starts to push the platinum ring up and over my knuckle to the base of my ring finger where I hope that it stays for as long as I live.

"You own me." His voice sounds hoarse with emotion as he stares at me.

"You love me."

"I do. Should I have done that in private?"

I shake my head no and melt into his chest again as he holds onto me like I'm going to magically vanish.

"We should go say hi to Hadley and Wade."

I pull back and wipe at my face again before nodding. "They're here?"

"Yeah. I told them that I'd be doing this the right way after Waylon and I spoke, and they wanted to be part of it."

"When did you decide to grow a pair, Jensen?"

"When I fell in love with you a decade ago."

I clear my throat as he leads me through a throng of people who congratulate us on our way over to where Wade is standing with his arms draped over Hadley's shoulders in front of him.

"Congratulations to the two of you," Wade says as we approach them.

"Thank you. I would hug you right now, but I don't think

that I can stand on my own," I tell them as Liam tightens his grip around me.

"Don't worry about it, Isla."

"Do you mind if I steal my fiancée away from her job a few hours earlier than we originally discussed?"

"Go for it, fucker," Wade answers over the noise of the library.

"Yeah, I'll fuck her all right."

"Liam," I try to chastise, but I know that it's no use while he's in this playful mood.

While he and Wade trade insults, I slip out of his grip and walk to my office to grab my things and come back out just as he walks up to me and grabs hold of my left hand to lead me out the front to the waiting car.

In the next hour, we drive to O'Hare where he has his jet waiting for us. As much as I want to look up at him and see that cocky smile light up his face, I cannot seem to take my eyes off of the diamond sitting pretty on my finger.

All of this seems surreal and impossible, but I'm in the midst of it. I'm living in this farfetched gem of a dream and loving Liam has never been so easy.

We're approximately two hours into the three-hour-and-something flight when I wake up from a nap and stretch out on the bed that's hidden at the back of his jet.

"Hey," he says in the darkness, "are you feeling all right?"

"Hmmm?"

"You were whimpering in your sleep," he says as he molds his frame to mine.

I can't help the sudden pink flush that seems to heat my body. The dream that I was just having was rather extreme with him using his finger, mouth, and cock on me in the most erotic ways.

I won't tell him that, though, because I'm not sure that he'll be able to meet the erotic demands of my dream in an hour before we land. What I want him to do to me may take all day long and result in aching limbs for days to come. I cannot wait to play.

"I'm okay. Promise."

He rotates my body so that we are face-to-face before his lips brush against my collarbone.

"Grady will meet us at the hotel when we land. I'll have him set up in the room next to ours, and I'll have another two men at my parents' house. I just wanted you to be aware of them."

"At your parents' house? Liam, what is going on?"

He lets out a breath of hot air against my skin before nipping at it and speaking again. "RW's central office was broken into, remember? Nothing valuable was taken, and the files that were taken were later found a couple of blocks away."

"Well, maybe they didn't find anything that they thought they would. I'm sure it's just some teenagers fucking around, but what does that have to do with my having to have a bodyguard?"

"That's the thing, though, doll. I think that they found exactly what they were looking for."

"Why do you say that?"

"The only thing that's missing from the office is my personal file. Remember?"

"Yes, I remember, but why would they . . . what's in the file, Liam?"

"Not much that just anyone would be interested in. It's mostly personal information. Information that if gotten into the wrong hands could possibly cause some issues for me."

"I don't understand."

He clears his throat and pulls my body tighter against his. "The only person that Coop and I can come up with who would want that information is a leader of a ring that I've shut down."

"A trafficking ring?"

"Correct."

I chew on his logic for a few moments before realizing that he thinks that if they find him and see him with me, the biggest way to hurt him would be to take me. To sell me. To abuse me. To harm our child.

"That's a lot to take in."

"I understand, but we're working with my security team to figure out who did this, and you have my word that I won't let a single thing happen to you."

I can only nod because as much as I don't want to believe it, I know that I could be in a lot of trouble if this gets perilous.

It's not like either of us has nothing to lose anymore. Each of us has more on the line today than we did a week ago; as much as I love what's happening, it's also scaring me.

I close my eyes and breathe in all of his masculine scent because I know that it's the one thing that will give me the relief that I'm currently seeking.

It's just past six in the morning in Key West when we check into Casa Marina. According to the front desk agent, we'll be staying here for a week, and after the news Liam laid on me a couple of hours ago, I couldn't be happier.

We're met at the door to our suite by a man who should truly be classified as a living work of art. He straightens up when Liam and I approach him and removes his hands from his front pockets.

"Took you long enough," Liam says as he and this giant shake hands like old friends.

"It's good to see you shaved and showered after what we went through in that jungle."

Liam chuckles and pulls me into his side. "Doll, this is Grady Kent. Grady, this is my fiancée, Isla Madden."

I reach out my hand in greeting, and he takes it willingly, shaking twice before letting go. I can see his sinewy muscles move as he simply folds each of his arms over his chest. I'm sure if I gawked, Liam wouldn't appreciate it, but it wouldn't be gawking in a sexual attraction type of way. This man is just too much of everything. His body is past the point of being well built and athletic. He's intimidating as hell, and I'm almost glad that he'll be the one to ensure my safety when Liam isn't around. If I had to guess, I probably make up a fourth of him in total.

"Fiancée, huh? I'm glad this shithead took some of my advice. It's nice to meet you, Isla. If you don't mind, I'm going to clean up before we proceed with our day."

"I'm going to go over a few things with Grady before we leave. I'll be back in a couple of minutes, babe," Liam says as he unlocks the door for me and lets go of my waist.

"Don't be too long," I speak in a slow drawl. I need to relieve some of this tension before I meet his family, and I know just the way to do it. If I close my eyes right now and think about him burying himself inside of me, I'm pretty sure that I'll be able to get myself off by just standing here.

"Be good," he growls low against my ear before he lets me slip through the door to where our bags have been delivered. I close it behind me and survey our suite. It's decorated in neutral tones, but somehow still captures the beachy feel of any vacation home. It's stunning, and I'm not sure that I'll ever be leaving.

The next thirty minutes that he goes over whatever it is that he needs to go over with Grady, I use to get dressed and snack on some dry toast from room service. I've been struggling to keep anything down these last few days, and I'm praying that I'm at least able to keep the toast before meeting his family in person.

Once I've managed to swallow both slices, it comes straight back up. *Surprise, surprise.* I clean myself up again and walk out onto the balcony and take in the turquoise views. After sitting in the sun for a couple of minutes, I return to the room and leave the balcony doors wide open to fill the suite with the great relaxation that the ocean and beach always seem to provide.

Thirty minutes turn into two hours, and I can barely keep my eyes open any longer, so I lift the corner of the comforter off of the end of the bed and drag it haphazardly over my lower body before lying down and closing my eyes.

"Isla?"

His voice stirs me from the wrapping of deep sleep as I feel him move some of the hair out of my face and push it behind my ear.

"Wake up, baby doll. I'm sorry that took me much longer than I expected it to."

I groan and attempt to flip over and ignore him. All that I want to do is sleep now, but he seems to be insistent on waking me up.

"Isla? Come on. We need to meet my parents at the restaurant."

"Go away," I mumble, but of course he doesn't listen. He lifts my limp body up from the mattress and places me on his lap where he's able to cradle me and shove his face into my neck.

"Forgive me."

"I will if you just let me sleep."

He places a solitary kiss on my lips before responding. "I know that you're tired. I can't imagine what that dewdrop is doing to you. I'll call and cancel with them, and we can meet them for dinner instead."

He shifts his body on the bed so that he's able to reach his phone that's in his left pocket.

"Liam, wait, you'd actually do that for me?"

"I'd change the time for you if you needed me to."

I sit up on his lap and take his phone from his hand before setting it down next to his jean-clad thigh on the bed.

"You don't have to do that. I can try and stomach something now. I'm actually starving. I got sick again after eating that toast."

"Fuck. How long does this go on for? I'm sure that they'll have something that you'll enjoy."

"I don't know, but it's driving me to insanity. Do you think that they will have ice cream?"

"If that's what you want, then I'm sure they will."

"I could go for some gelato right about now, actually. Anything that has a substantial amount of sugar and cream in it, I'm game to swallow."

He taps my ass playfully to get me up and moving. "I could give you something creamy."

I giggle and smack his chest. "Trust me, that won't be welcomed right about now."

"All right then, let's go get this craving crushed before you starve yourself."

Fifteen minutes later, Liam has changed into shorts and a light shirt, and we're walking out into the outdoor dining area at Casa Marina for lunch.

To my surprise, his dad, as well as his father, are seated around a table sipping wine with his mother and sister.

Remember that thing I was saying about starving? Well, it just vanished. *Poof.*

I misstep as we get closer, and Liam steadies me before we reach their table. Every single one of them is just as beautiful as my fiancé is. I'm stunned, really. I could stare at this family for hours and not concern myself with anything else in the world.

Hopefully, our little dewdrop will look something like them.

"Look who has finally decided to join us," his biological father says as he stands and walks around the table to slap his son on the back and hug me once.

"How's it going, old man?"

"Well, Liam, it's going fucking great now. You, little lady, must be Isla."

"I am, and you must be Connor."

"Indeed. Welcome to Key West. Have you been before?"

"No, actually, this is my first time."

"Good to hear it. I'll make sure that Liam shows you around the place."

"Thank you," I tell him as he steps aside and allows Liam's non-biological father to introduce himself. It's easy to tell who is who because Liam must get his dark and brooding vibe from Connor and not his mother.

"It's good to finally meet you, Isla."

"As it is you, Mr. Jensen."

"Ah, no, sweetheart. Liam took Connor's last name years ago. Call me Mr. Burns."

I flush. It's something that I should have known, but Liam leans over and kisses my cheek to ease my racing heart before hugging his mother.

The next couple of minutes are spent doing introductions that don't really need to be done. His mother watches as I'm greeted by Liam's older sister, but for some reason, his mom doesn't come up to me at all. She just takes her seat again at the head of the table after greeting her son. We've spoken before via video chat, so I do not entirely understand why she's being so standoffish.

I glance down at my feet and try to calm myself down by counting the number of laced loops on my Converses. Surely she's just being obtuse. Liam doesn't come down here often, and I'm sure that she just wants to spend some time with him without having me around.

I take a seat beside Liam and his sister, Delaney. She glances over at the two of us, smiling as she watches him move his hand to my thigh, securing his fingers in place as he orders a tumbler of whiskey.

"Isla, I don't mean to be rude, but I didn't know that you two were engaged."

Fucking hell.

Way to call out the elephant in the room.

I shift uncomfortably and lift my head to glance at his mother, Adaline, before speaking.

"It's relatively new, actually."

Liam finally comes to my rescue when he squeezes my thigh. "She officially said yes last night."

"What?" Delaney almost shouts but manages to hold back at the last second. "Holy shit, am I about to gain a sister?"

"As well as a niece or nephew."

For the love of all things, Liam-fucking-Jensen.

He cannot keep his damn mouth shut long enough for me to get comfortable. Is it just me, or is the ocean starting to recede with my dignity?

"Excuse me?" his mother asks as she sets down her glass of rosé.

I knew she was awfully proper, but not pompous . . . or so I thought, but she's starting to prove me wrong by the damn second. *Just swallow your pretty pink wine and shut the fuck up.*

Holy hell. I need to tape my mouth shut before some of these thoughts decide to shoot out like everything else does with this morning-sickness bullshit. Whoever decided to call it morning sickness can shove it up their ass—it's an all-day-all-night thing that never stops.

Liam looks over at me and leans in to place his lips against my cheek. As soon as the warmth of them leave my skin, he speaks while still looking at me. "We're expecting."

Hello?

What happened to waiting until I'm twelve weeks along before announcing such things?

His mother doesn't smile, but she nods once. Just once because why would she bow her head once more in my direction at the expense of her bogus poise? I'm sure that she assumes that it is the only reason why he asked for my hand. She turns her attention back to her menu while Connor leans over the table to shake Liam's hand. This is why I cannot trust women. She's the epitome of every bitch that has held me back over the years.

"Congratulations, son. Isla, welcome to the family."

"Thank you," I manage to say before picking up the menu and turning to the back page to where I know I'll be able to find their desserts. I'm craving sugar like crazy, and it might be the only thing that will help me keep my mouth shut right now.

As I read over my few choices, I try to breathe in deeply and bring my mind back to my body instead of sprinting away from here in whatever direction is the safest.

When it's my turn to order, I just go for it, not giving a fuck what anyone says. "I'll have the Chocolate Island Volcano, please."

"Yes ma'am, and for your main?"

I glance over at Liam when the waitress is done speaking.

"That'll be her main. I'll have the All-American Burger, medium-rare."

"Oh. Of course."

I watch her scamper away from us and around the table but she continuously casts glances over at Liam as she takes Connor's order from the other side of the table. Jealousy is not my thing. I've watched all kinds of women fall over Waylon and Liam for years, but right now, I want to shove my fork between her eyes if she looks at him once more.

She does.

My entire body tightens as I reach for my fork, but Liam's hand moves over mine, dragging my attention to him. "What's wrong?"

I don't say anything because now I'm appallingly self-conscious, and I don't want him to know what these hormones are doing to me so I just look over at her while she watches him before looking down at my lap again.

Keep your shit together, Isla.

"You own me," he says as he tilts my chin up and locks his lips with mine, kissing me with a heated hunger and more need than what is appropriate in front of his parents or even in public.

He doesn't stop when I try to pull away, nor does he stop when I speak his name against his lips. He kisses me like it's the last time he'll ever get to be this close to me until his mother interrupts.

"Honestly, Liam."

He chuckles and replaces his hand where it seems to belong on my thigh, only, this time, it appears to be higher up than it was earlier.

"There's just you, Isla," he says in a whisper against my ear, and I want to rip off his shorts right here and ride him at the table until I can't hear anything but the low buzz of an orgasm roaring through my body.

"You didn't have to do that."

"I did, now relax before I take you upstairs."

I'd much rather he does that than sit through this lunch, but I nod and lean back against my seat as the conversation starts to flow at the table. Delaney starts telling everyone about how much work she has to catch up on at her law office, but that she took this *precious* time just to come and see us.

Are they all this damn smug and self-absorbed?

"Isla?" Connor asks, and I look up at him. For some reason, I know that I'll more than likely get along with him the best.

"Yes?"

"How far along are you with my grandchild?"

"I'm not very far along at all, really. I'm at ten weeks today."

"You take care of that little one, you hear me? That baby already has a large fund in his or her as yet undecided name. You let me know if you need anything at all that my son isn't providing."

"I might take you up on that. He's been slacking in a few areas today."

That earns me a pinch on my inner thigh, and I suck in a breath to help ease the pain, but it does nothing to stop it from traveling up to the apex of my thighs. Okay, so Connor won't be able to help with my current needs, but I need tending to. Soon.

Our lunch arrives then, saving me from having to further embarrass myself and I don't even bother waiting for everyone to be served as I dip my spoon into the vanilla ice cream and bring it to my lips. I don't mean to moan out loud, but I seem to have because Liam is staring at me while I still have the spoon between my lips like he wants to strip me down and then attack me.

Game on, sucker.

"How is it?" Liam asks me, his voice coming out more hoarse than I'm sure he means for it to.

I pull the spoon from my mouth and lick the remainder of the white cream off of it while watching him. "So good."

"Yeah?"

Connor's booming laugh almost makes me lose my self-control, but I hold onto it a moment longer as I scoop up another bite of my dessert and lift it up to my lips. Slowly, I move my mouth around the spoon and flutter my eyes closed.

"So, *so* good."

"Fucking tease," he says for everyone to hear before I'm able to open my eyes and stare at him while he adjusts himself.

"You deserve it for holding out on me."

Everyone is watching us now, and I know I should feel self-conscious about what I'm doing in front of them, but I don't. I know what I can do to Liam, and I'm enjoying toying with him right now. Serves him right, the lousy bastard.

He doesn't say anything back as his mother's eyes bore into him, and I know that he's got a firm grip on his tongue right now because I can almost taste the lecherous energy rolling off of his sturdy build.

"I don't mean to intrude, but how is everything this afternoon?" the waitress comes from nowhere to ask.

"It's great, thank you," Liam says dismissively as he picks up his burger and takes a bite from it.

Lunch passes while Liam teases me with slight touches the entire time. Once we've said our goodbyes to his family, he grabs hold of my hand with more force than I'm used to and pulls me through the lobby, past Grady, and into a closing elevator. The doors jerk open as he nestles us into one of the corners, surrounding me in his scent.

I stare up at him from the position he has me locked into at his side. A slow, menacing smile spreads across his face.

Oh shit.

The intense anticipation that whips itself through my body is almost too overwhelming.

"Can you physically feel what I'm thinking about doing to you?"

Before I can respond, he grabs my hair with confidence as

we ascend and kisses me like the world might lose its gravitational pull if he stops. His tongue runs along the length of mine before he tilts his head in the other direction to get a better claim on my mouth.

"You were never supposed to mean this much to me."

I pull away from him just enough to look up into his almost-black eyes. "You know that I didn't expect it. I just wanted you to fuck me, but I got greedy when it came to you. I wanted to love you."

"Show me," he demands.

Fuck the butterflies—I can't feel my entire body.

"Show you that I fancy you?"

"Show me what you want from me."

I bow my head and bite down on his arm, leaving my bite marks on him like a love note on his skin. "I want you to chase me. I want you to fuck me passionately and love me deeply."

"Hell, a little naughty never killed anybody."

"Not anyone that I've known."

When we come to a stop, he actually runs out of the elevator and down the long hallway while holding onto my hand, rushing to our suite where I know he plans on keeping me occupied this time.

We collided in a haste of need and want when we got back to the hotel suite, and he satisfied every single ounce of sexual frustration in me. I'm now lying out on the beach on one of the hotel's loungers as my skin drinks in some much-needed vitamin D.

I can still smell him on my skin, and it makes me shift on the cushions.

Liam is dozing on his stomach beside me, and I'm able to feel Grady's intense stare every once in a while, but I try to look past it. He's here for a reason, and I know that now.

One of the outdoor bartenders who have been walking up and down the beach all afternoon comes up to me and asks if I'd like anything.

"A large glass of ice water, please. Oh, and what are your premium whiskeys?"

He lists off a couple of them, eyeing me speculatively. I glance over at Liam before turning back to him. "He'll have the Glenfiddich Janet Sheed Roberts Reserve. It should be the 1955 bottle."

"I'm unsure if we have that. I'll go check for you."

"Great. If you don't have it, then bring him the oldest Macallan that you have in house. Straight, please."

He nods and walks off before I turn back to Liam and run my hand through his slightly damp and salty hair. It causes him to stir and open his eyes. He blinks away the sleep before he pushes himself up and moves his top half over mine to stroke his lips along mine.

"I didn't mean to pass out on you."

"I don't mind. You were rather active earlier."

"You deserved every second of it."

"Maybe . . ."

His easy laugh makes me giggle as he kisses me greedily again. You can't fake the chemistry that crackles between the two of us. It just seems to be overwhelming at times, but I wouldn't want it to end in the foreseeable future.

The waiter comes back with a tray and two glasses. He leans down as Liam moves off of me and offers me my water before handing Liam the Glenfiddich. I know that he'll enjoy the floral, fruity, and sweet taste of his pale whiskey, and it's sixty-something years in the making.

"They had the Glenfiddich, Mrs . . . ?"

"Jensen," Liam says before I can correct him.

Ass.

The waiter nods and moves on to the next couple seated in the loungers to the left of us.

"You're an envious bastard."

"It's a two-way street, doll."

"Shut up and drink your whiskey."

"You're all too feisty after what I did to you upstairs."

"Spare me."

"Never."

I roll onto my side to face him as his eyes roam up my body, pausing where the sweetheart neckline of my white bikini top dips well past my cleavage.

He takes a long drink from his tumbler before he leans in and runs his tongue along the seam of my lips. "Do you want to taste it?"

"I can't, Liam."

"I know that, but you're allowed to kiss me."

I start to giggle, but am quickly halted by his mouth. He starts exploring me, venturing inside of my body as I hold him captive. I'm able to taste the whiskey on his lips, and I groan in delight.

"It's a great year."

Instead of replying I move over him and straddle his lap as I start to kiss him again; tasting the liquor on his tongue is enticing. The creamy vanilla and smoke flavor balance each other out beautifully. The orange blossoms and violets join with toasted almonds the more I kiss him.

As much as I'm enjoying the taste, it's far from the best. Liam Jensen is my poison, and I'll never stop wanting for his flavor.

His hands slide underneath the still-damp material of my bikini bottoms to cup my bare ass in each palm.

"You better not get us kicked out of this resort. I like it too much."

"Who gives a fuck when I have you on top of me like this?"

"But I'm rather enjoying the ocean air and salty hair."

"I can give that to you at any beach, doll."

I shake my head and bite down on his lip. "I love this one. Plus, the sun seems to have kissed your nose, and since I'm half-naked, I'm going to need you to put some more lotion on my back."

"Sit up and turn around," he commands as he reaches for the lotion on the little table beside him. I do as I'm told and move to sit between his legs while facing the ocean. His hands start to move all over my back, pinching and nipping on my skin whenever he wants, and I love every semi-private moment of it.

We spend the remainder of the daylight on the beach, and by the time we make it through dinner, he's well past tipsy on the whiskey that I insisted he swallow without me. All right, so he's fucking hammered, but instead of the arrogant jerk that he turns into after one too many, he's been overly caring of me.

Grady walks up to us as we wait in the elevator bank after dinner. "Do you need any help with him?" he asks as he watches Liam lean his full body weight against my own. I push back against him to hold him up as much as I can, but it's no use.

"I wouldn't mind the help, actually. Thank you."

He chuckles and pulls my rather drunk fiancé off of me before helping me maneuver him into the elevator and up into our suite.

He hovers over me while I pull Liam's shirt, shoes, and shorts off. He's completely passed out now, and for some reason, I find him so goddamn sexy that I'm having to squeeze my thighs together to stop myself from getting on top of him and riding him while he's in his whiskey stupor.

"Can I get you anything else, Isla?"

I turn and smile at Grady. "No, not really. He should be good now. Thank you for all of your help."

"It's no problem. I'm going to head down to the bar and grab dinner if you'd like to join me for dessert. Liam informed me of your little situation."

"Sure. I'm always willing to have something sweet these days. Do you think that they'll have ice cream available to order at this hour? I know that it's late."

"I don't see why they wouldn't."

"Let me just get changed into something with more breathing room than this dress. I'll be out in two minutes."

"Of course," he says and turns his back on me before walking out of the suite to wait in the hallway.

I take my time getting changed into a pair of leggings, a tank top, and one of Liam's sweaters that I know he brought along just for me before I write a note to him and place it in the palm of his hand while he sleeps.

"I love you," I say as I lean in and kiss his whiskey-numbed lips. I walk out of the suite and close the door silently before turning and facing Grady who is leaning back against the opposite wall.

"That took a bit longer than I said, but I'm ready."

"Great, because I'm fucking starving, mate."

I can see why he and Liam get along so well. They almost remind me of each other, with the exception of Grady's Australian accent.

"How long have you known Jensen?" he asks as we get down to the lobby, and he leads the way to one of the hotel bars.

"I've known him since college actually. I guess it's coming up on ten years now."

He pulls out a barstool for me and offers me his hand while I get up on it. He doesn't let go immediately afterward and a little twinge of something pinches in my lower belly.

He lets go when he moves to take his seat beside me and orders himself a draught beer as I look over the menu for anything that will curb this sugary craving.

"Find anything good worth eating in there?"

"Uhm, just the ice cream really, but I think bacon and ice cream would be an incredible combination."

"Bacon ice cream? I believe that you've officially lost the plot, little girl."

I wince at his comment but push it aside as the bartender asks if he can get me anything. I decide to forgo my ice cream as Grady places an order for a rare steak.

"Maybe I shouldn't have left Liam alone in the state that he's in."

"He's a big boy. I'm sure that he's able to handle himself."

I chew on the corner of my lip and pull out my phone to check and see if he's woken up, but the only notification is from an Instagram picture I posted of the two of us and my engagement ring on my finger earlier today at the beach.

"So are you ready for all of the bullshit that comes along with marriage and a kid?"

This man obviously doesn't care about the emotional damage that he's doing when he says things like this, but I try to let the comment slide as best as I am able to.

"It will be a change of pace, that's for sure."

His steak arrives a couple of minutes later, and he takes the last swig of his beer. "And do you think that Liam plans on sticking around?"

I glance at my ring and then up at him, confusion settling over my soul. "I would assume so."

"Interesting," he says as he starts to eat.

"I, uhm, I think that I'm actually going to retire for the night. Thank you for your company, Grady."

"Be my guest. He won't be able to pleasure you in the way that you need him to, though. I can change that shit for you if you'd like."

I spin around to face him head-on with such force that I almost fall out of the seat. "Excuse me?"

"What does he call you? Doll, right?" he asks as he holds up his steak knife, inspecting it as if it can be used as a weapon. "Like a fucking porcelain doll who'll fracture into hundreds of pieces if she's dropped?"

I stand and start to walk away from him, but he reaches over just in time to wrap his thick, strong fingers around my upper arm. "Uh-uh-uh. Not so fast, *doll*. You wouldn't want me to break you, would you? It might be fun."

"Let go of me," I hiss out and try to pull my arm out of his sinister grip, but it's no use against his strength, and there's no one around us in the bar area anymore.

He pulls me back to him as if I really am a doll made from plastic and not porcelain as he squeezes my arm. *Holy shit.*

"What do you say we take a little moonlight stroll? It'll be like having a date with Satan himself. Only this time he won't be disguising the evil as good."

"N-no."

"It doesn't look like you have much of a choice, Barbie. I'll play Ken for the time being, and we'll go shack up somewhere pink and pretty."

Fuck him.

"You're no Raggedy Ann, are you? Shall we play house, Chatty Cathy? Are you intrigued?"

Who in God's name does he think he is? I believed that he was supposed to be protecting me from jackasses like himself.

How the fuck did he land in my lap, and why is Liam so trusting of him?

He stands and pulls me closer to his side as I watch a group of men dressed in all black enter into the bar area. Together they start to clear the space around us, and I swear that I can hear my heart make its last beat. "I would have preferred to finish my steak first, but since you're being a fucking petulant little bitch, we can leave now."

"Lea-ve?" I stutter as he walks me toward the bar's exit, forcing me to take step after step. I leverage my weight and shove him, trying to knock him off balance enough to let go of me, but it's no use. He simply continues as if I hadn't tried to escape his grip.

"Yeah, doll. I couldn't let Jensen take all of my girls without my taking one of his in return," he says against the back of my head as I feel the cold and sharp blade run down an inch of my spine.

"The plus side to this being a knife is that it won't make the noise that a gun would, and I'll be able to use it multiple times until I get you to behave. I heard that you weren't opposed to a little blood play. Am I right? Or do you need to be taught?"

"Why are you doing this?"

His chuckle is low and menacing as he steers me down into a vacant and dimly lit stairwell and out of the public eye as I push against his body and try to grip onto the doorframe. He manages to free my grip, pulling me further into the darkness.

"I've just told you, or are you more imperceptive than how you come across? An eye for an eye or in this case, a doll for a doll."

I do not know why it's taken me this long to figure it out, but it finally clicks.

This man.

The very one who has been specifically hired to protect me is the one that I should have been running from—the one that Liam warned me about.

The sudden realization of it makes my knees buckle, and as I'm about to hit the floor, his hand catches my head, and he chuckles. "I'm going to have fun breaking you in like the pathetic rag doll that you are. Maybe my clients will approve of the dark hair, but I think we'll bleach it, so you look more like the doll they are all after. I'll let them play house with you for a while before I do too much damage."

"Hel—" I start to scream but it's interrupted by a sharp pinch that pierces my skin, and I start to see large, unwelcome black spots as scorching fear pushes its way through my bones. I try to scream out again, but my body refuses to cooperate as he slides the stainless-steel needle beneath my skin and deeper until I cannot stand any longer and I'm separated from the world of the living and taken to an unconscious reality.

Sixteen

Liam

I GROAN AGAINST the memory foam pillow that my face is pressed against as a door opens too noisily for my liking. I can feel the bed pitch and sway beneath my body, and if it continues, I don't think that I'll be able to hold in the whiskey for much longer.

My brain is no longer charged with primitive endorphins. I'm fucking swimming in a sea of liquor and a suffocating atmosphere of existence.

I bring my hand up to my face to wipe the sleep away, but I'm met with the smooth surface of a folded piece of paper instead.

I manage to gather my wits about me and quickly realize that Isla isn't in bed alongside me when I reach over to bring her petite body up against mine. Fuck, I miss the cool of her skin.

"Doll?" I slur and reach over to turn the nightstand light on, but instead of successfully accomplishing my goal, I'm met with an awakening and brutal fist to the jugular. Every ounce of alcohol leaves my body the moment someone's skin makes contact with my own in the utmost vicious way.

My body reacts without my having to think about it. I ride through the pain as I get up faster than one would think was possible in my condition and deliver an uppercut to this fucker's jaw. The low groan and curse set my body alight as I reach for the lamp and manage to flick it on while he's still stumbling back-ward. A heavy thump sounds against the wall as his frame con-nects with it.

The swift moment of realization hits me like a bat out of hell as one of my security men that I've flown in from Sydney charges toward me. I know that he's armed, and his impassive stare lets me know that he's here to do more than fuck up my pretty face.

He manages to swing another fist at my face before I watch him pull a gun out of its holster, and then use the butt of the Glock to hit me. It connects with my cheekbone before I'm able to see it coming. In a matter of a second, the force of his impact makes my entire body fall back against the nightstand, which in turn sends shit flying. I grab hold of the base of the lamp and swing it around, using all of my force to bring it down on the side of his balding head. I hear bone fracture underneath the weight of the lamp as he falls in a pile of paralyzed limbs to the floor in front of me.

"I'm glad that we never agreed to play by the rules, fucker."

My breath is raging through my body as I wipe at the blood that's steadily trickling past my temple and into my eye. I lift my-self off of the floor and step over his bulky figure before turning the overhead lights on to get a better assessment of my current situation.

"Isla?" I call out, but I don't get a response. "Where are you, baby?"

I glance down at my feet and spit out a mouthful of blood onto the man on the hotel room floor.

"Worthless piece of shit."

I glance around the suite once more before grabbing my phone off of the nightstand, but I pause when I see the folded piece of paper lying in my now vacant spot on the bed. I reach for it and flip it open, scanning Isla's neatly printed words.

Liam,

If you wake up before I get back, don't miss me too much. Grady has agreed to get me ice cream because someone knocked me up and then passed out. I kind of, sort of still love you, though.

Yours,

Baby doll.

I ball my fists together and swing, not giving a fuck what I damage, just as long as I hit something. That something was the headboard, and my knuckles crack against it in displeasure.

After shaking out my hand to get a better hold on myself and what I'm facing, I grab my phone once more and dial Isla's number.

Where are you, baby?

Goddamn it, I won't allow this to happen.

It rings for longer than I'm used to, and just as I'm about to hear the tone of her voicemail, the ringing halts, and a distinct rustling noise replaces it. The line remains silent, and I know that I'm expected to go first, so I do.

"Who is this?" I demand as I make my way over to the closet and start pulling on a pair of jeans and a shirt.

"How much are you willing to pay for a doll, Jensen? One that might come back damaged. Possibly chipped and scared? What would you do with the pieces if you can't put her back together again?"

My mind narrows in thought and determination when I hear his low growl. The muscles in my body stretch and scream against my skin, waiting for me to detonate in an upsurge of fury.

"Grady."

"You have a keen sense of hearing, mate, but not a keen sense of who is fucking with you." I can hear his infuriating smirk over the line, and I'm on the edge of erupting.

"Where is she?" I grit as I grab my Glock from a hidden compartment in my suitcase and cock it.

"That, my brother, is not the issue. The issue is simple, really."

"Enlighten me, motherfucker."

"Gladly. You see, I've been sitting on your ass for years, steering you in directions that would lead you to shit-all during your pursuits. Fuck, you were so fucking intoxicated at times, I didn't even have to try to convince you of anything. You believed every word out of my mouth. That is until your buddy Cooper got word of my camp. *My* ring. Don't ask me how, because I have no fucking clue, but that piece of piss is the one that forced me to do all of this before I intended to."

"You son of a bitch."

"I wouldn't speak so poorly of my mother, Jensen. Not while I have your bride between my knees about to see just how much I'll be able to sell her for. How good is she with her mouth? Is she worth anything more than the price of plastic?"

"If you touch her, I'll fucking kill you."

His laughter is light, causing my accumulating rage and tacit fear to spill over. The urge to slaughter every single motherfucker in my way right now is stronger than it's ever been before, and I won't hold back. Not while he has my girl.

"I'd like to see you try. This," he groans, and I'm able to hear Isla whimper in the background. My entire body freezes up at the one sound. My world comes crashing down, and I know that he plans on fucking her up until I find her. It's the best way that he can get to me, and he's well aware of that fact.

"This is going to be fun, and this, Jensen, is what you call payback for all of my girls that you took. The best thing about it, though, is that half of them are ones that you'd previously saved. I took them back and branded them as my own. You've been doing a disservice to the world and one hell of a service to my compounds. Do you have any idea, though, how many years and how much money I've had to invest to grow my ring to the size that it was before you showed your pretty little mug and took some of my most prized possessions?"

"I don't give a shit. What do you want?" I hear my voice echo on the other side of the line, and I wrap my fingers around my phone tighter.

I'm moving once again, sprinting down the hallway of the Waldorf and down a stairwell. I can't stand still and wait for the mechanics of an elevator to click into place while the world moves on without me. I won't let one little thing take away what I need to do.

"I want to play in the dollhouse for a while. Maybe I'll record it for you to watch and then I'll let a few others inside to play as well. I'll get to see what no one besides you sees. How are you with sharing a toy, mate?"

His words sting and add an obscene amount of gasoline to the burn inside of me. *Jesus Christ.*

This cannot be happening. I'm about to reply when I hear her scream for me. It's a gut-wrenching cry that pushes my body off the edge, and I have to stop on the stairwell as my stomach forces me to rid itself of every ounce of liquid left inside of me.

"When I find you," I finally say through a granite jaw, "you'll pray for it to stop."

He chuckles again, seemingly enjoying my threats. I wipe my mouth off with my sleeve as I turn another corner of the stairwell.

"Ah, but the best part about this is that I get two for one. Are you having a little girl, Jensen? Should I cut it out and let you know the sex? Or should I wait a couple of months and be the one to watch her grow, and then raise the child in my world?

Would it be better if I taught the little fucker what I do? Or would you prefer that she or he is given the same fate as its mother? Huh? Tell me, pretty boy."

"Liam! Please!" Her voice comes through mutedly, and I have to stop and lean my forehead against the concrete wall to help keep my body stable. The slight confirmation of his having her edges its way underneath my skin with venom.

I hear an outburst of skin slapping against skin and his saying, "Shut the fuck up, you plastic piece of shit. Let's find out how you stack up." Moments before I hear her scream fill the air, he cuts it off by hanging up, leaving me in a torrent of rage.

Primal instinct takes control as a burning ire whips through my body as its own deadly poison. I push my way past the heavy metal stairwell door and into the lobby where I sprint to the front desk, ignoring the guests in line as I leap over the desk and grab the phone from the agent's hands, hanging it up and then hand it back to her. "I need to speak to your manager. Get the police on the line. My fiancée has been abducted."

I'm being engulfed by all of the boundaries of loyalty that have been furiously broken down and burnt, and the fact that this is happening all over again. The veins in my neck pulse with a wrath of pure black hatred as I start to type out a message to Cooper and Brass: *I need all of RW on the ground, and I need eyes covering every fucking airport in and around Florida. Isla is gone. Get me all of the information on Grady Kent that we have.*

As I hit send, I hear the agent speaking to the police on the other line. She feeds me some bullshit about having to wait twenty-four hours before reporting an adult as missing. I have to physically restrain myself from reacting as anger looms over me like a silent huntress in the fog of my mind.

"Motherfucker."

I'm barely able to register what I've said to the agent as my world comes to a stop and starts over again, this time leading me down the stairwell to the nine circles of hell. The first time a woman was taken from me, I had no clue where to start, but now, now I know this business backward and forward, and I'll get to her.

I have to.

I don't have another choice.

Seventeen

Isla

PLEASE, PLEASE, PLEASE.

The silences have become longer with each hour, and the bouts of adrenaline are no longer coursing through my system. The fear is now shutting down any ability that I might have had to think logically. I'm rooted to the spot and curled into a tight ball on the floor of some blacked-out and locked cramped room before the door bounces off of the back wall, pulling me out of my internal pleading chant.

Grady steps in front of me and bends down at the knees. I reluctantly meet his blank stare as he remains quiet. Instead of leaning down to pick me up, he aggressively grabs hold of a fistful of my hair, actively hauling me a few feet by it and causing my scalp to scream out in agony.

He's been carting me around from location to location because I can't find enough physical strength to carry myself. However, he's now dragging me across a well-worn carpet, down a jetway and into a cabin of a plane that I don't recognize. I feel numb, but the only thing keeping me going right now is the knowledge that my baby is in danger. We both are.

I clutch my stomach as he tosses me like I'm some flimsy rag doll against a leather seat. He takes the seat beside me and pulls out two guns and a knife from some holster on his body, setting them out in front of me as if it's some sort of scare tactic.

My body turns against me, and I dry heave at the sight of the knife with my dried-up blood on the tip. I pull my knees up to my chest and tell myself to keep breathing.

I'm denied a spike of salvation when no hit of adrenaline releases itself into my body this time around. My eyes remain wide as Grady reaches over to encroach on my space. I pull back from him as my paranoid mind silently cries for aid. I've screamed so much that my throat is burning and raw. I'm not sure that I'll manage another cry for help if I'm given the opportunity.

The lights dim in the cabin as the plane develops enough speed to lift us off of the ground and into the air.

Once we're high enough in the air and I can no longer see the ground below us, some man walks up to us and hands Grady a roll of silver duct tape and a package of zip ties.

"I thought that you might need these."

"With this little skank? No. The bitch can't even fucking stand up on her own." He takes them regardless and places each item in my lap. "You'll be good, won't you?"

"Fuck you," I spit out and move as far away from him in my seat as I possibly can.

He chuckles and grabs hold of my knee, digging his fingers painfully into my skin. He'll bruise me, no doubt, but I'm just grateful that he hasn't aimed his anger at my unborn child. Yet.

"It took your little hero two and a half hours to wake up before he realized that your fine ass was gone. He must think that you're a one-time-use blow-up doll. A fuck-and-chuck kind of thing, huh?" He turns his head to look at me, and I turn away, staring out the window and into the dark of the night.

"Shit, I got you as far as Miami before he woke up. You know . . . I got bored of waiting, so I sent in one of my men to pay him a little visit."

My eyes flick away from the window to the overhead light

before I close them in a silent prayer. Liam is the only one who will know who has me. He's my only chance. Our only chance.

Please, please, please no.

Please.

"Go cry about it, dirty doll. I'm sure that my clients wouldn't mind some tears leaking out while they take what they want from you. You know, a lot of them enjoy it rough. It's the reason why they come to me to get their needs met instead of their wives. I've got some high rollers who'd enjoy a little tease from you. You do anal, right? What about double penetration? Ah, or one of my favorites—playing with sharp objects around a wet clit. I've made a few women come with a knife. I'm sure I could do the same to you."

I don't respond to him because I know that's what he wants. He wants to see the fear in my eyes and drink all of it in while he tortures Liam from afar.

"Nice. The silent treatment. I'll add that to your resume when we get to my camp. You know, I knew that the fucker was coming for my girls, so I had the majority of them transferred out of Mexico to our current destination. You aren't afraid of a little moving around, are you? I need to make sure that he can't trace our whereabouts."

I close my eyes and try to imagine myself lying beside Liam on the beach earlier today instead of with this man beside me who tried to force his dick past the seal of my lips.

I bit him in the van earlier. I'm not ashamed to admit it.

It's why I currently have a deep ache on the right-hand side of my face. I remember him slapping and then punching me before my head knocked against the dashboard of the passenger seat, sending me into so deep an unconsciousness that I thought I was deceased.

I continue to ignore him as he rambles on about the types of sexual fantasies that I'll need to meet for these sick monsters that he keeps referring to as his clients.

"My highest bidder may take you. He has this sick fascination with fucking pretty little corpses."

My stomach heaves and this time, I truly get sick all over his worn leather seats.

"Fucking cunt," he yells out and grabs hold of the back of my neck before tossing me onto the floor. I hit a sharp metal edge of the chair in front of me and writhe in silent agony. Warm blood slides down the side of my face. It gently kisses the corner of my lips before it slides farther down past my chin. Thick crimson drops hit my chest, and I beg for all of this to be a nightmare from hell, but it's not. As much as I wish for it to be, it won't change the sudden turn in the course of my life.

I watch as his body moves over my now-seated position. He runs his index finger from my chin, up the side of my face that is covered in my blood before he places the tip of his finger into his mouth. I watch as part of who I am disappears between his lips and I want to die. Right here. Right now.

Instead of leaving me be, he grabs me by my neck and hauls me to a half-standing, half-seated position as he runs his tongue up the side of my face, cleaning me of my own blood before he discards me on the floor. He gets up with his cock now hard behind his jeans and walks to the front of the cabin.

As I sit in the dark cabin, I endure horrid visions of what my future holds. The knowledge that psychopaths run free around his compound instills a fear deep inside of me. The idea of grimy bodies taking control of mine makes my stomach lurch a second time, and I purge the last of the contents of my stomach.

I've been transferred to and from three different planes in the last twenty-four hours, and I'm currently strapped down to a seat in a helicopter as it hovers atop the deep blue sea. I have no idea how long it's been that he's been flying me around the world for, but it feels like I could fit a full lifetime into these sparse hours.

I lean forward to rest my aching forehead against the cool glass of the window. My actions pull on the restraints around my wrists, and they dig into my skin, but I choose to ignore it as the cool provides the slightest bit of relief against my bloodied temple. He tied me up after my failure of an attempt to knee him in his junk.

My impending future is hard to see through the haze of concern as the aircraft whips through the sky for a couple of hours before it lowers onto the roof of a low building in the middle of a city. I've never been here before, but I'm hopeful that I'll see it in the daylight again before my limited number of days are up.

As the propeller blades come to a stop, I try to prepare myself for what I'm about to witness and possibly take part in. From Liam's involvement in saving the women who survive these kinds of experiences, I know what to expect on some level.

They'll get pleasure from raping and torturing me, and my strongest defense will be to remain as neutral as possible. I don't know how I'll be able to do that while my dewdrop suffers along with me, but I have no other choice but to figure it out.

I'm hauled out of the helicopter like I'm cargo and not human.

"You're the one who had Chloe, aren't you? That's why he couldn't find her . . . because you knew what his next move would be before he even made it," I accuse.

"Well, would you look at this? The doll isn't completely made of plastic or porcelain. Now shut up, you useless bitch."

I start to speak, but his hand shuts me up as his palm swipes across my face once more. I collect myself enough to stop the tears from falling as I'm manhandled away from the aircraft and into the building. I almost gag on the thick air as I breathe in the sickening stench of involuntary sex and fetid blood.

Distant piercing screams fill my ears as I'm led down a hallway with closed doors on either side of me. There are no windows that I'm able to see as I'm escorted farther into their dollhouse. The acrid-smelling hallway comes to an end, and I'm shoved through an open door where I'm first cut free from my restraints and then left inside of the dark, empty, dank room. Instead of showing my weakness and sitting huddled up in the corner of the room, I move to the center and take a seat on the unforgiving concrete before folding my legs over each other and placing both of my palms against my stomach.

"I'm sorry," I say softly. "I'll fight for you, you know that I will."

I try my damnedest to remember anything from my self-defense classes that I took a couple of years back. A few moves come back to me, but I know that all of my efforts will be lost if I attempt to fight back. I'll be dealt double what I give out.

The malign walls of the room seem to be closing in on me at an alarming rate. I'm not sure what to do now that I'm here. I haven't known what to do since I was stolen from my life. From Liam.

This time I don't hold back the tears that well up in my eyes as Liam's handsome face appears in my mind. This experience could be detrimental to the baby and me, and I haven't done anything to fight for our lives as of yet.

How will I ever be able to forgive myself?

How will Liam be able to forgive me for giving up so easily?

Please, please, please.

Day two in this hole isn't much better.

They've left me alone for the majority of the time, keeping

me secluded from everyone is, in a way, a punishment on its own. I was allowed out once last night to use the restroom and when I returned there was a glass of piss next to a half-eaten sandwich mocking me in the middle of the floor.

I moved everything aside and sat back down in my spot, trying to keep myself warm by pulling Liam's sweatshirt over my legs as well as bounding my arms around my midsection. I fell asleep like that last night, and as I contemplate how I'll get some rest tonight, the door swings open with Grady and another man standing there looking down at me.

"What do you want from me?"

I shouldn't have asked.

I know because the smile that slides onto his malevolent face is one that I never want to see again in this lifetime. I know without a doubt, though, that it will haunt me in my dreams.

He takes the couple of steps he needs to in order to get to me and reaches down, fisting a handful of hair before dragging me to my feet by it. I wince as the unforgiving sensation spreads across my scalp, which in turn reopens the gash in my temple.

"Let's get you cleaned up. I have some clients that want to meet you, plastic bitch." He shoves me out of the door and into the chest of the man in front of me.

"Lead the way," Grady tells him as he starts to walk down the hallway.

I, however, stand my ground.

"She's resolutely perverse. Maybe I've got the wrong clientele lined up for you, after all, dirty doll." His hand moves back into my knotted hair as he starts to walk down the hallway, forcing me to follow beside him at a crooked angle.

I've lost count of the sheer number of doors that we're walked through, as well as which way I'd need to run in order to escape this place.

It doesn't take long until he pushes my weak body against a solid wall in what seems to be an unaired communal bathroom. I take note of the multiple nameless women in the large open showers, each one shadowed by a man that is twice her size as they all try to scrub off another man's sins from their skin.

My heart nearly stops beating when I see that some of them are entirely vacant of life as they look over at me. Their eyes tell me more than their words ever could, and I mourn for their lost lives. They seem to have put a tremendous distance between what they are experiencing and a life that they once lived.

My eyes search each of them before I stop at one woman in particular. She stands out to me because her eyes are still alive. She's shaking her head to and fro while teardrops fall before she starts mouthing something at me. It takes me a second to realize what it is that she's trying to tell me, and the second I do is the same second that I want to forget while she continues to mouth, "I'm sorry, I'm sorry, I'm sorry."

I duck my head down before I can set aside the images of the women in front of me. After a moment of reprieve, I stare up into this brute's sin-filled eyes.

"I can see through your bullshit. He'll come for me, and you know that he will."

"Oh, but dolly, he won't know where to start with the amount of evidence indicating your presence everywhere we stopped on our way over."

I don't reply. There's really no use in riling him up. If he hasn't been taking his anger out on me, then he's been using one of these other women as a punching bag.

"Are you done with your pussy power?" He chuckles and points at the far wall. "There's bleach on the rack over there. I'll leave you to get started."

I glance at the wooden shelving unit that he's referring to

that contains a number of cheap bathroom products before shaking my head in refusal. "No. I'm pregnant."

"And?"

"I can't put that on my skin. It will harm . . ."

"All the more reason to do it then, huh? I'm sure that your cocksucker Jensen wouldn't mind."

Fuck.

I need to learn to keep my mouth shut. I don't move from my spot as he watches me carefully. I know that the more I refuse, the harder he'll come down on me when the time comes, but I'd rather not bend to his every command.

"All right. Pick one of these sluts to help you if you can't do it alone, you indolent bitch."

Pick one? What will that mean for her? That she gets a reprieve from being raped long enough to bleach a pregnant woman's hair? Or will she suffer for helping me? *Oh God.*

I concede and point in the direction of the one who was in tears mere moments ago, telling me how sorry she was, as she's being led out of the room.

"Stop." His repellent voice fills the expanse of the room, which causes every person in the washroom to pause in what they are doing to look over at him.

The man holding onto the rope she now has secured around her neck stops his movement and glances over at the three of us.

"Bring her back," Grady commands. "She has a job to do."

I watch as the man holding onto the end of her rope tugs on it, which causes her to gag.

Grady turns his attention back to me once they approach us. "Strip."

I watch her eyes dart to mine as pure confusion and withering fear fills her red, swollen eyes.

"Please," she whispers as she gets closer to me.

"Strip, plastic. I don't have the fucking time to watch you bitch about being pregnant again. Instruct her on what to do. I look forward to seeing the transformation once you're done," he tells me as I pull each item of my clothing off and set it aside. Once I'm done, he hands me a bracelet to put on. It's a plain stainless steel piece of shit with a number-engraved bar on it: 236698.

In this brute's world, I'm a mere number, but I refuse to let him use me like I'm next in line.

"I can see why Jensen is so fucking drugged up on you. I might be the first one to take my turn on you before these assholes ruin you." He grabs me by the hair and pulls me to him. He inhales and takes in my scent as he runs his nose up the column of my neck and stops at my ear.

"Even though it will be forced, I'll still be able to make you come harder than any motherfucker has before me. Just you wait, dolly."

It takes every ounce of restraint I have in me not to bring my knee up to his nuts. His attempt at seduction isn't lost on me. I'm not some stupid loon who enjoys anything that any man tells me. If he meant to get a rise out of me, then the asshole better think again. I won't fall into his little trap or his lap for that matter.

"You remind me of her," he says as he runs his tongue over the shell of my ear.

"Of who?" I grit out.

"236698."

I glance down at my wrist, which is now ringed in silver.

"You know, don't you? That's why I gave you the same number. The same bracelet. She was my favorite and my first."

I wince as his hand moves to cup one of my breasts. "You're smaller than her, though. You were the runt, weren't you?"

I don't mean to, but I slap his hand away from my body as fury rises like bile in my throat.

He shoves me away, causing me to fall into the girl that's going to help me with my hair. We both land on the unforgiving concrete floor, causing the dimensions of my bruises to grow. Grady hacks and then spits on me before turning and walking out of the room.

"I'm sorry," I whisper as we both right ourselves and stand on unsteady legs.

"Why . . . why does he want me to stay?"

I note that she's British.

"Where are you from?" I ask as I'm handed the shit for my hair.

"Bristol, it's in England."

"I know it," I tell her as I take a seat and hand her the products. "I need a little help, please."

"To bleach your hair?" she asks as she reads over the bottles.

"Yes, and I was hoping that you'd know where we are."

One of the burly giants clears his throat and takes a step toward us as a silent warning.

"I have an idea of what country this is, but that's the best that I can do."

I take a seat and run my fingers through the knots in my hair. "Please, when you do this, try not to get it on my scalp. My baby . . ."

She gasps and covers her mouth, speaking to me through her fingers. "You're pregnant?"

I nod and cover my stomach with my palm as she moves behind me. She leans forward and says quickly. "I was in Greece on vacation when I was first taken. When I was sold again, I believe I heard Macedonia."

Her words flow so tightly together that I almost don't

understand her, but I do the second she cries out in agony as one of the two men watching us pulls on the rope around her neck in an attempt to close off her airflow.

"Let her go! Stop!" I cry out. "Grady won't be happy about this," I insist as if I know anything about these malicious monsters and their protocol.

Two more seconds pass as she struggles against the rope before he lets the tension on it go slack.

"I'm sorry," I say underneath my breath and turn back around. I can't put these girls at any more risk than they already are. I know that if Liam comes for me, which he will, I tell myself, he won't leave a single one of these women behind.

The two of us remain naked and silent while she applies the thick mixture to my hair. I don't know how, but she manages to keep the majority of the product off of my roots before wrapping the length of it around itself.

"Done."

"Thank you," I say when I turn to look at her, but she's pulled away from me by the rope and led out the same way that I came in.

I shut my eyes as I wait for the bleach to warm and change my naturally pitch-black hair to ash white.

I don't know if I'll see her again, but I'm unbelievably appreciative for her at this moment and will be for the remainder of my life—however long that might be. I'm left to my own devices to wash the bleach out of my hair and then thrown a bar of used soap to clean the remainder of my body with. I run the waxy bar through my now snow white and brittle hair. I force myself to focus on something outside of this building. Closing my eyes, I stand underneath the cold water and travel back to the moment Liam made me his in front of everyone at Blended.

These men might be able to physically scar me and mess

with my soul, but they'll never take away what I have waiting for me at home.

I should have kept track of how many days have passed since I got here, but my heart just wasn't in it after the first five went by and my door remained locked.

Whenever I close my eyes, I'm transported back in time to a padded room and the dire need to get out of the hell that holds me. It may feel like I'm dying, but I can't focus on much else than the unrelenting discomfort in my abdomen.

All I know is that I'm constantly famished, and the stabbing pains in my stomach cannot mean good things for my dewdrop. I haven't been sold or taken advantage of as of yet, but I know that when it happens, it won't be pretty.

I lie down on the floor of the silent concrete box that's morphed into an isolated prison cell. The rough flooring is hell against my back, but it's nothing compared to being someone's private sex slave.

I understand now that there is a difference between having your own demons and being one. I refuse to think of my disease as a monster any longer. I've been through my personal hell with it each step of the way, but never once did I allow it to affect others, not like these men who are holding so many women captive. These men are the stuff of nightmares: they are the reason that things go bump in the night; they are the demons that live in the world with us, not the dark and murky disease inside of me.

Over years of fighting an internal battle, I've come to this miraculous conclusion in the most unlikely place. I realize now that I've been off of the medication that kept me in a deep fog for awhile now, and regardless of my issues in this last month, I'm still breathing.

I wallowed in despair for years.

I survived depression when everyone told me to give up and take the drugs.

I survived my own wounded soul.

I will survive this.

Eighteen

Liam

PERSPECTIVE. FUCK THAT word and how others view the world. Right now, everything is fucked, and it's once again my burden to carry. My current view of the world is distorted and pathetic as I sit in the cabin of my jet that will lead me to yet another fake sighting or suspicion of where the current location of Isla is.

It's been two weeks. *Two fucking weeks* since she was taken from underneath me, and I fucking detest myself for it. Self-destruction kicked in the moment I received a call from Wade. He drilled into me and chewed me out until I was fucking manic. I've allowed the darkness in, and I'm eager to use it on Grady Kent. I'm slowly immersing myself deeper and deeper as the days move on, and he better be ready for me to extract my revenge on his goddamn life.

My stoicism has welled up and run out, but I won't let her go. I'll never let her go.

I haven't been able to get much sleep since the night in the hotel in Key West. Before the police arrived, I went back to the room and searched the still body of the fucker who tried to take me out. Kent must have known that the fucker would not have a chance against me, which is why he sent him. He got sick of waiting to hear from me after successfully fucking up my life.

Grady must have known that I would end the guy before

he did me because he planted Isla's engagement ring in the poor fucker's suit pocket with a slip of paper in the middle of it.

Catch me if you can.

He's toying with me, and I don't doubt that he's watching from afar. I'm sure that he has more of my men involved in this bullshit than I care to know about, but I cannot let that stop me from moving.

The moment I find her, I'll castrate the fucker, as well as anyone else who has laid a single hand on her.

Needless to say, I've halted all other recovery efforts that RW was in the middle of working to have every fucking person in my organization focus on finding her.

I got news this morning that they've narrowed it down to one of two locations. I've not ventured into sex trafficking in either country before, but if they've gotten supposed sightings of her there, then I'll make it work. I cannot allow a single lead to go to waste when she could be anywhere in the world right now.

Two weeks is a long time to go without hearing from someone, and a lot of searches would usually be called off by now, but I won't stop searching this time. I'll remain in the thick of it until I find her dead or alive. There's no cease-fire this time around, and fuck keeping the peace when it comes to these raids. I'll personally put a bullet hole in every fiend's head as I take over their compounds.

There have been many times over the last fourteen . . . now fifteen days that I've almost lost who I am to a heart of stone. This is one of them when I have to force my racing mind to stop and solely focus on finding her instead of what I'll do to him when I find him.

I blow out a heavy breath as the plane hurtles through the foreign skies.

There are multiple men and women undercover in this dank

world, and word spreads quickly when one of our own is taken. I've seen men blow through years' worth of undercover secrecy to save one of our own. I'll do anything to make that happen for Isla.

This morning, we received two hits from two separate agents working the field under the guises of slave handlers. One of them is located just inside the Greece border and the other in Macedonia. I'm unsure if this is the continuation of the rat maze that Grady has sent me on, but I cannot ignore it.

In the last two weeks, I've added thirteen stamps to my passport, and I'm fucking hoping that these will be the last two for a while.

I've forced myself to get up and hold myself upright when I've lost all faith. She's the reason that I've sworn to both myself and Wade that I won't give up trying to find her. Not until my life is taken from me for trying. I don't plan on going home until I have a pregnant Isla Madden in my arms.

"Prepare for landing," my pilot says over the speakers, and all of my men open their eyes before buckling up and sitting upright in their seats.

I take the last swig of whiskey in my tumbler before slamming the glass against the marble table in front of me, causing it to shatter. Pieces of what once was whole settle at my feet. I throw my head back against the headrest and try to focus on what steps I have to take next.

When we land, the captain of my team calls the handler who provided us with the information as the SUVs are being loaded up with our gear. I keep glancing over at him as I supervise the equipment transfer.

"And you're sure?" he asks as he looks up at me from his laptop. "Delay it for as long as you can. We'll be there." I watch him hang up before he speaks again. "She's not in Greece, Jensen.

There's an auction scheduled for later this evening in Macedonia. We don't have a lot of time to get there, and we'll have to go in unnoticed."

"Then what the fuck are we waiting here for? Get the shit back on the plane. Let's go!"

I start pacing the length of the cabin once I'm back inside, as they start to reload everything into the hole of the jet.

"You're sure about this?" I ask as he types out some shit on his laptop.

"I'm not, but I know this guy, and he's gotten more women out of this situation than I'd like to count. He said that he's pretty sure that it's her from the picture I sent him."

"Pretty sure? What the fuck does that mean?"

"It means that she's been through some shit, Liam."

"Jesus." I take my seat again, glass crunching underneath my boots, and shove my face into the palm of my hands. "Let's get going."

Keep fighting for me, baby doll. I'm coming.

To understand me, you had to understand why I kept myself back. You had to figure out why I did the things that I did, and having Isla taken from me is exactly why I was living my life on the edge of a deep, dark, and dank pit of nothingness. Life has a fucked-up way of bringing back our insecurities, and this right now is the most fucked up life has gotten for me.

I won't allow this to be the end of us. I refuse to let this be my final void in this wicked game of life. I shake with the trepidation of not finding her in time.

What am I living for anyway if I don't find her?

Nineteen

Isla

I'M DELIBERATELY GIVING up.

He has brought every negative part of my past to the surface at this point, and I'm unsure if I'll be able to take one more malicious dig from Grady Kent.

Especially now when he has me naked and handcuffed against an oversized wooden crucifix that has held many slaves before me. There are multiple men around the room starting to bid on me. No, that's wrong. They are bidding on my body and not on who I am. I glance down to my toes that are barely able to hold up my body to reach the shackles when Grady clears his throat.

"Use the neck restraint," he says to the handler who's currently standing beside me. A moment later, my head is forced back against the rough wood and held in place as a rusted collar is brought around the column of my neck, securing me tightly before the bidding continues.

The shackles that have me bared to these sick fucks are digging into my skin as I hear number after number called out. I force my eyes to close as the numbers grow and my faith in humanity dips with each additional digit.

How can I cling to anything good when I'm about to be broken in like a little bitch? When I'm being pulled back into my past? This, however, is so much worse than a secure padded room.

"Let us try her out," a heavy voice calls out from the back of the room. It's more like an auditorium, and no, these men are not in days' old rags. They are dressed to the fucking nines in designer outfits tailored specifically for them.

"Damaged goods don't sell. If you'd like to get a closer look, be my guest, but I don't do returns. You know the policy by now," Grady spits out.

My eyes fly open as I watch multiple men step forward to the slightly elevated stage.

I shut my eyes and keep them closed as man after man runs his disgusting hands over my exposed skin. As much as I try, I can't hold back my emotional reaction as the thought of never seeing Liam again runs through my mind. I'm about to disappear without a trace, and there won't be a hope in hell for my survival.

The microphone pops before Grady's voice is heard over the speakers. "Seeing the number of bids I've just been offered for this plastic piece of shit, I'm going to change the way I handle things for this slave and this slave alone. I will take the top five bidders and allow each of them an hour alone with her on my property. She is, however, still worth the value of a full sale. Anything less will not be considered."

The last strand of hope that I was holding onto snaps as the last of his words leaves his mouth.

Numbers are shouted throughout the men, and I keep my eyes closed as the final five bids are secured. Involuntarily my eyes flip open as my wrists and then neck are released from the shackles, and I'm carried off of the stage and to a room that I've never been in before. I'm set down on the bed, and the rope around my neck is removed and set aside before the two men who brought me in here leave.

I stand up and glance around at the ornate furnishings and fixtures, surprised that such a beautiful room can be kept in such a malevolent place like this.

Grady steps into the room and takes a seat at the far end. His eyes are trained on me, taunting me with his stare. I give it back to him. Although he may have sold me to five soulless thugs, I refuse to let him be the one to see me crumble.

"I'm going to enjoy this, dolly."

"Go to hell."

"Ah, but you're already in it. Now don't you worry your pretty little head: the fucker who enjoys his women unresponsive is last in line today."

There's a single sharp knock on the door then, and my body freezes up on me, willing me to become one of those vacant souls.

"Enter," Grady calls out, and the door swings open and an oversized man steps over the threshold.

My blood runs cold as one of his guards closes the door behind him while he undoes the burgundy tie around his neck.

"And what do we have here? I was told that I'd be able to enjoy you. My men know what I like and you, dear, are exactly that."

I can see the iniquity in his eyes as his pants tent around his crotch. I remain in my place as he strides toward me.

"What do you say we have some fun?" he asks but doesn't get a response from me, so he prods again. "Do you not speak English?"

"She does," Grady answers and crosses one leg over the other.

"Good. I like to hear their pleading screams while I take my time."

He reaches out to pinch one of my nipples that refuses to

pebble at his touch before he undresses. I swear I have to repress a laugh at the size of him. He's a pathetic excuse of a man.

I'm shoved backward and onto the bed that has soaked up hundreds of screams before it will do the same for mine. I gasp in pain as strong arms flip me over and then hold my neck in a chokehold.

"Kent, retrieve the gun from my slacks."

There's a shuffling noise before I'm forced up onto my knees with my ass in the air and the cold metal of what is unmistakably his gun runs up my left inner thigh. He pushes my thighs apart as the gun runs up over my sex and up past my ass.

I'm breathing heavily as he tightens his arm around my neck to cut off some of my airflow. "I've paid a lot of money for you, and if you don't cooperate . . ." He shoves the nose of the gun against my puckered opening. " . . . then I'll make this hurt."

Before I have the words to reply, the cool metal is moved down and pushed into my sex. My vision begins to blur from the tears and pain that course through me.

"Easy," I hear Grady say before this man starts to pull the gun out of me and then shove it back in as if the odd shape belongs buried deep inside of me.

The cold metal is harsh and unforgiving, and I don't want to feel any of this.

His arm loosens around my neck, and for the first time since entering this world, I force myself to slip away, to let an unconsciousness willingly take me away from here in order to spare myself what I'm about to experience.

Now, I completely understand the vacant stares of the women in the shower room. I don't want to remember this. I won't. He can dwell on the surface fear that his false perceptions let him see, but I'll save myself by not letting them see me break.

With my mind made up, I close my eyes and allow myself

to drift away from these men, this room, this life as who I am is stolen from me.

Muscular arms are locked around me when I surface from my internal prison, but my mind refuses to focus on what's going on as I open my eyes. My body is being jostled from side to side as door after door passes by. I close my eyes again and will death to take me. I know that I've given up, and I know that Liam will never forgive me, but I can't do this.

I don't know how Chloe survived all of those years, but if there's one thing that I do know, it's that I'm not her. I do not have her strength, and I never will.

"To your left," a voice says, and a round of shots are fired. I blink my eyes open again in the dim hallway, as the body carrying me doesn't stop moving.

"Heads up, we've gotten control of the chopper, and it'll be the fastest way to get her to the hospital right now," a deep voice that I don't recognize says. I understand what he's saying, but none of it makes sense in my current predicament.

"Hold the fucking door open."

That voice.

Oh God. I know that voice. I force myself to focus, but it's so hard to when I've only eaten a couple of bites every couple of days since I've been here, and my body seems to have given up on me now as well.

There's more shuffling as I try to focus my double vision. I lift my head and close my eyes before forcing them open again, hoping for more clarity than what I've been given.

"Liam?"

His eyes dart down to mine and relief fills his stern face as he carries me out of the warmth of the building and into the winter night air.

"Isla. God, baby doll, I'm here, but I need you to keep those eyes open for me, all right? Do we have a deal?"

I don't know if I'm imagining this or if he's actually found me, but I manage to respond through chattering teeth. "Deal."

I turn my head into his chest as my body moves with his and close my eyes regardless of what I've just promised him, because I'm too exhausted to keep my body functioning, let alone think right now.

I don't know if this is real or not, but if these seconds are my last, then at least I've conjured up the feel of his body against mine. He smells like home, and I breathe in a lungful before forcing myself into that deep, dark, and quiet place that I was in before I imagined him up.

Please.

Please.

Pl—

Twenty

Liam

THE SLOW BEEP of her heart monitor is the only thing that has been able to keep me from going back and slaughtering every motherfucker whose heart is still beating in that compound.

In the two weeks that he had her, he's managed to bruise and starve her. Her hair is fucking white-blonde, and blondes don't do it for me, but on her . . . *fuck*. She still manages to look radiant after everything that she's been through. The biggest things that are bugging me right now as I inspect her is how her skin clings to the outlines of her bones, but I'm thankful that she's alive.

The entire fucking stint feels like a dream now as I remember watching from the rafters as man after man laid his dirty fucking hands on her during the bidding process.

Grady must have done his homework on her to know what would make her fall off of the high wire that he had her strung up on. He knew exactly what he was doing with each step that he took in his attempt to torment her. I clench my fist at the thought of what else he put her through, or possibly made her relive.

It took us longer than I would have liked to find the room that she was taken to after the auction, but when I did, nothing could have prepared me for the sight. She was on her hands and knees, head bowed in submission as some old geezer shoved the barrel of his revolver in and out of her.

I recall Grady struggling against one of my men as I charged at the sick fuck who touched her in ways that no one besides myself should ever be allowed. He was too big to react in an acceptable manner, and I got ahold of the same gun that was inside of her and shoved it between his lips before firing a single shot that ended his pitiful existence.

I blow out a heavy breath as the only female doctor in this small hospital walks in after doing a full-body exam on Isla when we first arrived. I insisted on it being a woman. I couldn't stomach another man touching her again, regardless of his occupation.

"Mr. Jensen?" she asks in heavily accented English.

"Yes?"

"Thank you for waiting as long as you have. It's difficult being the only doctor on staff when we fill up. Now, as far as physical harm, there are only minor lacerations and bruises on her body."

She moves to Isla and points to her temple, neck, wrists, and ribcage before pulling the sheet back over her. "Outside of that, I have not found any other injuries or forced penetrations."

"How can you be so sure?"

She clears her throat and gives me a weak smile. "This is my profession, and I thrive on helping those who need it. She'll be all right."

"And the baby?"

She shakes her head and sets her clipboard at the foot of Isla's hospital bed before answering me. "Currently our ultrasound equipment is not functioning so I cannot give you a definitive answer to your question. The fetal heartbeat is strong at 164 BPM but based on a manual exam, the fetus is small for its age. You said she is about twelve weeks pregnant?"

"Yes."

She nods before continuing. "This is a small private hospital that survives on what little government funds that we can get. You'll need to transport her to somewhere better equipped to do a more extensive exam on her than we can here."

"Thank you," I say as she leaves the room. I take my phone out of my pocket and dial Wade's number.

I don't give two shits what time it is back in Chicago. This is important.

"Jensen?" he answers on the third ring.

"I've got her."

There's a long moment of silence that we share before he speaks. "Thank fuck. Where are you?"

"Just inside of the Greece border. I need to get her to a more secure hospital, though."

I can hear him typing between our lines of communication. "Did he have her? Did Grady Kent have her?"

"Yes."

He clears his throat before he starts to speak again. "You better have ended his goddamn life."

"The team is taking care of it as we speak. I needed to get her somewhere, and you'll be fooling your CEO ass if you thought that I'd leave her in the hands of someone I believe that I can trust again."

"Good. Get her home when you can. I'll have RW take care of the women that the teams are pulling out."

"Thank you."

"No. Thank you for putting your life on the line and finding her."

We don't say anything for another moment because he already knows that I would take many more bullets than I have these last two weeks to get to her.

"How's the baby?"

"We're unsure, which is one of the reasons that I need to

have her moved. They don't have functioning equipment for ultrasound."

"Get moving, Liam. Get her as far away as what you deem her capable of traveling."

"Already am, and I'm thinking that the United Kingdom may be my best bet right now. I'll call you again once I have her out of this fucking area."

"Thank you," he says before I hang up and stuff my phone back into my pocket.

By the time the doctor returns I have my jet on standby, waiting for us to arrive so that I can take her away from here.

"Here are her discharge papers, as well as everything that I found while examining her. I'm hoping that it will help when she arrives at the next hospital. Please keep in mind that I've already given her some pain medication for the flight. As for yourself, Mr. Jensen, I'd prefer it if you allowed me to remove the bullet before you left."

"Don't worry about it. Thank you for what you've done."

I take the papers from her and intertwine my fingers with Isla's as one of my team members starts to wheel her bed out of the room and down the hallway to the waiting van right outside of the exit.

I haven't so much as moved from her side since the plane ride to London, England. Isla is currently under the watchful eye of the talented doctors at the Greenwich Hospital. She's woken up a few times, but she hasn't exactly been present enough to acknowledge the fact that she's no longer in the throes of hell.

A doctor walks in, and I stand in greeting as he offers his hand out to me. We shake briefly, which causes me to wince, before he moves to the other side of Isla's bed.

"It's my understanding that the police in Chicago and Key

West have been notified of her being found?" he asks before checking the readings on her monitors.

"That's correct. Is your ward ready for the remainder of the women who are currently being flown in?"

"We are as prepared as we can be. We will, however, need them to share rooms if your count is correct."

"That won't be a problem. Please make sure that all of them are somehow registered under Remission Worldwide. The last thing I need is one of them disappearing on me."

"Of course. They have started preparing the 197 bracelets for them already."

"Good. Now, please tell me something good about the condition that she's in."

He smiles up at me and nods. "That I am able to do, Mr. Jensen. Are you the father?"

My hands begin to tremble out of anxiety when he says that word. My stomach lurches and my head begins to ache at the sudden onslaught of dire information.

"I am," I get out as my voice cracks underneath the pressure of the situation.

"Good. The baby is doing just fine. It may be slightly malnourished at this point in time, but we are providing it with all that it needs through her IV lines."

My over-caffeinated body seems to sag as the tension that I was carrying leaves my shoulders. The festering guilt that had infected each cell of my body seemingly disappears at the knowledge that they will both be okay for the time being.

"Will there be any future complications?"

He lets out an exhalation before adjusting Isla's bed height. "That is something that we are unable to predict at such an early stage in pregnancy. The important thing, though, is that for now, you and Miss Madden will be parents toward the end of the year."

I turn away from him to glance down at Isla whose eyes are still closed, but she seems to be sleeping peacefully now, unlike she was earlier.

"I'll leave you be for the time being. I'll be back when the women start to arrive, and we'll go from there."

"Thank you for agreeing to host us."

He nods and walks out of the private hospital room, closing the door quietly behind him. Yes, he'll be receiving a payout from RW, but that's beside the point. He, as well as the owners of this hospital, understands the threats that come along with helping an organization like mine, but Brass was very convincing nonetheless. Contracts were created and signed before I even stepped foot onto the premises. It usually takes a lot of coercion and manipulation to get a private and independent hospital to agree to our terms, but seeing how they did this so willingly, I know that Brass threw more money at them than either of us has before.

With Isla's well-being on the line, I would have done the same thing. Fuck ethical behavior while her silence is deafening.

I lace my fingers through Isla's and watch her still body rest and attempt to catch up with itself. It's probably the most sleep that she's managed to get in the time that we've been separated. I lay my head down on the bed and place a light kiss on the inside of her wrist as my free hand moves to rest on her flat stomach. I resent my failure to get to her faster. All of my hope of finding her had been diminishing into the darkening distance of the next day when I was flying from country to country.

For the first time in days, the loneliness that was eating me alive has let up and allowed the circulation of the blood in my veins to return. If I was drowning on my own, I hate to think of what her isolation put her through. I don't know what she'll be like when she wakes or what terrible truths will spill from her lips, but I won't let her sink on her own. Not now or ever.

My fingers caress her stomach as a reminder to myself that she's present. She's here, regardless of my failure.

"You're safe, doll."

I shut my eyes for a minute to regain my slipping composure as I get as close to her as possible from my seated position, but I'm given respite as a profound exhaustion wraps me in sleep.

When I force my eyes to peel open, gentle fingers are being run through my hair in a repetitive motion. An instantaneous and unwelcome dread fills my mind, and I have to force myself to breathe and remember where I am. My subconscious mind had me battling to get to her again. Hypnagogia keeps me at arm's distance from fully waking until I hear her.

"Liam?"

I tilt my head to look up at her bruised, yet beautiful face as she watches me pull myself into a conscious state.

"You found me," she says quietly.

My carousel of erratic and unwanted thoughts leaves as I sit up and cup one of her cheeks before leaning in and taking her lips with my own. I kiss her with every ounce of apology that my body can physically give her. I'm able to tell just how exhausted she is by the weakness behind her kiss. I won't let what happened break her through her healing process.

"I would have never stopped looking for you."

"I know, but I gave up. I wanted to disappear."

I shake my head and lock my lips with hers again before pulling back and searching her eyes. "You were strong enough. I'm so sorry that I made you wait as long as you did."

Her smile is slight, and it kicks up the endorphins in my body. She reaches her fingers outward and back into the short mess of my hair before responding. "I knew that you wouldn't give up. How long has it been?

"Just over two weeks. I would never, Isla. You're safe now."

"Thank you," she says as she leans into my touch.

"Did . . ." I inhale deeply before preparing myself to ask her what I'm dreading to hear. "Did anyone touch you?" I know that I should give her more time, but not knowing is eating at me from the inside out.

She turns her head away from me as her eyes swim with tears. It's as if she's disgusted with herself and would rather I look elsewhere, but I can't.

"Isla?" My fingers run down her jawline before tilting her head to look at me once again. "Please answer me."

Unchecked tears flow down her cheeks and drip onto her chest from her chin. She mercilessly tries to wipe them away. Fear and sadness seep through my bones while she attempts to stop each fresh torrent of tears that threaten to fall.

"I don't know," she says once she manages to swallow a sob.

Out of nowhere, her eyes widen in profound distress. She grabs at her stomach while her heart machine starts to expel loud and frantic beeps. I throw a glance up at the machines and then look back down at her as panic seizes her.

"Hey, hey. Isla? Look at me."

She does, but she's still panicking as thoughts accelerate inside of her head. Her eyes bore into mine as I cup her cheek.

"The baby is fine, Isla. I need you to relax."

"It is? What? Are you sure?"

I shift my body as close to hers as I can get while a bed separates the two of us. "Listen to my words. It's healthy and alive. You kept our dewdrop safe."

I watch her intently as brick by brick her wall starts to crumble down against her, and the tears intensify. I'm expecting sobs to punch through her and rip straight through me, but when they don't come I get up onto the bed and pull her body onto my lap.

"Shh."

She buries her face into my chest and holds onto my shirt while pearls of tears roll down from her wide, luminous eyes. A hurricane of emotion threatens inside of her and shackles her to her worst fears again.

She was terrified.

My stomach contorts as I realize that Grady was chipping away at the person who she's pushed herself to become. He was attempting to break the best parts of her.

I pull her closer as too many waves of sentiment pass between the two of us as I think about the pure devastation that losing this child would have done to the two of us.

She speaks to me with words broken up by silent sobs. "N-no one. No one t-touched me unt-til the auction. Th-then this man put a g-gun inside of me. I don't r-remember anything that happened after that."

She tries to stop her tears by muffling them with the palm of her hand over her dry and cracked lips. She's crying ferociously and silently, and I know that nothing will stop it as her entire body quivers in my arms. She needs to get it out, and I need to be the one to provide her the secure place to do so. If I could physically wrap my body around hers, I would, to provide her with a safe place.

"That's when I got to you, Isla. Nothing happened beyond that. I wouldn't have been able to live with myself if someone hurt you in that way. I love you," I tell her as I rest my lips at the crown of her head. "So much, Isla."

"I know," she sputters out and wipes at her bloodshot eyes. "Just promise me that you won't let go."

"You have my word."

We both go silent for a couple of minutes until I hear a bustling of commotion outside of her door. I know that my teams must have just arrived with the women, and I say a silent prayer that she'll be able to look past the outburst of screams that are now coming from down the hall.

"Oh God. Where? Where are they?"

"Where are who?"

She sits up on my lap and adjusts her IV lines before looking up at me. "The women. There were so many of them. You have to go back for them, Liam. I can't let them stay there."

"Hey . . ."

"Please! I need you to go!" Hysteria starts to take over as I lock my arms around her petite frame.

"Isla, I need you to breathe."

"I can't. Not when they are suffering."

"Every last one of them is either here or currently en route to this hospital as we speak. I don't leave people behind, doll. Not now, not ever."

That seems to calm her down for the time being, but I know that it will be just the start of her panic attacks that will purge her system.

I know that I need to try and distract her from what is going on outside, but I also need her to fight the thoughts that I know are currently racing through her head.

"Tell me what you remember. Can you do that, or would you like to wait?"

She shakes her head, and I think she's telling me no until she answers me out loud. "I'd rather tell you and just get it out of my head."

Fuck, this woman is stronger than I've ever given her credit for.

"I'm all ears, but first, I need to call a nurse or doctor to let them know that you're awake."

"You're leaving?" she asks as panic causes her body to start trembling again.

"No, doll." I reach over and press the button on the side of her bed before righting myself again. "I won't be leaving your side for a long damn time, so you better just get used to my annoying ass being around."

"You're the only one I want to be with."

"It's a damn good thing that you've promised that you'll give me forever then, huh?"

"Liam," she says as she sits up as a fresh batch of tears start to well up and then leak from her eyes. "Grady. He took my ring."

"I know." I consider keeping the information from her, but I know that she will need to hear it all in order to heal. "He planted it on one of my security guards to toy with me. It's in my safety deposit box in Chicago."

"To toy with you?"

I nod as the nurse first knocks on the door and then opens it, saving me from explaining my brutal slaughter of one of the many men that I took out in the last two weeks.

"Welcome to London, Miss Madden," she says with a smile and starts to adjust Isla's IV cords, untangling the mess that we've apparently created.

"London? Where was I?" she asks me as the nurse busies herself.

"Macedonia. I needed to get you to a better-equipped hospital than could be found just inside of the Greek border. Cooper and Brass both suggested that I bring you here instead of flying you back home first."

"I love London," she says as she nuzzles into me.

"You'll have to spend some time in the city before you head home to the States then," the nurse comments as she moves about the room while Isla stays silent in my arms. I'm not sure if being around others has turned her into this quiet woman, but I'll break her free from it eventually. I have to.

Fifteen minutes later, the nurse exits but not before leaving a strict set of instructions for Isla to get as much rest as possible as well as to try to eat something solid.

"Do you think that they have ice cream here?"

I chuckle and pull her tighter against my chest. "I'm sure I can bribe someone to go find you some."

"You'd do that for me?"

"I'd do anything for you."

She nods and nips at my jaw before pulling me down by the back of my neck to plant her lips on mine. "Thank you for coming."

"Don't thank me, Isla. I'm the sole reason that you were in that situation."

"Stop. Please. I don't think that I want to talk about it any longer, but I do have a favor to ask, besides the ice cream."

"Anything, doll. You know that."

She winces but continues to speak. "I need you to find one of the girls. I don't know if she was sold outside of the compound, but I'd like to speak to her."

"What's her name?"

She bites at the corner of her lips and shrugs. "I don't know. She's from Bristol, though. She's got light curly hair, and that's as much as I can give you about her."

"I'll find her. You have my word."

"Thank you."

I place a gentle kiss to her temple, and she sags in my arms. I know that she's exhausted from this life-altering experience, and now that the shock of being found is starting to wear off, she's completely worn-out. I can see it through the sluggish movements of her body.

"Of course. Why don't you try to get some more rest?"

I can tell that she doesn't particularly want to close her eyes and be surrounded by the darkness again, but the recovery process has to start somewhere and that somewhere is here and now. I won't stand by and watch her suffer through memories that should never have belonged to her in the first place.

"I can try," she murmurs, and I move her out from my hold and back onto the mattress before taking my seat beside her bed again.

"I won't leave. Close your eyes."

She nods and rolls onto her side to face me before her eyelids flutter to a close. I watch as the world around her quickly fades and sleep takes her into a weighty and much-needed slumber.

The coffee that was brought to me earlier this evening has gone cold. Not that any amount of caffeine would help me at this point in time. I pull out my phone and curse myself at the depleting battery before shooting a text off to one of my men asking him for a charger, fresh coffee, and gelato when he has a free moment.

Isla manages to sleep through the next day. Her body has been relaxed and her breathing steady, oblivious to the physical world.

Conflicting thoughts have skated in and out of my mind during the soundless hours, which have been slowly draining me of what diminished energy I have left. It feels as if my muscles are finally giving in to the world's gravity, and I'll soon be plastered across the floor as exhaustion takes over. I may be overtired, but I'm delighted that I'm no longer deprived of Isla.

While she slept, one of my men managed to find the woman that she mentioned—at least I'm hoping that it's her. She's fucked up beyond belief and is currently on a ventilator to help her breathe after the blows she received to her ribs, which in turn punctured her lungs. The color of her skin is a tint of yellow and green as well as black and blue due to the vast amount of fading and fresh bruising that covers her.

It does not matter how much of this I see: I will never get used to it or the disgust I feel in my gut at these fucking fiends. The majority of the complicit men have been taken care of, except for Grady Kent. I have yet to decide on what to do with him. He's currently in an empty auditorium, chained up in the same position that he had my fiancée in.

If I hadn't sworn to stay beside Isla, I would be the one laying into him right now. However, I believe that making him sweat while he waits for his comeuppance might be daunting enough. The fucker. I should have been the one to end him.

He's apparently confessed to housing Chloe for all of those years. He has yet to shut up about the tales of what he did to her . . . with her . . . and what he watched others do to her. After the first repeated story I received from one of his personal *handlers*, I refused to listen to the ones that followed.

I'm unsure if any of it is the truth, but I'd rather not dwell on it when I'm doing all of this because of Chloe.

My eyes travel up the length of Isla's body as she stirs beneath the sheets. I reach out from my seated position and take her hand in mine while focusing on her face as she blinks the remnants of her deep slumber away.

"Hi."

"Hey beautiful. How'd you sleep?"

She stretches out her limbs, and I swear that I can hear them whine with each measured movement.

"As good as I can in this bed."

"Understandable."

"Did you get me ice cream?"

I chuckle and squeeze her hand. "I did, but it melted at least twenty-two hours ago."

"Wait . . . what?"

"You've been asleep for a while, doll."

"I didn't mean to," she sputters and grips onto my hand as if she needs to apologize.

"Stop. You needed the rest more than we each realized." I move my hand to her stomach, and she wiggles underneath my touch. "I can't wait to see you grow with this little one."

She smiles and groans as her stomach rumbles. "I think that I need that ice cream now."

"Yeah? I'll get someone to grab you a tub or two."

"Or two?"

"Yeah, it's really fucking good."

She gasps and smacks my forearm. "Dickweed. You ate a pregnant woman's ice cream, didn't you?"

"I won't say that I'm sorry about it either."

She giggles and I swear to God, I could hear that sound for the remainder of my life, and I'd never once get sick of hearing it.

"We'll grab you some more."

"Thank you," she says as she settles back against the pillows. "Oh, are they all here? The women who were in there with me? Did you find her? The one that I told you about?"

I nod and lean over to kiss her forehead before giving her the news. "I believe that I did, but she's not in great shape. She'll need to stay here a lot longer than you will."

"Why? What's wrong with her?"

"The doctors said that she was beaten pretty well for a couple of days. She's got some serious injuries."

"Oh God. Please tell me that it's not because of me."

"Why would it be because of you, Isla? You did not do a single thing wrong."

She chooses not to answer me. Instead, she swings one leg at a time off of the side of the bed before attempting to stand. I jerk to my feet to steady her as she sways.

"Easy, baby doll."

"I need to see her, Liam. Right now. I need to."

The panic in the pitch of her voice would be evident to anyone who has the capability to hear.

"All right. I need to find out where they are holding her, and then we can take a walk down to her room."

I know where she is, though, because I wanted her to have the best fighting chance. She's a couple of rooms down from the one that we are currently occupying, but I need Isla to relax and not panic before we go in there. It won't be good for her or the baby if her body isn't strong enough to walk, let alone handle a mental breakdown.

My arms lock around her before I lift her up, cradling her against my chest. I manage to contain my physical reaction to the strain on the bullet wound as she reaches out for the rolling IV stand.

"You weigh next to nothing. I need to get some food in you."

She kisses me underneath my jaw as I carry her to the nurse's station and ask if we're allowed to go check on the woman who Isla wants to see so badly.

"That won't be a problem. She woke up earlier today."

I nod my thanks before turning and walking Isla down the hall to a closed door. "I'm going to need you to knock for me, babe."

She reaches over and knocks on the modern glass door before a nurse pulls it open from the room's interior.

"Can I help you?"

"Yes. I'm lead in Remission Worldwide, and I'd like to reunite these two women."

"Of course."

She moves out of the doorway, and I step past her and to the bed where this fragile girl is lying.

"Oh God," Isla gasps and lets go of the IV stand once I stop moving and slowly lower her onto her feet. I don't let go of her for two reasons, though. One, I'm an infatuated asshole, and I need the reassurance that she's still here with me. Two, I'm unsure how physically strong she is right now.

The woman tries to smile around the tube in her mouth but fails miserably.

"Oh no, no. Please don't push yourself. I just . . . I needed to see you. I needed to know if you were okay."

She nods and reaches for Isla's hand. I watch my girl hesitate before she grabs hold of this woman's hand in what seems like a death grip.

"Thank you," Isla whispers and leans down to move the hair from the woman's face. "I'm Isla Madden, and this is my fiancé, Liam Jensen."

The woman nods and signals for a pen and paper with the one arm that isn't currently in a cast.

"Hold onto the bed, Isla. I'll go grab some from the nurses' station."

"Thank you," she says before kissing my cheek and placing her hands on the bed before I help her take a seat in the one available chair before walking out of the room faster than I probably need to. The nurse offers me a pad of paper and blue pen, and I make my way back to my girl.

When I walk back in, I pull the door closed and move to Isla who takes the pen and paper from me before I move behind the chair that houses my world.

"Here," Isla says as she hands both objects off to the woman, helping her steady the pen in her hand. "What's your name?"

We remain silent while she scribbles her name on the white paper before ripping off of the stack and handing it to Isla. *Quinn Welsh.*

"It's nice to meet you, Quinn."

She nods and rests her head back.

"Liam and I will make sure that you get home to your loved ones, okay?"

We watch her write out two words before tears start to trickle down her cheeks.

Thank you.

Isla reaches back for my hand, and I take it willingly. I'm glad that she understands the fact that I'm here for her. Here to support her and to bring her back up when she feels as if she's had enough.

"We should allow her time to rest, doll."

Quinn's eyes go wide and shoot to Isla's, but Isla doesn't say anything about it. I'm unsure if it's the fact that I'll be taking Isla away or if Quinn will be alone once more. Neither of them says anything as they communicate through the silence.

"We won't be far. I'm sure that you will be able to ask the nurses to take you to Isla's room once you're off of the ventilator."

Her eyes don't stray from Isla's once as I speak, and it's at this moment that I know there's something I'm missing, something that Isla is keeping from me, and I will, regardless of what I have to do, get the truth out of her.

"Isla? Are you ready?"

She nods and just as she starts to stand, I move to the front of the seat and lift her up into my arms. I grit my teeth and breathe in deeply as the wound seems to reopen on my shoulder.

She blows Quinn a kiss before grabbing hold of the IV stand and we leave the room. Not even two minutes later, we're back in her room, and I've closed the door and dimmed the lights to give her some kind of reprieve. I watch her close her eyes as I sit beside her, but a loud knock on the door startles her, and I have to contain my fury toward whoever is on the other side of the door right now.

I get up and pull it open with more force than necessary. I'm met with the tired eyes of one of my team members. He holds up a brown paper bag, and I take it.

"Go get some rest," I instruct, "and thank you." I nod toward the bag as he walks away from the door and I close it quietly before walking back to Isla's side.

"What's in there?" she asks as she lifts her head up from the pillow.

I smirk at her and unroll the top of it to cast a glance inside. I chuckle to myself and reach in to pull out the first tub.

She groans when she sees the pint of vanilla gelato and reaches for the remote that will adjust her bed. I reach out for the rolling table and pull it toward her before placing the vanilla and two other flavors in front of her.

"I guess he didn't know what to get you."

"Are you kidding? This is going to be the best meal that I've ever consumed. Give that guy a raise, Jensen."

The rise and fall of her voice puts a slight smile on my face. It's one of the few times that I've heard my Isla come back from her hell-induced monotone.

"What flavor do you want to keep out? I'll ask the nurses to keep the rest in their break room."

"What flavor?"

"Yeah, which do you want now? Vanilla, chocolate, or salted caramel?"

"Uhh, all of them?"

I chuckle as she opens each container and scoops some of every flavor onto her spoon before placing it in her mouth and groaning in delight.

I have to fucking chant my grandmother's name in my head in order not to get fucking hard right now.

"Want some?"

"More than you know."

That makes her blush and look down at the tubs before turning her attention to me again.

"Can I tell you something?"

"Of course."

"You have to swear to me that you won't do anything about it, though. I just want to get it off of my chest. It's got nothing to do with the compound or Grady, though. It happened before then."

"What is it, Isla?"

"Well," she says but pauses to place another spoonful into her mouth. "Do you remember when we met up with your family for lunch in the Keys?"

"I do."

Where the fuck is she going with this?

"Well, when I went to the bathroom, your mother joined me." She looks up at me while reaching for my hand and lacing her slim fingers through mine. "She cornered me and pulled out her checkbook, asking how much it would take for me to end our relationship and make the baby disappear."

That smile on my face that was there not even a second ago? It fucking vanished.

"Excuse me?"

She sighs and shakes her head. "I shouldn't have said anything."

"Isla, yes, you should have. What the fuck did you do?"

"I told her to go fuck herself. Needless to say, I don't think that she likes me very much."

I start to laugh because in the history of knowing my mother, not one person has ever been as brash with her as my fiancée apparently was. "Fuck, I love you."

"What?" she squeals as I stand and angle my lips over hers for a brief moment before I pull back again.

"Do you think that anyone has the balls to say shit like that to my mother?"

She beams and leans forward, asking for my lips. "I did."

"All the more reason why I'm going to marry the fuck out of you."

I lay my lips against hers gently. Instead of pushing the kiss, I allow her to take the lead, and she doesn't hold back as her tongue prods my lips for entrance. With the knowledge of her wanting this, I run my tongue along the smooth surface of hers before deepening the kiss and taking my control back. Fiery demand and passion envelop me in all things Isla as I delve into her mouth. This is the one woman who has had the innate ability to take all of the wind from my lungs with her lips, and I won't ever complain about that shit.

She inhales sharply against my kiss, and I'm completely unprepared when she pushes the table away from her and tugs on my shirt. My breath quickens and I tilt my head to get better access to her parted lips. I pull back for a moment to take her in. In place of the shy smile that she's been hiding behind since I found her, her face lights up as she leans up again, hungry for my kiss. I refuse to keep it from her even though I know that I should.

Nothing about this kiss is obligated or overthought. Each of us seems to be locked in the present moment as warmth radiates between us. I push the rolling table completely out of the way before taking my chances and lying down beside her. Her warmth slowly seeps in through my skin and spreads throughout the rest of me.

"Liam," she moans, and I pull back for a couple of seconds to ensure that she's still enjoying this moment.

She is. I can see it in the glittering golden flecks in her eyes.

"Isla?"

"I want you. I want you to touch me."

Her captivating demand almost leaves me fucking breathless with euphoric ecstasy.

My Isla is back, and she's still mine. She will always be mine.

Twenty-One

Isla

HIS LIPS FEEL implausible as they envelop mine, and tease my heart with pure bliss. "Please?" I ask again as he adjusts me and my IV lines. I move deeper into his hold and slide one of my legs between his.

I can see him overthinking my proposition as I pull back and stare at his handsome face. "Liam?"

He parts his lips to speak, but it takes him a moment longer to find the words that he's in search of. "Are you sure? Here? So soon after . . . ?"

I give him my affirmation with a smile because we could be under a freeway bridge in the middle of winter and I would still need to feel the release that his body provides mine with.

"Let me get you out of here first. Please?"

My smile falls, but I try to keep it together while he wraps me in his arms and keeps me steady.

"You don't have enough energy for what I want to do to you. The moment you do, though, I'll lock us up in a hotel room and ravage you until you can't breathe."

"All right, deal."

With his saturated love, he gets me to smile again as I nuzzle into his shirt. Every inch of him is immeasurably fine. He's done much more than piqued my attention over the years: he's won my heart over without having to try. His love and warmth spill out from his heart and flow into mine as we lie soundlessly together.

It is said that it usually takes three things to make something intertwined, and here we are with our third resting between the two of us.

Though one may be overpowered, two can defend themselves. A cord of three strands is not quickly broken.—Ecclesiastes 4:12.

A repetitive rap on the door draws me away from an unpleasant dream of rope burns and the sickening stench of involuntary sex. I shift in Liam's arms before taking note of the dark skies just beyond my window.

I lift my head when the sounds startle me again.

"Mmm," Liam groans, and I have to repress a laugh. I slide my fingers through his dark hair before moving them down his sideburns to his jaw. I tilt my head up and place my lips against his and try to wake him with a kiss, but it doesn't seem to work too well.

Someone raps lightly on the door. "Miss Madden?"

I hear the door open and let my eyes adjust to the light streaming through the doorway before I lift my finger to my lips, asking them to keep quiet.

I get a questioning look from a nurse who I haven't seen before, but the doctor just shakes his head with a smile on his face and moves to my side.

"He's been through a lot. He was telling me about the number of countries that he traveled to in the last two weeks. It's astounding, really."

I look back down at Liam and snuggle a little further into his body than I was before. I knew that he'd be searching for me, but I didn't know just how hard he's been looking. I don't know if I'll be able to thank him enough for searching the world for me.

"He's one of a kind."

"I'm glad that you see that. While he's asleep and not arguing with me, I'll replace his bandage and check on his other stitches."

"You'll what?"

The doctor moves away from the machines keeping track of my body after noting down a few things and walks around to the other side of the bed where Liam is lost to sleep.

"Miss Madden?" The nurse asks before the doctor has a chance to answer me, "Would you like to use the bathroom and take a shower?"

I cast a gaze at Liam as she helps me stand up from the twin-sized bed. I watch as the doctor adjusts Liam so that he's fully lying on his side before pulling his black shirt up his torso and removing his right arm from the sleeve.

I almost pass out on the spot.

I would have hit the floor if the nurse weren't already supporting my weight. Scrambling to regain my balance, I watch the doctor remove the tape from a large bandage that is covering his shoulder.

"What happened?" I choke out. I'm going to be sick; I can feel the bile threatening at the base of my throat.

There's dark blood covering the once-white bandage and my stomach lurches.

"Miss Madden, I'm going to need you to calm down."

"What happened?" I demand as I pull out of her grip and hold onto the bed as I move around it to where the doctor is working.

He looks up at me and sighs. "He'll need to be the one who explains exactly what happened, but from my treatment, I can tell you that he was shot while he and his teams invaded the Macedonian compound. I removed the bullet when you two first arrived."

I watch as he washes the wound before starting to cover it up once again.

"Shot?"

"Three times actually. He has a knife wound as well and two more gunshot wounds in his abdomen. I'll check on those as soon as I'm done with this one."

"Two more?" I squeeze out and cover my mouth with a cupped hand.

"Yes, but that's as extensive as his wounds have been over the last two weeks."

"All of this happened while he was saving me?"

"Once again, Miss Madden, I'm unsure of the details, but the only bullet that I've removed was the one in his shoulder. The other wounds were taken care of by someone else. They had occurred before this one did."

The tears burn down my cheeks and seem to sear my soul as I begin to realize how much his life was on the line while searching for me.

"Will he be all right?" I ask through a deluge of silent tears.

"He'll need to be careful with this arm until the wound heals, but he should be fine since no bones were shattered, and no major organs were damaged."

"Be careful?"

"Yes. He has a list of restrictions that I've been over with him on multiple occasions now. One of them he seems to have already broken, according to my nurses."

"What did he do?"

He gives me a gentle smile before pulling Liam's shirt back on. "He's not allowed to lift anything heavier than five kilograms."

"Five?"

"Yes, which is approximately ten pounds."

"I had no idea."

"Which is understandable. He's been far more concerned about your and the other women's well-being than his own."

I sob and reach for his hand as the doctor and nurse move my sleeping fiancé onto his back to check on his older wounds.

"Miss Madden? Shall we see about that shower now?"

I nod, but I don't want to leave his side at all now. What did he see while he was looking for me? What did he do? How has all of this affected him? How have I not thought about any of this before now?

I don't know the answers to those questions, but I know that it's something that we need to speak about. I also know that I need to tell him about Grady referring to me as his plastic bitch. It's the one thing that I wasn't going to share with him, but I know that I need to if I want him to divulge any information that he seems to be holding back.

The look that Quinn gave me when he called me his favorite nickname, one that he has called me for years, was unmistakable. She was scared for me, but there's no reason to be. None at all. He's my salvation, and I refuse to let a monster diminish my relationship with Liam just because of a slice of personal information that he was able to get ahold of.

Screw the assholes who tried to steal my life away from me. I know that in the end, they will be reduced to nothing, and I'll be sturdy enough to continue living my life. After watching the doctor check over his other wounds, I let the nurse lead me away from Liam and into the en suite bathroom. She helps me out of the too-big hospital gown and into the shower once the water heats up.

I manage to wash up without her assistance, and I know that it's the first step in the right direction. I cringe when I run the shampoo through my straw-like hair. It's just another thing to fix before I am able to completely move on from the turmoil in my head. I know that it's just hair, but it's part of who I am. It's the visible stain on my body of what I've been through and I'm ready to have it covered up.

When I'm done washing up, I stand under the spray for a full five minutes before the nurse asks me if I'm done for the hundredth time. Instead of ignoring her this time, though, I nod and accept the towel that she offers me. It's warm when I wrap it around myself, and it only makes me want to get back into bed with Liam.

Once I'm dried off and dressed in a clean hospital gown, I make my way, without help, back to the bed and to the man who will obligingly put his life on the line for me.

The doctor is no longer in the room, and Liam's masculine scent of sleep and cologne fills my lungs as I crawl into the bed and nestle myself against him.

"Hit the call button if you need anything else, Miss Madden. I'll be on duty for the next nine hours."

"Thank you," I tell the nurse as she leaves the room silently.

I pull the sheet up over my body in an attempt to get my toes warm before I run my hand up the front of Liam's shirt. I lift it up and lean back to get a better look at what he put himself through to ultimately get to me and his baby.

I run my fingers along the line of healing stitches to the left-hand side of his abs and then to the right-hand side of his torso where two bullet wounds seem to be stitched up as well. I want to kiss each healing wound on him and thank him for being the unwavering and devoted man that he is.

There's no one else like Liam Jensen in this world. Not a single soul.

An hour or two passes by while he rests. I've been falling asleep and waking up every couple of minutes because I'm worried that he'll wake up and leave me in the room alone. I know that I'm being preposterous, but I need him. I try to stay awake as he dreams beside me until he jerks awake and clutches onto my body as if I'm trying to escape his grip.

"Isla," he grunts before blinking the sleep away from his open eyes.

"Liam?"

"Jesus. You're . . . fuck."

I don't wait for him to fully recover from whatever dream he was having to wrap my arms around his neck and swallow the remnants of his dream by kissing him until he's pure again.

His arms lock around my waist as he kisses me with his eyes open, too afraid to close them because of the chance of my disappearing. I pull back and run my fingers into the back of his hair in another attempt to calm his demons.

A rare spate of goose bumps breaks out over his skin before he leans his forehead against mine. "Focus on me," I tell him as I feel his heavy breath meet my cheeks with each exhale.

"I missed you."

A hundred lifetimes with Liam Jensen would not be enough right now. He doesn't expect a thing from those around him, but he gives his full heart without being asked for it.

"I missed you," I return as he pulls the bottom half of my body against his. His solid limbs feel unworldly as he stares at me in dignified silence.

He unties the gown that I'm wrapped in and moves it aside so that he's able to run his fingers along the bare skin of my back. "I just need to touch you. I need to know that you're here," he says as my fingers continue to move through the back of his hair, down the thick column of his neck and then back up again.

We lay innocent touches on each other for a long couple of minutes before he pulls a few strands of blonde hair between his fingers and twirls the hair around the height of his index finger.

"Do you remember my telling you about those nightmares that I'd have about Chloe? The ones that I tried to banish with the use of recreational drugs?"

"I do," I say softly as he concentrates on the hair around his finger.

"They've now morphed into something worse. Instead of Chloe . . . it's you."

"Liam."

He moves his tired gaze to meet my eyes and a pitiful smile moves across his face. "You don't have to worry about my delving back into that kind of shit. Not when you alone are enough to put me on my ass."

"Are you sure about that? That dream didn't seem like something you should brush off."

"Damn sure, doll. You do trust me, right?"

"Why wouldn't I?"

"I don't know. I'm still learning to trust myself. You've also been through more than you ever should have experienced, and I see the way you look at others now when they come close to you."

"Do . . . I don't look at you like that, do I? I just don't know what they want. I don't want them to touch me if I can avoid it."

"No one will ever touch you again without your consent. You have my word."

I move as close to him as I can get and bury my face into his warmth. "I know," I say against the material of his shirt.

Liam-fucking-Jensen has my heart locked up. I trust him to a point that I don't think is either sensible or legal, but I do. Call me senseless or unseeing, but I don't care. He's not the hell that was holding me. He's my refuge.

"What can I get you to eat, Isla? You're wasting away in my arms."

The thought of food makes me raise my head and smile. "I could go for the largest, greasiest, slightly charred double cheeseburger in London right about now."

His deep laugh vibrates against my body. "Let me guess. You'd like ice cream on the side?"

I think about it for a moment and then scrunch up my face in distaste. "Nope. I'd really like fried pickles, though."

"Do they even make those outside of the States?"

"If not, you can just tell them to batter them up in their beer batter and fry those babies up." I'm trying my best to be strong for him as well as for myself. It has to start from somewhere, right?

I got my miracle, and now I need to live it out.

"I'll see what I can do."

My heart sinks when he says that particular grouping of words. "You're going?"

"If you'd like it done right, then I might have to. I believe most of my men are at the hotel getting some much-needed rest."

"You need your rest as well."

"I'll get it when we're home. Right now, though, my pregnant fiancée needs food." He shifts on the bed and dislodges himself from my intense hold on him before standing and running a hand through his now-tousled hair.

"Would you like a milkshake as well?"

I chew on the corner of my lip as I watch him collect his phone and wallet from the counter that holds numerous medical supplies.

"A chocolate shake and fries to dip into it."

"You're disgusting," he says before pulling on his leather jacket and walks back over to the bed to kiss me mercilessly. I reach up and yank on his hair as he devours my mouth. When each of us is able to pull back, we're both breathing heavily.

"If you don't go and get me food right now, I'll make do with your cock and the cafeteria chips and gravy.

"Fuck, doll. I'll be back before you know it. Do you want me to take you to Quinn's room so that you're not alone in here?"

"I'd like that, thank you."

I get off of the bed and move next to my IV stand where I wrap my fingers around the cool metal. He strides toward me and I freaking swoon right here. Right in my hospital room. I swoon at the way he's looking at me with such hunger and love in his eyes. He's the only man who has made me feel so beautiful in his presence when I know I look like complete and utter shit.

He bends down to try and pick me up, but I stop him. "Liam," I chastise. "You know that you're not supposed to be carting me around this place."

"What?"

"The doctor was in here earlier to check on me, and he changed out your bandage as well."

He looks down at his feet to try and compose himself before he can look into my eyes again. "I didn't want to worry you."

"It's okay. I understand, but will you tell me what happened?"

"Yeah. I will when both of us are ready to hear it again."

"Do you swear it?"

"I do."

"Thank you."

Since I've been with Liam, I've had to learn how to compromise. Relationships are not about what one person wants, but about caring enough to make it thrive in delivering what the other person wants or needs. The gestures that we show each other, outside of the physical ones, are those that seem to speak louder than words actually do.

He reaches for my hand, and I take it willingly, feeling like I need the physical contact with him more than the air that's keep-ing me alive.

Once he has me settled in the seat in Quinn's room, he plac-es a blanket over my legs and kisses my forehead. "Keep those feet warm for me."

"I'll try," I joke, and he takes my lips quickly while Quinn watches before he leaves me alone with a woman who took the physical beating that was meant for me.

"I think that you've got a good one in your court. It's Isla, right? Am I saying it correctly?"

I lean back against the chair and smile at her. She's still bat-tered and bruised, but they were able to remove the tube from her mouth earlier today, and she's apparently been talking the ears off of anyone who will listen.

"Yes, you are, and yes, he's passionate, but somehow he still manages to be a conceited asshole."

That gets her to laugh for a beat, but she winces a second later. I pull my feet up underneath me on the chair to warm up a little more since I don't have my personal body heater on standby.

"How long have you been together?" she asks as she adjusts the angle of her bed, giving her a better position to sit in.

"Together?" I sigh as I try to figure out which parts of our friendship have been more than we thought it was. "Honestly, I'm unsure, but I've known him close to ten years now. He's been my best friend since college."

"Oh. That's incredible, Isla. He seems so caring." She sighs. "He must be knackered, though."

I squirm in my seat and move my hand to my stomach. "I know that he is."

"Since college . . . that's a long time, right?"

"Yeah. There've been plenty of trials and tribulations be-tween the two of us, as well as individually, but through it all, we found each other. What about you? Is there someone waiting for you at home or someone that you'd like me to contact?"

She rests her head back and shakes her head from side to side before replying. "Not entirely. I was orphaned at a young age, and I've been in and out of orphanages all of my life. When I was shoved out of the door at eighteen, I made a run for it and never looked back. I worked for a while in a coffee shop in a little town called Chippenham. I was able to save up enough money to go to Greece for a week on holiday. Well, I don't think I need to map out how the rest of it went when some todger got his hands on me."

"Eighteen? If you don't mind my asking, how old were you when they took you?"

"Twenty. I wasn't sold into trafficking immediately. The arse whose goons captured me kept me locked up in his house to do with as he pleased for three years before he got bored of me and sold me to the highest bidder."

"I'm so sorry. How long were you at the compound for?"

She shrugs and looks down at her fingers. "It was hard to keep track, but I think a week had passed before I saw you enter the shower room. It was a lot worse than being in that house with him."

I nod and reach out for her hand. She takes mine in return, and I squeeze. "Thank you for helping me in there. I realize that by doing so, though, they put you through hell."

"Don't worry about it. It's not your fault, and it won't ever be. How's the baby doing?"

I smile and look down at my other hand, which I have resting on my stomach. "So far, so good is what I'm being told."

"I'm glad. By the way, we might need to pay someone with a little more experience than I have to fix the muck-up of your hair."

We laugh together before she starts to talk about what she'd like to see herself doing in the future—none of which involves her hanging around here or going back to where she came from.

I must have fallen asleep to the sound of her voice because the next thing I can comprehend is being lifted up and carried back to the hospital room that I've claimed.

"Liam," I groan and swat at his chest.

"Still my grumpy doll, huh? I'll take it," he says through a smile that I don't need to see to know is present.

"The doctor said . . ."

"Yeah, yeah, I heard what he said, but I don't care."

I tsk as he sets me down on the bed and readjusts the blanket that's still around me.

"I managed to get you those pickles that you wanted."

"What?" I squeal and sit up. Fuck sleep. I need pickles . . . like *right* now.

He actually rolls his eyes at me before pulling the table up to me and opens up the large bag of food. I groan when the scent of grease, cheese, and pickles fills the air.

"Eat to your heart's content, babe."

"Thank you so much for getting all of this greasy food. I'm going to blow you the second I finish up."

He takes a seat beside me on the bed while chuckling and unwraps one of the two burgers before kissing my lips as I chew on a French fry.

"You're welcome."

A little stuffed may be a gross understatement, but I feel like I could eat double the amount of what I just did. I lost count of the times that Liam told me to slow down but it was just too damn good.

"How's that stomachache treating you?"

"Like shit," I gripe and the bastard laughs at me as I curl up into a ball on the bed. "When do I get to sleep in a more comfortable bed by the way?"

"Once you're feeling well enough to leave."

"Well, I'm good to go. Get me the fuck out of here, Liam."

"Calm down there, baby doll. I'll get you out once your stomachache subsides, and I have a hotel room. I can have us flown out as well if you'd like."

I think on it for a minute before straightening up and squirming into a seated position. "This is going to sound reckless and foolish, but I want it. It might just work."

"What is it?"

I wring my hands together before looking up at him through my lashes. He's stopped his cleanup efforts and is facing me. His shoulders are broad, and if I didn't know him personally, I actually might be afraid at how dauntingly handsome he looks right now. "I want to elope."

"Elope?"

"Yes."

"Here? In London?"

"It doesn't have to be in the city. I'm sure that there are a lot of gorgeous places around here."

"Isla," he says as he takes a seat beside me on the bed again. "You'd want to do this away from everyone back home? There's no need to rush any of it."

I think on it for a minute and shrug. "Brass will be peeved about it, but he'll get over it faster than he can get inside of Hadley, and my mother, well, fuck her. She wouldn't attend regardless. It's just your family, really. It doesn't have to be anything fancy. I just want what we have to be concrete."

"There she is," he chuckles and kisses the side of my head. "It already is as concrete as it could get."

I giggle as he scoops me into his arms and plants a big one on me.

"Well? Do we have a deal?"

I watch his dark eyes as he thinks it through for a quiet moment. "Deal."

"Wait, seriously?"

"Seriously, babe. Name the time and place and I'll be there."

I throw my arms around his neck and capture his mouth with mine as he kisses me in return. He tastes of the breath mints and everything Liam as his tongue massages mine. I pull back and rest my forehead against his.

"Tomorrow. Can we do it tomorrow? Please?"

"If that's what you want. I just have one condition."

"Anything," I say as I move my body onto his lap until I'm straddling him. I can feel him grow hard beneath me, and I want nothing more than to seal our plans with raw, unabridged sex right now.

"When you said yes to marrying me, you said that you would wear white for me, and I'd like for you to see that through."

"Promise. Wait, what time is it now? Will I have time to get a dress?"

"It's just past noon. I'll go get things arranged for your release. I need you to change into some clothes that I picked up for you today as well. I'm not even sure if I got the right size, but I tried."

"I love you, thank you."

He pats my ass before moving me off of his body, kissing my temple, and walking to the door. "I'll be back as soon as I can."

"All right."

I'm glad that he sees through my facade of fake strength. He knows that I need him, and he understands my reasoning for not wanting to be left alone or with someone who I don't trust.

I love Liam more than I can put into words. He's everything to me. *Everything.*

I watch his back retreat from the room, and I want to scream and call everyone on my phone list. I frown, realizing that I no longer have my phone . . . or my engagement ring.

I try to push aside the negatives—they're minor—and bask in the knowledge that Liam-fucking-Jensen wants to get married to me *tomorrow.*

Twenty-Two

Liam

THE BLACK CAB pulls up in front of the Four Seasons Hotel in London, and I get out to check in with what few belongings we have between the two of us. We're shown to our suite, and as soon as we walk in, I know that Isla wouldn't mind staying in here for the remainder of the day, but we're wasting the day.

I walk into the bathroom where she's washing her face and gaping at her reflection in the mirror as if it's about to jump out and bite her. She was prescribed some medication before we left, but she's refusing to get hooked on medication again now that she's finally off of it after years of taking the shit.

"Everything all right?" I ask as I lean against the doorframe.

"Yes. I just didn't take my hair into consideration."

"I'm sure that they'll have an opening at the salon down-stairs, and if not, I'll arrange for someone to come up here."

She dries off her face before nodding and walking back over to me in a too-baggy shirt. I can't see her slim, gorgeous figure, and it's beginning to bother me. Isla is a beautiful woman, and I don't approve of it when she's hiding from me. I managed to get the right-sized jeans for her to wear today, but the rest I royally fucked up on.

"We'll grab you some clothes to wear for the next few days while we're out."

"Thank you."

I grab her by the waist and pull her against my chest. "If you thank me one more time for being the man you deserve, then I won't be held responsible when there's red handprints covering that pretty ass of yours."

"If you insist."

"I do. Now listen, I was emailing back and forth with the event coordinator here, and she said she'd be happy to help us put our elopement together, so I took her up on the offer. The only thing that I need to know from you is what kind of flowers you'd like to hold as you walk down the aisle to me."

"Are you serious?"

"Very."

She chews on my question while I lead her out of the suite and hotel and onto the streets of London.

"Well?"

"I think that purple orchids would be beautiful."

"Purple? You're sure?"

"I think so. Why?"

I pull her arm into the crook of mine as I lead her through the foot traffic on the sidewalk. "No reason, it sounds good to me. I also took the liberty of finding a place that will be able to at least provide you with a sample dress for tomorrow."

"Oh? Where is it?"

"About a ten-minute walk down Piccadilly. Is that okay?"

"Sure."

About five minutes into our walk, I notice that she's sticking as close to me as humanly possible as we pass by hundreds of people. Her eyes are darting in every which direction and I want to help her escape from her apparent fear. Fuck, I'd do anything to help her forget and not have the past two weeks leave an effect on her life. However, it happened, and now she needs to work on the monsters in her head just as I once had to. Still have to.

I move my arm around her shoulders and pull her against me as we maneuver our way through the crowds.

"Trust me, Isla. I won't let anything happen to you."

Her wide eyes dart to mine, and she nods once before swallowing her fear.

The short walk is anything but and it feels like fucking hours have passed by the time we're standing outside of Alexander McQueen's store just off of Old Bond Street.

"Liam, you can't be serious."

"By knowing both Wade and I, you should be well aware by now that money can get you into anything that you want."

"Holy shit. Can we go in?"

"Seeing as we have an appointment, I don't see why we shouldn't."

She takes the few steps forward to get to the door as excitement radiates off of her body. I reach around her to pull open the door and watch her face transform just as it did when she stepped foot into Harry Winston.

We're greeted immediately and then she's taken from my grip and propelled toward the back of the store—where apparently I'm not invited.

"Wait," she says as the salesperson turns the corner. "Liam?"

"What's wrong, doll?"

"Nothing. It's just." She looks over her shoulder at the salesperson before taking a step toward me. She shrugs and holds her hands out in front of her while she thinks of a way to explain what she wants to say.

"Okay, listen, I know that it's supposedly bad luck for you to see me in the dress before the, er, wedding, but I want you with me. This is our unconventional journey, and I don't want to do this alone." She takes another step toward me before continuing, "Plus, I'd rather not have someone else's hands on me to zip me up right now."

Shit. I didn't even think about that. I take quick strides until I'm in front of her, and she automatically reaches for me, needing the physical connection that we share to calm her down. "All you had to do was ask."

"Thank you," she says before getting up on her tiptoes to lay a quick one along my jaw. Her fingers lace between mine as we follow the clerk to the limited number of dresses that she has on hand for us to purchase.

There are a few racks pulled out, all of which host three or four white dresses each.

"Take your pick, beautiful."

She lets go of my hand and reaches out to touch the material of an ivory-colored dress before clapping excitedly and listening to what the salesperson has to say. It's something about her size, height, and preferred fabric, so really, it's like speaking a different language to me. I spot a couch off to the side and take a seat on it as I watch Isla enjoy this moment that she's allowed me to be a part of.

I take the opportunity to email the event coordinator at the Four Seasons Hotel with Isla's flower preference before sending out requests for favors to a couple of others as well. By the time I'm done, Isla walks up to me and shimmies her hips in front of me.

"Are you ready to see me naked, Jensen?"

"More than ever."

Ninety minutes and eight dress changes later, Isla is standing in front of me and behind a mirror with tears in her eyes as she turns to her right and then left over and over again.

I walk up to her and wrap my arms around her midsection as I lean my chin on the top of her head.

"You're beautiful. Do you know that? How the fuck did I get

so lucky to land my best friend, huh?"

She chokes out a laugh and watches the two of us in the mirror. "Well, if I had to end up with my best friend, I didn't really have another choice at this point in the game."

"You would have ended up with me even if I was an altar boy."

She wipes away her tears while smiling at me in the mirror. "Have you ever actually stepped foot inside a church?"

"Once or twice when my mother dragged me in by my ears."

"She didn't."

"Oh, but she did."

She giggles and turns in my arms, and takes her time sliding her hands up my chest until they are locked at the back of my neck. "This is for life, Jensen. Are you sure you want me for that long?"

"I may have to reconsider since you put it that way," I joke and get rewarded with a smack to the back of my head.

"I'm being serious here, dickweed."

"I'm sure, Miss Madden."

"Good because you weren't going to be able to get out of it."

"Is that a challenge?"

"Nope, it's the truth. Plus, I don't share well with others."

"You'll have to share when our dewdrop comes along."

She scrunches up her face and shrugs. "I'll think about it."

"Deal."

"Deal," she replies before untangling herself from my hold and looking at herself in the mirror again. "We need to add something to that deal, though."

"Yeah?"

"You have to swear to stop me from dying my hair any shade

other than my natural color. I look pathetic as a blonde."

"I beg to differ, but I do prefer my natural beauty."

"Suck-up," she quips.

"You sure as fuck will be sucking on something tonight."

"Assume all you want. Just because you're paying for one of the most comfortable beds in all of London doesn't mean that I'm going to allow any snuggling, never mind the idea of penetration."

I pull her ass against my now-hard cock. "I won't settle for anything less," I seethe before pinching her cheek. She steps out of my hold with a radiant smile beaming on her face.

"Can we pay for this and get back to the hotel?"

"We can. My tuxedo should have been delivered by now."

"By now?"

"Yes. What was that thing I was telling you about money?"

"Shut it and take me back to the hotel. I need to be taken care of in more ways than one."

"I figured that we could grab food on the way. Would that be okay? Or would you prefer room service?"

"I'm wholly against anything that stops us from getting back to the hotel in the next ten minutes and my getting laid in fifteen."

"Well, get your ass out of this dress, and we'll grab some clothes for you before we leave."

Fifteen minutes later, I've paid for the dress that will be delivered to our hotel suite tomorrow morning, four pairs of jeans, a couple of black shirts, and sweaters. I hail a cab, but instead of instructing the driver to take us to the hotel, I have him stop at La Perla. This earns me a sidelong glance as I help her out of the cab and into the store.

"I cannot allow you to go bare underneath that dress."

"You're spoiling me, Liam."

"Allow me to enjoy it. If this is what you'll allow me to provide for you on our wedding day, then I'll take it."

"I love you, you dickweed."

I lean in to kiss her, but get distracted by a bustier that's a few feet behind her. I move past Isla and pick up the bustier's hanger before turning back to her.

"Now this is something that you can wear for me in private."

She saunters over to me and touches the fabric before blushing.

"You'd like this?"

"I'd like you in anything and in nothing, Isla."

"Regardless of my bruises?"

I set the hanger back on the bar before pulling her into my arms and tilting her chin up to look at me. "You are the single most hauntingly beautiful woman that I've ever had the pleasure of laying my eyes on. A few bruises don't do anything to diminish that beauty. Do you understand me?"

She tries to nip at my finger, but I pull it away in time. "I understand, so would you like to pick out what you get to see once you peel my wedding dress off of me tomorrow?"

"You'd let me do that?"

"Duh."

We spend another two hours at the store, completely forgetting about our anticipation and need to return to the hotel to get naked. Once we're done checking out with the salesclerk, I pick up all of the shopping bags and chuckle at the sheer number of shoes, handbags, lingerie, and loungewear that we've purchased.

"We're going to have to get you your own suitcase to fly home with.

"I think we might," she says as she pushes through the front doors of La Perla and out onto the London street where I flag down a taxicab to make our way back to the hotel.

When we arrive, the bellhop greets us and leads the way to our suite with the bags in his hands as Isla runs her thumb up and down the back of my hand.

It's making me rather impatient to bury myself inside of her, actually, and she seems to notice but doesn't once stop her silent yet deadly attempt at seduction.

Once we make it to the suite, I tip the bellhop and watch him take another desperate glance at Isla before I close the fucking door in his face. The douche is lucky that I need her right now and that my gun is not in reach.

"I'd like to say that I want it easy, but honestly . . . I need us. I just want what we are and what we provide each other."

"Did you think that I'd deny you?"

"Possibly."

"Not a chance, baby doll. Just don't go scratching at my injuries when I make you come."

"I make no promises."

"You play dirty."

"I always have, and you know it."

I sweep her up into my arms and walk her backward until I'm able to lay her down on the bed and move on top of her, kissing down the column of her neck until she whimpers in need beneath me.

"Liam, please."

"I know, babe. I just need you to lie back and enjoy this."

She nods and runs her hand down my neck and underneath the fabric of my shirt to get to my skin before she starts to gather the shirt in a fist, at the base of my neck. I lock my teeth on her and suck lightly until she curses under her breath.

She pulls on the fistful of fabric that she's holding until she's able to get me to sit up for a long enough period of time to get my shirt up and off. I set it on her side of the bed knowing that she'll wear it to sleep in, before moving back down on her and breathing in everything about this gorgeous woman.

"I'm so in love with you," she says against my lips and wiggles underneath me.

"Yeah? Well, then it's a damn good thing that I'm in love with you too, huh?"

"Probably."

I pull her shirt up and off of her before burying my face between her perky breasts, nipping at them as I reach around and undo the clips that are holding her new bra in place. Once I'm able to get it off of her, I toss it to the side and run my tongue around one of her nipples as each one pebbles in the cooler air.

"Liam."

"Isla," I breathe against her nipple, and she arches her back off of the bed.

"Please?"

"Be patient with me, baby doll. It's been a while since I've touched you like this. I'm going to savor every second."

"All right."

I close my eyes for a brief moment to gather all of the emotions over the last couple of days, but when I do, image after image of her shackled to a crucifix fill my vision. *Goddamn it.*

I pull back and move onto my back beside her, rubbing my eyes before looking back over at her. "I'm sorry."

"What happened?" she asks as she leans up on her elbow.

"I've just seen too much, doll."

"Too much? Are you talking about Chloe?"

"Chloe? God, babe, no. I'm talking about you."

"Me?"

"Yes. I've told you that you've replaced all of the images of her, but it doesn't make it easier. Fuck, I want to kill every single one of those bastards who had their hands on you. And any other man who looks at you now."

She moves her body into mine and throws one leg over my waist to grind herself against my straining erection.

"Try not to think about it. Okay?"

"Saying that and doing it are two very different things."

"I know, but it won't happen again. I know that I'm safe when I'm with you."

"You should have been safe the night that he took you."

She shifts and tilts my face so that we're looking each other in the eyes. "Do you blame yourself?"

I watch her as I run the pad of my thumb over her now-red lips. "I do."

"You shouldn't."

"I shouldn't have been drunk," I retort and pull her closer to me.

"Liam, you've put your life on the line to find me. To save me. None of what happened is your fault, all right? What you do for the women who have been taken is monumental, and what happened to me should not deter you from focusing on getting more women out."

"I cannot bring myself to go out there with the thought of not coming back to you and the baby."

"Then don't go out into the field. Be there for the women when they are brought to the safe houses. Be what RW needs you to be. You started all of this, and hundreds of women would be either dead or still suffering if it wasn't for you. You can't stop just because I'm pregnant."

"I'll do what feels right, and right now, what feels right is being with you."

"So work from Chicago, but don't give up on what you're passionate about."

I chuckle and run my hand past her waist and up her ribcage. "Deal."

Her body melts against mine as I shut my eyes and try to fight the demons that are pushing themselves deep into my soul, fighting every detail about me. They push against my own experiences to get what they want from me—which is to get me to stop the actions that RW takes against trafficking. It won't help. Not now and not ever.

"I can hear you thinking from here, Jensen."

"Yeah? Try not to worry about it. Just know that I won't let you go. Keep calling me Jensen, by the way, because come tomorrow you won't only be referring to me but to yourself as well."

"Cheeky bastard."

"Don't complain. I know that you're excited to take my name."

"I am. More than ever, really, and by this time tomorrow I'll have it, and your ass better believe that I'm not giving it up."

"I wouldn't want you to."

"Good. Now kiss me before I fucking combust."

Twenty-Three

Isla

LIAM JENSEN IS currently waiting for me at the end of an aisle.

My body feels like it's in one large knot and despite the bruises, it's the only thing that I can feel right now. It's an overpowering emotion of love and want that I need him to fulfill. It's one that I know that he'll selflessly achieve in a few moments even if it will be just the two of us.

I know that what we're about to do goes beyond a ring and a mutually signed piece of paper. It's something that I'll savor as my life goes on. It's the union of two hearts that beat better as one.

I blow out a breath of air as I stare at myself in the mirror with knowledge that the best is yet to come. I check my nails that were done earlier this morning and think back to when Quinn called from the hospital around noon today. We stayed on the line for a couple of minutes until one of the nurses needed to get her back to her room. Liam and I will be stopping by to see her with a care package before we head back to the States after our nuptials this evening. I cannot wait to see her and let her in on our secret elopement.

There's a lighthearted knock on the door, and the hairstylist pauses for a moment to walk over and answer it. When she comes back, she's carrying a small white gift bag that she hands to me.

"I believe that this belongs to you."

"Thank you."

I pull out the first layer of white tissue paper and take a card out. It has my name written on it in black in Liam's slightly messy handwriting. I pull the simple white card out from the envelope and curse myself as the tears start to fall before I can get to the end of the single sentence that's scrawled out on the card. I reach for a tissue and dab the underneath of my eyes before my makeup can run as I read his words again.

Today, I have loved you for 3,652 days.

The attempt to stop my tears fails miserably as I'm handed more tissues from the makeup artist.

I take them and set them aside as I dig into the gift bag and pull out a Harry Winston navy blue box and snap the top open to reveal my engagement ring.

"Oh God . . ."

"Is everything all right?" the hairstylist asks as she pins the last curl into place.

"Everything is faultless. So beyond perfect," I say with a sniffle.

She smiles at me in the mirror as I slide my ring onto my left finger then hold my hand out at arm's length to inspect it as I did a hundred times before it was pried away from me.

"I need to see him," I tell the two women and begin to stand from my position.

"Oh, no, no, no. I need to fix your makeup again and then we have to get your dress on. Only then can you go."

I huff out a frustrated sigh before taking a seat again. My knees bounce up and down as I think about his touch. When these two ladies first showed up, Liam refused to leave me alone with them, but I swore to him that I'd be able to handle it for the short period of time.

Right now, though, I wish that I listened when he insisted on staying. I need him.

It takes them an additional twenty minutes to finish up before each of them takes one of my hands and helps me step into my heels. I remove the plush hotel robe when my dress is brought over. I close my eyes and keep them shut as they work together to get it correctly positioned on my body. I cringe at the feel of their fingertips against my bare skin, but I manage to remind myself of where I am before a panic attack ensues. Before I'm allowed to leave the room, the makeup artist applies one more coat of blood-red lipstick before they insist on taking a handful of images, which they'll send to Liam once the ceremony is over. I know that he asked them to do it, so I'll indulge them for a moment.

I thank each of them before walking out of the suite and to the elevator bank on our floor. Once I hit the down button, I stare at myself in the full-length mirror on the far wall.

The iridescently white material hugs my curves flawlessly with the beading and lace flowing down from my breasts to my hips in erratic yet precise patterns. The mermaid cut fits closely to my body until it flares out at my knees. The sweetheart neckline with spaghetti straps gives a great view of my girls for Liam, and I'm eager to see his reaction to the finished product.

My hair is swept over to one side of my shoulders where half of it is pinned up, and the other half lies softly over my left shoulder. I know that he'll like it like this because he'll be able to see the column of my neck . . . the side that he didn't leave a hickey on yesterday.

My favorite thing about the woman staring back at me in the mirror, aside from the fact that my hair is back to its natural color, is that I see myself. I don't see the damaged and haunted woman that I thought I would. I see someone who is thrilled about the next steps in life and who she has waiting for her downstairs.

I run my fingers through the curled locks of black hair as the elevator opens and I step into it, immediately impatient for it to take me downstairs. It makes a lot more stops on the way down than I'd like, allowing more and more passengers on each time.

My heart starts to beat wildly in my chest, and I have to remind myself to keep breathing as they stare at me like I'm locked up behind bars or . . . or shackled to a crucifix.

Liam. Oh God, I've never needed him to save me from anything so inconsequential before like I need him to right now. I shouldn't be panicking. I shouldn't be afraid of their smiles, but I am. I don't know what they are thinking or what they might do. All I know is that I need to get out of this thing.

My palms get sweaty while I hold my bouquet and my entire body starts to tremble as we continue to pass one floor at a time. I shut my eyes and start to count backward from a hundred, and once I've reached eighty-nine, I feel us come to a complete stop. I wait to hear the rustling of bodies leaving the confined space before I even attempt to open my eyes, let alone step out. Once I leave the confines of the elevator, I'm able to breathe in the untainted air. I turn in the direction of the private room where I was told to meet Liam but halt my movements when my heart crashes against my chest.

He's here.

This cannot be happening.

We've traveled so far away, but yet he's here. Right in front of me.

I don't know whether to run or walk, but he's here, and he's watching me as if I'm something to behold. I look back over my shoulder, wondering if I'm seeing things, but when I glance back in his direction, he's taking quick and purposeful strides to get to me from his position in the hotel's lobby.

I seize up and start to hyperventilate all over again.

"Holy shit," I say under my breath as he finally reaches me and pulls me against his hard chest by my arms before wrapping me in a tight hold that I can't escape from.

His light chuckle fills my ears, and it's only when he's touching me that I allow myself to take a breath.

"Brass."

"It's good to see you, Isla."

"You're here?" I look up at him and try my damnedest not to burst into a torrent of tears at the sight of my best friend dressed to the nines in a tuxedo.

"Did you believe that you'd be able to get married without my being present?"

"I mean . . . I gave it a good shot, right?"

"And you failed miserably." He holds up my left hand and smiles. "Plus, I had to make a special delivery."

"You brought me my ring?"

"I doubt that anyone else would have the uncanny ability to get inside of another man's safety deposit box, Isla."

"Thank you," I say as I squeeze him with my right arm.

"Come on. I've got a job to do and delivering you to Liam is first on that list."

"Delivering me?" I pull back and stare up at one of my best friends, one of the two people in my life that saved me from sinking. "Are you . . . you're not . . . are you?"

"Am I walking you down the aisle? Yes, if you will allow it."

"Of course I'll allow it. I cannot believe that you're actually here."

"Liam was rather insistent when he told me what you wanted to do."

"He's such a shit," I mock.

"Hey, you're the one who's about to get married to that shit. Not I."

I laugh and hug him once more before moving out of his arms and straightening myself up again. "Okay. I'm ready."

"You look stunning, Isla. I'm glad that you're safe. I cannot begin to—"

"Please don't. We can speak about it, but not here. Not today."

"All right."

I shy away from him as we walk to the ballroom that Liam managed to secure for this afternoon. Wade stops us at the door and offers me his arm. I slide mine into the crook of his and beam up at him as the door starts to open.

"You've got this, Isla."

"Definitely."

I know that I should be terrified at what I'm doing, at making such a significant commitment, but the truth is that I cannot wait to do it. I'm beyond ready to start our life together.

The faint sounds of *Kiss Me* by Rebel start to get louder as the doors open wider and my heart starts that hammering-against-my-chest bullshit again.

Liam's eyes find mine the second he looks up, and if Wade was not by my side supporting me right now, I would have crumpled in a mess of love onto the floor.

The smile on my groom's face is one that I haven't seen him wear before as I make my way toward him. I would so much rather hike up my dress and sprint down the aisle into his arms, but then again . . . I'm unsure whether I can feel my legs right now.

Liam's gaze drops to the floor in front of his feet for a second before he looks up at me again. The rest of the world seems to fade away at the moment I see a solitary tear leak from his eyes and then another, and I'm suddenly not moving fast enough to get to him.

It takes me a moment longer to reach him when Wade places my hand into Liam's outstretched one. I gasp at the physical reassurance I feel from him at his touch.

"Liam."

"Isla."

I reach up and wipe the tear from his jaw before placing my lips on his and kissing him slowly. Screw the order of nuptials and any bad luck that it may bring me. I need him. *Always.*

A clearing of a man's voice brings me back from the world that only Liam and I reside in when we're alone with each other. He cups my cheek and smiles down at me. My entire body lights up from his touch, and as much as I was looking forward to this, I want it to be over now so that it can be just the two of us again.

"You're beautiful, doll."

I lean into his touch and blink up at him, loving the way he's watching me.

"Shall we proceed?"

Glancing up at the man standing in front of us, I nod as Liam lowers his hand and takes one of mine in each of his.

"Ladies and gentleman, we are gathered here today to celebrate the union of Isla Madden and Liam Jensen."

I hear someone whoop, and I shoot a glance over my shoulder. I'm astonished when I see Hadley sitting beside Wade, Eden, and Liam's family in front of us.

"Liam," I say interrupting the nuptials once again.

"I wanted to surprise you. You deserve this and much more."

"Thank you," I mouth as the ordained minister starts to speak again.

I must have gotten lost in his gaze because the next thing I know Liam is squeezing each of my hands to get my attention.

"Doll? Are you okay?"

"What?"

He chuckles and leans in to place a kiss on my cheek while whispering, "It's time for our vows."

"Oh. Right."

I blush as he pulls away from me. I don't even need a mirror to know because my cheeks scorch under his ogling.

"If you'll repeat after me," the minister says, but I shake my head.

"Actually, can I just speak from my heart? Please?"

"Certainly."

I clear my throat and look up into my groom's eyes before spewing the contents of my heart out to him and those around us.

"Liam-fucking-Jensen, I choose you." He laughs with me and his eyes brim with unshed tears once more. "I choose you to give my whole heart to. I choose our unconditional love. I choose our forever. I take you as my best friend and my faithful partner. These vows will seal me to you in front of our friends and family, but I've belonged to you since the day we met. With you, I will celebrate the journey of life and provide you with more compassion, laughter, and support than you'll know what to do with. This is a once-in-a-lifetime love, and I swear to never forget that as long as you provide me with an adequate amount of whiskey along the way. I'm yours for always. I love you . . ."

"Liam," the minister instructs, and instead of repeating the first line that the minister feeds him, he follows his heart.

"Isla Jens . . . Madden, I have called you my best friend, girlfriend, fiancée, and soon, my wife. I swear to love you all of today, tomorrow, and the next. All that we are and all that we will become is something that I hold close to my heart. I will lift you up in the bad times and celebrate with you in the good. I'd choose you and our mutual weirdness above anyone else. Our future not only contains each one of us but together we have something precious on its way. I'll be there by your side through every single moment of diapers, screams, tears, math homework, and first dates. We, Isla, are for always. Shit just got real, baby doll."

Everyone laughs along with us as we exchange rings that I didn't know that he had. To make it official Liam pulls me closer and bites down on my lower lip before locking our lips together in front of those with whom we shared our souls.

I lock my arms around his neck as he lifts my feet off of the floor and spins me around, all the while kissing me. "You truly own me now, Isla Jensen."

"Deal?"

"Deal."

Instead of the usual reception, Liam had the event coordinator set up an early dinner for all who were in attendance. We're currently seated in the Hamilton room at the Four Seasons Hotel, and I cannot get over how gorgeous everything is. Surrounded by walls of windows, we sit at the long table that has cascading purple orchids in the center of it with gold accents everywhere.

I'm seated beside my *husband* while he plays with my fingers, and I try to take this day in.

"I was enough for you after all, huh?" he asks.

"You've been enough from our first kiss."

"I remember," he says as he squeezes my hand.

"You do?"

"Yeah. I just had this little fucking crush on you that I couldn't drop. I was supposed to be hooking up with my girlfriend at the time, but for some reason, you walked into the bedroom at the house party instead of her, and I knew that I had to do something to finally settle what I was feeling toward you."

"You did?"

"I did. I don't know why you came upstairs to me, but I remember getting up and walking toward you. I locked the door behind you, and before you could protest, I had your lips locked onto mine."

I giggle and squeeze his hand. "You can thank Waylon for that shit. He was the one who told me to go up and see you. He said that you weren't feeling well or some BS."

Liam glances up at Wade and shakes his head before turning his attention back on me. "That little crush turned into a lot more with every touch you laid on me."

"You kept me coming back for more."

"I always will, Mrs. Jensen."

I rest my head against his shoulder and smile up at Wade. An odd feeling of serenity settles over me in knowing that Waylon had a hand in setting us up. We might not have known it over the years, but when I look back, I can see it. He always used to push us together. I mouth, "Thank you" to him, and he gives me a single nod, confirming my suspicions.

"Are you happy?" Liam asks as champagne is poured for everyone while I settle for sparkling cider.

"Incredibly. Thank you for doing all of this. I don't know how you did it, but thank you nonetheless."

"You're welcome, baby doll."

A clinking of glass and silverware sounds and Liam leans over to take my lips before the noise stops and he pulls back, running his fingers through my once-again dark locks.

Liam stands up and draws everyone's attention to him, including his mother's for a change. For the first time since I've noticed her, she's not throwing daggers at me with her gaze.

I look up and watch as Liam clears his throat as he raises a flute filled with golden bubbling champagne. "I wanted to say thank you all for being here and dropping everything in your lives to help us celebrate the love we share for each other."

He looks down at me and reaches for my hand. I don't hesitate to lace my fingers with his before he continues. "As of today, May 21st, I've promised my life to one woman who hasn't left my side in ten years, and I imagine that the next ten will be the same. Neither of us are the same people we were ten years ago. We've made mistakes that served a purpose, but ones that ultimately taught us how to live and grab hold of each other. I won't define her by the worst things that she's done in life, but only by the best as we take the next couple of steps forward."

I squeeze his hand as he continues. "You've promised to be by my side through the tough shit, Isla, and I want you to know that regardless of our past or future, I'll always have you by my side and in my heart. Both you and our child."

My free hand moves over my stomach as the tears start to fall once more.

"Stupid hormones," I ramble as everyone turns to look at me. It gets them all to smile, and I get to my feet to lay an innocent-looking kiss on my husband.

My *husband*. Holy fucking shit balls.

"Isla?" Connor says from across the table. "I want to be the first to welcome you into our family. Some of us might be renegade bitches, but our love is still the same."

I almost choke on my water as I take a drink. "Th-thank you," I stutter.

He nods and holds up his champagne flute to me. "Cheers, Mrs. Jensen."

"I'm assuming that the two of you have discussed where you'll next be moving," Liam's mother pipes in from nowhere as I take my seat again.

"Moving?" Liam asks as an answer.

"Yes, Liam. With a baby on the way, I don't think that it would be wise to do it alone. Surely Isla hasn't cared for another human being before."

"Mother, you can go fuck yourself because Isla and I will be staying in Chicago, and she's going to be the best goddamn mother—one who will not lie about our child's upbringing and relationships. She won't abandon the child either. I'm going to ask you politely to leave if you cannot keep your mouth—as well as your checkbook—closed."

That earns a gasp out of her, and her eyes move to mine again, burning into me until I shift and look up at Liam.

"I'm sorry," he says and places his hand on my stomach, "you're going to be a remarkable mother."

I watch as his mother excuses herself, and Delaney follows her out of the room just as our meals arrive.

I jump when my seat starts to move until I notice that Liam is pulling my chair up against his, but he doesn't seem satisfied because he reaches out for me and lifts me onto his lap effortlessly. I lean against his chest and breathe all of him in. He smells like mine. Masculine. Delicious. Mouthwatering. Jensen.

"I can't wait until I get to curl up with you on the couch and just be," I say.

"We'll get there tomorrow. Plus, I have a gift for you."

"For me?"

"Yeah."

I sit up as a weary smile crosses my face. "Are you going to tell me or do I have to get down on my knees and blow you right here, right now, and suck it out of you?"

He casts a glance to the others who are eating and involved in their individual conversations before attempting to answer me.

"I'd prefer if you got down onto your knees, but seeing as neither one of us likes sharing, I'll compromise."

"And what would that involve?"

"If your dress wasn't so damn long and tight, I'd ask to touch you, but seeing as it is, I'm going to ask that you allow me to bury myself in you on our plane ride home whenever and however many times I want."

"You've got yourself a deal, dickweed. Now tell me what you've been holding back."

He reaches into his pocket and pulls out his phone. With a few taps of his finger, he pulls up a picture of a beautiful four-story home with a white stone face and black window frames. It's a modern build, with two windows as large as rooms looking out onto the street. It's undeniably stunning.

He swipes a finger across the screen to the next image. This one is of the back of the house, and it's just as gorgeous. There's a large garden and a private pool area as well.

"What is this?"

"This, Mrs. Jensen, is our new home."

"What?" I squeal and grab the phone from his hands. I go back and forth between the two images for a minute before I stare up at him. "Is this . . . is this the house that you were building?"

"It is, with two slight differences."

"Oh?"

"Yeah. Firstly, it's ours, and secondly, there's one room in there that has yet to be decorated. Its walls are white, and the room is empty. I wanted you to decide what goes into our nursery."

The words that I want to say refuse to come, so I do the next best thing. I kiss him. I kiss him because I'm more than grateful for everything he does. For who he is. For marrying me today.

"I want you happy, Isla."

"I'm beyond happy."

"What do you say that we get out of here?"

"Right now? I haven't even eaten."

"Ah. I keep forgetting how fucking important food is to you now. Eat up, doll, because I need something sweet to eat later."

I squirm on his lap and reach for the roll on his plate, place a little butter on it, and bite into the warm French bread. It's possibly the best bread that I've ever had.

"Liam," I groan once I've swallowed, and he chuckles before leaning in and taking a bite of what is now my roll.

"Hey! Back off, buddy."

He reaches over and pulls my plate over as well. I finish up my bread roll and grab the second off of my plate before he can.

"Don't fuck up my dress, dickweed. I'm going to have it framed."

"Framed? Can they do that?"

"Yes, of course they can."

"Where's it going to go?"

"In our closet?"

"Ours?"

"Is that okay?"

"Yeah. I just liked hearing you say that something was ours."

I smack his chest, and he reaches for the glass of whiskey that was just placed in front of him.

"What is it?" he asks.

"It's a Balvenie 50-Year-Old," Wade says as he and Hadley each take a drink from their tumblers.

"Assholes. All of you are assholes, and in seven and a half months, I'm going to outdrink all of you. Be prepared to drown in my whiskey while you sink underneath the table."

"I'm unsure if you'll be able to handle much after giving birth, Isla," Wade says, and I give him the best damn evil eye that I can manage.

"That's cute."

"Fuck you," I hiss out through a smile and turn to Liam.

I lean over and kiss Liam after he takes a drink of the lus-ciously fragrant liquid. He tastes of lemons, oranges, honey, and vanilla, and I swear, I'm about to drool.

"Good, huh?" Liam asks as he licks my lips.

"So good," I croon.

"That's cheating," Hadley says through a giggle, and I stick my tongue out at her.

"Trust me, nothing tastes better than whiskey and Liam."

"I beg to differ. Nothing tastes better than whiskey and Wade."

I roll my eyes as the two of them lock lips before stealing the bite of steak from Liam that he was about to place into his mouth.

"Keep that up, and I'll spank this ass on the plane as well."

"Is that a dare or a promise?"

"Both," he growls into my ear and just for that, I grind my ass into his crotch, feeling his semi turn into a full-on erection. I shift on his lap until I can feel his length resting against my sex. I decide to stay in this position until he moves.

All throughout dinner and dessert, though, he doesn't shift an inch.

My panties are soaked, and I'm only going to guess that I'll be able to lick up his pre-cum as soon as he unzips his tuxedo pants in the hotel room.

Liam forfeits his ice cream to me, and I've never been more grateful because each scoop came with a gooey chocolate brownie, and I'm in a bliss-filled heaven. It's almost as good as sex. *Almost.*

We say our goodbyes to everyone after dinner. Connor swears that he'll be sure to make plans to visit us in Chicago. I get a hug from his dad, but not from his sister or mother. I wasn't surprised that she simply ignored me.

The stale bitch.

We say our goodbyes to Wade and Hadley who will be staying in London for the remainder of the week. Maybe we'll inspire them and Hadley will come back pregnant.

I'm tempted to say screw the plane ride home as his strong fingers run down my bare back as he strips me of my wedding dress in our hotel suite

Once he's done, I turn around in his arms and allow my dress to pool at my feet. His lips quirk up in one corner at seeing me in my panties and nothing else.

"I'm a fortunate bastard."

"That, my husband, you are."

He runs his fingers down the center of my torso until he reaches my damp white panties. He flicks my clitoris, and I jump in his arms at the sudden jolt of pleasure.

I watch him get down on his knees in front of me and lift my heeled feet one at a time so I could step out of my dress before he shoves my legs apart and covers my panties with his mouth.

"Liam."

"Let me have this, and we'll go. I need to taste what belongs to me."

"Okay," I whimper as he slides my panties to the side and sucks me into his mouth. My hands scramble to hold onto his hair as he begins to eat me. My legs start to tremble and go numb as the pleasure swims through my veins. Liam moves his hands to my thighs to hold me steady as he takes what he wants from me.

"You taste incredible."

"Liam!"

"Don't worry, baby. I'll take care of you."

The moment his tongue runs up my sex again, I swear I can see the light because he intensifies how hard his tongue is working me, and I want to scream out in decadent pleasure.

"Give it to me, Isla. We made the deal of a lifetime today. You owe me this."

His tongue starts to flick against me at a faster pace, and I can't breathe anymore. I start tugging on his hair and moaning as my orgasm builds up from the very tips of my toes.

The moment it hits me he glances up to watch as I throw my head back and scream until I can't fill my lungs with a sufficient amount of air to scream any longer.

He doesn't remove his tongue from me until my body stops twitching with each touch of his.

I loosen my fingers in his hair as he helps me out of my wet panties before standing up and pulling my naked body against his tuxedo-clad one.

"I love you, Isla."

"Love you," I whisper back and rest my head against his stout chest.

"Do you have another pair of panties? Ones that I can ruin on the plane?"

"I do."

He smacks my ass before picking me up and carrying me to the bed before he grabs my new suitcase, which is filled with clothing, and places it beside me.

Instead of wrestling with clothes to get dressed, I watch him remove his tuxedo, and I want to jump him right now, but I know that if I do, I won't have time to stop by and see Quinn before we have to be in the air.

"Stop staring and get dressed, doll," he says without having to look over his shoulder at me.

"Fine," I grumble and pull out a matching pair of white silk

La Perla lingerie items, a gray knitted sweater, and black Capri pants.

I get dressed slowly as he pulls on a pair of jeans, a black shirt, and his favorite leather jacket. I take my time as he picks, zips, hangs, and bags up my wedding dress for me to take along with us.

Once I get up, I decide to slip my feet back into my white wedding heels and gather what little I have around the hotel room before ducking into the bathroom to pull the pins from my hair and ruffle it up a little so it falls around my shoulders.

When I walk back out, Liam is looking at the wedding ring on his finger, spinning it around and around before he looks up and stands.

"Are you ready?"

"Take me home, Mr. Jensen."

"It'll be my pleasure, Mrs. Jensen."

We're allowed back into the hospital where some of the women from the compound are still recovering. The majority of them, though, have been flown to the safe houses closest to their homes.

"Go right on in," the nurse says and pulls the door open.

"Thank you," I tell her as Liam and I walk into the dimly lit room.

"Quinn?"

She turns over and the smile on her face is beautiful when she sees us.

"I didn't know that you two were coming back."

"Do you honestly think that I would have left without saying goodbye?"

"I wanted to think that you wouldn't."

"Well, we're here, and it was Liam's idea to bring you some

things. I guessed on clothing sizes, but he insisted on a phone and ID."

"An ID?"

"He has his sources, apparently."

Liam sets the basket on the seat next to her bed before running his hand around my waist when he moves beside me.

"I'm glad to see that you're well. Isla was telling me that you weren't sure what you wanted to do once you get out of here."

"I really have no idea. I've completely lost the plot."

"Well," he says, "I've programmed both my and Isla's information into your phone, and when you're ready, I'd like to be the one to help you get started wherever you'd like. You'll find a credit card in there as well. Please use it to get started on your new life. You saved my wife as well as my child. I owe you my life, Quinn."

"Your wife? When did . . . I didn't know that you two were married?"

"It happened earlier today," I tell her and hold up my left hand for her to see my two rings kissing each other.

"Bloody hell, congratulations, you two."

"Thank you," Liam replies, and I smile down at her.

"We need to get going, but please know that we're in your corner."

"Sure, and thank you for everything."

"You're welcome," Liam says and kisses the side of my head before pulling away and letting go of me long enough so I'm able to lean down and hug her once more.

"Promise me that I'll see you soon, Quinn?"

"I have no doubt. Now go have fun with that gorgeous man of yours and if you find someone who doesn't mind dealing with a damaged girl, send him my way."

"You don't have to rush into things, Quinn. It's been years

since you've been free. Right now, you need to live your life for you and only you. Focus on what you want out of life."

"Thank you, I will. Text me when you land?"

"I'll text you from Liam's number since my new one is back in the States."

"Sounds good. Have a safe flight."

"We will, thank you." I hug her once more and then step back into Liam and we lace our fingers together before walking out of her room and out of the hospital that has helped start the healing process for so many women.

I didn't believe that many things about Liam would ever surprise me, but he did. I had no idea that he was going out of his way to make today as beautiful as it was. So, yeah, I owe the dickweed a blowey or two.

On our flight back to Chicago, he managed to ravage me a total of three times, and each time he made my body scream with tingling nerves on multiple occasions.

I'm currently curled up on my side against his gloriously naked body as I run my fingers up and down the ridges of his abdomen. He pulls me closer and adjusts the blanket over the two of us on the couch.

Liam is someone who I've always let my guard down with, and he's one of the few people who show me that he's okay with it. He loves me with no regrets, and if you told me six months ago that I'd be married to this asshole, I would have bet my life savings against you, but here I am.

I'm not hurting, and I'm not suffering while he holds me like this. I'm safe.

"Does it feel good to be home?" he asks as he kisses the top of my head.

"It does, but nothing feels quite as incredible as being in your arms. What are we going to do with the loft, by the way?"

"We can keep it or rent it out. I'll leave that up to you. I know how much this place means to you."

I close my eyes and nuzzle into him. "I'll need to think about it, but I cannot wait to see our home."

"We can head over after I sleep off the impressive number of endorphins currently vibing through my system."

"Deal."

When I wake up again, I'm alone on the couch. I stretch out my sore limbs before tossing the blanket off of myself. Walking naked into the kitchen, I smile when I see Liam opening a Chinese-takeout carton and I perch on the barstool just as he looks up.

"I don't think I'll ever get sick of seeing you like that."

I reach over the island and grab a fortune cookie, open it, and take a bite before Liam shoots me a glare.

"What?"

"Aren't you supposed to open those after we eat? Surely that cardboard shit can't be good for the baby."

I look down at it in my hand before pulling out the fortune and casting the remainder of the cookie aside.

"What does it say?"

"Something about counting my blessings. What did you get us to eat?"

"All of your favorites. I wasn't sure what you'd still enjoy."

I lean over the kitchen island and crook my finger at him to come closer. He complies, and I kiss him once before sitting back down and opening one of the three containers he takes out of the carrier.

Thirty minutes later, I'm stuffed, but still craving something. Fried pickles? It's hard to say, really.

"Go get dressed, and I'll take you home."

"Is it done? Like, can we stay there tonight?"

"Would you like to?" he asks as he steps between my bare thighs.

"I'd love to."

"Go pack a bag, baby doll."

I squeal and push him back slightly so that I'm able to jump off of the stool. I run up the flight of stairs to the bathroom and turn on the shower to clean off the residual sex before I start packing.

As the water falls on my skin, I think back to what we've both endured, and what ultimately brought us together. The steam slowly fills the room as I bathe my skin in a fragrant body wash. The hot water seems to calm me down after the orgasms that consumed me earlier, but my mind keeps drifting to the *how*. How we got to where we are today, and if anything would be different if life took each of us down a different street.

"Liam?" I call from the shower, and minutes later, I hear him step into the bathroom, and he pulls the shower door open.

"Are you okay?" His concerned eyes flash down my body in search of something out of place.

"Yes, I was just wondering."

"About?"

I massage the shampoo into my hair and sigh as the water hits my breasts at the perfect pressure. "Do you think that she would mind?"

"Who? Quinn?"

"No. My sister."

I move underneath the water spray and let it wash away the suds laced through my hair. The regimented routine of showering doesn't slow as he replies to me.

"As in Chloe?"

"Yes."

He opens the glass shower door wider before he steps in under the spray with me, wrapping both of his arms around my naked body.

"I'm not sure how to answer that, Isla. What I do know, though, is that she would have done anything to finally meet you. I should have made it happen before everything took place. I should have pushed her more after each excuse that she fed me, but I didn't."

"Liam, none of what happened is your fault. Not with what my mother chose, nor what happened to Chloe. Plus, without you, I wouldn't have even known that I had a sister."

He reaches out to grab the bottle of conditioner, squeezing some out into the palm of his hand before returning it to its place. He starts to massage my scalp with his fingers as he begins to speak.

"A lot wouldn't have happened if I wasn't around, doll, but I cannot change the past."

I can tell that he's trying to figure out what to say, so I let him have a moment of silence as I close my eyes and enjoy the feel of his fingers massage my scalp.

"Honestly, I don't think that she would mind. What I do know, though, and as fucked up as this is going to sound, I believe it to be true. I think that my initial attraction to her was because she looked like you. Sure, I loved her, but when I think back to those emotions that I felt for her all of those years ago, none of them compare to what I currently feel for you. Not even in the slightest."

"Liam."

"Trust me, Isla."

"I do, you know that."

"Good, now listen to me and absorb what I'm going to tell you wholeheartedly."

I nod and move back under the warm spray as he helps me to get the silky conditioner out of the strands of my hair.

"I recall the first day that I saw her. I was drunk and high out of my mind at a beach bonfire, and you walked up to me in a fucking string bikini. I about fucking flipped to see you in Australia, but when you opened your mouth . . . it wasn't you, and then I drunkenly noticed all of the differences."

"Like what?"

"There were a lot. Her voice wasn't as velvety smooth as yours, she had a good four inches on you, and her hair was cut just above her shoulders. As long as I've known you, you've never had it that short, and I doubt that you ever will."

I chuckle because he's right. I love my locks too much to haphazardly chop them off.

"We sat and spoke for a long time. I remember showing her a picture of you, and she froze up on me. I'm not sure if that's when all of the pieces fell into place for her, but when I met her mother, I knew. I remembered seeing a picture of her in your dorm room—the one that you got after your grandmother's death. You would stare at it and give it the finger each time you walked in."

"You saw me do all of that?"

"Babe, I might have almost failed out of college, but I was fucking observant when it came to you."

"Just me?" I ask curiously.

"Just you."

I lean up on my toes and wrap my arms around his neck before I let him continue.

"Go on."

"Are you sure that you're okay with this?"

"I'm fine. Are you?"

"All good. All right, so, when we were finally alone later that

evening, I asked her what the hell just happened, and she told me
that she was told that you died right after birth."

"What?"

"Yeah. I was fucking fuming, so I left Chloe and went and
sought her out . . . your mother. I quite literally forced her to
take a seat and tell me exactly what was going on."

"And that's when you heard the story? The one that my
grandmother made into a nursery rhyme when I was a little
girl?"

"Yeah."

Both of us still for a moment as I try to recall the opening
lines of it.

"It was something like *'Souls alike yet plucked away, two children not meant together to stay. A girl with a smile, one with a frown.
A world upright, and one upside down,'* but I'm not sure if I can remember the rest of it."

He chuckles and kisses the top of my wet head. "That's kind
of fucked up. Did you ever find out what happened?"

"Yes. My grandmother had left a letter with her lawyers for
when she passed."

"And?"

I blow out a weighted breath because I've not shared this
with anyone before. "And she told me everything that was kept
from me. Both of our mothers were complete fuck-ups, Liam."

"Tell me what it said, doll."

"Well, what it comes down to is simple, really. She chose to
follow a man instead of taking care of her children. He told her
that it was him or the girls, and she somehow managed to bribe
him into allowing her to take one of us with her. She took Chloe,
obviously, because I was sick at the time and the doctors said that
I wouldn't make it. So she left me with my grandmother and
went on with her life. She disappeared and never looked back. It

also said that Chloe had passed away days after our separation, but it's because of you that I know it's not the truth."

"That's beyond fucked up."

"Tell me about it," I say with an eye roll and bite his jaw. "Enough with the heavy, though, okay?"

"All right, but answer me one more question."

"Shoot."

"If life was different, and you were able to meet your twin sister, would you have still married me if, for example, I dated but didn't become engaged to her?"

"Without a doubt, Jensen. Who knows? You could have turned out to be her in-the-moment man, but you're my happily ever after. That little college crush held more steam behind it than either of us knew."

"Apparently so. Thank you," he says as he kisses my wet collarbone before looking back up into my eyes. "Let me finish up in here, and we'll head to our place."

"All right."

I slip out of his wet grip and leave the confines of the shower to get ready to quite literally see my future.

We pull up to the house in Liam's Maserati, and I have to remind myself that this is ours. This is our life now. Fuck pixie dust and fairy tales. This castle deserves a princess, but I'm the best that it'll get.

"What do you think?" he asks as he shuts off the engine that seems to make me weak in the knees.

"It's gorgeous. Holy shit, I can't believe that this is it. I mean, all of this was your design, right?"

"A large majority of it was, yeah. I wanted to keep it as close to the house in Sydney as possible. I've missed the ocean views and all of the natural light, so I had to make sure that we would be able to see the lake as much as possible."

"Won't it get cold in the winter with all of those windows?"

"No, they're all custom-made thermals."

"You've thought of everything, haven't you?"

"Barely. Come on, I want to show you inside, and I need you to pick out some furniture as well. We can bring your stuff over, of course, but we need to fill a few more rooms."

"You just want my bed, you fiend."

"I do. It's the most comfortable shit that I've ever slept on."

I giggle and lay a soft kiss on his cheek before getting out of the vehicle and meeting him in front of it. He laces his fingers with mine and hands me one of the three house keys that he's holding before leading me up the stairs to the front door of our home.

"Open her up."

I insert the key into the hole and turn it; feeling the lock disengage, I push the door open and gasp at what's in front of me.

He leans down and whispers in my ear, "Welcome home, Mrs. Jensen."

Before I understand what's going on, he lifts me up effortlessly and steps over the threshold and into our place.

I look around as he carries me through the open floor plan. There are large canvas paintings hanging from the wall at the far end of the living room, and God, it's immaculate. The dark floors beneath us add a kind of depth to the room that I'm suddenly in love with.

I cannot believe that we're going to live here. *Together.* I cup his strong jaw and wait for him to look down at me. When he does, he lowers my body and sets me down on my feet without saying a word.

"It's stunning, Liam."

"You think so?"

"Without a doubt."

I turn around in a slow circle, taking in as much of it as I can. He's taken our new home, the one that he helped design, and turned it into much more than just a space to live. He's left his mark on every wall, corner, and surface. The house doesn't just express who he is as a person: it embodies him. He's captured me as well, and it's dauntingly beautiful. He's stayed with my color scheme of white, gray, and black with splashes of shades of red throughout.

Perhaps I had to live through all of that shit to be able to come back here and truly appreciate what I have in life. To see the beauty in everyday wonders rather than searching for it in places that won't ever transform into more. Instead of waiting for my happily ever after, I've been actively seeking it out.

Through all of the years, I realize that each road I took led me to Liam, and the moment I finally followed it instead of taking a detour, I started living.

We walk through the entirety of the house together. I've counted a total of six bedrooms and eight bathrooms throughout. My favorite room though is the only vacant one in the house.

He leads me into the vast, empty nursery before letting go of my hand and taking a step back from me as he looks around the large open space.

"I can see you in here. Seated over there by the window," he says softly, gesturing to the corner with an incredible view of the lake. "I can see you holding her in your arms." His eyes close as if he imagines it. "She'll look just like you, and I'll be able to come home to you and her every day of my life."

"Liam."

"Isla," he says my name in a whisper, and it's like he's calling for me.

I run into his muscular arms because I hate the couple of feet that distances us from one another. He catches me and lifts me up so that I'm able to lock myself around him completely.

"You're everything," I confess.

"You think so?"

"Definitely."

Twenty-Four

Liam

IT IS DEMENTED how time stretches and contracts depending on what's happening in life. The two weeks that it took me to find Isla and get her away from the sick fuck who took her felt like the slowest and fastest grouping of days ever.

The weeks that have passed since finding her have flown by and have been filled with an addictive amount of sex. If this little vixen wasn't already pregnant, then I'm sure she would have been after the number of times I've been consumed by that pussy.

As I finish up on my current project, I hear her arrive home as I run the wet paintbrush against the drywall once more to cover up the stark white color. I glance up from my position on the nursery room floor when she walks in holding two handfuls of shopping bags and looking guilty as hell. I throw a questioning glance at her, and she bites at the corner of her lip before speaking.

"In my defense, I was left unsupervised."

I set the paintbrush down and close the can of cream-colored paint before I wipe off my hands and get to my feet.

"Yeah? What did you get?" I cross the empty room to get to her and wind my arms around her midsection, holding her against my shirtless torso.

"I . . . uhm."

"You . . . ?"

She swallows hard as I move my lips to her neck and nip at her earlobe.

"I wanted to be prepared once we came back from the sixteen-week appointment today."

"And what happens at this appointment?"

"You . . . uhm," I can feel the muscles in her neck work to swallow as I lay my lips against her skin. "You . . . Oh God. Liam."

"Isla," I breathe out against her as she drops the bags of baby stuff onto the floor to wrap her arms around my neck. I lean into her and brush my lips against hers in a tease of demanding passion.

"Please?"

"Right here?"

She runs her hands down the column of my neck, over my shoulders and to my chest as I prolong the moment before kissing her.

"Anywhere."

"Are you sure?"

"Definitely."

"Then allow me to take you on your honeymoon."

My statement seems to catch her off guard because she pulls back and scowls at me. "I've told you that I don't feel comfortable with traveling yet, Liam."

Here we go again.

"What if I take you somewhere that you've already been?"

She stares up at me as I lean my forehead against hers.

"I mean, I suppose that wouldn't hurt."

She's compromising?

"It won't. I know that you're scared to leave again. I understand why and all of your reasoning behind it, but don't overanalyze this, doll. Let it be, and let's go have some sex on the beach before I change my mind on taking you where I plan on taking you."

"Where are we going, Jensen?"

"Hmm, would you really like to know?"

She smacks my chest, and I lean toward her to steal a kiss from her harlot-red lips.

"All right. I was thinking about heading down to Sydney. We can spend as long as you'd like back at the house down under."

"You'd want to do that?"

"I would. Plus, I forgot my guitar there. I need to grab it if I plan on playing for that little squirt inside you."

"Yes," she squeals and hugs me harder.

"Good. Now, get your shit together, or we're going to be late to another doctor's appointment."

That earns me a smack to my chest again. "Liam, it's not my fault that I needed to have you make me come in the parking lot before we went in."

"Of course not, doll." I wink and pinch her ass before moving my hands around to her stomach. She started showing around thirteen weeks. We just woke up one day and instead of her flat stomach, her midsection grew with our child. She places her hands over mine and beams down at me.

"Are you ready to find out what we're having?" she asks eagerly.

"I have already told you that it's going to be a girl."

"You're absurd. Are you ready to go?"

"I am." I let go of her to grab my shirt off of the side of the ladder that I was using earlier and watch as she walks in front of me.

Fuck, I've loved watching her unfold and become the woman she was before she was pulled into the depths of slavery. She's thriving lately and unquestionably glowing despite her vulnerability. I cannot control what I feel for her when she smiles at me as she is right now from over her shoulder.

She lights something up inside of me that I'd like to think has always been present, but I chose not to acknowledge it. Now, though, it's all I can fucking think about. There's no controlling these damn emotions around her.

Once we're shown back into an examination room, she strips down in front of me, and I have to say my grandmother's name on repeat again, so I don't get a damn woody before her doctor walks in.

It's highly unsuccessful.

She hops up onto the table but halts her movements when she sees my cock struggling against my jeans.

"If you bring that joystick over here, we'll definitely get kicked out today."

I take a step back and give her my most innocent grin. "We don't have time for that if you want to find out what we're having and make it to the Cubs game on time."

She grumbles to herself as she lies down and pulls the paper blanket over her lower half just as there's a knock on the door. It swings open, and her doctor and a nurse walk in to greet us.

"Welcome back, Mrs. Jensen. Are we ready to find out what the gender is?"

"More than ever. I'll even bet Liam over there that it's a boy."

"Oh yeah?" I say. "What are you wagering?"

"If it's a boy then we get to stay home for our honeymoon. If it's a girl, then we'll travel to Sydney for as long as you want and do whatever you want."

I chuckle and step closer to her to take her hand as the doctor moves the sheet out of the way and applies a good amount of gel to her raised stomach.

"Deal?" she asks.

"You're going to lose this one, but deal."

We each watch the monitor as the picture comes to life on the screen. The three-dimensional image is sepia in tone, and I'm almost brought to my knees at the small human being in front of me.

Isla squeezes my hand as the doctor moves the wand around to get a better angle.

"Well?" Isla asks impatiently.

The doctor looks up and smiles at us before speaking. "Mr. and Mrs. Jensen, I'm delighted to tell you that you'll both be traveling to Sydney for your honeymoon. You're having a little girl."

"What?" Isla squeals and almost jumps up from the bed as the tears brim around her eyes. "A girl? We're having a girl? Liam . . . she's . . . are you sure? It's a girl?"

I chuckle and lean in to kiss her slowly. "I hate to say that I told you so, but I told you so, baby doll."

"I don't even care," she cries and reaches up to wrap her arms around my neck. "We're having a girl," she exhales.

"We are. You and me, babe."

"Always," she counters.

The remainder of the appointment passes effortlessly as we listen to her heart beat and I try to convince Isla that our little girl won't leave my sight until she's fucking forty.

Twenty-Five

Isla

THE SHADOWS THAT once tied me down in a captive fog have died out. With the help of Liam and a therapist, I've managed to stay off the depression and anxiety medication. Sure, I still have way too much emotion to handle at times and being pregnant doesn't help that for a second, but I'm pulling through.

I'm merely glad that the poison that once filled my veins with venom is no longer in sight. My body is no longer just a heart beating warm blood through my veins. It's filled with so much more logical hope and tangible love. Liam has helped me through the impenetrable darkness since day one, and he's finally brought me up and into the beams of light.

I'm not a defective person. I'm not the darkness that lived inside of me. I'm not the nagging, clawing, mind-numbing disease. I'm simply myself. I run my fingers over the pink Chicago Cubs onesie that Liam and I bought before the game yesterday and smile to myself.

This little girl is going to become the definition of spoiled. I haven't even met her yet, but she makes me feel complete. I might have been terrified of her when I first found out about the pregnancy, but I believe that she was the final piece in my armor to shut out the murky darkness. For her, I'll do more than survive. I'll live.

I'm currently seated in one of the wingbacks in Blended when Eden walks up to me. "Hey, I thought that Liam was coming by?"

I check my watch and shrug. "I'm sure that he'll be here soon. He was insisting on meeting here before we head out to lunch, though. Maybe he just wants some whiskey before we leave."

"I'm sure that he'll be here soon. Do you need anything?"

"Just a glass of water will be great, thanks."

"Sure thing, then you better show me that new ultrasound that you got yesterday. I cannot wait to see her little face."

"How did you know the gender?"

She pauses as she's about to step away from me. "Uhh. Lucky guess?"

"Liam?" I ask, and she regretfully nods her head. "The bastard."

She laughs before walking away, shaking her head.

By the time Liam walks into Blended, Wade is here as well, and we're deep in conversation about when to have the next member's social.

"Hey doll," Liam says as he rounds my seat and kisses me on the cheek. "How's it going, Brass?"

"It's going well. Your wife here was just telling me how much of a fucking ass you are."

"Was not," I counter and reach out to take Liam's hand. "What took you so long?"

"Do you really want to know?

"Of course I do."

Wade excuses himself with a smile on his pretty mug before he walks over to where Hadley is seated reading a paperback with her legs drawn up to her chest. She beams up at him when he approaches her and makes room for him on the couch that she's occupying before leaning into him and taking his whiskey tumbler.

I look away then because it just seems too personal to watch. "Doll?"

"Hmm? Sorry, I got distracted."

"I noticed." He pulls something out of the small bag that he was carrying and hands it to me. "This is why I was late."

I look down and take it from him, unfolding the soft white material before realizing that it's another onesie with the words *Whiskey Made Momma Do It* on it.

"Oh God," I giggle and lean over to lock our lips together, taking my time to explore his mouth. "I love it. She will as well."

"Good. There might have been another reason why I was late, though."

"And what would that be, Jensen?" I ask as I fold the onesie and return it to the bag he brought it in.

"Me," a voice says from behind me. I know exactly who it is before my body can even move, her accent giving her away. The tears spring to my eyes as I get up and face her head-on while cupping the palm of my hand over my mouth.

"You're here? Holy shit."

Quinn shrugs and walks around the seat to pull me into a full hug. Between the two of us, I'm not quite sure who is crying harder. Her shoulders shudder as we share an overwhelming amount of emotion. We've kept in touch since I got my new phone, but I had no idea that she was planning on flying over.

I pull away from her but don't let go as I inspect her up and down. I feel like it's the first time that I'm physically seeing who my friend is for who she is, and she's gorgeous. Her light blonde curls are tight and silky smooth. A dusting of freckles pops against her fair skin that looks incredibly vibrant and healthy. With what little makeup that she has on, she hides the scars that

I know are there, but even if I could see them, it wouldn't matter. She's beautiful in a classical way. "You look lovely, Quinn. How long will you be staying? You're staying with us, right? Right, Liam?" I turn to look at him.

He stands and walks up to me to place a kiss on my cheek. "If that's what you both want. Once she's gotten on her feet, I thought that she could take care of the loft for us."

"Wait, what?"

"Surprise?" Quinn says and smiles up at Liam. "Your husband has been helping me a lot more than I've been letting on. Aside from paying for therapy and my medical bills, he was paying for my apartment in London as well. But after a long conversation with him last week while you were passed out beside him, we came up with the idea of moving me here. I don't have anyone back in England, so really there's no point to being there when the only two people whom I trust are here in Chicago."

"How . . . Liam? How have you not told me any of this? You couldn't keep your mouth shut about my being pregnant, but you can make all of this happen?"

"Just know that I care and that I love you, Isla," he says as he places his arm around my waist.

"He stated that he'd help me find a job here as well, but I'd like to talk to you about that, though. I'm not so sure that Liam will be able to help me with it."

"Of course. Holy shit, you can work here. I wouldn't mind hiring you on at Blended."

"Here?" she asks as she looks around the library. "What is it? A pub?"

I giggle before answering her. "In a way, yes, but it's more of a library. We sell the world's best whiskeys here."

"Whiskey? Oh no, I cannot stomach that shit stuff. I'm actually more into fashion than anything else. I'm sure that there's something that I'll be able to do in the city, right?"

I gasp and clap my hands excitedly. "Holy—I have the best idea."

"Yeah?" Liam asks.

"Oh yes. Come on, I know just the person that we need to talk about it."

"Right now?" Liam asks and squeezes my side.

"Yes, and then we can go get lunch or whatever she wants to do."

"All right, eager beaver."

"Okay, good. I'll be right back."

Liam watches me warily as I turn around and march my pregnant ass over to Wade and Hadley who look like they are consumed in their own whiskey-laced world.

"Brass?"

Wade looks up at me and grins. "Is everything all right?"

"Yes. God, yes. That's Quinn Welsh. She was in the hole with me, and she's possibly one of the reasons that I got out of there in one piece and with my baby girl in tow."

"A girl?" Hadley pipes in and moves to the edge of the seat.

"Yes, it's a girl. We found out yesterday." I beam at the two of them.

"Holy shit, congratulations. So does this mean that I can get Lola Marc to make her little outfits? And Wade here gets to put up with a little Isla."

"Absolutely, and that's kind of my reason for interrupting your little lovefest."

Hadley turns away to look at Wade. They stare into each other's eyes for a moment before she turns back to me. "What is it that we can help you with?"

"Well, I was hoping that Lola might have a spot open at her boutique for a new employee? Quinn said that she'd love to delve into that industry."

"I know that Lola would love to help. I'll send her a text and ask if she's there. Maybe you can swing by now if she is."

"I'd love to do that. Thank you, Hadley."

"Of course."

I watch her exchange a couple of text messages before she looks up at me again. "You're all set to drop by."

"Thank you!"

I kiss Wade's cheek before walking back over to Liam and Quinn who are deep in discussion about her moving into the loft.

"All right. We're all set, and we need to make a stop after lunch."

"Where are we going?" Quinn asks as she blows a spiral curl out of her face.

"It's a surprise."

After lunch, Liam left the two of us to head over to Lola Marc's Boutique, claiming that he had some work for RW to do, but I know otherwise. That man is probably off buying even more baby shit than what I walked in with yesterday.

My phone goes off as I put my Porsche into park. I pull it out of my pocket to check it as Quinn glances out of the window.

Does this mean that I'm getting some serious head tonight? We might have to keep it down, though. I might appreciate your screams, but I doubt that Quinn will.

I can't help but giggle as I type out my reply: *It means that you'll be up all night, yes. You might need to gag me in order to stop my screams. I enjoy what you do to my body too much.*

We jump out of the vehicle and walk over to the entrance of the store.

"Welcome to Lola Marc's. It's relatively new, but everyone who is anyone in Chicago now buys from here. It's well on its way into the national market, and the next sector that they plan on overtaking is international. It's thriving, really."

"It's stunning," Quinn says as we walk inside. She turns to face me while walking backward and bumps right into a tall, scruffy-looking man.

"Jesus," he says as his phone is knocked out of his hand.

"Bloody hell, I'm dreadfully sorry." Quinn spins around on the balls of her feet, and I watch as the two of them go speechless. They both stare at each other in a brief moment of silence as I get a better view of this gorgeous man.

I know that I've seen him before, but for some reason, I cannot place his dark blonde hair and hipster-looking outfit.

"Good God, Holden, don't scare my customers away," Lola yells from behind him.

He doesn't turn around.

He doesn't even respond as he refuses to take his eyes off of Quinn.

I chew on my inner lip and walk around the two of them to Lola as she watches them take each other in.

"Hey, it's good to see you again."

"It's Isla, right?"

"It is."

She gives me a polite hug and folds her arms over her chest. "I'm sorry about that dummy. He was just picking up Owen's phone. He left it in my purse after we had breakfast this morning."

"Owen? The man that you were dating on New Year's Eve?"

"The very one. Holden's his brother. We're still not official or anything, but I guess that we're together. I don't know. He's got some commitment issues."

I turn back to her as Quinn and Holden start to speak to each other.

"I'm sure that he'll come around. I mean, I didn't expect to get married to Liam-fucking-Jensen, but here I am."

"Wait . . . you two got married? Does Addy know?"

I bite down on my lip and shrug, and it's now that she notices my pregnant belly.

"Holy shit . . . he knocked you up?"

"That he did," I say with a giggle as I start to braid my hair over my shoulder and tie the end off. "So I wanted to talk to you about Quinn. She just flew in from England today. Now, I'm not sure if you know what happened to me, but she was involved as well."

"I know, and I'm so sorry. Hadley told me about it, and she texted me about Quinn. I just wanted to meet her before I said yes, but she seems to be preoccupied with Hold."

"It's all right and thank you. I know that she's going to freak out. I'll grab her before Holden over there tries something on her."

Lola laughs as Holden hands Quinn something before shaking her hand and walking around her and then out the front door. I watch him throw a glance over his shoulder at her while he walks away from the storefront.

The faint curve on Quinn's lips that's slowly turning into a beam is one of the few times that I've seen her smile from the heart.

"Well, well, well, what was that about?"

She tries her damnedest to wipe the cheesy grin off of her lips, but it doesn't work worth a shit. "I don't smoke, but I could do with a fag right about now."

"A what?"

"A smoke. A cigarette."

I giggle and nudge her side. "While you're in the U.S. you might want to refrain from calling it a fag . . . and yeah, he's not bad looking."

"Holy balls, he is flipping gorgeous. Isla, I would shag him."

I burst into a fit of laughter, and she joins in with me just as Lola walks up to us. I manage to straighten myself up, but Quinn is still flushed and blushing at the same time.

"Hi, you must be Quinn? I'm Lola Marc."

"Oh, goodness, I'm sorry, yes, I'm Quinn Welsh. It's nice to meet you, Lola. You're the owner, correct?"

"I am indeed, and I would like to offer you a position here if you'd like it."

"That'd be brilliant. I'm so sorry to meet you like this—I'm knackered after that flight."

Lola smiles and shakes her head. "Nonsense. You look great, and I'd love to have you help me out. I'll have you work every aspect of the boutique as well as my private orders, and you can decide on what you enjoy the most."

"I'd love that. Thank you."

"You're welcome. Shall we trade contact information before you fall asleep on me or maybe fall into a daze and follow Hold out the door?"

They laugh together as I look around and pick out a few items while they trade information and small talk.

A little over three hours later, Quinn is passed out in one of the guest bedrooms while Liam is asleep on the couch with his head on my lap when his phone starts to ring. I glance over from my position next to him to see if it's anyone I know. My stomach drops at the sight of Adriana Hugh's name and bikini-clad body on his screen.

I look down at him and ruffle his hair a bit. "Liam?"

"Mmm?" he grunts out and turns to face my stomach. He places a kiss on it before opening his eyes and moving a hand underneath my loose-fitting tank to touch my bare skin.

"Adriana is calling you."

"Huh?" He gets up and rubs his eyes to clear them of sleep just as his phone stops vibrating. I hand it to him anyway and get up to cross the room to the kitchen where I pull out a pint of chocolate ice cream and a spoon before leaning against the island counter to dive into the thick, decadent treat.

"Isla?"

"Mmm?" I answer as I put a spoonful into my mouth and close my eyes as the sweet creaminess starts to melt on my tongue. It's silky . . . heavenly . . . blissful . . . and luxuriant until it's interrupted by my dickweed.

"You're upset with me because she called?" he asks from a few feet away.

I tilt my head to the side and shrug as I scoop another spoonful into my mouth. I moan out softly as the wintry mixture overtakes my taste buds again. Just as I'm about to suck down another mouthful, he grabs the spoon out of my hand and takes the container off of the counter before stepping back and leaning against the opposite one while facing me head-on.

"Don't you dare, Jensen."

"Or what?" he asks as he loads the spoon up with my favorite flavor.

"Or . . . I won't blow you for a month."

"Nah, doll, you're too horny to deny me that. I do, however, want you to speak to me. Why are you upset?"

I sigh and throw my head back before providing him with the truth, knowing that he's going to think of me as a pathetically covetous wife. "You have a picture of her in her bikini as her caller ID."

"Mrs. Jensen, do I sense a hint of jealousy?"

He sticks the spoon into the pint container, leaving it on the countertop, and closes the distance between us, lifting me onto the island before running his thumb over my bottom lip. His other hand pushes my legs apart so he can stand between them.

"Possibly, but why do you still have that picture?"

"Honestly? I didn't set it as her caller ID—she did. And I don't even recall taking it."

I stare down at the floor because I know that I'm being petulant, but I cannot help it. He's mine, damn it.

"You own me, Isla. Nobody else has ever had the privilege."

I cough out a laugh and nudge his chest. "I think that I need a little more chocolate."

He steps away from me for a moment, and when he's back, he's holding a spoonful of the chocolate goodness up to my lips.

"Take some."

I lean in to take a bite, but he pulls the spoon back and meets me with his lips instead. I move my hands up his defined chest to his rounded-out shoulders before he pulls back and places the spoon in front of me.

This time, he allows me to get the spoon into my mouth, but he pulls it out soon afterward. I moan once my lips slide closed and he leans in to place a peck against my now-cold lips before he feeds me more.

"Do you like it?"

"Yes."

"Given the choice, would you want my lips or more chocolate?"

"You," I whimper as he teases me with his lips against my neck when Quinn walks into the kitchen.

"Oh shit, I'm sorry. I have the worst timing out of anyone I know."

I pull away from him as she steps closer to us with her arms folded over her chest. I give her a welcoming smile as Liam places the remainder of the ice cream on the spoon into his mouth and runs his other hand up my bare thigh to the fabric of my spandex running shorts.

"You're fine. Can I get you anything?"

"Actually, I just came for some cold water, but I wouldn't mind a bite to eat."

"Help yourself," Liam says as he pinches my inner thigh and kisses my neck before moving back to the couch to grab his phone. I watch as he heads down to the basement where I know I'll hear the pounding of his fists against a leather punching bag soon.

"What would you like? I've pretty much got the entire store in here. Liam is great at meeting those late-night cravings. I could make us some pancakes?"

"He's pretty great, isn't he?"

I blush as I return the ice cream to the freezer. "He is."

Only once we are done cleaning up does Liam emerge from his workout session with a damp T-shirt and wet hair. He takes a seat on the couch, looking even more stressed than he was when he left to beat some sense into an inanimate object.

I walk over to him and sit on his lap while Quinn opts for the recliner to the side.

"What's eating at you?"

It takes him a few seconds to look up at me, and when he does, I can see that he's fighting to keep something in. "Liam? Please?"

He shakes his head, and I cup his face. "Talk to me? At least tell me what it's about?"

"I received an email from my new head of security at Remission Worldwide concerning Grady Kent."

My blood turns cold at his name.

"And?"

"And the fucker escaped from prison."

"Wait, I thought that your men took care of him?" I glance over to Quinn who is now listening to our conversation.

"No. Every other fucker who was down there met his fate the day we seized the compound, except for Kent."

"You spared him?"

"Not exactly. I wanted him to suffer, and he will. My men were the ones who found him after he escaped, and now he is in the sole custody of RW. They flew him down to Australia this evening. It's now my decision as to what happens with him. Before I was able to give them orders after the raid, the authorities got involved, and it was too risky to kill him in cold blood."

I glance at Quinn whose eyes are as wide as saucers.

"What are you going to do?" I ask and angle his face so that he'll actually look at me instead of speaking to the wall across the room.

"I have no idea, Isla. My killing a man has never been premeditated before, and I'm not entirely sure that I want to start that now."

"Then don't. I'd rather not have you lose yourself because you feel as if you owe me his heart."

"What do I do, Isla?"

I pull his lips to mine and kiss him gently before giving him my answer. "Have him locked up as far away from me and our baby girl as possible."

"Are you sure? You don't want more?"

"Yes, I am sure. He deserves to suffer, even if it's from a prison cell rather than a pain-filled death."

The following day, Liam and I make arrangements to head to Sydney, Australia, which is a lot earlier than we'd planned on going. We need to get there before they decide to move Grady again. I don't believe that Liam got an ounce of sleep last night, and I don't blame him for it either. I believe that he's made up his mind on what he's going to do in regard to Grady, but he hasn't said anything to me about it yet.

Quinn has told us multiple times that she'll be fine to watch the house on her own, and with her position secured at Lola Marc's Boutique this morning, I'm thrilled for her. She's taking the next step in her life, and I'm pleased to be part of it with her.

After going over the lock codes and the security details of the house, and giving her Eden's and Wade's phone numbers just in case, Liam and I left.

The flight to Sydney was uneventful. I spent half of it sick in the bathroom. Apparently, our little girl is not a fan of eating and flying at the same time. Currently, we're driving through Sydney toward Liam's house.

I watch as he reaches over the console and places his hand on my thigh before sliding his fingers farther down my inner thigh between my legs.

"Why do you do that?"

He glances over at me from the road for a second before turning back. "Do what exactly?"

"You lock your fingers between my thighs whenever you can—or when you can't touch me in any other way. Especially when I'm sitting with one leg crossed over the other."

He glances down at his hand that rests dangerously close to the apex of my thighs before he offers up an answer. "Well, you're warm here. You're mine, and I enjoy touching you in this general area as often as I can."

I shift in my seat and lean over to bite down on his bicep, which causes him to inhale deeply.

"All right. I guess that's a fair reason."

"I'll get you for that, Mrs. Jensen."

"As if." I giggle and place one of my hands on top of his as he drives.

"Are you comfortable?" His fingers dig into my inner thigh in a short gesture of love as he speaks, and my insides liquefy.

"I'm fine now that we're on the ground. I did, however, want to ask you about Adriana. Did you call her back last night?"

He shakes his head and squeezes my thigh again. "No, baby doll, but if she calls again, then I'll answer and make sure that she understands that it's just you."

"You don't have to do that."

"I do, Isla. It's the least I can do to make you feel comfortable."

"Love you," I say as I lean my head against his shoulder and pull my feet up onto the seat so that I'm sitting crisscrossed.

"I love you, doll."

"Oh, and Liam?"

"Yeah?"

"Thank you for taking care of Quinn when I was absorbed with the baby and trying to get through things on my own. I know that I still have a long way to go, but I just wanted to thank you for being the man that you are."

"You know that I'd do anything for you. You're welcome, and I'll be here for the remainder of your recovery. I won't let you delve into that shitty place that I found you in all of those years ago. Plus, I like the way you make the bed, so I'm going to need you to stick around."

"The bed? Are you fucking kidding me?" I laugh and look up at him.

"Barely."

"Well, if it's any consolation, I love that I can smell you on the sheets when you're not in bed with me."

"Fiend," he mocks as he pulls into the beach house's driveway.

"Duh."

We've barely slept off our jet lag by the next morning, and now I'm watching Liam pour himself a third mug of black coffee and then continue to pace around the room. He seems to be consumed in an indefinite limbo of thought as he takes his steps, turns, and walks back toward me. Just watching him is making me anxious.

"This shouldn't be how our honeymoon starts. I'm sorry, Isla."

I shake my head and push my bowl of cereal aside. "You have nothing to apologize for. I enjoy being here, and this is something that neither of us has had to deal with yet, but now it's staring us in the face, and we'll quickly get it over with."

I can see the festering guilt in him even though he's managed to keep his inner dialogue to himself. I know that an electrical storm named Liam will surface soon, and I may be prepared to tame him with my mouth at a moment's notice.

"Are you ready?" he asks as he stops pacing in front of me. "Did you eat enough?" He casts a glance at my half-eaten breakfast and then back at me. "You don't need to come with me if you'd rather not be in the same vicinity as the fucker."

"I'm fine, dickweed. The only reason that I'm going along with you is to be your support. You've been mine for the longest time, and I'm here to show you that I'm yours as well. Now, how about we get this shit over with so I can enjoy this honeymoon? Although, I didn't think over the fact that I can't lie out on the beach in this weather."

"I'll take you somewhere else, doll—just name the place. Yeah, I think that I'm ready or as ready as I'll be. Let's get going."

With that, we leave the sound of the waves that we're able to hear inside of the house and make our way to where the security team at RW is holding a tremendously impatient Grady Kent captive.

The thirty-minute drive goes by before I'm able to inhale or blink. As we're walking into a warehouse, my heart screams in my chest, and it's like my entire body knows that I'm going to be close to the man who almost ruined my life.

Neither Liam nor I say anything aside from minor greetings to the men around us as we're led through the large empty rooms.

"Liam?"

His motions are almost robotic as he turns to me and captures my face between his hands.

"You don't have to go farther, Isla. I won't be long, but I need to do this. I need him to suffer in a way that I did. I need to know why he fucked me over. I just need to understand this cruel fucking joke."

"All right," I say as his lips come down to mine, and I realize only now that Liam trusted Grady as a brother. They were so close, but the entire relationship was a lie. Liam might not have anything to prove to the stupid fucker, but he needs to heal, and this is the first time that I've been able to acknowledge that need. I don't know how I haven't put two and two together before, but now that I have, I completely understand why he's been on edge, aside from the obvious reasons.

"Stay here. I won't be long."

"Be careful."

"Always, baby doll, always," he says against my lips and then I'm watching his back retreat from me. His broad shoulders move with each step that he takes, and just watching him take on something like this makes me fall in love with the asshole all over again. My hands automatically go to my midsection to protect our little girl while Liam goes to get his slice of peace that has yet to be granted to him.

Twenty-Six

Liam

SHIT ALWAYS SEEMS impossible to do until it's done. I'm done limiting myself when it comes to what I ultimately want. Right now, I need to cross a boundary that's been in place for a while, and I'm walking into this fucking room with a loaded gun and the idea of hurting this fucker in any which way possible. I refuse to allow another woman to live in fear of him finding her again. This bullshit that surrounds him ends now.

Naturally, my phone goes off as I'm about to step into the bare room that contains the man whose life I'd do anything to end. I dig the phone out of my pocket, hoping that it's not Isla asking me to return to her because I'm unsure that I'll be able to. I sag in relief seeing that it's just Adriana Hugh again. Two fucking birds with one stone, huh?

Without any preconceived notions, I answer the call. "Adriana, this is not a good time. Let me call you back."

"Hey you, I'm sorry. I've been trying to reach you for days now."

"Yeah, I know. I've seen all of your missed calls, but I have yet to understand why you keep calling when you know what my life entails right now."

"Liam, quit being a jerk for one minute and let me talk, okay?"

"I don't have much time. Spit it out."

She sighs into the phone before speaking again. "Listen, I was just calling to say congratulations on the wedding, on the baby, and on finding someone who will help you disconnect from what you've been through. You seem to have made peace with who you became and who you are now. I know that without having to even speak to you about it that it's finally happened. The man who I used to mess around with would have never gotten married to his best friend, let alone be having a child so soon. He was too consumed by his own grief to give a shit about anyone else."

I remain quiet as she takes a slight pause from her little speech.

"I'm just proud of you for pulling through after all of this time. Gratitude seems to have taught you a thing or two. You have a heart of gold, Liam, and I've always seen it, but you've finally found it on your own. I don't think that you're holding yourself back anymore, and regardless of where we stand, I'm happy for you. Truly, I am."

I clear my throat as I run a hand down my face, my lips parting to reply to her. "I wasn't expecting any of that. I figured that you had more to say regarding the fact that I'm with Isla."

"I will admit that it took me some time getting used to it once Wade got back from England, but as your friend, Liam, I couldn't be happier for you. You deserve a life full of love that you have continually denied yourself. As much as I didn't like it at the time, I believe that she's what you needed. I'm just glad that you have her. I think that she's good for you in more ways than one."

"She always has been. Listen, I know that I haven't always been decent to you over the years, but please know that you had an enormous impact on my finding myself. I appreciate all that you've done from day one."

"I wouldn't have done it any other way. Now get back to your pregnant wife, and once she's ready to speak to me and feels comfortable enough doing so, I'd like to get to know her some more. I just know her as Mr. Brass's full-of-shit best friend, but I know that she's more than that. I'll talk to you soon, all right?"

"Yeah. That sounds good. Hey Addy?"

"Yes?"

"Thank you. Honestly."

"Of course. I need to get going. Call me if you need a babysitter, all right? Goodbye, Liam."

"See ya around, Addy."

We hang up and I stand there for a moment to collect myself as one of the security guys watches me from the door that contains the sickest motherfucker who I've ever crossed paths with.

"Open up."

Satan has a message for Grady and it's coming through me. The amount of physical violence that I want to unleash on him is almost degrading to myself. I know that regardless of what he says, I need to keep myself in check while I'm in there. I cannot allow him to take control of this situation, but I will permit myself to do what feels right at the time of the encounter.

I take sturdy and powerful strides into the room to where he's seated in the middle of a dusty warehouse, gagged, handcuffed, and tied down to a steel chair. He looks well-worn with patches of his clothing a darker color than the rest, stained by what appears to be dried blood.

His eyes open and he glares up at me as I approach his pitiful presence.

"You're fucking pathetic, Grady, my brother."

He tries to speak against the cloth that is gagging him, but I can't hear a damn thing. I kneel down in front of him and rip the duct tape off of his face and then remove the cloth from his dried-out mouth.

"What was that? You missed seeing me?"

"I said," he repeats, clearing his throat before continuing, "how's that pretty pink pussy doing? Is she enough to keep you sated or does she not want to be touched anymore?"

The palm of my hand cracks against his cheek, snapping his head back with the force of the blow. I turn around from him and force myself to count to ten, but it doesn't help for a fucking second. I glance at him as a deep chuckle escapes me. "I didn't come in here to get violent with you, but once more wouldn't hurt."

On my eight count, I use the full weight of my body to throw a punch at his dirty, smug face, which causes him to spill over and the chair to lose its balance. I step over him, rubbing my knuckles as his clammy face contorts with the throbbing discomfort, courtesy of my fist.

"Tell me why you did what you did, cocksucker."

He spits blood up at me, but it lands a few feet away.

"You don't know shit, Jensen."

"I'm going to guess that I'm about to be enlightened by your pathetic ass."

He ignores my retort and stares just over my shoulder and up at steel beams that soar across the high ceiling of the abandoned warehouse. He seems to be a million miles away when he starts to speak again.

"Do you remember that cute little thing that was taken from you all of those years ago? Chloe Madden?" His sick chuckles echo against the vast walls of the warehouse before he continues. "Mmm, I bought her ass out before I ate it out, and fuck, she tasted good. She was what got me started in this beautiful world of buying and selling cunts. She was my first purchase—did you know that? She was also my last official toy, and I wouldn't have it any other way. Jesus, she was just as fucked up as I was because she was the one who encouraged me to purchase my first compound. She thrived in this world, and the greedy little bitch always wanted more."

My fingers go rigid as I curl them into fists at my sides. The words that he's saying are not making sense because I knew Chloe too well for any of this bullshit to be true.

"She fucking loved what I could do to her, and she would come just watching me sink into another woman who was unable to escape. She'd get so fucking wet watching me have my way with a slave or two—so much so that when I was done with a slave, she begged me to keep the bitch for her own purposes. She allowed me to do whatever the fuck I wanted to do with the both of them. She was one fucked-up little bitch, and I don't think that you would have ever been able to appease her the way I did."

Confusion by what he's saying fills my head because Chloe would never sink to his level of sick and demented actions against others.

"You're a damn good liar, Kent. You're the one who fucking killed her; don't spew this bullshit at me."

He coughs and tries to adjust himself on the floor while still secured to the chair. "Why would I kill a woman who satisfied my cock like no other? Huh, mate? The one woman who seemed to get pleasure out of the same twisted shit that I did? I didn't fucking kill her, Jensen. I fucked her until she was raw every night or until she begged me for more. She didn't belong to you, and despite my payment, she did not belong to me either. She was my fucking girl, though, until she was stolen from one of my compounds when I had a sale. That's the one and only time that I took your digging seriously."

I glare at him and search his face for any type of hidden

agenda, but all that I'm able to see is the deep and unwanted truth in his eyes. "You're full of shit. She wouldn't hurt another woman."

"No? I've got pictures and video recordings of her doing just that. She wasn't who you thought she was, Jensen. She was my fucking queen, and she ran those goddamn compounds. She was the one who would push me to open a new one in a different country after she got bored."

"You motherfucker. She wouldn't have done any of this shit. You had a fucking wife and kids. What the hell happened to them?"

He chuckles and glares at me. "All of that was a façade, brother. None of it ever existed."

I stare at him in silence before he starts to speak again.

"She had the option to go back to you, ya know, but she didn't because she did not want to. She chose to stay with me and never once tried to contact your sorry ass. I guess that she knew you'd always had something going on for her sister. When I refused to stop *working* for you, she's the one who insisted that I help you on some level, but what's the fun in that when you enjoy ruining what I live for?"

"You stole women, you fucker. You watched them fucking drain of life just as Chloe's life was drained from her body. All of this shit is because of you."

He seemingly ignores me as he continues his pathetic little tale. "Once we found her body, I had to get my fucking revenge on your oblivious happiness, as well as the dirt wipes that did what they did to her. Fuck, I was the one to find her body, Jensen. I was there. I smelt her. I touched her cold skin. I was the one who carried what was left of her back to the fucking vehicle and held onto her rotting corpse while we transported her to your goddamned jet. I'm the one that killed those fuckers with my bare hands, and she would have loved to watch."

He chuckles before adding, "She would have blown me while I did it."

I'm unsure if he's giving me the truth, but I cannot help but feel fucking sick with the knowledge. I won't let him see me cower from his detailed story, so I change the subject. I take a few steps away before turning on him again.

"So you thought that Isla would be your round two? You thought that you'd see if she was like her sister? To see if she liked it the way you wanted her to?"

"It might have been genetic," he says through a fit of coughs. "I wasn't sure until I saw her pull away from the dick with the gun inside of her and then I knew she wasn't what I wanted. She's fucking feisty, I'll give you that, but she's no Chloe."

"Fuck you."

"Chloe did. Plenty."

Jesus. I want to fucking strangle him with my bare hands right now and watch him leave this world the way he took those other lives. I want to watch as the life leaves his frantic eyes and his pulse stops beating underneath my grip, but I won't put myself in that situation. I won't reduce myself to a piece of shit when I cannot turn back time to find out if any of this is true.

I won't risk my life when I have a wife and a healthy baby girl on the way. I might not be the one to break him, but the knowledge that he also suffered the loss of Chloe settles something perverse within me.

"You expect me to believe all of this shit?"

"No, not even for a fucking second, which is why you'll find an amusing little video in the central office of RW. Consider it a little parting gift from Chloe and me."

"Rot in hell."

"Ah, I'll see you down there, brother."

It takes every ounce of strength that I have to turn and walk away from the fucked-up son of a bitch and toward my future. I won't allow him to break the best part of who I've become. I won't let a single soul have that kind of hold on me again.

I'm led out of the room that contains the malevolent darkness of my life and across the warehouse into one that holds my light. I had no goddamn clue that I was following a repetitive pattern that Grady was laying out in front of me for years. Fuck, the ones that he and Chloe were plotting out. The only good thing about it is the fact that he brought those who killed Chloe to justice, and I fucking hope that he made those pieces of shit suffer.

Do I forgive Chloe for sinking into the world of hell if what he said was true? I do not know. It would mean that she delved into the world willingly and probably did as much unspeakable shit as Grady did. How do I forgive her when she was one of the brutes of the underground world that I've been fighting against?

Do I still mourn who she was? Of course, but right now, I'm not sure of whom she truly was, and I won't get the opportunity to find out. The thought of that video planted within my organization is already haunting me.

As we walk through the abandoned warehouse, I send a quick email to Gage and my security heads who I instruct to pull the office apart until they come across something that does not belong there. Out of the two of us, Gage will be the one who has his head on straight about the situation when I may be too emotionally involved.

All of the years of searching seem to all boil down to Chloe's selfishness, but throughout it, I've been able to pull out an obscene number of women who needed me to find them because others are too afraid or apathetic to go looking in the dark.

I won't fault Chloe for her mistakes, but I also will not

change what I'm doing. I will continue to fight for those women who are unable to fight for themselves, and I'm hoping that it may come easier now, without having someone constantly plotting against my every move.

The invisible scars that cut deep into me may not heal completely, but I've let the past go. Scars fade over time, and with Isla's help, that healing process is well on its way.

"Liam?"

I'm broken away from my inner thoughts as I step over the threshold of another door, and into a well-lit yet dank room. Fuck, Isla's voice is a pure fucking sanctuary, and I could live in it.

"Are you all right?"

I can hear the concern in her voice. I'm able to physically feel the nervous energy radiating off of her in the small space as I close in on her. This woman grounds me when not even the most potent cocktail of drugs would do it for me. The second I lock my arms around her petite frame, the majority of the world fades to static gray.

The endless cargo of shit that has been weighing me down seems to be supporting me right now instead of imploding. Her arms latch around my neck as I lift her up and off of her feet to carry her out of the room and then out of the warehouse in silence.

The negative space between us is the only thing that's keeping me upright as I walk into the cool air.

"I love you," I say into her ink-black hair as I hold her close to me.

She wraps her body around mine as best as she can as I stand beside the rental vehicle and take the moment to breathe in everything about her. My battered fucking soul might not be able to handle the truth of the past, but it can revel in the truth of the future. This woman owns me, and that malevolent force that I was burdened with is losing its power after Grady's words, more than I thought it ever would.

If his words are true, then he's freed me. If he lied, he freed me as well, but the truth will be revealed once that video is found—if it's found.

I groan as Isla runs her fingers up the column of my neck and into the back of my hair. Isla Jensen makes me feel again, and she's been here the entire time. I just didn't give a shit enough to look around and see what I had.

"Liam?"

"Yeah, baby doll?" I answer her in a hushed tone while my face is still buried in the crook of her neck.

"I need to tell you something that happened when I was down there."

I pull back and look at her as a nauseating sensation settles over me.

"It's nothing serious, but I'd like for you to know."

"All right."

"Grady . . . well, when he first took me, he called me his doll. He continued to call me your nickname for me the entire time I was down there. He kept degrading me and referring to me as a plastic bitch. I think that he was pushing me to see just how far I could go without breaking, but instead of that name becoming something cruel and menacing, it's what made me pull through some of the tough times. Especially when I was alone in that concrete cell. You're all that I could think about. I just wanted to hear you say it again."

Every muscle in my body tightens up and squeezes at the misery that I know I've inflicted on her by continuously calling her my doll. I place my lips against her neck and tighten my grip on her. "I'm sorry. I'll learn to stop saying it."

"No," she almost shouts as she pulls the back of my hair

with her fingers so that I'll look up at her. "You've always called me that, and I don't want you to stop. It's our thing, and I won't let him take that away from us."

I don't know how I got fortunate enough to share the life I do with this indomitable woman, but I never plan on taking her for granted. "Are you sure? I have no doubt that I can come up with something else."

"I am, and nothing else would ever be the same. I won't allow myself to be a casualty of my own mind."

"If anything else that I do evokes anything from that hell, I need you to swear to me that you'll tell me about it. I want to be the one to help you work through it and not cause you any more damage. I know that we see the therapist for that kind of shit, but I need to know that you're okay a lot more than the two times a week we sit down on a chaise together."

"You have my word."

"All right, thank you. Now, I'm going to need your help with some things before we leave Australia."

"Wait, why are we leaving?"

"I need to, babe. I'm going to sell the house, and I'll buy you another wherever the fuck you want, but I need to be away from the reality of what Grady just confessed to me. I don't want to be surrounded by anything that had to do with Chloe."

She scrunches up her face as I hold onto her and reveal what he told me. She offers up so many apologies that I've lost count of them. She tells me the same thing that I've thought—that he lied—but somehow, something deep inside of me knows that he's telling the truth about this shit. I've decided that I won't fault Chloe if it's what actually happened, but I need to put it all behind me instead of overanalyzing every ounce of information. The second we find that video and I get to see the truth, I won't need anything else. I just want this outlandish bullshit to be over with. I've given too much of myself to live in a hole of lies.

Isla seems to sense my mind running away from me, and she pulls me back in with her spell. "Will you take me on our honeymoon afterward?"

I raise my eyebrows at her unexpected request. I know that she's internally cringing at her own words, but I'll save her from it all. "Where would you like to go?" I ask as I lean my forehead against hers.

She shrugs her petite shoulders and kisses me leisurely. It's a kiss that's filled with too much passion, but yet not enough. I gradually move one of my hands to the underside of her thigh as I'm consumed in her heady presence. Her compassion is otherworldly, and she has extended so much of herself to bring me back to the place where I should have been living in all along. Our tongues slide against each other as we live in the kiss that seems to heal the parts of us that have been taken advantage of.

She pulls away from me and runs her thumb over my lips in an attempt to remove the painted streak that she always seems to leave behind. "Take me anywhere. I just want it to be the two of us for a little while."

A vision of her on the beach in a bikini and pregnant comes to mind, and I know exactly where I'll be taking my wife. I agree with her. We need to be untouchable for the time being.

"Do you trust me?" I ask against her harlot-red lips.

"Implicitly."

I move my lips up her jaw to her ear before replying. "Good," I murmur against the shell of her ear and tongue it once before setting her on her feet. "Let's get this shit going, and we can leave. Deal?"

"Deal."

Isla is asleep on the couch as I sit beside her and slowly strum the individual notes that together make up my baby girl's lullaby. My fingers move along the strings of the guitar like second nature as I play a piece that I've been writing out for the last month. It's the one thing that has been able to soothe me after dealing with Grady.

Once the song ends, I move my hand over to the side of her stomach, loving how she's grown. "I cannot wait to meet you, little girl. I know that the moment we meet, the gravitational pull on my world will move to you, but don't tell your mother that just yet. She's been known to be a bit covetous a time or two before."

Isla draws in a deep breath and stirs underneath my hands. "Liam?"

"I'm here, baby doll."

"Mmm, I was dreaming that we were far away and on a beach and naked underneath the sun."

She pushes herself up, and I can't help but chuckle at the crease that the pillow left on the side of her face.

"We'll be leaving tomorrow morning to an island that I'm sure I'll have to drag you off of."

"I cannot wait. Do you need to do anything else with the house before we go?"

"Nah. The movers will be here later this afternoon, and it's already listed on the market. Now, tell me, if you could have a house wherever you want, where would it be?"

"Anywhere?"

"Anywhere."

"I think a place in the Keys that we can take our little dewdrop to whenever we want without the hassle of staying at a hotel would be great. I'm sure that Connor would love to be involved in her life. Other than that, I like the idea of having a house like this somewhere far away from Chicago. It would give us an excuse to get away from life and enjoy each other's company."

"Like where, babe?"

"Uhm, I'm not sure. Somewhere in Norway would be ideal."

"Norway? I didn't know that you wanted to go there."

"Well, I went with Wade on a business trip once, and I fell in love with the country as well as the culture. I'd really like to go back."

I shift her onto my lap and move my hand underneath the fabric of her shirt to touch her naked stomach.

"I'll get us a house in the Keys to be closer to my fucked-up family, but I'll also cave and get you your dream vacation home in Norway. However, you have to allow me to extend our honeymoon and take you house hunting in Norway after a week or two of staying where I currently have a hotel reserved for us."

She chews on the inside of her lips as if she actually has to consider my proposal.

"It seems to be a win-win situation, dickweed."

"Good because I would not have taken no as an answer. Now get your pretty ass naked so I can kiss you in places that I know you constantly dream of."

"Oh yeah? Prove it."

"With pleasure, baby doll."

I spend the next two hours meeting her darkest sexual fantasies on every surface that we're able to get to before our bodies implode in mind-numbing orgasms.

Epilogue No. 1

Isla

NO BOUNDARIES, REGARDLESS of their geographical limitations, could stop me from loving Liam Jensen the way I do. Everything about him is infectious, and I cannot wait to spend a lifetime of dedication with him. He's the cage that surrounds my heart, which protects me from the world around us with a self-sacrifice and love that I never knew was possible.

This man will not let me down, and he'll keep me grounded when I start to lose myself. Do I believe that life throws shit at us until we're able to grow and accept our own situations enough to thrive in them? Being what I've been through now, I can say yes with a certainty that wasn't there before.

I would go through every nightmare that I've lived through again if it means that I get to end up here with Liam. With this life. With this baby girl.

I run my hand over my stomach as I stare at myself in the mirror. I've just gotten out of the shower, and I cannot help but feel that every time I look in the mirror, I see the growth of my little girl in some way.

I'm pulled from my trance by both Liam's guitar playing and the sudden frantic movement in my belly. I stare at my reflection and dart my hand down to my stomach.

"Holy shit," I say under my breath. "Liam!"

"Yeah, babe?" he calls out from the bedroom.

"Get in here!"

I watch him charge into the bathroom with wide, worried eyes before taking me in. "What's wrong?"

"I felt her. She just kicked. I think that she did at least."

"What?" He takes cautious steps to get to me as if he's going to scare her off. He reaches his hand out, and I take it and place it around the same area that she kicked a moment ago.

"Give her a minute. I've never felt her do it before."

Between the two of us, we remain silent until a whirlwind of movement occurs beneath our hands.

"Holy shit. That was her?"

"Yes," I sob out and lightly push down on my stomach. "Hi, little girl."

Liam chuckles and smooths his hand over my swollen belly.

"I cannot wait to meet her."

"Neither can I."

He places a kiss on my lips before walking out of the bathroom to take a minute for himself. I stare at my stomach and internally beg for her to move again, but I think that it's all that she's going to give me at the moment. Stubborn little thing.

I walk out of the bathroom while towel-drying my hair to find Liam, who is naked, strumming away on his guitar on the bed again.

Fuck, my husband is gorgeous.

"Are you going to miss this place?" I ask to distract myself from my now-throbbing sex.

He stops playing and sets the acoustic guitar down before looking up at me. "I think that a part of me will, but I'm ready to move on and beyond it with you."

"And you're entirely sure?"

"I don't have a doubt in my mind, Mrs. Jensen." He gets up and stands to his full height, and it's a wonder that I don't simultaneously combust into an orgasm on the spot. I hope that he'll always look at me the way he is now with such an extreme longing. A sweltering desire breaks out over my skin as I take in his dark eyes and slightly flawed skin.

The bullet wounds have mostly healed, but it's the jagged scar from the knife that will always have an effect on me. He surrounds me in his bare skin in a warm hug before stepping around me to grab a towel to dry off his still slightly damp hair before we both get dressed. Once we're ready to go, I step outside and give him a moment to say goodbye. Not to the house, but to the memories that live within those walls. Once he emerges, we leave the keys to his Sydney house behind us and go. Soon we're on the plane and the jet lifts us swiftly into the air and into a horizon filled with lavish colors.

Epilogue No. 2

Liam

I FUCKED AROUND and got attached, falling in love with a valiant and resolute beauty. I do not regret a fucking second of it either.

All I can think about while watching Isla walk toward me on beach of the Centara Grand Island Resort and Spa in the Maldives is that I want to fuck that tight little body in the sand. If I allow myself to imagine it, I can see the sand sticking to her wet skin as I bury myself to the hilt. She'd be gripping onto the grains of sand instead of sheets, and I know that I need to make it happen at least once while we're here.

She joins me on the double beach lounger and runs her hand over her midsection. I know that she's yearning to feel our little girl kick again, and I don't blame her.

"I've been thinking . . ." I say as I take a drink of the Isabella's Islay whiskey that Isla brought over from the States. The liquid treasure explodes in my mouth as a campfire burns across my taste buds and then down my throat, the authoritative combination of flavors seductive. Light suggestions of peat and campfire smoke linger on my tongue, and it's the closest I've gotten to the shores of Islay without actually being there.

"Do I even want to know what that involves?"

"I believe that this will interest you more than you know, but first, how the fuck did you score one of these bottles? There weren't that many produced."

"I have my ways," she says with a smile. "Actually, Waylon gave it to me as a gift when he first opened Blended. I haven't opened it until now because I was saving it for something."

"Something?"

"Yes. Something that would make me realize just how much I love life."

"And that something is me?"

"It became you a while ago, Jensen."

"Thank you for sharing it with me. Do you want a taste?"

"Always," she says as she moves over me to straddle my lap. She leans down, and I take her mouth, allowing her a taste of this awfully rare vintage.

"So good," she moans and comes back for more. After a solid minute of her drowning against my lips, I pull back and smirk. It takes her a moment to find her balance after her libido disturbs it, and when she does, I try again.

"Now, let me tell you what I was thinking about."

"Oh Jesus. Spill it."

I chuckle as the sun starts to set on the horizon in front of me while Isla has her back to it. "I was considering names."

"Names? For her?" she asks as her hand covers her midsection again.

"Yes."

"Tell me? Please? Everything that I've come up with just doesn't seem to fit."

"All right. I was thinking about Rilynn."

"Rilynn? That's . . . Liam, that's stunning."

"I thought so too. It's a variation of Ryland, which means island meadow. It reminded me of you, so I thought I'd change it up a little just as you did yours."

"Rilynn Jensen," she repeats, and her lips curve up into

a ravishing smile while she looks down at her stomach. "Hi, Rilynn."

I chuckle and lean forward to place my lips against her bare stomach. "She's going to have your feisty spirit, baby doll."

"As long as she gets her father's looks, I'm all right with that."

"Nah, I'd like a little more of you in her."

She rolls her eyes and moves off of me to relax back into the plush cushions and watch the sunset with me. I reach over and take her hand in mine, toying in silence with the rings that I placed on her finger.

By the time either of us makes a move to get up again, the sun has completely set, and the sand before us is glowing with what looks like green-blue stars scattered along the shore.

"Did you know that this happened? Everything is glowing."

"Yeah, it's why I decided to bring you here."

"It's so damn pretty."

"Maybe, Isla, but nothing compares to your splendor. The hauntingly stunning beauty that you see in front of you is what you embody."

"I love you," she says as she smacks my chest softly.

"I know."

She snuggles against me as we lie there together and watch the small waves move the glowing particles around before us.

"Liam?"

"Yeah?"

"What happens next?"

"Next? We live our intertwined lives and strive for embodied perfection."

The End

Thank You

THANK YOU FOR reading this novel. Always remember that it's never too late for your chance at love. Love who and what matters to you, regardless of what others think and what the world expects from you. Don't be ashamed of your own story, and don't judge others because you walked in during a debauched chapter in their book.

With love, *Sasha*

www.ingramcontent.com/pod-product-compliance
Lightning Source LLC
Chambersburg PA
CBHW071158250626
47159CB00001B/127